# Cambridge
# Thrillers

## Peter Wadsworth

**Cambridge Thrillers**
by Peter Wadsworth

first published in 2016
Copyright © 2016 Peter Wadsworth

Front cover illustration by Mark Lee Jones
© 2016 Mark Lee Jones
www.markleejones.co.uk

ISBN 978-1534780361

To Ruby and Maureen...

*two older sisters, the first I never knew,*

*the second I knew and loved dearly.*

This first story in the series concerns a fresher at Magdalene College, Cambridge. A seemingly parochial case – but not so...

Cambridgeshire Police
Crime Investigation Unit

# Case 1: the intern

# Prologue

'Come out with your hands in the air.' The police loudspeaker barked out its unambiguous command, loud and clear over the disorderly noise of a police stand-off.

He'd made a pact with the Devil in his teens and now it was retribution time for all his victims; death by hell-fire, no more than he deserved.

If there was a place worse than hell then this was it. The heat was intense. Intense enough to cause his hair to spontaneously ignite; his leather jacket to melt like wax and to melt itself to his body; his jeans to be aflame, burning his legs, causing them to char and the skin to blister and peal. The many darting flames of eternal damnation behind him lacerated his whole body with weals of agonising burning flesh.

The pain was excruciating and the smell of his burning flesh acrid and revolting. All efforts to put the flames out with his hands were to no avail. The critical temperature was well-past and the heat all-consuming. With hot air rasping at his throat, he used a rag in his pocket to mask his nose and mouth from the smell and to stop himself from screaming.

It was a simple choice: being roasted alive or making a break for it. He preferred the latter and damn the consequences. With a parched and blistered throat that now felt like an inferno, he mustered all his strength to croak out loud, 'I'm coming out. Don't shoot.'

Throwing his Kalashnikov to the ground, too hot to even hold, he opened the large barn doors, taking all his strength to lift the cross-beam on the second attempt. He stepped outside. There was a momentary respite from the pain as a cold gush of air rushed to the flames, cooling his swollen face and giving his body a morphine-like numbness from the heat. He painfully raised his hands to show he wasn't armed.

A step forward and he felt a sharp pain in both sides of his neck. He knew instinctively it was a bullet entering and exiting. For a split second he thought himself immortal, but one more step forward and his knees buckled, hurling him forward face-down onto the bare earth with a grinding thud. He fell heavily and heard his nose crack. Still prone the blood spurted from his mouth, nose and neck in copious streams, first reddening the earth around his head, and then thirstily being absorbed by the brown soil.

With the few senses he had left he could hear the babble of muffled voices as they smothered the flames on his body. He felt the sensation of being turned over onto his back and dragged by his arms away from the burning building. Many inquisitive faces peered down at him as he heard the fading words:

'Is he dead?'

'Not sure.'

'Soon will be though, graveyard dead.'

'Good riddance, that's all I can say.'

Frederick Little, with his last efforts on this mortal earth, raised both his arms and stared at the palms of his blackened, blistered hands. He muttered his last words to himself through lips that had fused together, 'Useless, bloody useless!'

# One

Market Square, Cambridge, Wednesday, November 30th 2011, 11.30pm.
Weather forecast: snow flurries, increasing in intensity.

Amy's dream was a romantic meeting between lovers, somewhere exotic, where she lost her maidenhead to a romantic Latin lover. Amy's reality was awaiting a fellow student in a cold, freezing, wind-swept spot in the centre of Cambridge, romance scarce, about to lose more than her virginity.

Amy wrapped her long, woollen, Magdalene combi-scarf once more around her neck to keep out the cold and then pulled down her bobble hat over her ears for added warmth. She tightened the top button of her grey duffle coat and then wriggled her toes in her wool-lined boots. She was well prepared for the weather to get worse that evening. Preferably, she would have liked to have looked pretty and alluring on her first date but, at this very moment, warmth was her top priority. She gripped extra tightly in her gloved hand her grey-matching Cambridge satchel, a special present from her mother for winning a scholarship to Cambridge University, something to treasure all her life.

A quick glance at her watch, it had gone 11.30pm. He was late! How inconsiderate on their first date. He could at least have given her a quick call or a brief text on her mobile to say he was going to be late. Men! But she reminded herself that she hardly knew him, having met him only once before at the Freshers' Ball. She shouldn't hastily jump to the wrong conclusions because of his apparent tardiness. Anyway, she wasn't one to be always on time. It was just, in this case, she had made an exception and had hoped he would have done likewise. Obviously not!

Amy's imagination ran wild. Here she was, in an almost deserted market place, waiting for her mythical knight-in-shining-armour. It would make a good plot for her debut romantic novel. Her heroine would be clothed in furs and jewellery and be all apprehensive awaiting her suave, handsome hero in the dead of night. Bewitched by him, he would whisk her away in his powerful sports car to a helicopter pad and then to a private plane to Paris to meet the rising dawn, and then on to other romantic destinations. There would be a twist to the tale and he would turn out to be a gigolo blackmailed by a Chinese organ-trafficking ring. No! On second thoughts that would be a bit OTT!

Still, if she was to write such a novel, she felt she would need to absorb the feelings of loneliness, fear and insecurity, and trepidation she felt at this very moment in time. If she was to realise her ambitions of being a famous romantic author, then to experience these moments was invaluable for the story. With an absence now of romantic novelists perhaps, one day, the name of Amy Barraclough would be on everyone's lips. She sighed as images of success crossed her mind, the culmination of a childhood dream, of everything she ever wanted. Well, almost everything.

The sudden flapping and crackling of one of the stall's tarpaulins brought her out of her daydream and quickly back to reality. Amy shuffled about nervously. Where was he?  Fewer people were using the square as a short-cut between Market Street and Trinity, and the shadows of the surrounding buildings appeared darker and more foreboding by the minute.  What a stupid place to meet up!  Why couldn't they have met in a nice warm café?  Why Market Square of all places?

The sound of a clock in the distance chiming the witching hour refreshed her thoughts.  Another glance at her watch, it was several minutes slow.  She must remind herself to correct it as soon as she got back to the college.  Timeliness was of the essence now if she was to make a good impression with her tutors.

The canvas on the stall next to her flapped wildly in the gusting wind and Amy stepped between two stalls for added protection and raised her hood.  She looked around her once more, gritted her teeth and squealed inwardly as several large rats scurried out of a drain and slithered towards the stalls looking for food scraps.  She smiled to herself to deflect her anxiety and increasing fear of her vulnerability to anything untoward.

As was her nature, her mind wandered again.  The day had started so well.  A bright, early winter's morning and a satisfying jog around the atmospheric, cobbled streets of the University had put her in high spirits.  Being a fresher, everything was new and exciting and so different from her home town of Whitby, quaint though the town is to tourists, to Captain Cook fans, and as a Mecca for the thousands of Goths twice a year.

Being a fresher she'd been allocated a room near to the centre of Magdalene College and felt very secure, this being the first time she had lived away from her home.

Her room was Spartan comprising a single bed, a desk, chair, table and lamp, and a single wardrobe.  That was it!

But not forgetting, a single picture, a print of Magdalene College on the wall, as seen from the air, placed in every room! Spartan her room may be but for her it was a warm, womb-like space. It represented a hideaway from the real world, a place of solace for her studies and, most importantly, a cubbyhole where she could be herself and not be encumbered by her working-class roots.

This space, this tiny space, represented independence, a background weight being lifted from her shoulders, a social yoke that could now be removed. Throw in a few female bits and pieces like a cushion or two and several prized photographs and it would also be a very cosy home-from-home, so to speak. What more could she want?

She had taken an instant liking to the conviviality of her fellow students and their immediate friendships, both male and female. She loved the Cambridge academic ambience of learning and looked forward to her English studies with her tutors. It was to be a period of her life of widening horizons, personal experiences and life-long friendships. A period, also, she hoped, when she would lose her irksome and increasingly frustrating virginity tag. But only when it felt right of course, and only with the right man! Amy was a good girl, her mother had always said, but oh how that phrase had come to annoy her. Her virginity had become a symbol, not just of purity, but of puritanism, a person of strong moral beliefs who is critical of the behaviour of others, and that didn't represent Amy's beliefs. Not one little bit.

She had known her boyfriend, Neil, ever since she was a child, both of them living but three houses apart in the same small, whitewashed, terraced council houses within walking distance of the harbour. He was a Roman Catholic and had insisted no sex before marriage. She had respected his beliefs even though it was increasingly frustrating for her. Pent-up sexual emotions and rampant hormones were not conducive for good concentration of studies and certainly not for writing love stories. If she had never experienced making love herself, how could she possibly describe the emotions? Well, at least, that was her excuse for a good bonk when the time was right.

Amy's mind went back to the Sunday before last, when Neil had visited her in her new digs. She had taken this opportunity to visit the tourist sites with him, the Bridge of Sighs, Queen's College, King's College Chapel included. They had even spent half an hour leisurely, if cold, punting on the Backs. It had all started in a friendly, jovial way but had ended with a strong difference of opinions on the class divide.

Neil was outwardly pleased when she had been offered a place at Cambridge but deep down resented a parting of the waves between them. Cambridge was for the snooty toffs and elite, the white, posh, southern brigade, and he didn't want any part of it. He was a fisherman like his father and grandfather, and many generations before that. Fishing was in his blood as he constantly reminded Amy, to her continued annoyance.

Amy did not want to be as fisherman's wife like her mother. Not for her a stay-at-home housewife, worrying each time her husband was at sea. Her father had been lost at sea in a terrible storm when she was a child, a monstrous sea swelled by rage by all accounts, and she had seen the effect on her mother throughout the years.

No, that was not for Amy. There were many other horizons to explore and Cambridge gave her the portal, the door to another world, and she intended to step through it with all the energies and determination she could muster.

She wanted to experience all manner of things, especially those different from the norm, and to become a famous writer. Failing that, a top journalist for a leading national newspaper. Her sights were set high, just the way she liked it.

Neil, on the other hand, had left school with no qualifications. He said he suffered from Attention Deficit Hyperactivity Disorder, a term he would slowly and deliberately pronounce as though it was a badge of honour tattooed on his forehead. It wasn't his fault he couldn't concentrate on his studies and what was said by his teachers in class. In any case, he wanted to be a fisherman and you didn't need that kind of schooling. That was for school and not for the outside, real world. He was contented enough to be a good fisherman and his ambitions stretched no further than that. He was a working-class lad and he was proud of it. Fishing was his life and he could learn on the job, he didn't need teachers to "learn" him more.

Amy wanted to remove the shackles of her roots, to leave her past behind, to get away from the constant monotony and banter of football, game consoles, video games, beer, benefits, job centres, the dole, and getting "plastered" every Friday and Saturday night. And fish. Especially fish!

She loved Neil as a friend, a friend she had known from when they played together as children and had grown up together. But that was as far as it went. In her heart she was always frightened that Neil would propose marriage to her and she didn't want the heartache of turning him down. Cambridge, in a way, gave her the excuse to distance herself from him and to deter any thoughts of marriage whilst she was there. Her studies being a ready excuse should he use marriage to tie them together whilst apart these three years.

The tourist visit had ended acrimoniously. Amy had been lost in the history and architecture of Cambridge and the stuff of learning that seemed to seep from every brick and stone of every building. She had jokingly deflected Neil's quips and grievances against the working man in society and the social chasm. It had come to a head whilst visiting King's College. She had downloaded a history of the College on her ipad and was describing the place to Neil. He, in turn, couldn't have cared less and was impatient, petulant, rude and just downright irritable, not very companionable. He couldn't see what she saw in the place and irritatingly drummed his fingers on his black motorbike helmet to Amy's distraction.

Buying a brochure on the way out, Amy had flounced out of the building with Neil following in her wake. She had had enough and just wanted Neil to get back on his bike and go home. She hadn't been in Cambridge very long, a mere few months, but already she felt their two worlds were miles apart. She was now independent, free from her family ties and customs and would no longer be intimidated by Neil's wisecracks and sneers at her every remark.

'Amy, don't go off like that.'

'Why not?'

'Because we've known each other a long time and you're my girlfriend.'

'*Was* your girlfriend.'

'Amy, I'm sorry. I've been acting like a pig. Forgive me? Please.'

'Neil, I don't think we're ever going to see eye to eye. You're besotted with class divisions and can't see beyond your nose. You're a bloody fool to yourself. Everything doesn't revolve around your boat. If that's all you care about, I suggest you marry that!'

Amy was now building up a head of steam and resented the words coming out of her mouth, but there were many things between them that had been unsaid and the Cambridge environment had given her the courage to speak of her convictions. Fishing, boats and Whitby were not the be-all and end-all of life. Her mother, her father, when he was alive, her brother and sister, had all taken this parochial view of life and had tried, in their own subtle ways to persuade her that there were worse things in life than being a fisherman's wife. She was sick of it and now all her pent-up emotions exploded in Neil's face.

Amy calmed herself and addressed Neil coolly as though talking to one of her professors. 'Let's face it Neil, I don't think we should see each other for a while. Go home and good luck in your fishing but please leave me be for a while. Let me be the person I want to be, not the person you think I should be. For a short time I have the opportunity to be happy and to be lost in my studies. I know it is not a world you understand or even care about, but for me it is a big new world and I want to be a part of it. I don't want your lifestyle, can you not understand that?

'The last two months have been the happiest days of my life. I have the opportunity to learn about myself and to learn about others, to learn and to love. When I was a little girl I would look out of the window and watch people walking by. All I wanted then was to love someone and for someone to love me. I still want that, but now I want to experience life to the full, to discover my inner-self and what makes me tick. Cambridge has given me the opportunity to do just that. For God's sake, Neil, please try to understand.'

'Well, if that's the way you think then good luck to you. I don't want any part of it.' With that, Neil turned round and, without looking back, strode purposefully, clutching his helmet, to the car park where he had left his motorcycle. Amy's words had hurt him but he didn't want to show it. It was not a manly thing to do.

Amy bit her bottom lip and blinked back her tears. Neil wasn't a bad boy and she hadn't meant her words to be so piercing. It did have to be said sometime or other, she couldn't get away from that. Better now than later, she thought to herself. He'll get over it. He's pretty thick-skinned anyway.

She watched Neil disappear from sight, without even a wave goodbye, and with a heavy heart she walked back to her lodgings. Visiting the other sights had lost their meaning for the moment and it was best to lose herself in her books. She'll make it up to him when he visits her next time was her final consoling thought.

Amy recalled Neil's visit and altercation with him with a certain degree of sadness, but she was still determined to strike out on her own. In that sense, she didn't need a man, any man for that matter, to be her own person. That icy determination, at this very moment, was being matched by the icy conditions around her. Sort of ironical she thought to herself. Here she was, waiting in freezing conditions, late at night, waiting for what? A man! How ironic was that? Nay, stupid!

One other person who did come to mind, however, was her long-time school friend and confidante, Susan. She was now a single mum with an autistic child, Sarah. Amy was Sarah's godmother and she knew she would miss her

11

dreadfully whilst away from home. She had helped Susan whenever she could financially, particularly when her husband had left, and had also made regular contributions to the Autistic Society. It was something close to her heart, a cause she strongly believed in and, when she was famous and rich, she would dedicate part of her royalties to the Society in perpetuity.

It was for that reason she had already arranged for a part-time job in a local McDonald's. It didn't pay very much but it meant she could continue to give financial aid to Susan. It was not a lot but by adding to it from her maintenance grant and student loan she could send some regular money home to Susan and Sarah and see them right as best she could. Her heart was heavy with such thoughts of her friend and godchild battling against Asperger's syndrome, a milder version of autism which often left the child clumsy, shy and tongue-tied, and looked forward to seeing them again soon in the Christmas break. It would be a lovely and Christmassy reunion and it couldn't come soon enough.

Amy looked at her watch for the umpteenth time. It was now 12.15am. I'll give him another fifteen minutes and then I'm off, she thought. No man in the world was worth it if he couldn't even turn up on time; fifteen minutes and no more.

As her thoughts turned to this new man in her life, her heart skipped a beat and all her feminine emotions came to the fore. He must be late for a reason she persuaded herself. Maybe she was even in love with him. She wasn't certain of her feelings. She had only met the man once before at the Freshers' Ball, but she could be in love with him. It wasn't beyond the realms of possibility.

Pleasant thoughts crossed her mind and she smiled to herself as she recollected the day of the Ball. Amy had gone with several girlfriends, fellow students from her dormitory, to what turned out to be a raucous gathering of drink-fuelled students gyrating to a local live band. The noise was loud enough to burst the ear-drums and drink was cheap, served at the Union bar. Not a large imbiber herself, she watched as her friends lost all inhibitions and made several advances to fellow male students.

'Come on Amy, join in' mewed Natalie who lodged in the next room to hers. 'Have another drink.' With drink-fuelled bravado Natalie disappeared into the throng of sweaty students. She emerged pulling a man by the arm. 'Amy, let me introduce you to Joseph. I'll leave you two together, got to get another drink.'

Joseph was a more mature student and Amy was quite taken by him. Tall, dark, athletically built, she was quite bowled over by his looks. Looks aren't everything she thought to herself, but it will do as a start.

For the next fifteen minutes they both gyrated together for what was called dancing. Joseph's body movements were hilarious to watch, with arms, head, hips and body moving in directions that God had never intended as he flung himself around the dance floor with Amy in tow. Amy split her sides with laughing which seemed to encourage him even more. Eventually, exhaustion took its toll and they both sat down on chairs in a quieter spot of the hall to catch their breath.

'Let me introduce myself again,' shouted Joseph above the din. 'I'm a PhD student in my last year.'

'And what are you studying?'

'Medicine, I'm studying medicine. I want to be a research scientist.'

Above the noise of the Ball-room, Amy could detect a slight American accent to his voice. 'Are you English?' she enquired.

'No. I'm an American, over here in your beautiful island.'

'Have you travelled much in the UK?'

'Not a lot, but I intend to do so before I go back home.

Amy, wrongly or rightly, immediately compared him to Neil. Neil had rarely left his home town except to go to sea. The more desolate his surroundings the more Neil liked it. Here, on the other hand, was a young man who had left his country to study in England. In some ways they were worlds apart and Amy was intrigued by this new man in her life. He fitted her fantasy for someone older, more sophisticated, more established. Someone older and wiser was a glamorous notion.

The evening passed with more dancing, more talking and more drinking. At 1.00 o'clock in the morning they had left the Ball together and Joseph had seen her back to her lodgings. A peck on the cheek by Joseph and a brief kiss on the lips by Amy and they had parted saying good-night to each other.

'OK if I give you a ring sometime,' asked Joseph, remembering at the last moment. 'Can you give me your mobile number?' Amy told him her number and he keyed it into his mobile. Amy did likewise for Joseph's number.

They parted with a little love in the air. Amy couldn't wait to see him again. In truth, she fancied the pants off him but, at this stage, their two worlds seemed leagues apart and she didn't want to be seen as too forward. Let the man make the first move, her mother had repeatedly said to her. But to Amy, that was old-fashioned. Women of today were much more likely to take the lead in courtship, pursuing lovers with phone calls and texts. Romantic relationships are driven by women she thought to herself. It is they who make the decision and once they have made their mind up they just go for the poor bloke until he keels over and gives in. Anyway, that's what she had read.

Several days later, in her desire to see him again, Amy tried to call him on his mobile, but all she got was a wrong number. She was puzzled. She assumed he had given her a wrong number or else she hadn't entered it into her mobile correctly, probably the latter. It was her fault, not his.

His call came two weeks later. It was a text message and read: *"meet me in Market Square at 11.30 tonight. Joseph."* Strange time, strange place thought Amy, reading the message again and again as though there was some hidden meaning to it. Still, she couldn't wait to see him again and, what the hell, one place is as good as another, one time as good as any other time. He was probably studying during the day anyway. In any case, the strange rendezvous appealed to her sense of adventure and romantic outlook on life; something different, something worth exploring further, something worth remembering for a novel perhaps.

So there she was, standing in the market place, freezing her bum off, waiting for Joseph to appear. And he was late! Fifteen minutes more and that's it she thought, Joseph or no Joseph.

The place was now desolate and surreal as if becalmed on the open sea as Neil had described. There were bright lights in the distance but the market place was uncomfortably dark. A fox barked in the distance sending a shiver down her spine and her imagination into overdrive. For the first time, she was frightened and a feeling of isolation entered her thoughts. The weather wasn't helping her mood and now snow flurries, whipped up by the swirling wind, seemed to be the order of the night. Amy pulled her hood further over her head to shield her face and waited impatiently. Where was Joseph? Where the hell was he?

Enough was enough. She would wait no more. On the brink of giving up, she suddenly heard the throaty sound of a motorbike coming her way. She cheered up immediately as the motorcycle drew alongside her. She recognised it as a Suzuki, the same as Neil's bike, and suddenly there was a puzzled expression on her face. What on earth is Neil…?

Stepping off the machine, the figure in full leathers and black helmet, moved towards her. Amy could see her reflection in the helmet's visor and thought of what a sight she must now look with her hooded duffle coat and squinting eyes to see who it was. She brushed aside the cold, matted, wet hair from her face and peered more closely.

The figure slowly raised the visor; a protective bandana covered the nose and mouth from the worst of the wind and snow.

'Oh, it's you,' gasped Amy, you frightened the life out of me.'

No sooner had those words left her mouth when she felt herself take an involuntary step backwards. It was those eyes. There was something in that icy stare that frightened her. She was instantly gripped by a spine-chilling unholy fear, an indescribable feeling which made her body stiffen and her heart to beat wildly. The rushes of adrenalin in her body spiked her blood. Her mouth opened as if to issue a strangled, nightmarish, blood-curdling scream, but no such sound escaped her lips.

She found herself taking another step backwards and her female instincts and brain screamed at her to turn around and flee the scene, to run for her life, to get away, to leave now, but she stayed her ground out of shock and curiosity and became rooted to the spot.

'Don't be frightened Amy. It's just me and I've a present for you…'

# Two

Earlier in the year.
Alexander Gardens, off Victoria Road: a small park with
bowling green and play area.
Cambridge, Friday, September 16th 2011, 8.30pm.

Charles Waley-Cohen shuffled his bottom on the thin,
wooden slats of the park bench nearest to the entrance gates
to achieve a modicum of comfort. He wore a Savile Row
pinstripe business suit, a dark blue waistcoat, an expensive
yellow Charvet tie and a white shirt with bones in the collar
and silver cufflinks on double cuffs. Beside him, neatly
folded, was a knee-length creamy-white Danimac on which
he'd placed his fold-up umbrella just in case the weather
took a sudden turn for the worse. Charles inhaled deeply.
The smell of autumn was in the air with its heavier, deeper
mustiness, a special treat for his office-bound sinuses.

A small oval, bronze plaque pinned to the back rail of
the bench caught his eye. He took a closer look, brushed
away some of the grime with his hand and read the words
slowly and deliberately, "This bench is in remembrance of
David Smiley, 1941–2001: Father and Husband". Brief
but poignant epitaph he thought to himself. I wonder if my
life will be annotated so succinctly when I die. Hope Not.
Perhaps I could be remembered by a plaque and a bust at
my club, or maybe even a painting, life-size of course. Or
maybe even a tree, a newly planted sapling growing into a
sturdy oak with squirrels running up and down my body

and birds nesting in my hair, and insects crawling all over me. Not so sure about that now that I think of it. A painting is probably best. I'll leave instructions in my will.

Adjusting his posture yet again, Charles looked across the park and watched studiously as people, near and far, some with their dogs in tow, scrambled for the exits. They hurried with a gait as though seemingly frightened of what the dusk and waning moon might bring. Clearly the fading light had dangers all of its own and the park was not a place to be after a certain time.

Charles buttoned his jacket. This autumn day had been reasonably warm but was now, with wisps of cloud veiling the setting sun, turning out to be a cool, slightly chilly evening. The park closed its gates at 10.00pm prompt and Charles steeled himself for a long wait. The fragrance of the summer flowerbeds, now seemingly more pungent than ever in the cool of the evening air, filled his nostrils with an agreeable scent, putting him in a relaxed frame of mind. He inhaled deeply again, stretched out his arms, and relaxed his body.

The shafts of late sunlight coming through the tree canopies were now weaker in intensity with sun-dappled shadows of the trees and shrubs lengthening, merging into each other to form a soft blanket of semi-darkness. In some ways it was a pretty sight as the street lights and car headlamps illuminated the road skirting the park, bringing the darkened trees and shrubbery to life with moving, magic-lantern type, phantom shadows. He could hear voices and traffic noise in the distance but it didn't detract from the solace and beauty of this place, especially at this time of the evening, provided you overlooked the detritus of people using the park during the day and the spill-over at litter bins, as evidenced by the one close to hand.

Why on earth do people not take home their litter? Why leave it to the park wardens to clean up the mess of tin cans, bottles and paper? And why don't all owners clean up their dog's mess each time? Why are some people so discourteous and unconscionable to others? Enough questions, Charles thought. I mustn't get on my high horse over such matters. Having reminded himself he checked his own Oxford brogue shoes, took out his handkerchief and gave them a quick polish. That seemed to settle his mind once again.

To pass the time, he took out an ebook reader from his jacket pocket, pressed its buttons to switch it on, retrieved Dan Brown's 'Digital Fortress' and tried to read the screen. Its luminescence wasn't sufficient to read the lines clearly and the fading light only made things worse. He was about to switch it off and put it back into his pocket when he was alerted by approaching rackety voices. Three youths in hoodies and Nike trainers swaggered into the park, each holding a can of liquor to their mouths. They took a final swig and then threw them simultaneously into the flowerbeds. Unzipping their flies they urinated on the cans, laughing and joking as to which one of them could reach the farthest can. "High-fives" followed as one was acknowledged the winner.

Having satisfied themselves with this banal amusement, they spotted Charles and swaggered their way towards him. The big, burly youth was white, the other two black. They stood menacingly in front of him. Charles sensed trouble lay ahead.

'Hey mister, what are you doing?' shouted the white youth, staring at Charles with a mouthful of teeth.

'He's watching porno, he's a perv,' said the smaller of the two black youths with a flattened nose that filled his face, hiding somewhat behind his bigger white mate.

'Are you a porno mister waiting for your boyfriend to come, are you, are you? The white youth jabbed his fingers into Charles's chest and then into his forehead. 'We don't like your type do we mates?'

'Nah, we don't. We don't like your type,' said the second youth again, like a parrot mimicking its master; they all high fived each other again for added amusement.

Charles guessed what would happen next. The white youth withdrew a serrated blade from his sleeve and brandished it in front of his face. 'We could cut you here and now; wouldn't be a pretty sight.' The tip of the blade could be felt on both cheeks and a tingling sensation felt all over his body. 'We'd soon make a mess of that pretty face, won't we guys?'

The tip of the blade was pressed into Charles's chest. 'Hand over whatever it is in your hand and give me your wallet.' The blade was pressed harder into his chest. Charles went to his inside jacket pocket and pulled out his leather wallet.

'Hurry man, hurry,' screamed the third youth who had been silent to this point, furtively looking around to make sure there was no one in sight, a permanent squint in one eye.

Charles stood up, all six foot of him, head and shoulders above the youths. He placed his wallet and ebook reader onto the park bench and then turned his back on the youths who had all stepped back one pace as they suddenly realised this was going to be no easy mugging.

'Turn around mister or I'll cut you. I mean it. I'll cut you.' Charles felt the tip of the blade between his shoulder blades dig a little deeper.

'Bore him... bore him,' screamed the third youth, now dangerously over-excited, his eyes seemingly moving in all directions.

Charles did turn around but swivelled swiftly on the ball of his left foot with great dexterity, raising his other leg and kicking out with his heel at the hand holding the blade, sending it spinning from the hand into one of the bushes. In another split-second, another high turning kick smashed squarely onto the youth's jaw, sending him reeling backwards onto his backside with several bounces.

The other two youths, seeing their leader overpowered in this way, holding his jaw and groaning, had rapidly come to the conclusion that fleeing the scene was their best option. Charles watched them disappear into the darkening gloom. He knew that policemen had been posted at every exit and they wouldn't get far.

The youth on the floor had also decided to exit the scene and was rising to his feet with uncanny haste but another kick to his midriff soon had him buckling up again in howls of pain. In a matter of seconds, Charles had overpowered him whilst applying hand-cuffs. Charles lifted the youth off the ground and pulled down his hood to get a better view of his face. 'I can see why you wear a hood,' he said, 'it's not a pretty face, is it?'

'Go to hell mister, you slimy perv.'

'Now, now, let's not have that kind of language.'

'Piss off. Go to hell you bastard.'

'I said less of that language.'

And, in a more submissive tone, 'What was all that about mister? I never meant you any harm. I was just pretending.'

'Of course you were.'

'I'll sue you for GBH, you dickhead.'

'By the way, it's Detective Chief Inspector to you, and I'm not pretending.'

'Piss off.' The youth spat in the Inspector's face.

Charles cleaned his face with a second handkerchief and, with a foul-mouthed tirade of abuse still ringing in his ears, frog-marched the youth to the exit gate where a marked police car awaited. Another globule of spit directed at him fell short at his feet onto the pavement. He was swiftly and unceremoniously bundled into the car, moaning, shouting profanities, counting his teeth and nursing his wrist.

'Well done, sir,' remarked one of the two policemen assisting the Chief Inspector. 'These youths have been troubling this area for some time and we'll be glad to see them behind bars before they end up murdering someone.'

'Amen to that. Make sure you get the CCTV footage from the camera overlooking the park bench. We'll need it for the courts.'

'That's already been arranged, sir.'

'And you can tell Detective Sergeant Ruskin he can come out from hiding behind that tree.

'He was only watching your back, sir, just in case.'

'I know, like a mothering hen.'

Charles looked down at his brogues, took out yet another handkerchief and gave them a quick polish before stepping into the car's front passenger seat, the youth now more passive in the back with the other policeman, bemoaning one loose tooth. He stepped out again when the second police car pulled up behind them and indicated for Sergeant Ruskin to lower the passenger window. The other two youths, both cuffed, were sitting on the back seat looking somewhat ashamed of themselves, a complete contrast to the hatred in their faces just a few minutes earlier. He looked at their young faces more intently and thought to himself what a waste, what a terrible waste, why do they do it? Why don't they get a life?

'You OK, Sergeant? I saw you chasing these two.'

'I'm fine, sir,' he replied, still catching his breath, 'and you?'

'No problems, Sergeant. Now let's get these three to the station and throw the book at them.'

~

Back at Parkside Police Station the burly Desk Sergeant jabbed his pen in the direction of the Chief Constable's office. 'The Chief would like to see you straightaway in his office, sir. He's not in a good mood. I'll book these three youths and get your details later.'

'Thank you, George.'

Charles knocked on the Chief Constable's office door.

'Enter.'

Charles opened the door to see his father pacing up and down the room, feeling his chin now and then as if contemplating what to say next.

'Yes, father?'

'Please don't call me father in office hours. It's Chief Constable or sir.'

'Sorry sir.'

'Oh, for God's sake, take a seat.'

The Chief Constable took his seat behind his desk and stared at his imponderable son. 'Charles, oh for God's sake, you've got me at it now. Detective Chief Inspector, it is my formal duty to give you a warning. These antics with the youths in the park. These things have got to stop. This isn't the first time I have warned you about putting yourself at risk, not only as a policeman but also as my son. These things have got to stop. Do you hear me? Get someone else to do it. You are giving me and your mother nightmares and it will all end in disaster one of these days.

'It wasn't long ago you disarmed several youths on a bus plagued by muggings of passengers. I know the bus company was very grateful for your personal intervention but that could have ended in serious injury to yourself.

'And then again, that time in the warehouse with armed robbers where you kicked the gun from his hand. What if you had missed? He could have shot you dead. You were a bloody fool. A bloody fool! Do you hear me?'

'It was a toy gun. I wasn't fooled. I know when they're real.'

'And while I'm having my say, why on earth do you let your colleagues call you "Inspector Tae"? It's not proper.'

Charles had learnt not to interrupt his father when in full flow. Experience had taught him when discretion was called for.

'I know you're an expert in the martial arts of Taekwondo and Karate, and can handle yourself in a tight situation, but I still worry about you taking a lead in everything, both as your police superior and as your father. You have an appetite for risk-taking that could one day be harmful to you. By the way, how often do you teach Taekwondo at the Police College? Is it still once a week?'

26

'No father... sir. Once every two weeks. In fact I am there tomorrow.'

'That's all I've got to say. Keep me informed of how the case against the youths progresses. With them off the streets at least the crime rate figures should improve.' With a peremptory gesture of the hand, he indicated the end of the meeting and Charles went to leave the room.

'And by the way, whilst we're having this heart to heart conversation, why aren't you married yet? There are plenty of pretty WPCs out there. How old are you now? Twenty-eight is it?'

'Yes, father.' The conversation having become more personal Charles felt that he could address his Chief Constable as "father". 'I'm married to my job father.'

'Rubbish, I was married to my job but I could still find time to have... err... you know what, with your mother.'

'It's called sexual intercourse, father.'

An icy stare from father to son to put him in his place, and then a quick change of subject: 'And what's your new car?'

'It's a Porsche 911, Carrera 4GTS PDK,' said with a slight childish impudence.

'And why yellow? Why not red or blue? Can't stand yellow?'

'Because, as you are well aware, yellow is my favourite colour, since you-know-what, and I thought I would indulge myself for a change. Bit expensive, but what the hell, you only live once.'

An awkward pregnant silence followed. The Chief Constable, having run out of questions for his son, and having exhausted his paternal, pent-up emotions, made another wild wave of his hand and Charles was summarily dismissed from the office. The yawning gap between father and son, between experience and youth, between conservative and risk-taker was still evident.

Charles smiled to himself as he closed the door behind him. The father-son relationship had a humorous side to it with most discussions ending in a family banter between them both, but there was a serious side to it too which he had to respect.

His father was both a distinguished academic and policeman, holding the post of Chief Constable for the Cambridge Constabulary for over seven years. Operating from Police Headquarters in Huntingdon, he was responsible for sixteen hundred officers and four hundred police community support officers. He had a lot on his plate and he deserved respect.

A product of the Police College at Bramshill, he was a strong advocate of community policing, deploring the "dehumanising" of the police with guns, rubber bullets, tear gas, water cannon, pepper sprays and stun guns. He constantly called for greater co-operation between community workers, probation officers, teachers and the police in the fight against crime.

Charles held similar views to his father about the dehumanising of the police in general, but acknowledged there were instances where armed police were needed. A product of the Police College himself, excelling in his studies, he had been fast-tracked to the rank of Detective Chief Inspector at the young age of twenty-seven, a remarkable achievement. He had been told by HR that with a few more years' experience under his belt they would offer him a post of Chief Superintendent.

As ever, the downside to his rapid promotion on the lips of most of his police colleagues, junior and senior, though rarely said, more in the mind than on the tongue, was the inevitable subject of nepotism, favouritism due to his father's seniority and family connections. It seemed he was always having to prove himself to everyone and that included his father. The increase in rank was proving to be an increasing burden on his young shoulders and there were times when he thought of leaving the police force altogether and taking a job in the City.

Charles set aside such negative thoughts for the moment, took a large intake of breath to clear his head and headed back to the Desk Sergeant to give George the details of his fracas with the three youths and their arrest. There were boxes to tick, the paperwork being an all-important part of the job nowadays if he was to testify against the youths in court and to secure their conviction. The CCTV coverage should guarantee their conviction though.

His spirits did lift, however, when he recalled that tomorrow was Saturday and he was due at the Hendon Police Training College. He was gifted in the art of Taekwondo, a sport he had practised since he was a boy. So good that he had achieved a gold medal at the 2008 Beijing Olympics, beating a Korean, bringing honour to the police force in general and the College in particular. He was given leave every fortnight to teach the new recruits the art of self-defence. Whatever his mood, he always found it an uplifting experience.

It was at the College, during one of his sessions, that, jokingly, he'd been called "Inspector Tae" by one of the new recruits. The name had stuck and now, mainly by his junior colleagues, in more informal situations, he was addressed as Inspector Tae. For Charles it was a sign of endearment, of respect in some ways for his sporting achievement, knowing it was meant in a non-derogatory way. Depending on his mood, everyone knew when to address him formally. His father didn't like it but hadn't kicked up too much of a fuss about it, despite his usual abrasive comments on the subject.

~

Charles drove his Porsche 911 through the towering wrought-iron gates of the Police Training College at Hendon; gates that Charles thought always gave the impression that visitors were not welcome. He headed for the visitors' car park and there found his reserved parking space, identified by a blue plaque on the wall of the building in recognition of his sporting achievement. He used to attend the College weekly, now fortnightly, and the plaque with the Olympic logo was always a boost to his confidence, as much if not more than his Olympic medal. It always brought a smile to his face and a quickening heartbeat.

Stepping out of the car, he unlocked the boot and took out a pair of Armani shoes to replace his driving shoes. He eased on the left shoe and then the right, always in that order. He had a bit of a liking for shoes – boots, brogues, sandals, trainers and loafers – and only the best would do. Ever since he had told family and friends of such an interest, it seemed that every other present for Christmas and Birthdays was a pair of expensive shoes. He had run out of space in his flat for all of them and was now in the process of giving some away to charity, rather reluctantly it had to be said.

He removed his casual, cream sports jacket from its hanger and looked for any creases, smoothing them out with his hand before slipping it on and "shooting a cuff". It was important to keep up appearances; clothes maketh the man. Although not one strictly for sartorial elegance he had, he admitted to himself, a keen eye on the latest fashions. A quick check of his white shirt, crisply ironed the night before, fitted with silver cufflinks engraved with an Olympic logo presented to him by colleagues as a good luck charm, a tightening of his College tie, a hitch of his chinos, and he was ready to do himself justice in the "College Hall of Fame". First, though, his shoes needed a quick polish. He always kept two clean handkerchiefs in each jacket pocket for just that purpose, a habit that had evolved from his sporting days; illogical behaviour maybe but one of his many superstitions.

He took a quick glance around the campus. The formal gardens, attended by the inmates of the local prison, were immaculate this time of the year, and the park beyond was a restful sight for sore office and desk-tired eyes. The campus itself was a buzz of activity as new recruits were directed in parade-ground manoeuvres, some in full uniform and others in full riot gear, practising the controversial tactics of "kettling". It wasn't so long ago that he was doing just that himself.

His thoughts were interrupted by a resonant voice shouting his name. 'Charles. Hello old chap, nice to see you again.'

'Hello David,' replied Charles, pressing his hand into his.

Police Sergeant David Blake was the chief training instructor and had spotted Charles getting out of his car whilst busy on the campus. It was a cordial greeting, it always was. They had known each other from their Eton days and were the best of friends. David's golden-brown, leathery face screwed up in pleasure at seeing his friend again.

'We've had to delay the session by half an hour so perhaps you'd like a cup of coffee in the refectory first.'

'Thanks David. Lead the way.'

They both entered the hallowed hall of the College and went directly to the refectory.

'Take a seat Charles and I'll get you a coffee. Milk no sugar, I believe?'

Charles found a suitable table and looked about him. There weren't too many people in the refectory at this time of mid-afternoon.

'There we are, one cup of coffee. Mind if I join you?'

'Please do.'

David took a seat and fidgeted with his tracksuit before addressing Charles. 'Haven't seen you in a while, a couple of months, maybe? Been on holiday and doing other things. The college keeps you busy. Everything OK with you Charles?'

'Fine, everything's fine. Busy but that's how I like it.'

'Last time I saw you, you were sporting a beard, a growth of some kind, didn't suit you.'

'Oh! That was for the prostate cancer charity. I was glad to shave it off, can't stand the hairs tickling my face.' Charles fingered his smooth face and chin, the result of a close wet-shave that morning, rather than his normal dry-shave.

David glanced down at his watch. 'Must leave you now Charles. I need to prepare the gym. You know, of course, where the changing rooms are, will see you shortly.' He gulped down the last of his coffee, sprang to his feet and headed towards the gym.

Charles, left alone at the table for a few minutes, couldn't help reminiscing. He looked about him again. He was conspicuous by his smart appearance, a far cry from his student days. His immediate thoughts harked back to his days at the College. He had spent so much time in the gym, it seemed he was never out of his tracksuit, whether in the refectory or in the classrooms. That wasn't true, but it seemed like that. When it came to his sport he'd had tunnel vision and every available minute, day or night, would find him in the gym.

He knew his upbringing was privileged. Eton, Oxford, where he had gained a first class honours degree and was an Oxford Blue. Then, to the surprise of his parents who had expected him to go into the City as a banker or lawyer, he joined the Police College, following in the footsteps of his father. There he was fast-tracked for senior management. Now he was one of the youngest Chief Inspectors. A whirlwind of privilege and he knew it.

Despite all of that, he constantly wrestled with pessimism and he blamed his upbringing. If he could change his life, he thought to himself, he would like to change the way he grew up. Around every corner is disaster, it is lurking, it is increasingly negative. Some of the things, the gutterish things he had experienced in his limited time as a policeman had done nothing but increase his pessimism of life. A pessimist by nature and at times, introspective, he sometimes struggled to sleep at night and drank too much. But when it came to his sport he knew that was different, very different, requiring an unsullied, one-track mind.

His watch told him it was time to change for the gym. A last sip of his coffee and he headed for the changing room. There he found his Dobok, his white uniform, ironed and neatly folded just as he liked it, ribboned with his black belt, under a peg on the wall with his name on it. The college did him proud. Pessimistic in life maybe but, when dressed in his Dobok, he was a different person entirely being determined, competitive, high in optimism and adrenalin. Sport was different, very different. It brought out the best in him and he wanted to be the best, the very best in his chosen sport. He was well aware that sport tests the line between sanity and genius and between teamwork and individualism. When the call came he was up for it, willing and able.

He entered the gym to be greeted by David with a handshake and the applause of twenty new recruits sitting on the floor. Charles made an informal bow to acknowledge the hand-clapping and smiled a broad smile. He was now in his element.

David introduced Charles to the new recruits. 'Let me introduce you to Chief Inspector Charles Waley-Cohen, our gold medallist at the 2008 Beijing Olympic Games in the art of Taekwondo. You men take a breather after your exercises and watch an exhibition of the martial art of Taekwondo by the master himself…Inspector Tae. After Inspector Tae has shown you the various moves you might like to try it yourself, but I must warn you to be careful, very careful. Most of you have difficulty raising one leg six inches above the other without rupturing yourselves, so be careful, it is not as easy as it looks. Charles: over to you.'

Using several armless and legless mannequins set up for him by David, Charles went through his repertoire of kicks to the heads and torsos. He was in a world of his own as he demonstrated the battle of kicks and punches.

First the "Roundhouse", a flying kick to the head; then the "Axe" kick, where the heel drops to the head; followed by a "Skip" kick where the leg is swapped in mid-air; finally, the "Lottery" kick, which is a spinning hook to the opponent's head.

'Taekwondo,' as Charles explained, 'translates into English as "the way of the foot and fist" and it is exactly that. A battle of kicks and punches. The protagonists compete on a mat inside an eight-by-eight metre zone, over three rounds of two minutes. The aim is to land accurate kicks and punches on the scoring area of the opponent. A kick or punch to the opponent's torso scores one point, an additional point being awarded if the attacker has his back to his opponent at the point of contact. Spinning kicks score two points. Punches to the head are illegal but kicks score three points.

'It is more a sport about speed of thought and of execution than brute force, not a slugging contest but a battle of wits, the perfect synthesis of sport, game and art. It is all about passion, on a good day it leaves you mentally pummelled and physically aching but elated; on another day you might be knocked flat.'

He ended the exhibition with a formal, deep reverential bow. The applause was like a shot of adrenalin in the arm and he could have repeated it being on such a high but, at his age now, he needed to quieten his instinctive tendencies. Like an actor, applause is addictive and the food and drink of life. Now, he needed to watch his "appetite".

David resumed control of the group and the next half hour was spent by the recruits trying to emulate Charles's kicks and punches to the mannequins. Needless to say, with great mirth among themselves, most unable to stay on two feet the higher they raised their legs. Most ended up on their bottoms with a jarring sound and a painful yelp.

Charles left the gym to another round of applause and headed back to the dressing room. There, he had a shower and dressed before heading back to the refectory for another coffee.

David joined him several minutes later and thanked him for his attendance, always with a ready smile. 'We'll see you again in a fortnight's time?' enquired David as a passing remark.

'Hope so,' was the reply, 'but as the office workload increases, it becomes more difficult to find the time. I enjoy it mainly because it keeps me fit although in future it may be at monthly or greater intervals.'

'Well, good luck anyway and see you again soon.' David returned to the noisy throng of his new recruits whilst Charles headed back to his car.

Driving home to his Cambridge flat in the quietness of the car, Charles became more subdued and negative in his thoughts. Once again, he blamed his upbringing for his pessimism in life and the reason he seemed to be always proving himself to others. Being an Old Etonian can be a curse, a stigma. It is a label that sticks with you whether you like it or not.

There was always a certain expectation on the part of his parents, his friends and colleagues. He needed to constantly prove himself, go beyond the pale, outside and beyond the boundaries of acceptable behaviour. To others, it was leadership, to him it was a point to prove, a blurring between his sport and police work, making him a leader in some people's eyes and a fool with others. His focus and determination was often wrongly confused for an aloof manner. He believed there were two types of public

36

schoolboy: the self-hater and the arrogant git. Whilst cherishing the education it gave him, he bitterly resented the entrenchment of privilege. Extreme comparisons he still had to come to terms with. As with his own world of privilege, and the people he had had to deal with on a daily basis: some violent, some criminals and the disreputable or obstreperous or unpredictable such as the drunks, addicts, rowdy teenagers, prostitutes, loiterers and the mentally disturbed.

It was as though his upbringing had defined his future, his fate in life decided in advance. His social contacts via both his parents had opened more doors than he could walk through and in his Olympic success, yet more. In his confusion he was being led by the nose by unseen hands, his life no longer being his own. He was conscious of seeking out the riskier elements of police work to prove himself worthy of his promotion to Chief Inspector, particularly to older colleagues who had taken twice, even three times as long to gain the same rank. Junior colleagues, on the other hand, tended to be more sympathetic and chummy and, in an affectionate way, would address him as Inspector Tae, the master of Taekwondo. It was his nickname, his soubriquet, and he didn't mind it one little bit. In fact, in a funny sort of way, it levelled the social playing field between himself and his juniors.

Thinking then of his sport, his mind-set totally reversed. Nice guys finish last, he thought. In sport, you have to be bold to be a winner. Whilst sport is King, pessimism will never be my undoing. What he didn't have now though was the single-mindedness necessary to make it to the top of his sport again. He was resigned to being good, but not that good. Those days were over. The magic had not flickered and died, not yet, but it was a reminder in sport, as in life, that great moments do not last, all the more to appreciate them whilst we can.

Memories of his victory flooded over his consciousness. His throat constricted as the happy, smiling faces of David's twin daughters, Sarah and Susan, appeared in his mind. He was their godfather. He had adored them and had loved every minute of their short lives. Aged three, they had both died of a form of blood cancer a month before he was due to compete at the Olympics. It had put things into perspective and he hadn't wanted to go, but was finally persuaded by David and his wife to compete in honour of their children. Anna, David's wife, had presented him with a yellow ribbon as a good-luck token, an Olympic talisman, being the twins favourite colour, and her parting words to him were, 'Your heart and mind can only see the darker side of life at the moment, for the sake of the twins and your own sanity, open your eyes and face the future.'

Reluctantly, he had agreed, knowing the pain of losing the competition would never be as great as the pain of losing the twins. When push came to shove, his more relaxed but sombre state of mind had probably won him the gold medal.

The medal had been dedicated to the two little girls and given to their parents for safekeeping. The anguish of losing the twins, however, would forever remain in his thoughts. Seeing David had brought all those heartfelt feelings to the fore once again for the tousle-headed, red-cheeked bundles of joy.

As for the remark of his father about women, that stung a little. His experiences of the opposite sex were not favourable and they had made him wary of women to the extent that he had closed off all his innermost thoughts and emotions. Some would say he had a cold, somewhat aloof, stand-offish attitude to them, a man who hates women, even. He was not in a relationship and had no plans to be so. No woman was to get under his skin if he could help it.

He had no difficulty in attracting women, he knew he wasn't bad-looking and women would come on to him. Their main interest though seemed to be the social world he inhabited rather than the love in their hearts for him as a person. One day, perhaps, he might find that girl. Until then, his career was his main priority and women were to be kept low on his list.

He thought again about his experiences at Eton which had made him slightly homophobic. Then at university, where he had lost his virginity to an overbearing and over-demanding woman with a liking for bondage, domination and sadomasochism, the sexual pleasure gained by hurting others or of one's own pain. He wasn't into sexual pain in that sort of way and the experience had left him with a bad taste in his mouth. Subsequent sexual experiences had not changed his view of women and he had resolved to remain a bachelor until his dying day. Their "baggage" would not be deposited on his doorstep, not if he could help it.

Charles shook his head to remove all these negative thoughts and switched on the radio to soothing classical music. A sign of getting old, he thought, when I'm starting to prefer dead musicians. Perhaps I'm not meant to do this job forever.

The guttural sound of the Porsche drowned out his thoughts. He admired the wonderfully tactile, suede-clad steering wheel, and machined metal gear-change paddles for the seven-speed transmission. It was precision driving above all else with a top speed of 186 mph, and an acceleration from 0–62 mph in 4.4 seconds. He reflected on the precision of the steering, brimming with feel and feedback to provide the utmost confidence. Splendidly impractical, you either love it or hate it. Charles loved his new toy. A spot of self-indulgence, of retail therapy, always gave a boost to his self-confidence and feasted his well-cultivated senses and fantasies. Privilege does have its rewards sometimes he thought. It's not all doom and gloom.

Weeping skies overhead did not sour his mood.

# Three

'Female, caucasian, goes by the name of Amy Rachel
Barraclough, nineteen-years-of-age, a fresher at Magdalene
College. Marks to the neck but no other visible injuries.
Post mortem and forensics will tell us more in due time.
First estimate of time of death is midnight or thereabouts,
last night. The whole market place has been cordoned off
and the area secured. We have extra police on duty to ease
the traffic congestion and the local council has found an
alternative site for the market traders.'

'Rape?'

'Not obvious, sir. Her clothes don't seem to have been
disturbed.'

'Robbery?'

'Can't tell exactly. Her handbag, I think you call it a
satchel, is still here and contains a purse with money in it,
also a Cambridge Union ID card stating her name, age and
College.'

'A mobile?'

'Her mobile is still in the satchel.'

'Anything of significance in the satchel?'

'No sir. Just women's things, a pocket-map of
Cambridge, an English textbook and a membership card for
the Royal Autistic Society.'

The questions were from Detective Chief Inspector Waley-Cohen, the answers from Detective Sergeant Peter Rankin. The Chief Inspector mused at the crumpled body on the ground, absorbed in his own thoughts.

'Signs of a struggle?'

'Not evident, sir.'

'Any other signs around the body?'

'The overnight snow has obliterated most marks but forensics tell me there are faint signs of a motorbike's tyre marks. They have taken pictures and are attempting to make a mould. The forensic team is scouring the area.'

'Once forensics have finished have the cordon removed and allow the market traders back in. Arrange a space for the inevitable wreaths. Do the usual. Take statements from anyone who might have been in the area late last night, also take statements from her friends and tutors at the College. Let's track her whereabouts over the past few weeks and months.

'Arrange for yourself and WPC Morgan to visit her parents before the day is out. Explain why we have to hold the body. Where was her home?'

'From the Autistic Card, it is Whitby, sir, but I'll confirm that with the College.'

'Again, as usual, take statements from her parents, neighbours and friends, boyfriends of course.'

'Yes sir.'

'Has her room at the College been sealed off?'

'The forensic team did that early this morning as soon as they knew she was a student at Magdalene College.'

'Good. When I get back to the office I'll clear the red tape with the other police forces and I'll speak to the Provost at the University, to the Master of the College and to the Mayor. Best to keep them in the loop. A student

42

killed is not good news for the university or for the town, a rare event that will put the fear of God into all the students and their parents. No mention of this to the press until I can arrange a press conference.'

'Will that be soon, sir?'

'Just as soon as I have all the facts in front of me.

'Oh, by the way, check out the social networking sites that Amy may have been using. See if she was being trolled in any way, any defamatory or scurrilous rumours and allegations from internet trolls.'

The Chief Inspector took another long look at the body curled in a foetal position, lying on its right hand side. The hair was plastered to the face by the snow. The scene was harrowing. Around him, forensics were already erecting a tent to keep out prying eyes. As the shadow of the tent descended over the still body, it was as if a coffin lid was being lowered to separate the dead from the living. A fluorescent light was switched on and moved into position, the shadows bringing the body to life in a macabre sort of way. He was sick to his stomach at the pitiful scene and felt retching convulsions.

He stepped forward carefully and took a closer look at her face, now a pallid hue of death. Her hood and scarf had been removed and her gloves taken off just prior to her death, which was strange given that it had been a cold night. A pretty face, of fresh-faced ambition, now cold and staring, eyes bulging slightly, tongue projecting, a clenched fist whose nails had penetrated deep within the palm, and a left arm outstretched as if waving everyone a final goodbye or asking her God for help from her killer. It was not to be. Whoever had done this had been ruthless in her execution. The girl had had no chance of escape.

The gash to the neck was deep and cruel. This act was odious and could not remain unpunished. Barbarianism, savagery, cruelty cannot be allowed to win. Hate cannot win. He would be unflinching in bringing the perpetrator to justice if it was the last thing he did. He would find the killer and revenge the wrong for this girl.

'You OK, sir?' asked one of the Forensic team. The Chief Inspector shrugged his shoulders, jaw clenched, as he continued to stare through moist eyes at the corpse lightly covered in a shroud of pristine snow.

'We'll have a preliminary report on your desk by tomorrow morning,' added the senior member of the team, in a more reverential tone seeing the inspector totally absorbed and moved by the spectacle before him. 'Best not to take it too personally. It's a vision to make even the strongest man quail.'

A mute reply from the Chief Inspector: an affirmative nod of the head, a resigned shrug of the shoulders.

Still retching slightly, the Chief Inspector left the tent and headed back to the office in a waiting police car. This was his first homicidal case and although he'd seen dead bodies in the morgue before, a mix of anger, sadness and revenge had swept over him as he'd looked at the ashen face of that young slip of a student. He needed to get a grip of his feelings if he was to find her killer and to direct his team accordingly. The pressure was on to come up with a quick response, his seniors would demand it.

~

Over the next day, a deluge of information crossed his desk. Post mortem and forensic reports on the body, the market square and her college room including a full itinerary of its contents; statements from her family, her girlfriends at College and her tutors; statements from her intern work at a solicitors and a bank in London. One item that was missing was a statement from her boyfriend, Neil Robert Staines. He was at sea in a boat called "The Pride of Whitby". The decision had been made to wait for the boat to dock, expected in six days' time.

It was his job to make sense of it all. He called for a meeting of his team in the debriefing room for 3.00 o'clock that afternoon. Time was of the essence.

The conference room was buzzing with idle talk amongst the twenty team members but fell silent as the Chief Inspector entered the room. He got straight to the point.

'From the information given to me so far, this is what I conclude:

'The dead girl's name is Amy Rachel Barraclough. She was nineteen-years-of-age, her date of birth being the 17th July 1992. She was five feet six inches tall and weighed one hundred and twenty-five pounds. She was a slim, pretty girl, by all accounts, with auburn-hair and hazel-brown eyes. Other than an appendicitis scar there were no other marks on her body. She had been strangled. She was a virgin. There were no signs of a sexual assault. Further forensic and post mortem tests are being made.

'Amy's home town was Whitby. A bright girl, she had eight A* qualifications and had been offered a place at Magdalene College to study English. She took up residence on 1st of October this year. Prior to that, she had spent six weeks as an intern at Peabody and Sons, solicitors based in the city of London, but with many branches countrywide, also six weeks as an intern at the Meredith Investment Bank in Canary Wharf, London.

'She met her death at approximately 12.30am, the morning of Thursday, December 1st. Her body was found that same morning at 5.00am by a market trader setting up his stall. Forensics and Detective Sergeant Ruskin were on the scene by 6.00am and immediately cordoned off the whole market square with the aid of the police. As you know, it caused chaos in the town and traffic jams everywhere. I attended the scene at 6.15am.

'The snow flurries we had that night had obliterated the marks around the body save for a motorcycle tyre mark which suggests she might have been killed by a person riding a motorbike. It is too early to draw any conclusions.

'Her boyfriend of long-standing, Neil Robert Staines, is currently in a deep-sea fishing trawler working off-shore. We have spoken to the skipper of the vessel and they are due to dock in six days' time. The vessels are usually at sea for eight to nine days at a time. Neil will be apprehended to aid the investigation upon his arrival at Whitby. A senior decision has been taken not to force the boat immediately back to harbour.

'Needless to say, the manner of the student's death has had a major impact on the student fraternity, the University itself and its entire staff, and the people of Cambridge. Cambridge University has a staff and student population of thirty thousand. The press are baying at our heels for more information and so I have arranged a press conference for 9.00am tomorrow morning.

'Any questions?'

WPC Morgan raised her hand. 'You haven't said how she was strangled, sir.'

'I'd prefer not to answer that question at this stage. Are there any more questions?'

WPC Blake raised her hand. 'Was there any CCTV coverage at the market?'

'As you know, Detective Sergeant Ruskin and other members of this team have been searching for any CCTV coverage. Nothing at this time has come to light. The search will continue.'

'Any more questions?'

Total silence!

'In that case we'll adjourn and meet again when I have more information to hand. Continue with your allocated tasks. Thank you.'

The assembly dispersed in a hubbub of conversations. It was a presentation of salient facts by the Chief Inspector but one fact, one very important fact, known only to Sergeant Ruskin and his seniors, was withheld. He had in his possession Amy's personal daily diary. Amy's ambition was to become a writer and she had made copious notes on the events surrounding her life in addition to her personal diary. After the press conference of these same salient facts as given to his staff, he would arrange for two principal suspects to be interviewed, her boyfriend Neil, and Joseph the PhD student.

~

Neil blinked as the Chief Inspector switched on the recording machine and CCTV camera in the stark interview room.

'The time is 2.10pm on Thursday, 8th December 2011. Those present are Neil Robert Staines, his solicitor Mr

James Dixon, Detective Sergeant Peter Ruskin and myself, Detective Chief Inspector Charles Waley-Cohen. Mr Staines has already been cautioned.

'For the record, Mr Staines was apprehended at 6.15am this morning immediately his boat, the "Pride of Whitby", docked at Whitby harbour. He was allowed one hour to assist its crew to unload its catch before being brought to Cambridge police station here at Parkside, to assist in our enquiries relating to the death of Amy Rachel Barraclough.'

At the sound of Amy's name, Neil winced with the pain of grief. His head was throbbing and he wiped away the sheen of sweat from his forehead with a tissue. His mouth was dry and the palms of his hands sweaty, he reached for another tissue. He had never been in a police station in his life, never mind in an interview room. He was overtly nervous and the fact that his every word and body gesture was being recorded unsettled him even further. The hawkish eyes of the Chief Inspector and Sergeant seemed to note his every movement and emotion. He asked for a glass of water to soothe his parched throat and to give him a few more moments to control himself.

To settle his nerves, Sergeant Ruskin asked him to describe his job.

'I'm a crew member on the "Pride of Whitby", a ninety-foot, one-eighty ton, deep-sea trawler working off-shore with a five-man crew. It's a large commercial trawler, well over ten thousand horsepower, bigger than average worth one million pounds, and bottom trawls for the likes of cod, squid, halibut and rockfish. Other vessels midwater-trawl for anchovies, shrimp, tuna and mackerel. It's not cheap to run and so turnaround is only one day in harbour, sometimes two. It's eight days at sea each time to cover costs and make a profit to pay our wages.'

'And how long have you been doing that Neil?' asked Sergeant Ruskin.

'Since I left school, three years now.'

'And do you like it?'

'I love it. I'm a deckhand, mechanic and cook. It's in my blood you see. My father and grandfather were all fishermen. It's in the blood.'

'And you have another job, don't you?'

'You mean my other job at some week-ends and when the trawler is in port?'

'Tell me about it.'

Neil was in his element. He could talk about fishing all day long. He was an encyclopaedia for all things fishing.

'When the boat is in port, to earn extra money, I help out on a smaller boat, the "Dawn Rise", which can be chartered for deep-sea angling...'

'Fascinating! Tell me more.'

'With sea angling, trolling is a technique in which a fishing line is drawn through the water. Trolling from a moving boat is a technique of big-game fishing to catch large open-water species such as tuna and marlin.

'We use a nylon monofilament line made of a single strand with a steel trace. We use it because of its buoyant characteristics and its ability to stretch under load. This prevents the rod from being ripped out of the user's hand when given a sudden pull. We've been trying out the newer fluorocarbon lines which are less visible to fish and denser than monofilament so the bait stays closer to the bottom. The long-term management of fish stocks...'

Neil paused. He was suddenly self-conscious of doing all the talking and of being goaded into a sense of over-confidence and what might accidentally trip off his tongue. This enquiry was about Amy and not about his fishing. He stiffened his posture and waited silently for the riposte. He was right!

The Chief Inspector thrust a photograph of Amy's corpse lying in the snow. It was too much. The tears flowed and he blubbed like a baby. All his inhibitions, all his bravado, all his macho attitude had dissolved in an instant. His love for Amy welled up into his throat and he broke down in tears. His shoulders heaved with crying, his tear ducts overflowed and he buried his head in his hands.

A glass of water was placed in front of him as he dried his eyes with more tissues.

'I put it to you,' said the Chief Inspector, in a calming, measured, serious but with a quiet and effortless authority, 'that you had an argument, a difference of opinion with Amy on the afternoon of Sunday, 20$^{th}$ November, and suspected she had a new boyfriend. You were spurned.'

'I was what?'

'You were dumped. From the boat's Log, it was at sea for nine days from the 21$^{st}$ to the 29$^{th}$ November. On the morning of Wednesday, 30$^{th}$ of November, after unloading the catch you telephoned Amy to arrange another meeting here in Cambridge. She said she was busy with her studies and didn't want to see you that day.

'The same day, 30$^{th}$ November, you rode down to Cambridge on your motorbike, had another argument with her, lost control and killed her. You rode back to Whitby that same evening to sail with the boat the following morning.'

The Chief Inspector was guessing. Amy had made no entries in her diary on the day she died. However, from telephone records he knew Neil had called her at 10.32am.

'It's a lie,' blurted out Neil, now composing himself a little better from the assault on his character. 'I loved that girl. I wouldn't harm a hair on her head. I loved her with all my heart. We'd been friends from childhood and I wanted to marry her. I did ring her on the Wednesday to apologise for my behaviour, but that was it.'

'What did you do that evening Neil? We know you were late joining your boat the next morning. In fact, from the boat's Log, it departed from port at 7.00am, a delay of one hour. Where were you that evening and early morning? We know you were not at home.'

Neil hesitated in his reply, frightened of saying words that could be misconstrued. 'I went straight home after we had docked. My mother will confirm that. It had been a rough time at sea and the catch was poor. I was tired and irritable and took it out on Amy when I phoned her that morning, even though I only meant to apologise for my behaviour the last time we met. I was so upset at what Amy had said to me, I got on my bike and spent the evening riding along the coastal roads and then on to Saltburn to a place where me and Amy would look out to sea. I spent all evening there before riding back to Whitby in the early hours of the morning.'

'You are not normally late for your boat?'

'Somehow I lost track of time. I was upset.'

'Can anyone confirm your whereabouts that evening?' asked the Sergeant.

'No, I never met anyone. I wanted to be alone. I've just told you, I was upset.'

More questions followed but Neil stuck rigidly to his story. Then a bombshell of a question from the Chief Inspector. 'We found motorcycle tyre marks next to Amy's body. Forensics matched it to your motorcycle tyres. Can you explain that?' That statement was not true but it was worth a try. The Chief Inspector wanted to see Neil's reaction.

'I swear, I tell you, I never met Amy that evening. I can't explain the tyre marks. They can't have been mine. Please, I loved that girl.' Neil broke down once again.

'A final question Neil,' said the Chief Inspector in a more conciliatory tone of voice, feeling a little for Neil's loss. 'What did you argue over with Amy?'

'Silly things, really. I admit I was jealous of other boyfriends Amy would make at Cambridge. More well-to-do boyfriends and a higher class of society than me. I'm just a fisherman following in my father's and grandfather's footsteps. I wanted Amy to be a fisherman's wife but she wanted better things for herself. I knew I was losing her.'

The Chief Inspector nodded sympathetically. He knew Amy's diary had confirmed their differences. Nevertheless, Neil's occasional outburst at one or two questions showed that he was capable of an intense anger, possibly an uncontrollable anger resulting in violence. He was a strong, strapping lad from his labours at sea and, although he obviously loved Amy, it was, paradoxically, still a motive for killing her. If he couldn't have her then no one could. Love is one of the strongest motives to kill someone, even those closest to you.

The Chief Inspector concluded the interview. Neil remained a prime suspect. What hadn't been revealed was that Amy had been garrotted with wire, leaving a red weal around her neck. Her throat had also been slashed. Forensics had concluded from microscopic fragments that the wire was most likely to be a fisherman's line with a steel trace surround. It was damning evidence which pointed to Neil as the most likely killer. Not being able to account for his whereabouts that evening confirmed the assumption.

As Neil was about to leave the interview room he turned around suddenly to face the Chief Inspector and Sergeant. 'The first time I heard of Amy's death I was out at sea in gale-force weather. I felt like throwing myself overboard. I was sick to my stomach. I was useless on deck, you can ask the skipper.'

'We already have. Thank you Neil,' replied the Chief Inspector. 'You'll be allowed to join your boat the next time it sails but we will need you here for further questioning.'

~

Joseph Burnley was genuinely nonplussed and the furrows in his brow deepened. Sitting opposite the Chief Inspector he didn't have a clue as to why he was in a police interview room being taped and was uncertain how to react to questions. He knew, or surmised, the subject was Amy Barraclough who had been killed. It was all over the papers and the campus, but why him? Why had he been singled out for interview? He consoled himself that he was one of many students being interviewed.

'Tell me about yourself,' asked Sergeant Rankin, giving him a steely stare that frightened the life out of the student.

'I don't know what to say.'

'Your background… Tell us about your background.'

'Well, I am twenty-six-years-old and a first year PhD student at the School of Clinical Medicine here at Addenbrook's Hospital.  I hope to become a research scientist.  I graduated from Oxford University in Medicine. I was born in Tampa, Florida, and my father is a Senator.  I boarded at Charterhouse in Surrey before going on to Oxford.  I played rugby for Oxford you know.  Want to know more?'

'That's fine, thank you Joseph,' said the Sergeant, lowering his eyes to make Joseph feel more comfortable in his presence.

The Chief Inspector, again, thrust forward a picture of Amy's corpse in the market place.  'I put it to you that you arranged a meeting with Amy that evening, you tried to have sexual relations with her, she refused your advances and you lost your temper and killed her.'  Like in his sport, the Chief Inspector always believed in going on the offensive first to take the opponent out of his stride.

Joseph studied the photograph carefully and had a blank, if mortified, expression on his face.  A photograph of Amy's face was shown to him, another blank expression from Joseph.

'Do you know this girl?' asked the Chief Inspector.

'I haven't seen her in my life before, I've never met her.'

'You met her at the Freshers' Ball on the 12th of November, did you not?'

'I cannot recall.'

'But you were at the Ball were you not?'

'Yes, but I never met her.'

The Chief Inspector was puzzled. Amy's diary mentioned their meeting at the Ball and their subsequent date for the evening in question.

'You're lying,' barked out the Sergeant, making Joseph jump slightly with nerves at the tone of voice.

After taking a second to regain his composure, 'I am not,' retorted Joseph with a matching vehemence in his voice. 'I tell you, I have never seen this girl except for what I have seen in the newspapers - never, never, never!'

The Chief Inspector lowered his voice, cooling the situation, and asked Joseph to explain his whereabouts for the evening Amy was killed.

'I'm afraid I can't tell you that,' replied Joseph, lowering his eyes in a slightly abashed manner.

'And why not?'

'I just can't... I tell you I just can't.'

'Explain. You do realise that this is a murder enquiry and one way or another we'll find the answer.'

Joseph, taking a moment or two to realise the implication and enormity of his response, finally replied 'I was in my room at the boarding house, studying for an exam the next day.'

'All evening?'

'Yes, all evening. What else can I say?'

'Can anyone confirm it?' asked the Sergeant. 'Did you go into the kitchen late? Did anyone come into you room? Did anyone see you from 11.00pm onwards?'

'Sorry, no one.'

The Chief Inspector ran his fingers through his hair and scratched the top of his head. He was seriously puzzled by this student. Amy had clearly written of meeting him at the Freshers' Ball, had taken a liking to him and had received a text message from him asking to meet at 11.30pm in the market square.

The records from her mobile had matched with the entries in her diary but no telephone number of the incoming call had been noted. Presumably the caller had either withheld the number or it had been a private number. Permission had been sought to find the number from the records of the telephone company.

'What is your mobile number?' asked the Chief Inspector.

'I can't tell you that,' replied Joseph.

'And why not?'

'Because it's a private number for family security reasons.'

'I see. This is a murder enquiry and we can find out from the telephone company.'

'You will have to do that. I would need the permission of my father before I could disclose it. You will need to talk to him.'

This student is an enigma, thought the Chief Inspector. The description in Amy's diary matched the student to a T. "Dark curly hair in need of a haircut; a small, dark goatee beard; a tanned face with blue eyes; a small scar above his left eye; a handsome face with a fine jaw-line, unlike Neil's square-jaw and bull-neck; tall, athletically built". That person was sitting in front of him! Why was he so adamant that he didn't recognise her? Yet, here he was denying all knowledge of her. It didn't make sense. The Chief Inspector's instincts, however, told him that Joseph was lying about his whereabouts that night. He would need to question him again, no doubt with his father's lawyer to contend with, but the truth needed to be known before this student could be eliminated from their enquiries. He had to nail this lie.

'Joseph,' asked Sergeant Ruskin, 'do you own a motorcycle?'

'Why do you ask that?'

'Just answer the question.'

'I own three. My friends tell me I'm motorcycle-mad. A BMW R1200Gs, a Honda Cross Tourer and a Suzuki V-Strom.'

'Expensive bikes Joseph.'

'My father can afford it.'

For the moment, the Chief Inspector was making no headway in his questioning and decided, therefore, to conclude this initial interview.

As Joseph was about to leave, the Chief Inspector left him with a parting question: 'I must emphasise that this is a murder enquiry and if we find out that you are lying about your whereabouts that evening, we will charge you with wasting police time and perverting the course of justice, for which there is a jail sentence. You do realise that Joseph?'

Joseph hesitated in his tracks, realising the gravity of the situation but simply mumbled something under his breath before turning and leaving. He wasn't doing himself any favours and he realised that, but silence was for the best at the moment. He would need to contact his father as soon as possible.

# Four

'You're in early, sir,' remarked Sergeant Ruskin, peering into his Chief's office.

'Worms to be caught,' answered the Chief Inspector, 'worms to be caught. Take a seat, Peter.'

Charles looked at his watch. It was 6.00am on a cold, damp, squally Monday morning, with the rumbling of approaching thunder in the distance. He had been up all night and tiredness was beginning to show on his face. Sat behind his desk, he cradled his head in his hands and closed his eyes for a moment's peace.

'What sort of work is this Peter that shrinks our heads?'

'You tell me, sir.'

'It's like being taken to a cliff edge. Are you sane doing this job, Peter?'

'Sane–ish. Would you like a coffee, sir?'

'I'd love one, Peter. Thanks.'

Sergeant Ruskin knew to tip-toe gently when his Chief was in this mood, sullen, depressed, and irritable. After several years he had gotten used to the nuances in his voice. He sometimes wondered if police office work suited his Chief Inspector, bringing only bouts of pessimism, some would say depression. He knew his sport counterbalanced those feelings and made him more enthusiastic with life, a more gregarious and sociable individual. Pessimism was a pernicious condition that depressed the mind and immune system, leeching pleasure from life and purpose from the day. He was only too aware of that himself from his own personal circumstances.

The Sergeant left the office to grab a coffee from the machine in the corridor.

In his absence, Charles cradled his head again. The perimeter of his office seemed like an ever-tightening band around his head. He longed to get back to his Taekwondo sport as a release from the pressure, but all such exhibitions at the Police College had been stopped for now. He was under enormous pressure to make an arrest and he felt many colleagues were hoping he would fail so they could bring him down a peg or two.

It was Monday, the 19th of December, nearly three weeks since Amy had been murdered and progress was agonisingly slow. It seemed, at first, that it was a simple open-and-shut case, a domestic argument resulting in murder, a classical boy-girlfriend relationship that had gone wrong, but there were peculiarities about this case that left him baffled.

'Here's your coffee, sir.' Sergeant Ruskin placed the plastic cup on his desk and resumed his seat in front of it.

Charles took a tentative sip. 'Jesus, when will that bloody machine ever dispense a decent cup of coffee? Tastes like dish-water. We should sue the company under the Trade Descriptions Act.'

'Do you want me to make you a cup from the kitchen, sir?'

'No thanks, Peter. Just sit there while I get my head together. Let me recap on the progress made, maybe you can see something I'm overlooking. I can't see the bloody wood for the trees sometimes.

'Amy was garrotted with something resembling a fishing line that was strengthened with a steel outer covering. It's called a steel trace and there is an example of it on my desk,' Charles fingered it as if it was about to reveal some sort of secret. 'Her throat was then cut. No trace of the murder weapons has been found, even after an exhaustive search of the trawler and fish market.'

'...As well as the charter boat used for deep-sea angling.'

'As well as the charter boat, even though it sometimes uses the type of fishing line described. Amy's satchel - and I'm told it is called a "Cambridge Satchel" - was unopened when forensics first arrived. Nothing seems to have been stolen, not even an expensive mobile. Robbery does not seem to have been the motive for her murder. Even her room appears untouched. Nothing seems to have been disturbed. There were no signs of a break-in and nothing appears to have been stolen. All that can be said of the tyre mark near to the body was that it was of a touring type, a harder rubber of greater durability, and not a sports-performance type.'

'The tyre used by most bikers this time of the year.'

'That's right, and the tyre mark was too shallow to link it to a specific tyre.'

'That's right,' echoed the Sergeant, being a motorcyclist himself in a previous life, many years ago it seemed.

'Your team has done a lot of leg-work Peter, and a CCTV image has come to light of the incident. The image was far-distant and seriously blurred by the quality of the film and the falling snow, but a blow-up shows Amy being confronted by a motorcycle rider in full leathers and helmet though no facial features are visible. The bike itself has been identified as a possible Suzuki although with no great certainty, the image being too grainy for any identification of the number plate. We know a lot about Amy from her notes and diary, her likes and her dislikes, her ambitions and her fantasies even. Her characterisations have also been useful in knowing better the people in her life. Her boyfriend Neil ... you OK, Peter?'

Peter was fiddling with his tie and his eyes had an absent look, staring moodily into the distance through the office window. He recoiled with a start as his name was mentioned.

'Sorry Peter, I was forgetting. How is your divorce proceeding? I suddenly realise why you're in so early.'

The word "divorce" caused Peter to shuffle uneasily in his chair, stroking his tie as a means of comfort to his feelings. 'We've sorted the numbers... but the kids...?'

Charles looked sympathetically at him. He'd been his best man six years ago and knew the couple well and their two young children, Lily and Oliver. He'd acted as a go-between, an agony aunt, for Peter and Jane when their marriage was beginning to unravel. Things had gone too far and reconciliation was no longer an issue. He knew many policemen suffered the same fate because of the nature of their work. 24/7 police work was never conducive to a good family life.

'Let's meet tonight Peter for a pint. In the meantime, let's concentrate on the business in hand. I need your full attention.'

'Sorry sir'.

'Right, what was I saying?'

'... Her boyfriend, Neil...'

'Yes, her boyfriend, Neil, remains the prime suspect. Amy described him as a moody, divisive person, outspoken with a fiery temperament, and with rapid mood swings. He's been interviewed three times but has been steadfast in the defence of his initial statement and absolute in his love for Amy. It seems he adored the girl. I thought him rough and ready at first but first impressions can be deceptive. I think he's a softie at heart with a sensitive streak. There is no evidence to place him at the scene of the crime and no evidence *not* to place him at the scene of the crime.

'The distance from Whitby to Cambridge is about one hundred and sixty miles as the crow flies. A motorcycle tank holds about four gallons for the same distance. If he'd visited Amy that day he would have had to refill his tank at some point of the journey. Your team has visited every petrol station en route for CCTV evidence. None has been found as yet.

'Equally, the coastal route he said he took between Saltburn and Filey, which is about forty miles, has produced no CCTV evidence to confirm his whereabouts that evening. He said he stopped at a roadside vehicle café for a bacon sandwich and there was a new girl serving. The owner of the café confirms that a new girl was on duty that night and she even recalls seeing him. The time by her reckoning was 5.00am in the morning. That would have given him plenty of time to get back from Cambridge.

'It wasn't unusual for Neil to be out all night. His mother calls him her "night owl". He is a night-rider and parks his bike in a nearby lock-up garage and then walks the short distance to his boat. Not a single witness has come forward to confirm his whereabouts that evening, not even a speeding fine because we know there are several roadworks with a fifty mph limit on the route he took.

'Psychologically and statistically he's the one… and yet?'

'You forgot to mention, sir, that his bike is a Suzuki.'

'That's right, but it can't be uniquely identified as being at the scene of the crime. All the evidence is circumstantial and not enough to prosecute him in court. What do you think, Peter?'

'You're right, sir, there isn't sufficient evidence to charge him. We'll keep the team searching for witnesses. Something is bound to come to light.'

Charles continued, 'As for Joseph the PhD Student, he's a more secretive individual. Amy describes him as one of the nicest men she has met. Natalie Simpson, who had introduced Amy to him at the Freshers' Ball, has been interviewed and shown photographs of Joseph. She even picked him out at a police identity parade, yet, she remains uncertain because, in her own words, she was off her trolley with drink and the hall was dimly lit that evening. How, on the one hand, can she be so certain it was him and, on the other hand, excusing the drink element, be positively uncertain? There is some doubt in her mind. He could be the man! She wasn't sure! None of Amy's friends had seen Joseph subsequent to the Ball, so there is no other witness other than Natalie.'

'And Amy's description fits him to a T,' added the Sergeant.

'So why does Joseph vehemently deny meeting her at the Ball? He's been interviewed three times now and hasn't budged one inch. He swears he's never met her! At one of the interviews, under pressure from his father's lawyer, he had professed he was hiding the identity of the girl he had visited in her residence, late at night, against all the College rules. The girl turned out to be the daughter of the US Ambassador to London. The girl corroborated his statement but said he didn't appear until 1.00am in the morning. She knew for certain as she looked at her bedside clock.'

'Joseph also rode a Suzuki,' added the Sergeant, 'he could have made it to her residence in less than ten minutes after killing Amy.'

'True, but there's still insufficient evidence to place him at the scene of the crime. If we charge him, his lawyers will have a field day in court. Amy recorded that she received a text message to meet her that evening. The telephone number had either been withheld by dialling one-four-one before the number or the number was private. The court authorised permission to search the telephone operator's records which revealed that the number was private and belonged to a Richard Large, not Joseph Burnley, as we had hoped. The only Richard Large in the Cambridge area is an old age pensioner and a council official, both of whom have been eliminated from our enquiries.'

Charles paused again allowing the Sergeant to speak. 'Let's not forget that Joseph could have had a second mobile and given a false name to the operator.'

'Good point, Peter. Let's continue that line of enquiry with Joseph.'

Both men sat back in their chairs and took a breather, both their faces wearing puzzled expressions as the evidence was churned over in their minds.

'Everything's circumstantial and nothing conclusive,' quipped Peter, breaking the strained silence.

'Too right, too bloody right. We're getting nowhere fast.'

Charles had to harbour the thought that it was a random, isolated killing by a passing motorcyclist, an opportunistic killer. The licence plates could not be identified on the blow- up CCTV image because of the snow. So it could have been anyone. Amy's reaction though seemed to nullify this proposition as she seemed to recognise the rider when his helmet visor had been raised. It would be a waste of time and resources to concentrate on this line of thought. Amy knew her killer, he was certain of that.

Peter interrupted his thoughts. 'Amy was not using a social networking site, neither Facebook nor Twitter. What was disturbing though was that when we checked on the Cambridge University gossip website, known as "Library Whispers" allowing anonymous messages to be sent from libraries around the university, bullying and abusive messages were posted by a large number of individuals, a forum of hate by all accounts. We reported it to our e-crime unit.'

'Was Amy's name mentioned?'

'There was no reference to Amy.'

Charles shrugged his shoulders and sighed. 'Let's leave it at that for the moment Peter, my mind is going around in circles.'

'Why don't you go home, sir, and get some rest, I'll man the fort in your absence. You could do with a shave.'

Charles gingerly felt the stubble on his face and chin. 'No, not yet. More worms to be caught and they won't catch themselves.'

As the Sergeant left his office, Charles ran his fingers through his hair and scratched the top of his head, a habit formed over many years whenever he faced an opponent whose strategy he couldn't determine. His team were looking for guidance and he had little to offer at this stage.

He resigned himself to working out his speech for the TV appeal of Amy's mother and siblings, scheduled for 2.00pm the next day, and for the television crime programme. Maybe these public broadcasts would elicit more information but he had his doubts. For every genuine call there would be a hundred crank calls, calls that his team would have to follow up but would usually end up as a waste of police time. He felt he had no choice but to go this route and simply had to hope a bona fide call would make all the difference to his task – to find Amy's killer. Time was of the essence, he couldn't let the incident grow cold and let Amy's death fade too much into the background. His seniors would not tolerate that. It was important therefore for him not to take his eye off the ball with other such distractions.

~

*December 25th 2011.*

Charles spent the day at his parent's house on the outskirts of Cambridge, a mansion in several acres of tended gardens. A house he hoped he could aspire to, if, like his father, he achieved the rank of Chief Superintendent and beyond. At the moment, such titles seemed way beyond him. His father had been his inspiration which was in some ways a blessing and in some ways a curse. He had to plough his own furrow and not be so reliant upon his father's success. He had to be his own man.

His mother was also successful in her own right, being a playwright with several successes on the small screen. A woman whose default setting was always one of love and care, circumspect in everything she did. She had taught him that there was a life outside the police force and whenever he decided to take his nose out of the gutter of society, there were alternative avenues to explore. His education and sporting achievements would open many doors for him.

His younger sister, Faye, now divorced from her husband, the pragmatist of the family, and her two children, Mark and Leyla, were also sharing Christmas with them and brought a lot more gaiety to the occasion. For Charles, it was more a question of relaxing and catching up with family events, a respite from the intense pressure over the last month.

After Christmas lunch, father and son retired to the study to smoke a cigar and down a glass of port or two. Charles sensed from his father's demeanour there was something in the air, something that he wasn't going to like.

'Cheers,' said his father, clinking their glasses together.

'Cheers,' replied Charles gulping down a mouthful and watching his father carefully.

'I wanted to get you alone Charles, away from, the girls and the children so we could have a little talk.' He took a sip of port and drew heavily on the cigar. Charles guessed what was to come.

'I'll get straight to the point Charles. It is now over three weeks since Amy's murder and I'm under intense political pressure to come up with an arrest. I know you've been keeping me up to date and it seems to me you have come to a dead end in your investigation. The public response has offered no further lines of enquiry and you and your team have ground to a halt. I've given you a fair crack of the whip but now I've been asked to take you off the case for a more senior colleague. My pleas have bought you more time but if, at the end of January, you have made no further progress then you'll be relieved of your duties and transferred to other non-homicidal cases. I'm sorry Charles but you know what it's like.'

Charles nodded his head in thoughtful agreement. It was something he had expected. His father was only telling him how it was. Despite all the leg-work of his team, numerous statements and interviews, despite all the public announcements, there was not a shred of evidence, a final piece of conclusive evidence that would convict anyone in a court of law. His only reply to his father was, 'Let's forget it at the moment and enjoy the rest of Christmas with the girls and children. This is not the time to discuss it any further.'

~

Back at work in the New Year on Monday, 2nd of January 2012, saw Charles and his team staring at screens, flicking through computerised information in the search for clues, any clue that could advance their enquiries. It seemed a thankless task but the devil was in the detail, he was certain of that, it always was.

Charles, heeding his father's warning, was even more determined to stay on the case but gradually as the days had slipped by his pessimism had come to the fore. He would have to accept defeat and let another fresh mind take over.

He realised that he would be the butt of a few jokes but was prepared to take it on the chin. A sense of humiliation, yes, but a sense of pride, nevertheless, in what he had achieved so far. After all, the aim was to find Amy's killer and if a change in leadership could achieve that, so be it. It would be for the best.

It was the next day, early morning, when WPC Jane Wetherspool entered his office and approached his desk. She had only recently qualified as a policewoman and been made a member of his team for trainee experience.

'Yes, Jane, what can I do for you?'

'Sir, I've been going through the computer screens and I've noticed something strange. It may mean something, I'm not sure. You told us to report anything strange, anything suspicious immediately to you.' Jane looked uneasy and slurred her words slightly as if what she was about to say was too trivial, trivial enough to be embarrassing for her on her first day with the team.

'Well, tell me what you've spotted.'

Jane paused and added thoughtfully, choosing her words carefully, 'I checked the itinerary of items in the girl's room and there was no notebook about her internship at the investment bank. It might just be a clerical or input error but everything else is listed. We know Amy was a copious note-taker and it seems odd that something as important as that should be missing.' Jane smiled as she realised her comment wasn't as trivial as she had first thought. In fact, she was quite pleased with herself to see her Chief Inspector's reaction to the news.

'Thank you Jane, good work, could you ask Sergeant Ruskin to come in. I want to take this further.'

Jane left the room, said a few words to the Sergeant and then sat back at her desk all pert and pleased with herself, beaming a wide perky smile, blushing slightly. She quite liked her Chief Inspector but would never have the nerve to speak to him on a more personal level. For now, a smile, a compliment from him was a reward in itself.

Sergeant Ruskin entered the office: 'Sir?'

'Peter, WPC Wetherspool has informed me of an anomaly in the data, a missing notebook. Could you have the team check it out. Check for clerical or input error and ask forensics to do another search of Amy's room. I want a full inventory done again. It's still sealed off I believe?'

'To my knowledge it remains sealed until further notice.'

'Good, and if the notebook isn't there, check whether Amy left it at home or whether it was lent to a friend. Let's pull out all the stops to trace the notebook. You never know, it might just be the clue we've been waiting for.'

'Yes sir.' The Sergeant left the office to instruct the team accordingly.

Several days elapsed of thorough investigation but no trace of the notebook could be found. That was strange because in Amy's diary she referred to it and the statement from the Chief of Staff of the investment bank stated clearly that she took copious notes. It was one characteristic of Amy that everyone in the bank had noticed who had come into contact with her.

One possible suggestion was that it had been stolen from her room, but why would anyone want to steal such an item? The lock on her door had not been tampered with according to forensics so how had someone entered her room when she wasn't there? and what did the notebook contain to warrant such attention from a thief? All her other notebooks, including the internship with Peabody &

Son, hadn't been touched and were found in her room. All except this item. What did the notebook contain?

Charles knew this was a tenuous link to the investment bank but one he felt needed to be followed up and investigated further, even just to eliminate this new line of enquiry. The need now was to ask the Metropolitan Police to help him to interview the staff at the investment bank. For this, he needed his father's seniority to pave the way and cut through the red tape.

He took the first opportunity, since time was of the essence, to bring his father up to date with the new finding. He kept it formal and addressed his father as Chief Constable, but couldn't hide a degree of excitement at this new line of enquiry. He explained it was a tenuous link but his gut feeling was that this line should be pursued more vigorously, though what it might unearth he simply hadn't a clue. It was a last-ditch attempt to stay on the case and the Chief Constable knew it. He was taken aback therefore at his father's response.

'I'm sorry Chief Inspector, it just isn't strong enough. Amy could have lost the notebook, mislaid it somewhere. For all we know, it might have fallen out of her bag. She might even have destroyed it herself for whatever reason. An interesting new line of enquiry but not strong enough for me to contact the Metropolitan Police to re-visit and interview again the staff at the bank. There has to be another link to the bank before I will authorise it. Go through the records again to try and find another link for me to consider.'

Charles was stunned. He knew his father's decision was final. There was no way round it. There wasn't a second link. He'd had his team searching for it to strengthen his proposal. There wasn't one, not the slightest hint of any further connection and even then he couldn't imagine what that link might be, or even what it might suggest. He was resigned to being removed from the case at the end of the month. A pity because he felt he was on to something.

The following day, Charles entered the police station and for some reason or other something caught his eye on the noticeboard in the corridor. It was a note, recently pinned, of the suicide of an investment banker. The name immediately rang a bell. He'd seen that name before and the investment bank was the same one that Amy had visited. He rushed to his office. There, with nervous fingers, he opened the computer file and scrolled through the list of names that Amy had come into contact with whilst at the bank. He stared with incredulity. There, there was the same name. He had his second link. His emotions sobered a little. It could of course, be a coincidence, just a coincidence, nothing more than that. On the other hand, it warranted further investigation as he didn't believe in coincidences of this nature. There was a link, there just had to be. His spirits rose as here was the breakthrough he had been praying for.

---

*Extract from killer's diary:*
*He was an awkward bugger. Spent several days tracking his whereabouts and his daily commute from South Wimbledon on the Northern line to London Bridge changing to the Jubilee line for Canary Wharf. Stopped him at London Bridge station. Spoke to him about the need to switch his device for a newer version. He agreed to*

*meet me the next day at the same spot.  He gave me his device.  Gave him a blank.  Asked to borrow his bank security pass.  He refused at first but then handed it over after being threatened.  Easy for me then to give him a nudge in the back as the train arrived.  It was over very quickly.  The mess was disgusting. Better than my video game.  One down, three to go!!!*

# Five

New Scotland Yard, London.
Monday, 9<sup>th</sup> January 2012.

Charles stepped from the black cab outside New Scotland Yard. He paid the driver, smartened his appearance, glanced skyward at what appeared to him, at that very moment, to be a massive, uniform, uninviting and impersonal building. He entered, going straight to the reception desk.

'Would you please inform Deputy Commissioner Wyatt that Detective Chief Inspector Waley-Cohen is here to see him. My appointment is for 11.00 o'clock so I am a little early.'

'I'll ring the Deputy Commissioner's secretary to let her know you are here. Please take a seat.' The receptionist smiled to put Charles at his ease and picked up the telephone. A few seconds later, 'He'll be down to see you shortly.' Another fixed, strained receptionist's smile followed.

He was seated but for a few minutes when he was greeted by the Deputy Commissioner immediately on exiting the lift. 'Hello Charles, nice to see you again, long time no see.' He extended his hand to Charles, engaging him in polite conversation, all the while holding on to his hand, occasionally giving it an extra shake. Finally, Charles escaped his welcoming grasp.

'Nice to see you Robert, it's a long time since I was last here. Whilst I was in the Police College if my memory serves me right. Amazing how times flies.'

As a life-long friend of his father's Charles had met Robert on several occasions and had a sociable acquaintance bordering on the familiar. He was a gentle bear of a man with a softly spoken voice; a proud, old-fashioned man always reluctant to open up and discuss his real feelings; and not by nature someone who seeks out confrontations with politicians, but an erudite and intelligent policeman, not unlike his father. Strong views and a willingness to embrace change had won him many admirers.

Charles playfully patted Robert in his burgeoning stomach area.

'A stranger to exercise, eh, Robert?'

'It's difficult to find the time these days.'

'A lame excuse if ever there was one.'

'Cheeky sod, we can't all be Olympians. One day, you'll be like me you know. From a young Turk to a grizzled patriarch before you know it.'

'Never in a million years.'

'Come, come. Come this way and I'll introduce you to a colleague of mine to assist you in your case. Her name is Detective Sergeant Christine Moran. By the way, have you booked yourself into a hotel?'

'Yes sir, into the Palace Hotel in the Strand.'

'Good. I hope you enjoy your stay in London and you can make some headway with your case. Amy's death was terrible and I hope you can solve it soon.'

Charles was led into a conference room on the top floor, next to the Deputy Commissioner's office, where

Detective Sergeant Moran was waiting. They were introduced formally and shook hands.

'I must leave you now Charles but I'll leave you in the capable hands of Sergeant Moran. My office is next door should you want me. See me again before you leave London.' With that, the Deputy Commissioner left the room.

'Your reputation precedes you, sir,' said Sergeant Moran. 'We're all aware of your achievement in the Olympics and your training programme at the Police College. I was there myself and watched you in Karate and Tae...?'

'...Taekwondo; it's not an easy name to remember and the lesser known of the two sports. Call me Inspector Tae, if you wish. Many others do and I don't mind. It helps them to remember the name of the sport. The more publicity we can get for it, the better.'

'Yes sir.'

'Or just sir, if you prefer.'

'Yes sir.'

Sergeant Moran took an instant liking to the Chief Inspector. He was taller than average and rakish in a nice sort of way. He glowered rather than smiled. What attracted her was not so much his gloominess but his look of steely determination and what she interpreted as mild aggression. Some of the characteristics she surmised to become an Olympic Gold medallist and a Chief Inspector at such a young age.

'Take a seat, sir, and you can bring me up to date with Amy's case. The Deputy Commissioner filled me in on some of the details. Perhaps you could tell me the purpose of your visit here.'

'Thank you Sergeant. I would like to arrange a visit to the solicitors in London where Amy spent six weeks of her internship. I have the statement of Mr Peabody, the head of the firm, which you might like to read. I also have the notes Amy made on her visit and would like to clarify one or two points which give me cause for concern. Then I'd like you to arrange a visit to the investment bank to interview the Chief of Staff again. You heard of the recent suicide of one of the bankers there?'

'Yes sir. I read about it recently.'

'There may be no link with Amy's murder but whilst I'm down here I'd like to check it out. I'm staying at the Palace Hotel in the Strand and my telephone number is...'

'It's already programmed into my mobile, sir. I made contact with your team in Cambridge for the details. I'll telephone you as soon as I've made the arrangements.'

Charles stood up to leave. Sergeant Moran looked at her watch. 'It's 12.00 o'clock, sir. I don't know if you've made arrangements for lunch but, if not, I know a nice restaurant in Covent Garden where you can bring me up to date with your investigation in Cambridge.'

'No I haven't, and thank you for the invitation. I'll look forward to it.'

Sergeant Moran liked the Chief Inspector even more when he smiled slightly, a girlish crush on an enigmatic smile, deep blue eyes and a mop of unruly, deep-reddish-brown hair that just needs a woman's touch. He was as handsome as the other girls had said.

~

The Solicitors' firm was much bigger than Charles had imagined. It occupied the first six floors of a large building in Moorgate. After reporting to the receptionist, they were immediately greeted by Mr Peabody himself. Amy, in her notes, had described him in writer's terms as "a small squat man with a rotund waistline, a short-sighted, pint-sized, fiftyish-year-old with a bellicose, uncontrollable, throaty laugh. His waistcoat, singly buttoned, looked like it would burst at any moment. His double-breasted suit always looked creased and was too baggy for him as though allowing for further growth of his stomach. His florid face probably meant too much booze, with a nose becoming a deep plum-purple. His thinning hair was greasy and 'combed over'. His brown suede shoes didn't suit him at all although they did match his face in colour sometimes".

It appears, however, that she didn't like him one little bit. "There was something weird about him, something murky, something sinister", which her female instincts told her to steer clear of. In her words: "He was a puffed up old man, a self-made multi-millionaire, a man of self-importance".

Charles smiled to himself as he matched Mr Peabody's appearance with Amy's description. She would have made a good writer if she had been given the chance. Her characterisation was impeccable.

'Mr Peabody, nice to meet you,' said Charles shaking his hand. 'Let me introduce you to Detective Sergeant Moran.'

'May I see some form of identification?' was Mr Peabody's first response.

They both showed him their warrant cards. Mr Peabody studied them closely, scrutinising them inches from his face.

'Can't be too careful, you know,' and Mr Peabody laughed his bellicose laugh, his stomach undulating in sinuous rhythm.

Charles looked at Sergeant Moran and a wry smile crossed both their lips. Another time they would have both burst out in side-splitting laughter but, for now, dignity prevailed.

'We'll go to my office,' chirped Mr Peabody pointing to the lift. 'It's on the sixth floor.'

Seated on his red-leather seat behind a very large and what looked like a "one-off", exquisitely crafted antique desk with a red leather top and gold inlay around the edges, he puffed-out his chest and waited for the questions. The office space seemed huge for such a small man with more rich-red, leather-upholstered furniture which clearly reflected his status in the company and to one and all. He touched a button on his intercom.

'Coffee?'

'No thanks,' replied Charles and Sergeant Moran in unison. Mr Peabody relaxed back into his seat again, his head and shoulders barely clear of the desk top.

'It's an Italian designer desk, you know, very expensive.'

'You are Mr Thomas Peabody?' interjected Charles, quickly changing the subject.

'I am.'

'In your statement to the Metropolitan Police, you said you knew Amy Barraclough very little?'

'That's right. I met her twice, once when she joined the company and once when she left. She was a very bright, pretty girl, I remember that, and I assigned her to doing some conveyancing work with my son. It was a very busy period for us and I could not spare the time during her visit to have any further discussions. I did see her once when I passed through the department. She appeared to be taking notes. I'm afraid that's all I know and can't add further to my statement. I read about her murder in the papers. Shocking, truly shocking. Who would do that to a young girl?'

'Who indeed? Well, that's what we're trying to find out,' quipped Sergeant Moran interrupting the two men.

'So, other than the times you have mentioned, you never saw or spoke to the girl again, either in office hours or out of office hours?

'That's right, Chief Inspector. I'm sorry I can't help you further.'

Amy's notes had made no mention of seeing Mr Peabody at other times and there seemed little point in continuing this line of enquiry.

'Could we talk to your son in private?' asked Charles in a firmer, more commanding tone of voice.

Mr Peabody hesitated for a second or two before leaning across his desk to touch a button on his intercom. A crackly voice answered. 'Derek, if you can spare a few minutes, the Chief Inspector and the Sergeant would like to talk to you.' Mr Peabody prised himself from his seat as his son entered the room and, stretching on his toes, gave him a reassuring tap on the shoulder.

Amy had described his son as "tall, thin and wiry with mousey-coloured hair resembling a bird's nest. A weedy sort of character. He was always very smartly dressed in a suit and tie and wore polished shoes, clean at the heels. He was not bad looking in an ugly sort of way with a slightly crooked nose on which balanced a pair of platinum-framed spectacles and two ears which jutted out from his head, not cauliflower ears but something along those lines. His eyebrows were too thick, his lips were too thin and his chin too feminine. He very much had a clerk's appearance as portrayed on television and in cartoons. He was full of energy though and very diligent in his work. He impressed me with his thoroughness".

'Derek, please take a seat,' requested Charles gesturing to the seat opposite. Derek sat in his father's chair and gave a slight hitch to his trousers at the knee in order to prevent bagginess and to preserve a single vertical crease. There was no similarity in his looks or body demeanour to his father. Rather than relaxed, he was like a firecracker waiting to explode. His eyes were bright and alert. He licked his lips and his fingers drummed the desk as if patience wasn't one of his virtues. He fiddled nervously with his mobile, switching it on and off like a child. His behaviour had characteristics that both Charles and Sergeant Moran recognised in drug addicts.

'You are one Mr Derek Lawrence Peabody?'

No reply.

'I ask you again. You are Derek Lawrence Peabody?'

'Yes.'

'Derek, I believe Amy Barraclough was assigned to you for the duration of her stay here?'

'That's correct. Amy and I became good friends. She was a bright girl and I enjoyed working with her. She was a quick learner and was good in the detail. Between us, we got through the work very quickly. After Uni, I promised her a job in the firm, if she wanted it that is. I said all this in my statement.'

'Derek, were you in love with Amy?' asked Sergeant Moran.

Derek hesitated at this personal question. 'A little, I suppose.'

'Did you see Amy out of office hours?' asked Charles continuing this line of questioning.

'A few times, I took her out for lunch. I mentioned that in my statement too.'

'Did you take her anywhere else?' added Sergeant Moran.

Beads of sweat appeared on Derek's brow. He took out his handkerchief and wiped them away. His glasses were steaming up slightly and he cleared them as well. He began to fidget even more with his mobile.

'I'll ask you again. Did you take her anywhere else?'

'We went once, only once mind you, to a nightclub. Amy had never been to a nightclub and wanted to know what it was like. She was going to write a novel which involved a nightclub owner and she needed to know all the "nitty-gritty" details. Her words, not mine.'

'So why didn't you mention it in your statement,' asked Sergeant Moran.

'I must have forgotten. It was no big deal.'

'Are you a drug dealer Derek? Do you give drugs to other people?' It was a pointed remark but Charles thought the time was right to ask it.

'What sort of question is that?' He baulked at the suggestion and looked fiercely at the Chief Inspector.

'It's a simple question - yes or no?'

'Of course not! I'm not a drug dealer. How could you infer that?'

'Do you enjoy watching pornographic material?' asked Charles.

'No more than anyone else,' deflecting such an enquiry with a smile but shuffling nervously in his seat.'

'Are you a paedophile Derek?' asked Charles.

Derek exploded, stood up and waved his arms about frantically, and readied himself to leave the room.

'You people are unbelievable. Do you get off on giving people a hard time?'

'Sit down Derek,' commanded Charles. 'They are simple enough questions, you only have to say yes or no.'

'They're disgusting questions and you have no right to ask them. I'll make a formal complaint to the Met about your behaviour. You have no right to ask me those kind of questions. I'm not a criminal, I'm not under arrest and that line of questioning is out of order.' He ranted on, mumbling to himself.

Sergeant Moran looked at her Chief Inspector with a quizzical expression on her face, also not understanding his line of questioning. He must have a good reason she thought, and remained silent.

Derek calmed himself and used his handkerchief once again to remove the sheen from his brow, and once gain to clean his spectacles. A calmer mood enveloped the office.

'Does the firm have a branch in Cambridge Derek?' asked Charles, this time in a less assertive voice.

'Chief Inspector, this firm is large and we have branches in Cambridge, Oxford, Manchester, Leeds. In fact, a dozen branches throughout the UK. We employ many hundreds of people.'

'Were you in Cambridge on the 30th November 2011?'

That question brought a curt "So what?" from Derek.

'Just answer the question please Derek.'

'I would need to check my diary, but yes I think I was attending a solicitors' conference for three days in Cambridge.'

'Did you ring Amy to make her acquaintance again?'

'I might have done, can't be certain.'

'Why didn't you include all this in your statement?'

'I wasn't asked the question and didn't think it relevant.'

'You didn't think it relevant!

'Did you meet with Amy that evening?'

'No!'

'Can you remember what you were doing late that evening in Cambridge?'

'I attended some conference sessions, had a drink or two at the bar with some friends and then went to my room.

'Did you leave your room at any time?'

'No!'

'Can you confirm that?'

'Of course not!'

'Can you ride a motorcycle Derek?'

'…A motorcycle, a car, a tractor, a golf buggy and anything else that moves.' Derek was on firmer ground now and relaxed more in his father's chair. His fury at the personal questioning had abated and now was much calmer, not so much out of kilter with himself.

'Did you travel to Cambridge on a motorcycle Derek?'

'I did.'

'And what type of motorcycle?'

'A Kawasaki Versys 1000. Why do you ask?'

'Thank you for your time Derek. Sorry about some of the questions but they had to be asked. We'll leave now and see ourselves out. Thank your father for us if we don't see him on the way out.

Charles closed his notebook, stood up and left the room, followed by Sergeant Moran. Outside the building, the Sergeant asked her Chief Inspector about some of the questioning.

'In Amy's notes, and personal diary, she spoke about Derek offering her cocaine. He described the merits of the drug to her. He said he offered it to all his girlfriends. He frightened Amy with his talk of pornography. His firm were the solicitors for several pornography companies and he could arrange for her to appear in front of the cameras if she wished. She was disgusted at his suggestion and was even more disgusted when he spoke of paedophilia and what he had seen, and would she like to see it. She thought him a weird, creepy, tactile individual, a chip off the old block.

'They were the reasons that when he telephoned her in Cambridge for a meeting she flatly refused and said she would report him to the police if he ever came near her again.'

'What do we do next?' asked Sergeant Moran, satisfied with her Chief Inspector's explanation.

'We don't. I will ask my Sergeant in Cambridge to check on Derek's whereabouts in Cambridge on the night in question. My gut feeling is that he isn't our killer but I've already asked the Vice Squad in the Met to issue a warrant, based on Amy's notes, to search his house for paedophile material. He lives with his father in Kensington.'

~

'So many banks of computers! Row upon row of terminals in this one room. God! How many computer screens do you have here?' asked Sergeant Moran.

'At the last count, one hundred and sixty eight,' replied the Chief of Staff. 'If you think this is a sight to see, then you should see the cabling running under the floor and the back-up computers on the floor below with their own emergency electrical generators. It's one huge network complex.'

Charles and Sergeant Moran stood in the dealing room of the Meredith Investment Bank in Canary Wharf with a sense of awe. Neither had seen so much equipment in one room. 'More than NASA's mission to the moon,' remarked Sergeant Moran to the Chief Inspector.

'What did you say?' asked Charles, cupping his ear to hear his Sergeant.

'I said… not to worry, sir. The noise is deafening.'

The noise in the dealing room was an uncomfortable many decibels high with up to two hundred staff talking and shouting at the same time. Despite the myriad of telephones and intercoms, you still had dealers shouting at each other with high-pitched voices from either end of the room. Old habits die hard, thought Charles, in spite of the technology.

As for the computer screens, they had more lights than a Las Vegas gambling arcade. Coloured graphics and pie charts and histograms of every description flashed up on the screens with the merest finger touch of a screen or the slightest mouse movement on a tablet inlay.

'Seen enough?' queried the Chief of Staff. 'If so, we'll go into my office. It's a little quieter there.'

Sergeant Moran nodded earnestly and the three of them headed to an office in the corner of the room comprising nothing more than a desk, three chairs and a steel cabinet.

'Phew! That's some sight,' said Sergeant Moran sitting next to the Chief Inspector and opposite the Chief of Staff who had seated himself at his desk and had readied himself to speak.

'Dealing rooms were once quite small, handling essentially foreign exchange, but "they growed like Topsy", to be enormous beasts dealing in a whole range of instruments. The trend is still upwards.'

The Chief of Staff was Peter Ebdon, a young man in his thirties with a trimmed moustache and beard. Charles had expected an older man to hold such a position and was surprised how young he looked. He glanced at the statement he had made to the Met to note again his age and background.

Peter Ebdon interrupted his thoughts. 'It's a young man's game. All the dealers, well most of them, are in their twenties. Their life is devoted to those screens. They work 24/7 and burn out at an early age. If they can't be transferred to another department, they are made redundant. The bank gets its pound of flesh and then spits them out when they don't make the grade. The general public moan about the bonuses these guys make but they tend to be short-lived. You make it in your early years or you end up on the scrapheap.'

'The reason we're here is to talk about Amy Barraclough who was murdered in Cambridge last November,' said Charles, becoming suddenly very officious. 'The Met took one statement and that was from you. They did not take any statements from any of the dealers.'

'Well, you can see the number of dealers involved. It would have taken them months if they'd gone to each desk. As I said, once there were a few dealers dealing with foreign exchange, from spot deals to forward deals. Now, there are currency swaps, short and long-term, currency options and other option-based products. There are many markets dealing in certificates of deposits, re-purchase agreements, treasury bills, commercial paper, bills of exchange and other funds. Add to that the Euromarkets, Eurobonds, Euronotes and so on. Then, the domestic capital markets in government securities and equity markets. I won't go into the number of interest rate management products and derivatives. It's just one huge, complex trading operation which costs a fortune to run and equally makes a fortune for the bank, or loss as the case might be. Then you have the oil futures market, the...'

'Thank you. I get the picture,' said Charles trying to interrupt the lecture.

'You also have the support areas, the settlement department, the auditors, and not least, the financial control,' continued Peter Ebdon, not wishing for his forceful verbal explanations to be so easily interrupted.

'When Amy came to see me I showed her the development of a computer system I was working on, the programming and the like. But, within a day she got bored very quickly and wandered into the dealing room. Not surprisingly, she enjoyed talking to the young dealers and busied herself chatting and taking notes. She covered a lot of ground in the six weeks she was here and seemed to totally enjoy the working environment. At the end of the six weeks we spoke again and she gave me a resume of her stay here. It was most comprehensive and I was impressed. The girl was very observant and very meticulous in her notes.

'I said all of this in my statement.'

'You did indeed,' said Charles, flicking through the many pages of the statement. 'You did indeed. Tell me, did she go out with any dealer in particular, go out for lunch for example?'

'Not to my knowledge. There's a restaurant in the building for all bank employees and I saw her there occasionally, but with no one in particular.'

'The notebook Amy was using to make her notes in, has anyone reported finding it within the bank?'

'No. Not to my knowledge. Why? Had she lost it?'

'Changing the subject slightly,' said Charles deliberately not answering his question, 'tell me about the dealer, David Unwin, who committed suicide on the underground platform.'

'Not a lot to say really. A shocking incident. He was twenty-five, worked on the America's equities desk, North and Latin America, and, by all accounts, was very successful. He was due for a large bonus this year. It didn't make sense. There were rumours he was having problems at home with his fiancé, but I wouldn't have thought it justified what he did. Everyone was shocked at the news. You must understand also, that these guys are under tremendous pressure to perform, as I said earlier, and his death, however tragic, comes as no surprise. He's not the first and I suppose won't be the last to take his own life. I remember one dealer who threw himself off an NCP building. There was no bonus for him that year and he'd already spent it. That's all I've got to say really.'

Charles looked at the Sergeant with a thoughtful expression on his face. He had hoped for something that would have linked David Unwin's death with Amy's death. But, offhand, there didn't seem to be any link. It was after all, he thought, just a coincidence. Yet, his gut feeling was saying something different. He just didn't know what.

Turning again to Peter Ebdon, he asked if they could interview David's colleagues on the same desk, in private.

'By all means,' said Peter, 'there's John Bloomfield and Carla Bores. The two of them worked with David on the same equities desk. Do you want me to send them in, one at a time?'

Charles nodded. Out of all the dealers and support staff it was a wild gamble to interview just the two of them, but since there was no other way forward it was worth it as it might elicit some kind of link with Amy.

Peter Ebdon left the office and a few minutes later entered another young man, looking slightly harassed and what Charles could only describe as jittery.

'Please take a seat,' asked Charles calmly, eyeing the young man up and down to form a quick judgement of his character.

'You look a bit harassed and dishevelled,' said Charles to the young man, who by now was biting his nails.

'There's a big contract pending, multi-million pound arbitrage deal, and I need to get back to my desk as quickly as possible. My annual bonus depends on it.'

'Arbitrage?' queried Sergeant Moran, not understanding the meaning of the word.

'It's a widely used banking term to describe the process whereby advantage is taken of differences in price of some, or similar, instruments between one market and another. Happens all the time. Computers track the differences but you have to be quick before the markets equalise. Is that sufficient explanation or should I explain it further?' said the young man dryly, and in a somewhat superior tone of voice.

'Well, we won't keep you long and I'm certain your colleague will take care of it in your absence,' continued Charles. 'Your name is John Bloomfield I am told?' glancing at Sergeant Moran who was taking notes.

'Yes.'

'How old are you John?'

'Twenty-five.'

'And how long had you worked with David Unwin?'

After a moment's pause, 'Four years or so.'

'Did you notice anything odd in his behaviour, prior to his death?'

'Not really.'

'Did he have problems at home?'

'Not that I know of. If he did, he didn't mention it to me.'

The questions continued but the response each time was very succinct. If John did know anything he wasn't going to disclose it. Despite ever more probing questions, Charles could not find the slightest link with Amy. He was flogging a dead horse and there was no point continuing the interview. His gamble had failed.

'Well, thank you for your time. I hope the arbitrage deal goes through for you.'

John couldn't leave the room quickly enough. His general manner still puzzled Charles, even though he couldn't put his finger on what was troubling him.

He was about to consult with Sergeant Moran when the door opened again and in stepped a young woman. Dressed in a cream trouser suit and white silk shirt, she was stunningly beautiful. A striking brunette with her long hair tied in a bun at the back and slender tendrils of hair down each side of her face. Her features were Spanish or Latin American. She had an iridescent bloom to her face.

In contrast to John, she sat demurely on the seat and crossed her legs. She was calm, confident and impressively at ease. She looked Charles straight in the eye with a playful smile on her lips and an amusing, coquettish angling of the head. He was instantly bowled over by her charisma and self-assurance. He suddenly experienced feelings for a woman he had not had before. Sergeant Moran also noticed the change in his bearing and softening of his posture. She coughed to distract him from his fixed gaze.

Charles regained his composure. 'Your name is Carla Evita Bores?'

'It is.'

'And you are a dealer on the equities desk?'

'I'm a senior dealer.'

'How old are you?'

'I'm twenty-eight, and how old are you Chief Inspector?'

'Let's leave the questions to me Miss Bores.'

'It is Miss, thank you, Chief Inspector.'

A few more elementary questions from Charles and curt, nondescript replies from Miss Bores and Sergeant Moran decided to intercede on the repartee between the two of them, in what she considered was becoming a fawning interview. Whilst her Chief Inspector was still gawping at the girl in front of him the Sergeant waded in with her own questions. There was a hint of jealousy in her tone. She'd noticed that both their eyes were lowered on first introduction and he was plainly smitten by her charms. Her female intuition kicked in.

'Miss Bores, how long have you worked at the bank?'

The young woman turned her eyes away from Charles to look at the Sergeant. 'Five years, give a few months or so.'

'And how long had you worked on the equities desk with David Unwin, the young man who killed himself.'

'I'm aware of what David did and the answer to your question is three years.'

The questions came thick and fast from the Sergeant but Carla wasn't in the least bit phased and never lost her composure. The questions became personal.

'Did you have a relationship with David?' the Sergeant asked smugly.

'No. Certainly not. It was a strictly business relationship.' She bridled at the suggestion, seething inwardly but remaining calm.

'Did you meet with him after hours?'

'No. I've just told you it was strictly a business relationship. I might have had one drink in the local pub to celebrate a deal but others were always present. A team celebration, you know what I mean, you must have had several of them yourself, have you not?'

Sergeant Moran would not be intimidated by this serene, confident, and what she considered, unbearably smarmy girl whose face, in her opinion, betrayed a wry and mocking smile.

Charles brought a halt to it. He could see, once again, no connection with Amy's death and Sergeant Moran was becoming flustered and blustering in her questioning, Carla waspish and huffy in her replies.

'I think that's enough for now,' said Charles. You may go but we might need to interview you again.'

Charles had no idea why he said that. It was more wishful thinking on his part than to do with any connection with Amy's death. He was captivated by her - hook, line and sinker. He watched her leave the office with a certain swagger and swing of the hips. He'd never felt this way for a woman before and hoped he had hidden his feelings from Sergeant Moran.

They left the building after thanking Peter Ebdon and hailed a taxi to take them back to Scotland Yard where they would write up their notes. Sergeant Moran remained sullen, and silent throughout the journey, a hint of disgust written on her face. Why didn't he behave like that to her? She felt she was just as pretty as the other woman and she had first call on the Chief Inspector. She wasn't generally possessive by nature but in this case she would make an exception.

~

Charles sat alone in his hotel room the following morning with fairly pessimistic thoughts as to how Amy's case was progressing when there was a knock on the door. 'Service,' was the call. He opened the door to find Sergeant Moran standing there. 'Just joking, sir.' She entered and sat down opposite him. 'I'm told you're leaving tomorrow, going back to Cambridge?'

'That's right. There seems no reason for me to stay. I had hoped for a connection between Amy's murder and the investment bank but there doesn't seem to be any. My team in Cambridge is searching for witnesses to corroborate Derek Peabody's whereabouts on the night of the murder. Until then, he will remain a suspect. What he said to Amy was disturbing but was not illegal and he cannot be arrested on that basis.

'The Vice Squad has reported back to me to say that they removed the computers from his house and searched the files for paedophilia material. They found evidence of a paedophile ring and have made an arrest. But it wasn't the son they arrested, it was the father after he confessed to downloading the files. His son was just cautioned. It just shows you can't always go on appearances alone.

'As for David Unwin, it seems his suicide, or accident for that matter, had nothing to do with Amy's case. I had hoped it would be, but there you go, you can't win all of the time. A gut feeling that was wrong. So tomorrow morning, after I've reported to the Deputy Commissioner, I'll catch the midday train back to Cambridge.'

'The reason I dropped in to see you, sir, is that a friend of mine has given me two tickets to see "War Horse" at the New London Theatre. Something else has come up and she can't use them tonight. Would you be interested?'

Charles paused for a moment and the Sergeant expected a "no, but thank you". Instead, he answered in the affirmative and a broad smile crossed the Sergeant's face. She had told a fib about being given two tickets. She had purchased them the previous day and had taken the chance that he would agree. One way or another, she was still determined to try and find a way through the apparent thick skin of the Chief Inspector when it came to women. This was her last chance if he was leaving the next day.

'I'll see you 7.00 o'clock tonight then, outside the theatre,' said Sergeant Moran, beaming from ear to ear.

'I'll look forward to it, and we can have dinner at the hotel restaurant after the show.'

Sergeant Moran gently closed the door behind her as she left the room. 'Yes!!!' she said to herself, punching the air in a triumphant way and awarding herself a hundred "brownie points". She left her Chief Inspector still mulling over the interview notes from the bank and the solicitors, lost in his own thoughts.

At 7.00 o'clock promptly that evening, Christine Moran waited for her Chief Inspector, her mind in a state of fantasy. For a few minutes, there was a seed of doubt as to whether he would turn up but that was brushed aside when she saw him alight from a black cab and wave to her. She returned the wave.

She smiled when he came close and he smiled back, the first time she had seen him smile widely since they had first met. She noticed that he had irresistibly crinkly eyes when he smiled like that. She was more in love with him than ever. It wasn't reciprocated but she could work on that.

'Charles. OK if I call you Charles? And you can call me Christine.'

Charles nodded and smiled widely again.

During the show and the interval Christine deliberately made no advances to the Chief Inspector, maintaining their personal space, but her whole body tingled with his close proximity.

After the show, they both walked back together to the hotel in the Strand, discussing the life-like nature of the horses and how, after a while, you forgot or didn't see, the puppeteers manipulating the various parts of their bodies. Christine had blubbed a bit through the show and borrowed Charles's handkerchief to dry her eyes.

The show was followed by dinner as Charles had promised. Christine took this as another opportunity to show her affection. Whilst eating, she slipped off her shoe and rubbed her foot down the length of his leg. Charles retracted his leg smartly and his body stiffened, but he said nothing. Christine employed another tactic to get Charles to loosen up. Whilst he was distracted, paying the bill, she put her hand on his and squeezed it. Charles instantly withdrew his hand to his side and his whole bearing became cool and detached. Perhaps he's gay, she thought to herself. Surely not. She had seen how he had reacted to Miss Bores and was convinced he was not that. The sexual warmth was there, but it had sharp edges. He's intriguing, so much going on beneath the surface, but so temptingly out of reach.

'I'll order you a cab to take you home,' said Charles, after thanking her for the evening. 'I've got some more work to do and it can't wait.'

Charles saw her into a taxi and waved goodbye. Christine, out of sight, ordered the taxi to stop and paid the fare. She walked back to Charles's hotel and went straight to the bar. She wasn't defeated yet.

After a couple of vodkas and lime, and at several minutes past midnight, she went to Charles's room and knocked on the door. Charles opened the door dressed only in his dressing-gown and was surprised to see Christine standing there, pressing against the wall for support. Christine showed her feelings on her face and seemed not afraid to do so. It made her very vulnerable and, in some ways, rather endearing.

'Christine!'

'Do you find me attractive Charles?'

'Yes, you're a very pretty girl and easy on the eye too.'

'As pretty as Miss… Miss… Miss Bores?'

'You are both very beautiful women. You have lovely blonde hair and beautiful blue eyes. You have a very pretty face and trim figure.'

'Then why don't you kiss me?' she cooed as she staggered towards him.

'OK.' Charles gave her a chaste peck on her cheek.

Christine, in reply, threw her arms around his neck in a tight embrace and kissed him fully on the lips. Charles untied her hands, backed off and kept Christine at arms' length.

'Have you been drinking too much?'

'Err, sort of...,' she stuttered. 'I only had one or two teeny-weeny glasses of wine as a nightcap. I swear Charles, Inspector Tae. That was all.' She gestured with her fingers how small they had been.

'Come in Christine. I don't think you're in a fit state to go home. You can sleep here in my bed tonight. I'll sleep on the couch.'

Charles led Christine by the arm to the bedroom, helped her remove her coat and shoes and insisted she lie down on the bed. He covered her with a throw, kissed her forehead and told her to go to sleep, she'd feel a lot better in the morning. He grabbed a spare blanket, switched out the light and closed the bedroom door. He made himself comfortable on the sofa in the lounge and went to sleep himself. He had a busy day the next day.

Christine was woken up the next morning by the low hum of an electric razor. She sat up in bed and after a few seconds of realising where she was, was surprised that she was totally naked between the bed sheets. She couldn't remember undressing herself or that Charles had helped her undress, and her clothes were neatly arranged in a pile on the chair nearby! She pulled up the sheet to cover her breasts and surmised it must have been Charles who had undressed her. She peeped under the sheet at her body and a certain thought crossed her mind but she dismissed it, he wasn't that kind of man. He was perhaps a more devilish character than she had first thought though. Under that cool exterior lay the devil incarnate perhaps! He was a challenge to any woman and, to Christine, a prize worth winning and fighting for.

Christine was not a girl to be defeated so easily. She had one more trick up her sleeve. She slithered out of the sheets and tiptoed to the bathroom door which was still ajar. She could see Charles shaving, dressed only in his underpants.

'Is it tough being a "looker" Charles?'

'You tell me.'

'Charles, do you mind if I take a shower?' she asked in her best pillow-soft voice.

'Nearly finished and then you can have the bathroom.' Charles looked at his face in the large mirror over the basin and stroked his chin. 'Office worker pallor,' he shouted to Christine, 'desk work doesn't suit me. What do you think?'

Christine flung open the bathroom door and stood suggestively in the doorway casting brooding glances. Charles looked casually in her direction and then turned back to the mirror to continue his shaving. Christine, indignant at his indifference, walked sassily to the shower cubicle, brushing past Charles deliberately, and turned on the water. Charles continued shaving, seemingly oblivious to her presence.

'Join me if you wish,' shouted Christine above the noise of the flowing jet streams.

'No thanks. I've already had one.'

Charles couldn't help seeing the reflection in the mirror of Christine in the shower. He had resisted her so far but his resolve was wilting rapidly. The smell, the heady mix of perfume and fresh soap assailed his nostrils. That was it! His blood was up! She had taken him up to and beyond the point of no return for any man. He flung off his underpants and jumped into the shower cubicle with her. A man must do what a man must do, he thought to himself. She was a beautiful girl after all.

Christine's smile widened as she hugged Charles. At last, finally, she had won the battle. And, who knows, it might be a one-battle war! She sensed emotional scarring that made him hard to get close to, but she would change things and he would let go and "fall in love" with her. She would see to that and make it her mission in life. She was well aware that her own character was loud, strident and unashamedly effervescent but she could change that too to suit him given half a chance. She hugged Charles again even more tightly. She felt his hands on the inside of her thighs, reaching up and searching.

'Ooooh! Charles! Inspector Tae! What are you doing?!!'

They showered for much longer than usual and the wet kisses continued whilst both were towelling themselves dry. It was at that moment that the hotel telephone rang. Covered only in a big, broad smile, Charles picked up the receiver. It was the Deputy Commissioner.

'Charles. Come quickly to Scotland Yard. There's been another major development.'

'Should I bring Sergeant Moran with me?'

'No Charles, just you. Make it quick. We'll be waiting for you.'

---

*Extract from killer's diary:*
*Told he lived alone and kept the device in his safe.*
*Tracked his whereabouts for several days and waited until*
*he was alone in the house. Knocked on the door and he let*

*me in. We went to his study. Told him was there to replace the device with a new version. He went to the safe and handed me the device. Handed him a dummy version and pretended to leave. Turned around and shot him twice in the chest with a pistol. Shot him in the head, close up, to make sure he was dead and kicked over his wheelchair. Smashed up the place to make it look like a robbery. Retrieved the dummy device and left. It was soooo... easy and enjoyable. Two down, two to go!!!*

# Six

Charles was greeted by the Deputy Commissioner at the reception desk of Scotland Yard. The Commissioner's face was more serious and his deportment more officious. All suggested a sense of urgency. No joking from Charles this time.

'Charles, come quickly,' gesturing with his hand for the Chief Inspector to follow behind him. Charles said nothing and just followed in the quick steps of the Commissioner.

This time the Chief Inspector was led to the Commissioner's office. A new experience for Charles, he knew of but had never been introduced to the Met Commissioner. He was ordered to leave his mobile outside the room. 'Basic mobile phones, without specialist anti-eavesdropping security, can be converted into "listening devices" by foreign intelligence agencies,' he was told by the Assistant Commissioner. 'This briefing contains "strap" intelligence to be shared with only top officials.

'Let me introduce you to Stephen Beale from MI5 and to Douglas Home from MI6.' Charles hadn't noticed them sitting in the conference chairs at the other end of the office. He turned and shook hands with both of them, now standing to greet him.

'All be seated,' said the Commissioner in a slow, measured, soothing, paternal way, joining them at the conference table. 'I've asked my PA to bring in coffee and biscuits. There's no point in letting the seriousness of the business in hand spoil our morning coffee. Don't you agree?' His lightening of the mood and relaxed approach went down like a lead balloon, not even a smile crossed the lips of the MI5 and MI6 agents. If they could, they would have growled at the Commissioner.

Charles was bewildered. He didn't know what to say, he didn't know what to expect next. He had no clue as to why such a meeting was taking place and, especially, why he was part of it. He remained silent and looked intently at the two agents. The MI5 agent stared at Charles as if weighing him up, as if the Chief Inspector was a target for their deliberations. Charles glanced at the other agent. He too was staring at him as if he were an alien out of space. Charles felt uncomfortable and eased the shirt collar around his neck. Was he the subject of the discussions? Had he done something wrong to merit such attention? In any case, what had all this to do with finding Amy's killer?

The Commissioner, having shuffled himself comfortable, gestured at the MI5 agent to speak. The agent took from his inside jacket pocket a piece of paper and carefully unfolded it, seemingly grimacing behind the thick black frames of his glasses that gave him an academic air. Yet, in his spectacles and dark suit he looked neat and respectable, almost meek.

'We were given this report very early this morning of the death of Juan Carlos Bores. He had been murdered with a .45 calibre automatic pistol, shot twice in the chest and once, at point-blank range, in the head. Powder burns showed that the muzzle of the gun was touching the victim.

He was murdered at his office in Westminster last night at approximately 10.30pm. He was discovered early this morning by his cleaner.'

The name Bores instantly resonated in the Chief Inspector's head. Was he the father of Carla Bores, the girl at the investment bank?

The agent continued, 'Juan Carlos Bores was well known to MI5 and to MI6. He was a principal lobbyist in Parliament for Las Malvinas. He was head of an organisation, here in London, called the Belgrano Fellowship whose aim was to persuade members of Parliament to change their views on the sovereignty of the islands. There is nothing illegal in that but with the general ratcheting up of the subject by the Argentinian government of late we have been closely monitoring the activities of his organisation.

'The initial report suggests that it was a straightforward robbery that resulted in murder. A burglary that went wrong. The safe had been opened and the drawers emptied of their contents. Many articles and vases had been smashed as if the murderer was in a frenzy of anger. We think that Juan Carlos Bores met his death at the hands of a cold-blooded killer.'

The Commissioner then gestured to the MI6 agent to speak.

'Gentlemen, we have informed, early this morning, the Prime Minister and the Argentinian Embassy here in London. The Ambassador will have informed the President of Argentina by now. It may result in a greater slanging match between the two countries, more sabre-rattling, more exaggerated statements and propaganda by Argentina. The Argentine government has been unable to do anything about the humiliation of the existence of these British islands so it has embarked on an increasingly ludicrous and embarrassing PR offensive over the issue.'

The Commissioner interceded. 'The press has not got wind of it yet but it won't take them long. They are going to have a field day. I will arrange a press conference at the appropriate time, later today or possibly tomorrow. What is important gentlemen, is we catch the killer as soon as possible to dampen down the political speculation.'

It was Charles's turn to speak. 'I assume that Carla Bores, the girl I interviewed recently, is his daughter?'

'You assume correctly,' said the MI5 agent. 'In fact, she was used by her father to lobby with him. She was the "honeypot" to lure members of Parliament to private meetings and who knows what else. By fair means or foul, that is the way these organisations operate. She has been in our rear view mirror for some time now.'

'Then why wasn't I told of these things, and why am I here in this meeting?' asked Charles.

'We didn't think it relevant at the time, Chief Inspector,' said the Deputy Commissioner. We did not want to raise their suspicions that we were focusing in on them. Yours was a simple, local murder case and we wanted to keep it at that. As for why you are here in this meeting, the truth is we don't know. Your case has nothing to do with this one and would appear, at first glance, to be worlds apart. But, for some indefinable reason, you seem to be a catalyst for these events and we want to keep it that way. There is a slim possibility, a slim possibility I agree, that our route to the killer is via yourself. It is important, therefore, and we all agree, to keep you in the loop. We do not think there is any danger to you but nevertheless be on your guard.'

The Commissioner signalled the end of the meeting and they all stood up. Charles shook the hand of the Commissioner and then the two agents. He smiled. His smile was not returned. The two agents were sour individuals. They were just regular guys, nothing distinguishable about them, thought Charles. They were obviously smart and savvy working for MI5 and MI6, but you would not pick them out of a crowd, they would blend into any background. They both stared at him again as if they knew something he didn't.

The MI6 agent, in particular, his body language was so difficult to understand you could not tell what was in his mind. His facial expression wasn't giving much away either. Throughout the meeting it had been a picture of robotic blankness. When he had spoken, it was with a deadpan delivery. Rigidly inscrutable he stared straight ahead hardly blinking.

'Chief Inspector, can I have a word with you in my office?' asked the Deputy Commissioner. Charles followed him into his office. 'You are not to talk about this meeting to anyone,' added the Deputy Commissioner. 'Not even to Sergeant Moran. Because of the sensitivity of the information Sergeant Moran has been assigned other duties. There are times when the national interest requires secrecy and it is naïve to pretend otherwise. You do understand that Charles? You do understand that these events are not, and I repeat not, to be included in your enquiry of Amy's death.'

Charles nodded, taken aback somewhat by the changing nature of events.

'As for lobbying, Charles, let me add to what the MI5 agent said. Lobbying has a place in a democracy. Companies must be able to raise concerns with government but it needs to be an open and honest process. All too often the buying of power and influence can be murky, sleazy and unpleasant. They give money because they want something. A promised compulsory register of the four thousand or so active lobbyists has yet to materialise.'

Charles listened intently. Politics was not his forte but essential if he was to progress in seniority.

'I believe you were to go back to Cambridge today?'

'There was no reason for me to stay. We've drawn a blank in our interviews here …'

'Well, I would like you to stay for another week or so. I have spoken to your father and informed him of further possible developments. He understands the situation.'

As Charles was about to leave: 'And by the way, well done on your uncovering of the paedophile ring. That was an important bust and it will go on your record.'

'Thank you, sir.'

As Charles sat in the taxi taking him back to his hotel, his mind was absorbed in thought. It was a strange turn of events and he couldn't comprehend the enormity of it. He was here investigating Amy's murder which had somehow incomprehensively changed into an international affair. How weird was that? He recalled the interview with Carla Bores but couldn't find a jot of evidence of any sort, of any linkage to Amy's murder, no matter how many times he went through it in his head. If he had known her role in the affair, would he have interviewed her differently?

He smiled to himself when he thought about her. She was the sort of girl you could ravish as soon as setting eyes on her. She was so beautiful, serene and calm with an air about her which drew you to her instantly. Was that in her nature or had she developed it over the years working with her father? She was a girl of many talents. He wondered how many men had fallen for her. How many men had been compromised by her charms?

'We're here,' exclaimed the taxi driver, turning his head to waken Charles from his thoughts. 'We're here. That'll be eight pounds fifty.'

Charles spent the rest of the day in his hotel room, his mind befuddled by the course of events. Listening devices, anti-eavesdropping security, counter intelligence, "strap" intelligence. He was suddenly in a different world. He rang his father and Sergeant Ruskin in Cambridge, though he was careful not to mention the morning's meeting. His father had advised him they had put Chief Superintendent Adams in charge of Amy's case, on a temporary basis, until his return. On the one hand there was a pang of regret that he was no further forward in solving the case, on the other hand a fresh mind might do the trick.

The next morning, Charles read the morning newspapers. They were all full of the murder of Carlos Bores. Fact and lurid speculation made the headlines, especially, as expected, the President of Argentina would make political capital out of it. She had made a public announcement that she thought the British Secret Intelligence Services were responsible and it gave her the diplomatic offensive to raise the subject of the sovereignty of Las Malvinas once again. The Prime Minister had counteracted with a brief statement in the Commons. The Commissioner was right, the sooner the killer was caught the better.

All day, once again, Charles was at a loose end. He needed something to occupy his time, visit the London sights perhaps. Visit a gym where he could practice Taekwondo? He'd been ordered to hang around for a while so he contented himself with watching television and the unfolding news of the murder.

Late evening of the same day when he was about to retire for the night, there was a knock at his door. Not Sergeant Moran again, he thought as he opened the door, it would not be a surprise if she disobeyed orders to be with him again. No! It was not Sergeant Moran, it was Carla Bores!

Carla was in tears, her eye make-up smudged by her crying. She looked a little dishevelled, a far cry from the image she presented when they first met. That cool, calm, serene image of a strong woman was now replaced by a crying, snivelling little girl with a beseeching look in her eyes. Charles's heart went out to her.

'May I come in?' she blubbered.

'Yes, of course, come in.'

Carla entered the room, looked around her and sat on one of the chairs, her face lost under a tumbling mop of hair. Charles sat in another chair opposite her, gently lifted her face and held her hands in his. He lowered his voice to comfort her. 'I heard the news of my father's death this morning,' she sobbed, and burst out crying again. Charles stood up to comfort her and Carla stood up, hugging him tight around his waist and wailed. Her sobs struck the very heart of Charles. He held her close as if that would stop her crying. She nestled her head in his neck and sobbed more quietly.

Charles knew he shouldn't be doing this as Carla could, after all, be a witness somewhere along the line and he should keep his distance. But he found her instantly attractive and couldn't help himself. He held her more tightly and ran his fingers through her hair. She responded by giving him a peck on his lips. He wiped away the tears and kissed her fully on the lips, once, twice, many times.

Charles suddenly realised what he was doing, released his grip and stepped backwards. They both sat down on the chairs again.

'What are you doing here?' asked Charles.

'I was told the news of my father's death this morning. I had nowhere to go and then I thought of you. I had hoped you might be in your hotel room.'

'But how did you know I was here? I never mentioned it to you.'

'I'm not sure. I must have found it from somewhere. Perhaps your colleague told me. I can't remember.'

All his detective instincts had left him for the moment and he readily accepted her explanation. 'Have you eaten today?'

'No, I didn't feel like eating.'

'In that case, I will arrange for room service to bring you something to eat and drink.'

Charles looked up the menu on the table and ordered room service. He smiled at Carla. She smiled sweetly back, her grief having abated for the moment.

What happened that night he knew was wrong. He'd become infatuated with her. She was now under his skin in a way that no other woman had been before. He knew what she was, he knew what she'd done but it made not the slightest difference. It wasn't a case of her working her charms on him. He had just fallen for her totally. She was the most beautiful, ravishing girl he had ever met in his life. To hell with the job, he was just a man after all with the intense feelings for the woman and he wouldn't be cowed by his better instincts. It was against all the rules. She could be a witness. It would jeopardise a future conviction but he didn't care.

They spent the night together and made love several times. She responded to him with as much vigour as he had expressed himself. For one night they were in a world of their own - she, drawing comfort from his presence, which alleviated her grief; he, expressing a love for a woman for the first time in his life. A bonding made in heaven for one beautiful, tranquil night.

The next morning he woke up to find Carla's side of the bed empty and cold. She had left early and Charles was a little surprised he hadn't been aroused by her getting out of bed, getting dressed or leaving the room. For a minute he felt stupid about falling for her obvious charms. Maybe she was a welter of contradictions, of voluptuousness and vulnerability, innocence and experience, part angel, part whore. But in her eyes was an ever-present and underlying sadness. She was all contradictory and an enticing mystery.

Then he realised she had started a train of emotions in him that could only be satisfied when he saw her again. He looked forward to their next encounter. He loved her, he was certain of that, as certain as he could be.

Carla did reappear over the next three days. Beside the love-making, the discussions varied across a range of subjects including his involvement in her father's case and what knowledge he had of it. It was not an appropriate subject to discuss with her, he knew that, so he kept his replies to a general nature. In any case, he wasn't involved on the investigations so wasn't in a position to answer her questions. He wouldn't have told her if he had known. He was blinded by her charms but not made dumb by them. His only knowledge of what was happening was only what he had read in the newspapers and heard on the television news. He'd had no report from Scotland Yard. Even Sergeant Moran had been told to keep her distance from him and not to contact him in any way.

He had tentatively raised the subject of her lobbying but she was reticent and, because of her obvious grief, he had not pressed her on the subject. That could wait for another time.

He felt alone, stuck in his hotel room, somewhat ostracised by Scotland Yard, no calls being returned. Strange feeling, but he had Carla to keep him company and he looked forward to their next meeting.

# Seven

Kensington, London.
Wednesday, 10<sup>th</sup> January 2012.
The day before her father was murdered.

Carla Evita Bores did not consider herself to be beautiful. After applying her lipstick, she looked at herself hard in the dressing-table mirror. She had received many compliments from men regarding her looks but, for her, she would have preferred a paler skin, blonde hair and blue eyes instead of brown. Her nose was nice, possibly a different shape maybe, she thought as she lifted her hair above her head to reveal the nape of her neck. As for her mouth, that was sweet and her lips full and she wouldn't need to change them. More of an English rose type perhaps, a blonde-style, well-bred beauty with a heart-shaped face, rather than the sharper Latin-American features she possessed, a throwback to her Spanish ancestry on her father's side.

She looked closer at herself in the mirror again and then did a plumper and fuller pout, a pucker and then a purse, as she had practised as a pre-pubescent schoolgirl, but fell into fits of laughter and giggles at herself. Tears of silliness formed in her eyes.

Carla brushed her hair. That was one feature of herself that she did like. As she ran her fingers through it she could feel its softness. Soft, jet black and lustrous, it was shoulder length although she had thought of cutting it short. She lifted it up with both hands to imagine how she would look if it was short. Perhaps not. Well, not at this time anyway. She tied it in a bun at the back with a small clip in chignon fashion. She still thought black was too harsh for anyone over twenty-five – so ageing.

She stood up and raised herself even higher on her toes. She did have a slim figure and full breasts, and she was happy with what she saw in the mirror. Many men and even women had complimented on her tall, slim, willowy figure and ran her hands down the length of her hips to accentuate the fact. Where other women complained about the problems of staying slim, for her it came naturally. No matter what she ate, and she always had a good appetite, she didn't seem to put on an ounce of weight, even having several desserts in one sitting.

She put on her red high heels and straightened her back to reach her maximum height of five feet ten inches, slipped on her coat and prepared to meet her father who was waiting in the car outside. She waved goodbye to the servants as she slipped into her father's limousine, sitting alongside him in the back. She said a quick hello to the chauffeur.

This evening was typical of many where they would drive to Parliament to lobby MPs on behalf of her father's organisation, to put their case for Argentine sovereignty of Las Malvinas. She had been doing this with her father for the past five years and it was very much routine, second thoughts had never entered her head.

Carla glanced at her father's hands. It was a habit she had developed every time she met with him. He had had skin grafts and his hands were much improved, though stiffness still remained in the fingers and their joints were forever gnarled and swollen. She felt responsible for his infirmity and her guilt had never been assuaged after all these years.

Her father was born in Buenos Aires and had graduated from the university there. He had, after graduation, immediately sought better prospects elsewhere rather than in his own country. He had been offered a position at the London School of Economics as a lecturer in South American studies. He enjoyed it so much that he stayed in Great Britain and became a British citizen. It was in London, at the LSE, that he met his wife, Margaret Aspinall. She was English, a pretty brunette with some Spanish blood in her lineage somewhere, but very controlling in her nature. As a child, she had heard many an argument from her bedroom as her father tried to put his point of view, only to be over-ridden by her mother. Every time a difference of opinion occurred between the two of them, she would be sent to her bedroom. She was treated like a child, even in her teens, and her opinion was never asked for or considered. Maybe that was the reason she would take risks and play with matches under her duvet, the same risk-taking part of her nature that had made her a senior dealer in the bank.

But the consequences then were not just financial as now. For personal attention perhaps she had deliberately set fire to her duvet late at night. Her mother, hearing her screams had rushed into her bedroom first. Attempting to put out the fire her mother's nightdress had caught alight.

When her father had heard the screams of both his wife and daughter he had also rushed headlong into the bedroom. Initially, in his haste and panic and without thinking he had tried to put out the flames on his wife's nightdress with his bare hands before then using the fire extinguisher they kept in the house on the landing.

Carla had avoided any injury but her mother had suffered badly and died from deep burns to her body several days later. Her father had inhaled toxic smoke and that was the reason he now wheezed when he spoke. Seeing his hands always reminded her of this incident in her childhood. Her guilt would remain until the day she died. "If I had my time over again" was always a thought uppermost in her mind, a demon nightmare she could never banish.

She was beholden to her father in a big way for not blaming her for the incident and would do anything for him within her powers. She loved him dearly. She knew her father had taken advantage of that fact but she would brook no criticism of him.

That was fine until the Falklands war thirty years ago in 1982 in which over two hundred British service personnel and six hundred Argentinians were killed. Her father being sixty now, so he would have been thirty at the time, a senior lecturer at the university. She recalled, as a teenager, how her father spoke constantly of the Malvinas and his home country's right to sovereignty. His lectures at the LSE had become more fervent and his personal vendetta against the English had become evident to both staff and students. He had been cautioned several times by his peers and it ended up with him being sacked five years ago. It was then that he set up his organisation, lobbying MPs to change their minds about British sovereignty and hopefully, at some stage, to force a vote on the subject in the Commons.

Carla herself had attended an all-girls' school and then graduated from Oxford University with a first in mathematics. She had joined the bank as a dealer when she was twenty-three, five years ago, and was very successful at what she did being made a senior dealer two years ago. Further promotion was in the offing.

Her father needed money to fund his organisation and she had passed most of her earnings over to him, but he needed more money to grease a few hands and had told her a way to make more, a lot more, through the bank. She knew it was morally wrong but she had eventually, through his exhortations, agreed to his request. With ever more money needed by her father she had, against her better judgement, coerced her two colleagues on the desk, John Bloomfield and David Unwin, appealing to their greed to make more money for themselves. She did not tell them the cause. That she kept to herself.

All these events went through her mind as Carla sat beside her father. She knew she was the "honeypot" in these situations and she knew instinctively, and with some grooming from her father, how to attract and tease the men, make them feel important in her presence and speak to them as if they had a chance. She had learnt from her mother that the female tongue can be very cruel and unkind when used as a weapon; many a reason for separation, divorce, domestic violence and even murder. Women must learn to control their tongues. She would always remember that in her dealings with men.

She did not sleep around and, thankfully, was not a slave to her vanity. She was a "good girl". She would do many things for her father, his arm always being around her shoulder, but that was not one of them. She drew the line at that and her father was made totally aware of it. She knew he had thoughts in that direction and it disgusted her. Many a time she thought that men were horrible creatures.

Carla had been in a relationship with a student colleague at Oxford and that had continued for two years after they had both graduated. But, for one reason or another, their lives had drifted apart and they no longer saw each other. In fact, he was married recently in a civil partnership with another man. Since then, she had concentrated on her work 24/7 and had had no time for any such relationship. In any case, she had not met another man who she cared about sufficiently to strike up any sort of relationship. Her work and her father's obsession kept her very busy.

She was never bored. Her work was exciting enough in terms of the financial risks she took on a daily basis but, out of office hours, her role with her father brought excitement and glamour to her life. She didn't believe in Argentine sovereignty of the Malvinas and believed the islanders themselves should decide their own fate. It was fun and exciting to tag along with her father though and, as with her work, it gave her a sense of power generally and over men in particular. The closer dealings of her father she deliberately didn't wish to know or discuss and turned a blind eye and deaf ear to them, the subject of sovereignty would never trip off her tongue.

The limousine finally arrived at the House of Commons and both Carla and the chauffeur stepped out of the car and helped her father into his wheelchair. It was a cold January evening and Carla placed a blanket over her father's lap. They showed their passes and she pushed the wheelchair to the echo-sounding lobby area.

There they were greeted by two MPs and shown to an empty office. The MPs listened intently as her father smiled benignly and outlined the funds he had for their charities. The meeting lasted for half an hour with Carla smiling politely but not interfering with the men's talk. Both were invited to the late night party that was being held at her house, together with other guests who had been invited to meet senior figures from their charities. Somewhat reluctantly they both agreed to attend, albeit briefly.

Again, the routine was the same: drive back to her spacious home in Kensington where a catering company had been used to provide the buffet spread and to serve the drinks; mingle with everyone as hosts with a fixed grin and smile, and should expectations get out of hand, make her excuses and retire to her bedroom. What her father did subsequently, usually talking with guests late into the early hours of the morning, was up to him. She would have nothing to do with it. His advancing muscular dystrophy was no hindrance to his late night endeavours, if anything it spurred him on even further.

Carla had been told of her father's death at 10.00am on the Friday whilst at work in the bank with a telephone call from the Belgravia Police Station. She was furious that she hadn't been told earlier and had vented her spleen at the officer in charge, but an explanation or apology for the timing was not forthcoming. She knew her father wasn't in the strongest of health but it still came as a shock out of the blue. A shock further compounded when the officer in charge rather casually told her that he had been murdered. It looked like a robbery that had gone wrong. There would be an inevitable autopsy and investigation but in her confused and emotional state all that went in one ear and out of the other.

As she left the station she went pale, clutched her stomach and felt sick. Feeling dreadfully alone without her father who she had relied on so much for a meaning to life and for emotional support, she was more than bereft. Going back to work to occupy her mind was out of the question, she went home instead and there cried her heart out, lamenting her sudden loss. The one man in her life was now gone, not from natural causes but murdered.

There was also a lingering fear in her own mind that her life might also be in danger. Once, when walking from Kensington underground station, late at night, a motorcyclist in full leathers had veered violently to the wrong side of the road and had almost run her over. The motorcyclist had stopped next to her and the rider had quickly dismounted. He began to follow her on foot and had hailed her repeatedly to join him. She had run for her life. The motorcyclist followed for a while but then turned around to retrace his steps, to mount his bike and continue on his way. It was a very unsavoury episode. She did not report it to the police, perhaps she should have done. Perhaps her father would still be alive if she had done so. Who knows, he might have been her father's killer.

That evening, in a hazy mist of sorrow, she remembered the Chief Inspector with that dull, blonde bitch Sergeant Moran. He had a kind face and the twinkle in his eyes was very beguiling. When their eyes had first met there was a sense of mutual trust, an instant liking for each other, two souls of a not dissimilar nature. She knew he was captivated by her from the word go and she, in turn, felt something deep inside her. A feeling of love she had not experienced for a very long time. She would visit him that very same evening. His hotel room and number she had seen written down on a piece of paper by her father. She had always feared her father's organisation had spies everywhere as well as enemies. His murder was shocking, truly shocking, but not a total surprise and, in some ways, a blessed relief from his pains.

In her grief that evening the Chief Inspector had comforted her with remarkable tenderness and not taken advantage. Emotions had got out of hand, however, on both their parts and they had spent the night together locked in each other's arms. The last thing she wanted was to be alone and he had helped her to make it through the darkness of that first night. For that evening she had given in to her innermost feelings and for all she cared the consequences were of no concern. She needed a friend more than anything else. After that evening she knew he also wanted to take their relationship further and would visit him over the next few days before going back to work.

~

Carla returned to her dealing desk on the Wednesday. She still hadn't been allowed to see her father's body, not even to identify him. Neither had she been interviewed by the police, which she found strange. Her colleagues on the equities desk had helped her through the morning, her mind not at its best with the grief of the past week taking its toll. Her mind was also elsewhere as she thought of the Chief Inspector. After a few days with him she had found him charming, chivalrous, with a wicked sense of humour, just enough self-effacing to a point that is comfortable for other people but totally charming and engaging to where he makes you feel special - a real English gentleman.

She also loved his British accent. A good British accent had always melted her heart. She felt anything they say comes across softer. She was in love with him. For the first time in a very long time she was in love and couldn't wait to see him again. She had planned to take a day off work on the Friday to visit the sights of London with him. It couldn't come too soon.

At 3.00 o'clock that afternoon she took a call on her mobile. The caller was a senior Police Officer from the Belgravia Police Station telling her they had further news of her father's death and could she report straightaway to the station?

She notified Peter Ebdon of her absence, flung on her coat, and hurriedly left the bank to head for her car in the bank's reserved car park. It was pouring with rain, the heavens had opened with a vengeance and there were claps of thunder in the distance. She opened her umbrella and dashed to her car, splashing in a puddle in her haste, cursing under her breath that she hadn't been able to avoid it and the mess it had made of her shoes and ankles.

Carla pressed the fob to open the door – nothing happened. She tried a second time – again nothing happened. It was then that she noticed the door was unlocked and assumed that she had forgotten to lock it in the first place. Without hesitating and with the rain lashing her face and umbrella, she opened the door and scrambled into the seat, folding her umbrella at the same time. She closed the door with some relief, switched on the engine and automatically glanced in her rear-view mirror. A face appeared!! She let out a blood-curdling scream but it was not heard above the pounding of the raindrops and the car's engine.

---

*Extract from killer's diary:*
*She was a beautiful girl and regret having to do it. Some girls don't mind doing it to, other girls a waste of a life. A pang of regret quickly forgotten. Anticipated she would return to her car in the bank's car park. The security pass from Unwin got me through the barrier. A simple matter of*

*changing the photograph. It was easy for me to bypass her car's locking system and hide in the back seat but not very professional of me not to reset the car's lock. Must remember to do that in the future!!! Telephoned her on a temporary mobile phone pretending to be the police with more information about her father.*

*Raining heavily when she got into the car. She screamed when she saw my face and tried to exit the car. Too late. Put the wire around her neck and strangled her. She had her finger underneath the wire and the tip was sliced off. She struggled violently, shaking her head from side to side and grabbing at the wire. It was all over in a few seconds. Her last word was mummy. Sad, that. Grabbed her hair, pulled her head back and slit her throat just to make sure. One banker less. I hate all bankers. They all deserve to die.*

*Retrieved the device from her handbag. Her father told me she always kept it there. Destroyed it like the others.*

*Three down, one to go!!! Mission almost complete.*

# Eight

The Strand Palace Hotel, London.
Friday, 20th January 2012.

Charles shaved and then showered. He was in a good hearty voice as he sang in the shower, the more tuneful notes echoing and reverberating from every tile of the cubicle. He was expecting Carla to meet him in the hotel foyer at 10.00 o'clock that morning and for the two of them, as a tourist couple, to visit some of the London sights. He was as excited as a schoolboy on his first date and lathered himself with extra gusto.

He'd known Carla but briefly, but long enough for him to feel he was in love for the first time in his life. A love, he felt, that was reciprocated and, God knows, might lead to a lasting relationship. He had never been one for relationships he admitted to himself, but for some reason this girl had affected him like no other. With just a glance when they had first met, she had instantly lifted his spirits. When their eyes had locked he had felt an instant bond between them. He couldn't explain it. He didn't want to explain it. He was quite happy to accept it as it was. It was a lovely feeling.

He towelled himself and then dressed. Sitting in a lounge chair directly in front of a sunlit window his spirits were lifted even higher. He looked at his watch and waited patiently for room service. He didn't normally eat much for breakfast; a bowl of porridge and yoghurt was the norm. But this morning was different. He was hungry enough to eat a good English breakfast, a calorie filled bonanza to fuel his sightseeing trips around London, food to calm the nerves. The thought of seeing Carla again was a shot in the arm, the equivalent, if not more, than a sporting success.

Room service duly arrived and Charles tucked into his fried egg, bacon, sausage, black pudding, fried tomatoes and fried bread. He smothered his bacon in malt vinegar, just as he liked it; a sharp, tarty taste first thing in the morning. Toast and marmalade followed.

Having finished his meal, he relaxed in the back of the chair and poured himself a second cup of coffee. In so doing he unfolded the morning newspaper. He read the headlines which were catchy and inflammatory concerning the Argentinian President, the newspaper quoting yet another political and controversial speech by her, a string of provocative and pompous comments. She's a fine one to pontificate on moral issues he mused to himself. He sipped his coffee and read the column inches further. He could not believe what he was reading. He was shocked to the core. He put his coffee cup down and read the article again. His vision was obscured by tears welling up in his eyes.

He was reading about Carla's death, her murder, and the President was, once again, blaming the British Intelligence Services for a double murder, Carla's and her father's. He was initially calm with disbelief and shock but as he read further tears began to trickle down his cheeks. Gradually his incomprehension gave way to a boiling fury. A seething anger inside. His cheeks reddened with rage. The pain of grief ripped through his body and he clasped his head in his hands as tears flowed more copiously. It took several minutes to compose himself before the anger in him returned with a vengeance and knew no bounds.

Putting on his jacket hurriedly and slamming the door behind him as if that was to blame for his misfortune, Charles stormed out of the hotel and vigorously hailed a taxi. He alighted at New Scotland Yard, still in a rage, and stormed past the girl at reception who, at first tried to stop him, and then recognising him, returned to her seat. Seeing his demeanour she then had second thoughts and pressed a button on her desk. Instantly, as if from nowhere, two armed, stern-faced policemen stepped in front of the Chief Inspector and barred his way to the lift.

With the rage a dominant force in his head, Charles was prepared to create a fracas to vent his fury but, fortunately for him, common sense prevailed. He glanced appealingly towards the receptionist who was already on the phone to the Deputy Commissioner. After a few seconds, she instructed the two security policemen to step aside and let Charles through to the lift.

'Thank you,' said Charles in a calmer voice.

'You're welcome,' replied the receptionist with the same inviting smile.

The office of the Deputy Commissioner was his objective. He flung open the door and hurled the newspaper onto the conference table around who sat the Assistant Commissioner and the two MI5 and MI6 agents. Needless to say they were all taken aback at the violent intrusion and it enabled Charles to get his words in first.

'What the fuck is this, you bastards?'

'Now, now Chief Inspector,' said the Deputy Commissioner, getting hurriedly to his feet to bar his path, 'let's talk sensibly about this.'

'You bugger Robert. You couldn't even give me a ring. I had to read it in the bloody newspaper.'

'Chief Inspector, please take a seat.'

Charles whacked the newspaper onto the table, scaring the two agents who found their conference papers scattered with the force. The Deputy Commissioner sat down again and looked sympathetically towards Charles.

'I'm sorry Chief Inspector. I went on the advice of MI5 and MI6. There was a possibility that if we had told you sooner you might have made yourself a public nuisance and hit the headlines for all the wrong reasons. Do you understand Charles? We did it for your benefit?'

'What! Like hell you did.'

'We knew you were having an affair with Carla, her movements were being monitored 24/7. We know she spent several nights with you.'

'You wanted to know what she might say to me didn't you?' said Charles through clenched teeth and forming a fist with his hand, looking hard at the two agents as if wanting to goad them into a fight. He perceived unspoken guffaws on their faces but sense stayed his hand.

'Yes. Where she was unlikely to disclose anything about her father's murder to us, there was a possibility that she might whilst you were making love to her. I know it sounds crude Chief Inspector, but…'

'You dirty buggers. I loved that girl.' Charles never would have thought he could issue those last words in public, but in his heightened state of mind his conscience spoke for him without the slightest sense of embarrassment.

Charles sat down and buried his head in his hands and sobbed slightly. He raised his head with, once again, hot tears welling up and smarting his cheeks.

'What a lovely, bloody world this is. We're all gutter walkers. It's like working in a sewer. All the shit of the world flows towards you and you have to clean it up. I would leave it if I valued my sanity.'

The Deputy Commissioner nodded to the two agents to leave the room. 'Give us five minutes alone,' he asked.

Robert put a comforting hand on Charles's shoulder. 'This happens to be our business, Charles, you knew that when you joined the police force. I realise now that this girl meant more to you than I first realised and perhaps I should have followed my first instincts and told you as soon as we knew.'

'How did she die?'

'She was strangled, garrotted, in her car in the car park at the bank. For the moment I don't want to say any more.'

'Can I see her?'

'You know the routine as well as I do Charles. There's an autopsy taking place and until their report has crossed my desk I don't want to speculate or release any information. I promise I will tell you as soon as I know more.'

Charles knew Robert was right and shrugged his shoulders to acquiesce. By now, his boiling rage had subsided and the policeman in him came to the fore, his personal life becoming secondary in this situation. 'Gutter walkers,' he whispered to himself.

Seeing that Charles was a lot calmer, the Deputy Commissioner went to the door and asked the two agents to come back in.

'If I may say a few words,' said Douglas Home, the MI6 agent taking his seat, 'there is a much bigger issue here. It is paramount that we find this killer in order to refute the claims of the Argentinian President and to calm the relations between the two countries. With a warship and a nuclear submarine patrolling the sea around the Falkland Islands, and with the Prince on sea rescue patrol down there, we cannot afford to make any mistakes. We must find the killer and bring him to justice, if possible. You understand that Inspector?'

'It's Chief Inspector to you.'

'Sorry, Chief Inspector. You must put your personal feelings aside if we are all to work together.'

Charles glowered at him. He was as aware as anyone else about the emergency of the case. For him, Amy's death was just as important to solve as were the murders of Carlos and Carla. He did not like being spoken to like that, in such a belligerent way. He did not like the MI6 agent. He was poker-faced, showed little emotion and Charles was about to say something untoward but discretion got the better of him.

As for the geeky-looking MI5 agent, Charles didn't like him either. He had said nothing to Charles, hadn't opened his mouth even to say anything of comfort. He just looked at Charles with a mocking smile, a smirk on his face as if to cause Charles further discomfort. If the future of this country is in the hands of these two agents, then God help us, thought Charles. Finally, Stephen Beale, the MI5 agent did speak.

'We have spoken to the Commissioner and he has ordered you, Chief Inspector, to remain in London as long as is necessary. I…'

The Deputy Commissioner interrupted him as soon as he saw Charles's inflamed reaction to the agent's words. 'What Stephen is saying, Chief Inspector, is that you are being asked to remain at your hotel rather than go back to Cambridge. You don't mind do you?'

'No, I do not mind. Will you let my father know?'

'I have already arranged that.'

The two agents stood up, shook hands with the Deputy Commissioner and the Chief Inspector and left the room. Charles was about to stand up when Robert pressed his shoulder to remain seated. 'I am sorry for your loss Charles, I really am.'

'Thanks Robert.'

Lowering his voice slightly, Robert hesitated before saying, 'You realise you are being set up by MI5 and MI6.'

'I realise that.'

'Their thinking is that although Carla didn't say anything to you, her killer does not know that. He will assume that she has told you everything and will be gunning for you. They are expecting you to be his next target. Take care Charles. This is a ruthless killer we are talking about. Be aware of anything and everyone. We'll have another detective to shadow you, to give you some protection.'

'You didn't do a good job with Carla, did you Robert?'

'The killer was smarter than we thought. He was a professional hitman, not a random opportunist as we first surmised.'

'I understand what you are saying and I have a few scores to settle with him too, professional and now personal.'

Charles left the New Scotland Yard building and the thought of Carla's death scythed through his body, enveloping him in a cloak of sadness, of bereavement, of profound loss. The same feeling was there when he returned to his hotel room which now had the atmosphere of a morgue. He threw himself onto the bed where Carla's perfume still lingered, a pungent reminder of what could have been.  Tears welled up once again but this time he let them flow freely to purge his body and his soul.

# Nine

Three days later, Charles was sitting in his hotel room, busying himself as best he could. Thoughts of Carla would not go away and sitting alone only made his feelings for her that much stronger. Could he have prevented her death? They had discussed between them the possible dangers she might be in but she was a girl of great resolve and had insisted she go about her life as normal as possible. She knew she was being watched all the time by another detective and that had given her a certain amount of security.

Could he have done more? These questions would not leave his head. He lost many hours of sleep ruminating on the subject and if he could have unwound time he would have done so. Sleep would only follow after an exhaustive review in his head. As for Amy's death, he was no further forward in solving the case as he was when he first came down to London, several weeks ago. He was kept informed by Detective Sergeant Ruskin. Neil had been arrested for Amy's murder even though there had been no new developments, no new lines of approach. It was all a mystery just like Carla's death. The arrest of Neil was, in his eyes, more political than evidential and should not have happened. The team, he felt, would come to regret that decision in time, in particular the senior investigating officer. His thoughts were interrupted by a knock on his door. 'Room service,' said the voice.

Charles looked at his watch. It was 11.00 o'clock in the evening. He was ready to retire for the night and had not asked for any room service. His suspicions were instantly aroused. It could be Sergeant Moran, he thought to himself. I hope not. I'm not in the mood for any of Sergeant Moran's shenanigans, not now, not ever again. After Carla, he wouldn't let his heart rule his head. He would keep all women, and that included Sergeant Moran, at a suitable distance. It was best that way and less heartache.

The person knocked a second time. Charles was about to open the door when his sixth sense told him to look through the spy-hole on the door. As he did, he could see the sight of a gun being pointed at the aperture. His reaction was instant. He moved his head sideways to hear first a loud gun-shot blast, and then to see a bullet pass through the spy-hole and lodge itself in the opposite wall, passing through a framed picture with a loud cracking of glass. He swung his body round, away from the door so his back was to it, but wasn't quite quick enough. There was another "crack". The second bullet splintered the door and missed his body by inches. The third bullet, fired in rapid succession, grazed his left forearm. It was a stinging pain and the wound spurted copious warm blood. His immediate reaction was to cover it with his right hand and to press his thumb into the wound to stench the blood flow.

He could hear footsteps moving away from the door. He hesitated a few seconds and then opened the door to see the figure of a man in motorbike leathers and helmet dash down the corridor. He followed in quick pursuit, foolishly disregarding the fact that the man had a gun. Revenge for Carla obliterated his common sense. He ran headlong after the gunman, still holding his injured arm and trailing blood everywhere. He turned the corner of the long corridor and "screeched" to a halt. The gunman was waiting for him around the corner. Charles stood face to face with Carla's killer. The visor was down on the helmet and his features were masked.

The gunman hesitated to shoot, just for a second. He could see that Charles was injured and appeared to take pleasure in his discomfort. Under the visor, Charles could detect a wide smile on the face as he threatened to fire, to kill. That split second of hesitation was all that Charles needed. His right leg came up, raising the knee to chest height, snapping out the foot to smash against the gunman's right hand. The gun went spinning down the corridor. The gunman pulled a knife into his left hand, but a similar kick with the left leg sent the knife hurtling in the opposite direction to the gun.

Again, the gunman hesitated uncertain what to do next. A high turning kick delivered with the instep smashed his visor. He turned and ran for his life pursued by Charles, still nursing his wounded left arm. The gunman was quick and his escape route well plotted. Charles followed the man down the stairway but the loss of blood took its toll and he felt faint. Charles stopped on the stairwell and gave up the chase.

'You OK, sir? Detective Sergeant Purdy here.'

'Where the hell were you Detective Purdy?' Charles was panting, his breath catching.

'I was having a cup of coffee in the cafeteria when I heard a gunshot. I rushed up in the lift but it was too late to see anything. Should I go down to the foyer?'

137

'Oh for God's sake man, he'll be well gone by now. Help me to my room.'

Charles was helped to his room where he rang the Deputy Commissioner. 'Our hitman just tried to kill me in my hotel room. Send forensics to seal the place, there's a gun and knife to retrieve and several bullets. There may be some clues as to his identity.'

'Are you OK, Charles?'

'It's just a graze to my left arm, nothing serious. A quick bandage should suffice.'

'We're on our way.'

~

Charles found himself in an ambulance with two paramedics, escorted by two marked police cars. It was a short journey to Hammersmith Hospital. The Deputy Commissioner had insisted that Charles be checked out and to stay overnight in a private hospital room, guarded by two security policemen.

Whilst lying in his bed that evening, Charles went through the series of moves he had made. His reflexes were still good but not as good as he would have liked them to be. He would not have won an Olympic medal with those kind of reflexes. They were becoming dulled with age and lack of practice. The office work of late did him no favours in that respect.

His intervention, however, had resulted in the recovery of a gun, knife and slithers of shattered visor that might give clues to the identity of the hitman. That, at least, would be progress.

The next morning, washed and dressed, Charles was taken by police car to New Scotland Yard to meet the Deputy Commissioner and the two agents once again.

He entered the Deputy Commissioner's office to find all three of them in yet another huddle around the conference table. There were smiles all round, a pleasant change from the previous meetings. On seeing Charles enter the room, they all rose and shook him by the hand.

'Well done Chief Inspector,' said the Deputy Commissioner.

'Well done Chief Inspector,' said the other two in unison, reaching for his hand.

They all took their seats again. This time, the MI5 agent, Stephen Beale, spoke first in an excited tone of voice.

'We've had forensics work all night with the items found at the scene of your skirmish yesterday.'

'Skirmish!' Charles sucked in air. 'Skirmish,' he repeated. 'I nearly lost my life!'

Charles then stayed silent and the MI5 agent continued, noting the Chief Inspector's interpretation of the word. 'Let's just say incident then. Let me cut straight to the chase. Ballistic tests prove that the gun and bullets can be linked directly to the murder of Carlos Bores. We can say with certainty that the same gun was used in both cases. There were some blood traces on the shards of the visor and DNA analysis has revealed the name of the hitman. His name is Frederick Little, aka John Bird, aka David Reath, aka Michael Goodfellow, and many other aliases too numerous to mention. He is an American, born in Montevideo and is wanted in many States. He is known as "soft-face" because of his youthful looks, but don't let him fool you. He is aged 35 and is a cold-blooded killer, wanted for many heinous crimes. He has evaded capture so far and has a record of escaping the clutches of the law.

'A little more on his background: He was a student, believe it or not, at MIT, the Massachusetts Institute of Technology, studying law and electronic engineering. His father had hoped he would revitalise his ailing locksmith business. He dropped out of MIT to take over his father's business when he died. The business failed when his bank pulled the plug and he took a number of miscellaneous jobs including a spell as an extra on a film set. Somewhere along the line he went off the rails. An intelligent man who failed to cope with the pressure of living up to the ability he had.

'He is a ruthless and highly professional assassin. His methodology is to garrotte his female victims and to shoot his male victims. Don't ask me why. All assassins have signatures. Who knows what goes on in the mind of a psychopath? A sadist by nature, an assassin by calling. Your skirmish… your incident… with him in the hotel was unusual in that his killings are quick and clean, leaving no traces for forensics to identify him. In this case, we have been exceptionally lucky thanks to you, Chief Inspector. You have obviously riled him sufficiently for him to take greater risks and expose himself.

'He was well-known to the authorities and spent several years in jail for minor misdemeanours, mainly petty theft and threatening behaviour towards his banker. His girlfriends considered him weird with a very dry sense of humour, but were still attracted by his boyish looks and charm, his cool appearance and articulate nature. They were all concerned, however, about his codeine addiction which seemed bizarre to them.

'He's been linked to a number of contract killings around the world but nothing has been proven for a court of law. He is wanted for questioning on several recent murders but has been on the run for some time now. He would do his homework by observing his victims, working out the best place to strike, deciding the quickest way to escape. He is believed to be in this country right now; a cool, calculating individual, a master of disguises, as dangerous a person as you are ever likely to meet.'

Stephen Beale handed out police photographs of the hitman. Charles looked at it, was about to put it down, and then looked intensely at it again. He had seen that face somewhere, or a face very similar.

'He looks just like Joseph Burnley, the PhD student in Cambridge. I interviewed him immediately after Amy's death. He impersonated the student, the clever bastard. No wonder Joseph denied knowing Amy in any way. How clever was that?'

'A doppelganger, Joseph's double, eh, Chief Inspector,' quipped Stephen with a smug smile on his face, a smile which disappeared rapidly under an icy stare from Charles.

'And there's more,' interceded the Deputy Commissioner with a wide grin on his face. 'Listen to what Stephen is going to say next.'

Stephen coughed a polite cough to clear his throat and continued. 'What I was about to say is that advanced forensic techniques were used to analyse the knife and, although it has been thoroughly cleaned at some stage, they have discovered microscopic amounts, too small for the eye to see, of Carla's blood and...' he paused for a moment and looked squarely at the Chief Inspector, '... of Amy's blood.'

'Are you sure?' queried Charles with some incredulity.

'DNA analysis is rarely wrong. It's a proven, sure-fire, method of detection.'

'Any fingerprints on the knife?'

'No, there were no fingerprints. He used gloves or had wiped the handle clean; likewise with the gun.'

Charles sat back in his chair. For the first time he had conclusive evidence in the killing of Amy Barraclough. He was overjoyed. At last! At last! His instincts had been right all along. There was some connection between the bank and Amy's death. He then remembered Amy's face at the scene of the crime and her ghost-pale autopsy photograph. He calmed his exuberance and reassumed his demeanour as a policeman.

The Deputy Commissioner added: 'We have sent out an APB to all police stations and have sent his photograph to all airports, railways and shipping lines. Should he decide to leave the country there is a chance that he may be spotted but he is a master of disguise so we are not too hopeful. We have not informed the press. This morning's news was about a shooting at the Strand Palace Hotel and, for the moment, we prefer to leave it at that. Only if necessary will we publish a photograph to alert the public.

'Thanks to you, Chief Inspector, we now know who the killer is. Our problem is to apprehend him. We believe that he is still in this country, here in London, and still on a mission to kill you. For that reason, we will send you to a "safe house" for a couple of days. We think you have done enough already and do not want to put your life in any more danger than it is already. Are you happy about that?'

'Not really. I…'

'I'll hear no more on that subject. You are to go to a "safe house". I will not have your death on my conscience.

Charles stood up to leave. The Deputy Commissioner gestured to him to sit down again. 'There is more,' he said in an earnest, slightly hesitant voice. Stephen Beale interrupted.

'We have been informed by Carla's investment bank that John Bloomfield has, since Carla's murder, gone AWOL. He cannot be contacted at his home address and the bank does not know his whereabouts. No message was left, either on his answer-phone or in written form. He cannot be contacted on his mobile. We are working on the assumption that he has taken fright and left the country. Early indications are that he might have gone to Jamaica. There he could lie low for a considerable time. We have issued an international arrest warrant.

'In view of all that has been happening at the bank, we have requested all recordings of conversations and transactions for the last six months relating to the equities desk. The bank is currently organising this. Our banking experts will study it for any unusual patterns.'

'Don't some bankers have private accounts too?' chipped in Charles.

'Yes. We have thought of that and have already requested bank statements of all their personal accounts. It will be interesting to see what turns up.'

The MI5 agent was beginning to grow on the Chief Inspector. He may look a bit geeky but, by God, he was thorough and precise and had one hell of a calculating mind. He was no one's fool. He could now see why he was put on the case. If there was a puzzle to solve, then he was the man to solve it. Charles was most impressed.

The MI6 agent, Douglas Home, who had been silent up to this point, had the final word. In an unwavering, deadpan voice, 'We think there is a bigger picture here.

We do not know, as yet, the gunman's mission but it has something to do with the investment bankers and something to do with the Falkland Islands and Argentina. I can't say any more than that until we have completed our investigations. Our seniors have kept the Commissioner, the Prime Minister and the Foreign Office informed of the continuing revelations. The press have not been informed and it is not our intention to do so at this stage. We do not want to unnecessarily inflame the somewhat delicate situation between our two countries whilst certain events are taking place around the Falkland Islands at this very moment.

'We need more evidence in order to disprove the inflammatory comments to the international press by the Argentinian President. We need it, and we need it fast.

'We are also concerned that John Bloomfield is in hiding in Jamaica. As you know, Jamaica's Prime Minister said at the beginning of the year that he wanted to remove the Queen as Head of State, to turn the country into a republic. The "Party Prince" is expected to visit the island in this "Queen's Diamond Jubilee" year. We do not want to stir any more ill-feelings in our search for John Bloomfield. You understand what I am saying?'

Everyone looked at him with blank expressions. They all thought that was going over the top, just a little, even though his serious and unflinching stare suggested otherwise.

# Ten

Charles was making himself a morning cup of coffee when
the doorbell to his apartment rang. He had been two days
in the "safe house" and was fidgety, lonely and irritable.
He shouted from the kitchen, 'Who's there?' No answer.
He went closer to the front door and asked again, 'Who's
there?' He kept his distance and avoided being in line with
the door, just in case.

'Sergeant Moran,' came the reply.

'I don't believe it,' exclaimed Charles out loud. 'I
simply don't believe it.' He opened the door quickly,
pulled the Sergeant in without ceremony, and quickly
closed the door again ensuring that the latch was locked.

'What the hell are you doing here?' asked Charles,
angry at Christine's temerity. 'How on earth did you get
this address?'

'Wasn't that difficult,' replied Sergeant Moran coolly.
'A few questions here and there, you know what I mean.'

'No. I don't know what you mean. I could report you
for this.'

'But you won't, will you?'

'Don't push me too far, that is all I'm telling you.
Don't push me too far Christine.' On the one hand he was
pleased to see Christine, anyone for that matter, but on the
other hand he was annoyed she had disobeyed orders and

145

possibly revealed his location. Settling his mind a little from this annoying surprise he looked sternly at Christine. 'Do you want a coffee?'

'I'd love one, thank you.' Her lower lip drooping as if scolded by her father when a little girl.

In all seriousness, Christine had been told by her immediate superiors to stay away from the Chief Inspector and not to make any form of contact. She could be seriously reprimanded for what she had done. It was not a good decision on her part but she was willing to take the risk. Aware of his affair with Carla and of Carla's murder, her female thoughts and feelings for him were still as strong as ever. She knew he was in danger and wanted to help in any way she could. Female logic perhaps, but there again, she was a female and a female in love with the Chief Inspector.

'Did you know Carla well?' asked Christine, broaching the subject of her once perceived rival with a little care, not knowing how Charles would react to such a question.

Intimately, was the word that came into his head - 'Somewhat,' was the word that came out of his mouth.

'Take a seat,' said Charles. 'You have given me an idea. It's a long shot but it could just work. If you could find the address of this "safe house" as easily as you said, then perhaps the assassin could have done likewise. Carla's father had many fingers in many pies and via the underworld, or even by the police force, he could have been told of this address. A bundle of money can open many mouths. Corruption in the police is still rife in spite of the recent purges of the police, the press and the gangsters who roam the streets.'

Christine sipped her coffee. She had had more amorous intentions but realised she had stirred a hornet's

146

nest of police work in the mind of the Chief Inspector. She decided to stay quiet for the moment.

'I now know who killed Amy but not the motive. It seems a far cry from the fresher student but there has to be a strong underlying reason. It is all linked to the bank, but what? It doesn't make sense. The sooner we can flush this individual out the better. I can't just sit here waiting for it to happen. I know it's me he is still after so why don't I give him an easier target to aim at. I need a second chance to confront him and I can't do that hiding away in no man's land.'

Charles thought for a while. Christine preferred not to interrupt his pensive mood. Silence was preferable on her part.

'Shush, whispered Charles, putting his finger to his lips. He could be watching this apartment at this very moment. His track record is one of stalking his victims for days, weeks even, and then to make an opportunistic attack, making a quick getaway in the process via a planned route and then hiding low before stalking his next victim.'

Charles went to the window overlooking the street and surveyed the passers-by and the stationary vehicles. He saw several motorbikes parked. 'His motorbike could be any one of those,' he declared, pointing his finger towards the parked motorcycles and gesturing for Christine to observe. He closed the curtains, cutting out the light into the room and plunging it into semi-darkness. He peered furtively through the join.

Christine spluttered into her coffee and bit her bottom lip. In the last few minutes he had frightened the life out of her. She was used to such police talk but when it was horribly real, like this, the hairs on her neck would stand erect and her skin would tingle. The sudden semi-darkness had frightened her even more and given her goosebumps. She now had doubts about whether her choice of coming here had been a good one. The fire in her Chief Inspector's eyes suggested not.

'This is my plan,' said Charles calmly and reassuringly, not noticing the anxiety in Christine's eyes and her less than playful gesture of crossing her fingers on both hands behind her back, 'and this is where you can help me.' He outlined his intentions and after a few minutes of careful thought, Christine nodded her approval. Her customary smile was gone, however, replaced by a frown of concentration. There was danger in his scheme but she had the utmost trust in him and was fiercely loyal. If put to the test she would die for him, but hoped that wouldn't be necessary!

~

It was two o'clock in the morning when Charles slipped out of the front door. He wore a light raincoat and lifted the collar to shield his neck from the cold, biting wind. It would have been pitch-black save for the street lights and their eerie bright light this time of the morning reflecting off the wet pavement. He looked up at the moon which was now partially obscured by wisps of clouds diminishing its nightly glow. He looked about him for any sign of movement from a parked vehicle and then headed straight for Chelsea Bridge connecting Chelsea on the north side to Battersea on the south bank.

The elevated noise in London at this time of the morning was still surprisingly high, being mainly road traffic sounds in the distance. A number of pedestrians passed him by – a few late-night revellers, the homeless, drop-outs, deadbeats and insomniacs he supposed. It was spooky but fascinating at the same time as he listened to the echo of his footsteps in a relatively empty road. He walked slowly from Sloane Square down the Chelsea Bridge Road, the Barracks on his left, the Royal Hospital and Ranelagh Gardens on his right. At the end of the road he crossed the main junction and stepped onto the east side of the bridge, looking towards Vauxhall Bridge. He continued walking until he reached its centre and leaned against one of the painted lamp posts. He felt the draught of the Thames water on his face. It was smarting but refreshing, having been cooped up in the safe house for several days.

The bridge was brightly lit during the hours of darkness, more than he had anticipated, being floodlit from below and with towers and cables illuminated by light emitting diodes; would the lone gunman consider it too much of a risk?

Charles glanced at his watch. It was now 2.30 am. There were four lanes of light traffic on the bridge with one or two pedestrians on the walkways either side. A party of revellers passed him by, one of them shouting 'Don't jump batman, it's a long way down.' Another cracked a joke and they all did "high-fives", laughing loudly at Charles's expense.

He glanced at his watch again. It was getting on for 3.00 am, the dead of night. The traffic was far less and there was only the individual pedestrian. He thought that this was the moment when the assassin could take his opportunity. That is, if he was right. He was beginning to have his doubts as the cold wind numbed his skull and froze his face and more salubrious surroundings came to mind.

A Romanian gipsy woman shuffled towards him. A headscarf covered a wizened face, a shawl about her shoulders looked as though it had seen better days. She held out her hand as she passed by, asking for money without saying anything. Charles shooed her away. She shuffled a few yards and sat down on the pavement. He mentally cursed her as she lit a cigarette and stared at him. It seemed ages before she stubbed it out, put the butt in a tin box and continued her tromp to the other side of the bridge.

Even more frustration as a uniformed Police Officer and WPC in their fluorescent jackets approached him. 'You're not planning to jump, sir, are you?' asked the blank-faced policeman.

'No officer. Just can't sleep and wanted a walk.'

'Well, take care. There are many unsavoury characters around at this time of the morning. Can't be too careful you know.'

'Thank you, officer.'

That was it! The assassin would never approach him now, not if he had seen the two police officers. He looked at his watch again. It was 3.45am. There was barely any traffic on the bridge and he seemed to be the only solitary person there. Alone on the bridge his vulnerability to attack was self-evident. He straightened his posture and flexed his muscles to get the blood flowing again. 'Why didn't the assassin strike?' he mumbled to himself through frozen lips. 'Curse the bugger. I'll give it a few more minutes,' he mumbled again to himself, 'and then I'll call it a night, it was not to be.'

The Thames breeze was now more biting than ever and his whole body stiffened with the cold. He stamped his feet to keep warm and put his hands in his raincoat pockets to take off the chill from his fingertips. He was in no fit state to defend his person from a personal assault. He berated himself for not being better prepared. It was then that he heard a motorbike roar as it came onto the bridge. He kept looking out to the river but kept the cyclist in his peripheral vision. He knew that fear is at its greatest when a man can't see what he is fighting. Nevertheless it was important to appear distracted and unconcerned.

The motorcycle stopped a few yards from him and the rider, in full leathers and helmet, flicked the bike-stand nonchalantly with his boot. Charles kept looking out to the river but he knew this was the moment! The rider approached him with quick strides and he could see him pull a gun from his pocket. He recognised it to be a Glock 17, self-loading pistol. This was no toy gun.

Charles prayed to God that the rider wouldn't shoot until he was closer. A shot now and he was dead. Charles held his breath, his nerves at fever pitch, his adrenalin burning fiercely in his blood, every sinew strained! The rider came within range and into his zone and was about to fire when Charles spun around and with the full force of his boot, and with all the energy he could muster, smashed the gun out of his hand. He vented his fury with Taekwondo kicks and punches, causing the helmet of the rider to be dislodged and career across the pavement onto the road, clattering its way onto a deserted echoing bridge.

The rider tried to defend himself with a punch to Charles's left arm and his injury. It caused Charles to wince as he felt the wound reopen and hot fevered blood trickle down his arm. It made him react even more mercilessly with a ferocious kick to the rider's groin and another kick down on the rider's chin. 'That's for Carla, you bastard, and that's for Amy.' All his pent-up fury was released in a matter of seconds as his body reacted automatically to years of training. He stopped himself from applying a lethal terminal blow to his opponent.

The rider fell to the pavement heavily hurting his knee. Realising he was no match for the Inspector in hand-to-hand combat he scrambled to his feet and limped to his parked bike. He ran to no avail. Sergeant Moran was waiting for him, and being no slouch herself in the martial arts, quickly had him in an arm-lock and yelping with pain as she exerted the maximum force on his shoulder joint.

Whilst hand-cuffing the rider Charles panted his instructions to the Sergeant, 'Give the police a ring, Christine.'

'No need, sir, they are already on their way.'

Charles couldn't believe his eyes! Two patrol cars and a police van came hurtling from his left over the bridge, and three patrol cars and a police van came to a screeching halt from his right. Doors were flung open and dozens of armed police officers jumped from the vans, surrounding all three of them, all pointing rifles at the assassin, threatening to shoot and ordering him to the ground. It was ordered chaos as frightening to him and Christine as it was to the assassin.

The assassin's face was bloodied from the conflict and the vehement assault by the Chief Inspector. Close-up, Charles recognised the face from the photograph he had been given by the MI5 agent and thought he looked in real life even younger than his photograph. You could never have imagined from his looks how deadly an assassin he was and the thought most uppermost in his mind was the comparison with the youths in the park.

'That was close,' remarked Sergeant Moran to Charles. 'You were brilliant, sir. I've never seen anything as explosive as that in the martial arts.'

'Too close, a bit too close,' was the reply, handing a handkerchief to Christine whilst wiping beads of sweat from his neck and face with another. 'I thought he was going to shoot earlier. His mistake, thank God. You weren't so bad yourself Christine. Where did you learn to defend yourself like that?'

'You were a good teacher, sir. You just don't remember me.'

The rider was bundled into the police van with several armed officers and the doors slammed shut. The van sped away across the bridge and out of sight, preceded by and followed by the police cars, flanked by motor cycle outriders as a security escort, sirens wailing, ear-piercingly loud enough to scare the living daylights out of the London night folk. The motorcycle was levered into the second van and that, too, sped hurriedly away with police cars and outriders.

Charles brushed down his coat and checked his Oxford brogues. They had taken the full force of the attack and one of the soles was hanging off. He shrugged his shoulders. He would put a new pair on "expenses", the police at least owed him that. Shaking Sergeant Moran by the hand, he gave her a quick hug, more from relief than anything else.

He was then surprised to see the Deputy Commissioner approach with more than a suppressed smile on his face. 'Well done Chief Inspector, Sergeant Moran. A close thing but we've finally got him. Chief Inspector, you come with me back to my office and get that arm checked out.

Sergeant Moran, go to the car, they're waiting to take you home.'

~

It was 5.00 o'clock in the morning when Charles and the Deputy Commissioner sat down in their chairs in the office. A pot of coffee and biscuits were brought in.

'Coffee, Charles?'

'I wouldn't say no.'

Robert poured Charles a cup of coffee and offered the biscuits to him. Charles selected several custard creams and ate them hungrily. It was a way of calming his nerves. Robert waited a few minutes because he knew what he was about to say would, more than likely, infuriate Charles. When he thought the time was right, he began his speech.

'Charles, you won't like what I am going to say to you, but you were part of an elaborate sting operation by the Met, to provoke the assassin into doing something.'

'I was the bait wasn't I?'

'You were the bait, a pawn in a game of chess. You were expendable, you were being sacrificed for the good of your country. The plan was drawn up by the Commissioner, MI5 and MI6 and the Foreign Office. It was approved by the Prime Minister, though I would deny ever having said that.

'Plan A was to take the assassin alive. Plan B was an option but to be avoided as best we could.

'We knew all along you were the assassin's next target and we botched it up slightly at the Palace Hotel to put it mildly. We did not know who we were dealing with and underestimated the assassin's ability to escape from the clutches of the law. Fortunately, your confrontation with him gave us the evidence we needed to identify him and to place him at the scenes of his murders. You did well Charles but you could have been killed there and then.

'We sent you to a "safe house" for your own protection. We didn't tell you the whole truth. You were, once again, being set up as the sacrificial lamb. The notes found in Carlos Bores's office and his computer files made us aware of several moles in the Met, in senior positions, that were supplying inside information to him. We took advantage of that fact. A detective and three serving police officers are now under arrest and being investigated by the Independent Police Complaints Commission.

'We let them know the address of the safe house and set up a covert operation in an apartment opposite. It progressed as we hoped it would. The assassin was observed watching your apartment. We had snipers who could have taken him out at any time. But, as I said, Plan B was not an option.

'You'll be surprised to hear that Sergeant Moran was part of the sting operation. She was given your address and sent in to encourage you to step outside. She tells me it wasn't necessary as you had already made up your mind to do so. You were somewhat predictable Charles.'

Charles shook his head in disbelief at that piece of information. Sergeant Moran of all people! He poured himself another cup of coffee and helped himself to another custard cream.

Once Charles had settled again, Robert continued: 'You were under observation all the time you left Sloane Square, all the way down the Chelsea Road, and onto the bridge. The uniformed policeman and WPC was not part of the operation and nearly loused it up for everyone.

Fortunately, they moved on very quickly. Where's a policeman when you want him eh, and when you don't want him he's standing on your toes?'

That quip made Charles smile slightly. He'd heard it many times before but not in this context.

'The motorcyclist followed you and we had him on CCTV pictures. He crossed the bridge six times. Once stationary on the bridge we closed off both sides and had snipers trained on him. I was hoping, for your sake, that the assassin wouldn't shoot you from a distance with an automatic as he passed you on the road. We knew from his profile that he likes to get close to his victims. We took a chance. Fortunately for you, it paid off. You were brilliant in your self-defence. The assassin never knew what hit him.'

Charles lifted himself out of the chair and strolled around the office. His limbs were hurting from his exertions and his muscles were now stiffening from pushing his body to the limit. He wasn't at the peak of his fitness and such exertions were now taking their toll. Emotionally, he felt unimportant being sacrificed this way for the good of his seniors and their politicians. Only his self-preservation had kept him alive. So much for the police force working together and the camaraderie. What a joke!

'Finally,' said Robert, 'there are two further points to mention. First, the assassin, Frederick Little, will be on the first flight to the United States tomorrow morning. He is being surreptitiously extradited. The Prime Minister does not want him on these shores. Legal papers have already been drafted and signed by the two countries as part of the sting operation. MI5 and MI6 will interview him before then but they are unlikely to glean any information out of him. He is a professional killer and pathological liar and it will be a waste of time.

'Secondly, and this is more important to you. MI6 tracked down John Bloomfield, the other investment banker, to Jamaica. The world's a small place sometimes Charles. The local police arrested him and have held him in custody. He has given a statement which has just been faxed to us. I have it in my hand.' He handed it to Charles. 'This is your copy. I have highlighted the section you need to read now.'

Charles took the statement and read the highlighted sections. A broad smile crossed his face. It became broader as he read further.

'Charles, you now know who killed Amy, how she was killed and why she was killed. It has been an arduous, convoluted process. Get some rest now and then I suggest you go back to Cambridge. You will need to write up your report and wind down the investigation. I'll let you know the date for Carla's funeral. You will now be able to release Amy's body to her family for her burial. I will keep you informed of any further developments.'

The two men stood up. 'It has been nice working for you Charles. You are a bit hot-headed at times, and too much of a risk-taker, a bit of a "chancer" for my liking, but you are a policeman of great sincerity and, should I say, bravery, not easily fazed. You have a lot to learn, however, when it comes to politics and the craftiest of politicians plotting and conniving, as we all have done when we've stepped out of our local parish.

'There's a bigger picture here, just as the MI6 agent said, isn't there Robert?' stated Charles opening the door to leave.

'Possibly, but your job is done. Leave it to others to fill in the missing parts of the jigsaw. As I said, I will keep you informed of any further developments.'

# Eleven

Parkside Police Station, Cambridge.
Monday, 30<sup>th</sup> January, 2012.

'Let me recap,' said the Chief Inspector addressing his team. 'Amy Barraclough was murdered in the early hours of Thursday, the first of December in Market Square. She had been strangled. I couldn't tell you at the time but she had been garrotted and her throat subsequently slashed. There were no signs of a robbery or sexual motive for the killing. The autopsy has confirmed that she was a virgin. She was a bright girl with a glittering career in front of her, a life cut short by a sadistic killer.

'The killer had used a nylon monofilament wire similar to that used for fishing lines. This made us suspect her long-standing boyfriend, Neil Staines, a fisherman from the port of Whitby. As you know, he was arrested and charged in my absence with her murder with what I still consider to have been insubstantial evidence to place him at the scene of the crime. He could not confirm his whereabouts at the time of the murder in spite of all our enquiries. He was released as soon as further evidence came to light of Amy's true killer. He is a rough lad with a sensitive nature and was deeply in love with Amy. I hope his arrest has not had a lasting effect on him.

'Also withheld from public knowledge was that Amy kept a personal diary; in it she recalled her meeting with a

PhD Student, Joseph Burnley, and a text message from him for a rendezvous in Market Square on the night in question. In the interview with him he vehemently denied knowing the girl. We knew he was lying but subsequently we found out he was chivalrously shielding the name of the girl he was staying with. He was remanded in custody for perverting the course of justice but released on bail. A decision has yet to be taken on whether to charge him with wasting police time.

'Another suspect was Derek Peabody, a solicitor in London. We know he contacted Amy that evening to meet with her and that she refused to have anything to do with him. In further interviews he confessed to being at the Butterfly Club in Cambridge at the time in question.

'Surveillance was carried out on this club with disturbing results. There is evidence of sex trafficking, grooming, rape and prostitution, some as young as eleven with red, swollen marks on their small bodies from beatings. The owners have been arrested and Social Services called in. Derek Peabody has been arrested and charged for procuring and distributing paedophile material.'

The Chief Inspector coughed to clear his throat.

'I now want to read to you John Bloomfield's statement, given to the Jamaican police. John Bloomfield was one of the dealers on the private equities desk of the Meredith Investment Bank in Canary Wharf. He jumped ship after the deaths of David Unwin, the other dealer on the desk, and Carla Bores, the senior dealer on the same desk. They were both murdered as was Carla's father. John Bloomfield's statement is lengthy so please be patient.

'"I was a dealer on the equities desk of the Meredith Investment Bank in Canary Wharf, London, controlling

160

huge sums of money. My colleagues were David Unwin who reportedly committed suicide and Carla Bores, our senior dealer.

"Several years ago I was approached by Carla as to whether I wanted to make a lot of money. I said yes as long as it wasn't illegal, but suspected otherwise. She persuaded me it was a fool-proof system to make a bundle of money through my private account with the bank. The catch was that the proceeds had to be shared fifty-fifty with her. Each month, on the settlement of the account, I was to pay her half of the proceeds. I said I would give it a try.

"You have to understand the culture of the bank had become toxic and destructive. City careers are dead. You are forever competing and fighting against each other. Dealers would elbow each other out of the way and boast about who got the biggest bonuses. Coupled with the long hours, I regularly worked weekends until 10.00pm at short notice. After a while you begin to question what it is all for.

"I wanted out. If I could make a lot of money quickly I could ditch the world of banking and create a start-up company in Tech City. This is a bunch of start-ups clustered in and around East London. There I would be my own boss.

"Carla handed me a smartphone which she said had been modified with an expansion and communications port, called a USB flash drive, to accept a device which looked like a memory stick. It was only to be used on my private account and only in secret, away from the prying eyes of other dealers and staff. Any secretive behaviour was not to be seen by others otherwise the facility would be removed immediately.

"We took positions on our accounts, sometimes short, sometimes long. A long position meant we held the equity in question and if we sold it when the price went up we would make a profit on the deal. If the price went down we would lose money. If we had a short position it means we didn't own it at the time, it was borrowed, but had sold it anyway. If the price went down we would buy it back, return the share to the original owner, and make a profit. If the price went up we would lose money.

"I was told by Carla that the device would put us in contact with a hedge fund in Boston. We would notify our positions on the smartphone. If we made a profit from price movements then that was fine. If, however, we were liable to make a loss, the broker in Boston would buy and sell the equities, always at a profit to us.

"We therefore made substantial profits, very substantial, millions in fact, on our personal accounts. I don't know how the device worked. I was told to touch the "code App" to send the positions, the "decode App" on receiving messages and the "flash App" occasionally, once a week say, to erase the messages from memory leaving no digital footprints. It didn't seem illegal to me. If someone else, in this case the Boston broker, wanted to take a loss each time, so be it. That was up to them.'"

The Chief Inspector paused at this point and added, 'I know that's all a bit long-winded and banking speak, but it serves to put the next few paragraphs into context with Amy's murder. Please listen carefully.

"'One minute we saw Amy working with Peter Ebdon, the Chief of Staff, in his office, the next thing we knew she had crept up behind us to see what we were doing, peering inquisitively over our shoulders. She seemed a bright girl, taking copious notes. She worked with us for a while, just observing, and then sat with the other dealers on the other desks. She was very chatty and loved the excitement of it all and the aggressive, macho, gambling atmosphere of the dealing room. Being pretty, the young dealers in particular, would show off and engage her in conversation. I think many of them fancied her.

"We were concerned, both David Unwin and me, that Amy might have seen us use the memory stick device jutting out of the side of the smartphone. Being slightly larger than a normal memory stick it was very visible. In fact, at one point, she did ask us about it and what it did. We were caught short for an answer and bluffed our way out. She didn't seem convinced by our explanation that it speeded-up text messages to brokers and was a prototype being tested out by the Bank.

"The girl was too smart for her own good. She was no fool. The subject re-emerged some time later when she realised we were the only dealers using such a device and her curiosity had gotten the better of her. She had even made a sketch of the smartphone in her notebook. She should never have crept up on me like that.

"We mentioned our concerns to Carla. She said she would deal with it and to ignore the incident. We trusted Carla to sort it.

"The next thing I knew, I was asked to a business lunch by a man who said he was a friend of Carla's. He said he had been asked to check on the girl at Cambridge to find out what she knew about the device. He was not to harm her but just to ask questions.

"Several weeks later, I was asked out to another lunch by the same man. He said he had recovered her notebook from her digs, telling me that it was child's play to pick the lock on the door. He seemed pleased with himself. He said he locked it on leaving, nothing else being stolen from her room. No one saw him enter or leave, everyone was at lectures. He posed as a student. Nothing could have been easier. He posed as a PhD student he said, by the name of Joseph Burnley, who he had overheard in a pub, someone who looked very similar to himself. He met Amy at the Freshers' Ball and had tricked and charmed his way into her life; he later texted her to meet him in the Market Square.

"To my horror, he told me he had killed her. He told me that I should take that as a warning not to cream off more of the money I was making. He somehow knew I was taking 90% and only giving Carla 10%. He knew David Unwin was doing the same. It had to stop or else! There were no set limits you see and we were told by Carla to be sensible. But, we were greedy and took multi-million pound gambles. We couldn't lose so the bigger the gamble, the more money came into our pockets.'"

The Chief Inspector sipped from a glass of water and looked at his team. They were speechless. He coughed again to clear his throat and held his hand to his mouth. 'Last paragraph,' he said.

"'When David Unwin died, I was suspicious that it wasn't suicide but said nothing. When Carla was murdered, I panicked. I knew I was his next target. I didn't turn up for work the next day and sought refuge in Jamaica. There I had planned to keep low for a while, hoping he wouldn't come after me.'"

The Chief Inspector looked at his staff. There was an awkward silence.

'Any questions?' No answer. Everyone was just taking in the facts.

'You now know how Amy was killed, who killed her and why she was killed. She was a girl in the wrong place at the wrong time, a girl with a radiant and creative spirit who will be sadly missed by her family and the University. The man referred to in the statement we now know as Frederick Little, a contract hitman, a lone gunman from the United States. He has been apprehended and has already been extradited. I now know no more than you do. The case of Amy Barraclough's murder is to be closed. Her file is for the records. As from today, the investigation team is no longer required. Thank you for all your efforts during all these weeks. Thank you once again and well done.'

It was an emotional moment for everyone as they left the meeting, mostly in silence but for a few comments of disbelief on the tips of their tongues. The Chief Inspector went back to his office with Sergeant Ruskin. Turning to his Sergeant, 'The hitman was a locksmith by trade in his former life. He was able to unlock the door to Amy's room very easily. They are old locks and should be all renewed. We will inform the Provost at an appropriate time. With a staff and student population of some 30,000 to administer he will need to be seen to be doing something to reassure them. The murderer was equally adept at bypassing Carla's car-locking system. He was very clever throwing all the suspicion on to Amy's boyfriend and the PhD student. He made a right fool of us using the same type of motorcycle as her boyfriend and, with the snow falling he knew CCTV images would be blurred. He worked on the basis that circumstances can collude sometimes to frame a person even better and give him time to put distance between himself and the police. He was a master of disguise.'

'What do you think drives these people, sir?'

'Perhaps we shouldn't be asking why these individuals carry out these crimes because to seek to understand is in some sense to excuse. In order to understand you must have empathy. Sometimes, it has a lot to do with fame and the desire of someone who thinks they are invisible to become visible. Their undoing is to develop a greater urge for risk. He was a clever bastard and I hope he rots in prison.'

'Life is too short to care for the damned.'

'It sure is Peter, it sure is.'

'Why didn't you tell the staff that it was you who apprehended the assassin? They'll find out sooner or later. Rumours abound.'

'It's not in my nature,' replied Charles. 'We've closed the case and that's all they need to know. In any case, the applause would sound a bit hollow.'

~

The funeral of Carla and Carlos Bores on the following day was a sad occasion. They were devout Roman Catholics and the eulogies were read out by members of the family. Carla was buried in the same grave as her father and next to her mother; three souls in one grave, three very different lives on this earth.

The Chief Inspector was part of the funeral procession in a formal police role, but also as a lover of Carla. He had fallen for her in a big way and had envisaged a happier outlook than that which actually took place. She was the only woman in his life to brighten his world. Their affair was brief but no less memorable for that. How he wished he had done more to protect her. He knew she had turned a blind eye to her father's criminal activities but there would always be a place in his heart for her memory. 'May she rest in peace,' he whispered as the coffins were lowered into the earth, adding 'May God be her protector now.' Later, looking into the grave, 'Good night Carla, sleep well. I will visit you in my dreams.'

He left the burial site and its air of hushed gloom and walked slowly out of the cemetery. A car honked its horn and the Chief Inspector looked into the car. It was the Deputy Commissioner sitting in the back seat. He opened the door and beckoned Charles to sit alongside.

'I said I would keep you informed Charles of any further developments. Well, there have been a few.'

'First, I have to tell you that Frederick Little is dead. He somehow, once again, escaped from the police in Boston, a hijack by his mates taking him in a van between prisons. Two policemen were killed in the skirmish that followed. The police later chased him to a barn on a nearby farm. They surrounded the building and the result of stray bullets must have set it alight. He was shot accidentally by a sniper as he left the burning building. He came to a grisly end, apparently frazzled to death. He, like many people, will receive the notoriety in death that was denied to him in life. After so many murders he knew he would get the death penalty, so there could have been no moral struggle in his mind.'

'No more than he deserved,' quipped Charles. 'I hope he continues to burn in Hell.'

'Second,' the Deputy Commissioner continued, 'the analysis of the device retrieved from John Bloomfield by our Communications Intelligence Agency, GCHQ, was intriguing. I am a bit of a technophobe but the techies explained it to me in a simpler way.

'The device was developed in the Far East, using, amongst its components, nanotechnology. This is technology on an atomic or molecular scale. It's beyond belief but there you go. Anything seems possible these days, Charles. It included a GPS receiver, a battery, a mobile SIM card and had a memory and processing power equivalent to one thousand laptops! By using the nearest mobile cell, or if it can see a GPS satellite, it could track its own location meaning an operator in a far distant land could record the position of every one of these devices. Not only that, but a coded message could be sent to the device remotely blocking access, and, if necessary, could shoot a high voltage charge into its core, melting the chip.'

Seeing Charles's surprise reaction to this line of espionage, Robert sucked in a mouthful of air and continued describing the device, pleased that he understood it himself.

'Have you heard of Watson, Charles?'

'Is it a person? Can't say that I have.'

'In a way it's a person. It is IBM's supercomputer developed to tap demand from companies keen to profit from the growing volume of data they generate in this digital age. The supercomputer has the ability to understand human language and Watson shot to fame recently after beating all human competition on the long-running US quiz show "Jeopardy". Watson is now being sold to other countries.'

'What's that got to do with the device?'

'I'm coming to that. The firmware, the permanent software programmed into the device, a read-only memory, converted the text message in the smartphone to a form of anagram. Artificial Intelligence algorithms, you know, the software used to control robots and the like, then layered it in such a way to make a simple, meaningful sentence in English, far removed from what was input. Those algorithms were copied from IBM's supercomputer.

'So, the dealer input his positions into the smartphone as a text message. It was then coded into a message that could avoid any forensic analysis by the telephone operator, the police and GCHQ. The message was received by the Boston hedge fund broker and decoded. The messages to and from the broker therefore left no digital footprint of the financial positions of both parties or the source of the funds.

'It was clever, eh, Charles? But now listen to this. This will blow your mind. Argentina bought one of the supercomputers. The FBI and CIA investigation of the brokerage house in Boston revealed that such devices were used to communicate with a hedge fund in Buenos Aires run by the Secretaria de Intelligencia del Estado - the Argentine secret service, known to us as SIDE. It is now known as SI but still referred to as SIDE by the people. The Boston brokerage firm was, in turn, being compensated by the Argentinian hedge fund which was taking all the losses.

'Our deep-cover agents tell us that London was just one cell. There are similar cells in all the capitals of Europe, funding covertly all lobbyist organisations to persuade MPs to argue against the British sovereignty of the Falkland Islands. Argentina hoped to persuade all EU members to cast bloc votes against Britain. All these governments have been informed.

'It sounds implausible, eh, Charles? The dark arts of the Intelligence Service leaves us ordinary mortals scrambling for explanations when these things come to light.  God knows what is being developed at this very instance.'

Charles sat back and whistled through his teeth at Robert's explanation of the device.  Never in his wildest dreams did he contemplate such a level of counter-espionage.  'The mind boggles,' was his only remark to Robert.

'Our Prime Minister is to make a statement in the House of Commons tomorrow.  Let's see how the President of Argentina reacts to that!

'The other thing to mention is that an internal investigation by the Meredith Investment Bank has unearthed a number of payments of twenty-five thousand pounds from Carla's personal account to Peter Ebdon, the Chief of Staff.   They will determine whether Mr Ebdon abused his position of trust in allowing unauthorised trades for which he could be fired and banned from City jobs for life.

'The City watchdog is also involved in possibly fining the Bank for systems and control errors and whether anyone else was culpable in falsifying records and forging documents to aid Carla's activities.   Amazing what is unearthed when turning over stones, eh Charles?

'You stoked up a right hornet's nest on your visit to London, Charles.  Next time, come as a tourist.  It might be safer all round and involve me in less work.'

That comment released the tensions of the two men and they both burst out laughing, to the amusement of the chauffeur in front.

'And finally, I have in my hands your copy of the assassin's diary.  Yes, he did keep a diary.  He was as meticulous in keeping a diary as he was in murdering his victims. You might like to read his account of Amy's death on the way back to Cambridge.

'I think that about wraps it up. I am sure I'll see you some time in the future. Give my regards to your father. He's a splendid chap, a splendid chap. You could do worse than follow in his footsteps.'

That last comment slightly rubbed the Chief Inspector up the wrong way. It wasn't meant in a nasty way, he knew that, coming from Robert, but he did wish that other people wouldn't tie him to his father's bootlaces all the time. He was where he was on his own merits and would one day shake off the metaphorical supporting arm of his father from his shoulders. How many more times would he have to prove himself before people, like Robert, thought of him as a policeman in his own right rather than as a scion, a descendant of a notable family.

Charles thanked Robert and stepped out of the car, shaking his head in bewilderment that a device, not much bigger than a memory stick, can pick up unimaginably weak radio signals coming from satellites orbiting the earth at a distance of twelve and a half thousand miles, looking for a GPS signal, and how evil minds can use that to their advantage. He had a lot to learn still if he was to understand devious criminal minds.

# Twelve

London to Cambridge train.
Tuesday, 31$^{st}$ January 2012.

Charles read the diary extract of Amy's murder on the train back to Cambridge. It was frightening in its coldness. It made stark reading. A grim read indeed.

*Secured another contract through a friend of a friend with a brokerage firm in Boston. They want me to track down a certain girl in Cambridge, England, by the name of Amy Barraclough. She is a student at the university there. Not to harm her, just find out what she knows about a device and report back. They have hired me as a private investigator. Love that sort of challenge.*

*Now in jolly old England! Have studied her whereabouts for a while and that of her boyfriend. Make it my business to know these things. She is a fresher student. He is a fisherman in a place called Whitby. Get the impression they don't get on together.*

*Overheard another student in an English pub who looks like me. Have seen my opportunity. By disguising myself as him can get closer to the girl.*

*Befriended her at a party in the Uni. Forgot my ticket at the entrance was my excuse. No problem. She was a fresh-faced student blushingly innocent who saw the world through rose-tinted glassed. She liked me. Girls are all the same. Always looking for romance. Easy to discover exactly where she lived.*

*Waited until all the students were at lectures. Strolled past the Porter's lodge dressed as a student. Picked the lock of her room. So easy. Went into her room. Spotted the notebook nicely labelled and left the room. Job done.*

*Read the book. Contained a sketch of the device and several comments. Burnt the book. Reported back to Boston.*

*Got another call from Boston. Told me the devices in London have malfunctioned and can't be turned off and the dealers are not following the rules. Am to retrieve four devices at any cost. At any cost! Now that's my real business!! Take this to mean the girl is to be silenced too.*

*Have studied the boyfriend more closely. Can frame him for her murder and increase my chances of a clean getaway. By involving the other student can double my chances of confusing the cops to make my exit. The more false trails the better. Don't you just love this business!!!*

*Sent a text to her to meet with me in the market place at 11.30 tonight. Used a temporary mobile number.*

*Waited my opportunity. She became suddenly frightened of me and backed off. Other women have done the same, so offer them a present. A pretty necklace. No woman can resist it. Ask them to turn their back to me so can slip it around their neck. Kissed the back of her neck and replaced the necklace with a wire. The rest was easy. Most enjoyable.*

*Went to my bike. Heard her mutter slightly. The fishing line not as effective as thought it would be. It had stretched somehow. Panicked and had one of my seizures. Loosened her scarf and coat and slit her throat. Had to make sure*

*she was dead.  Botched it!!  Not as clean an execution as would have liked.  Not up to my usual standard.*
*They normally flail their arms and clutch at their throat but always to no avail.  Their screams become quickly garbled and the mouth gurgles as the wire tightens.  They make a last attempt to release the wire around their throat.  Their bodies go limp.  It's all over in seconds.  That's what happens when it's done properly.  The body...*

Charles stopped reading.  It was enough for now just to read the extract of Amy's death.  The other murders were all recorded and could wait until later.  There was a coldness about the killer which sent shivers down his spine.  He was used to nasty events in his police work but to kill like this was inhuman and barbaric.  What possesses a man to do these things?

He had noticed that the letter "I" was missing from the text, as though the assassin did not relate his actions to himself but to his alter ego, his alternative personality.  That was why he could be so cold and impersonal in his ruthless slaying of other people, burying his feelings by withdrawing from reality into fantasy.  It was frightening for ordinary mortals to understand, frightening that many of these people exist in society, frightening to think that so many murders are committed under such a veil of self-denial.

Charles shook his head with disbelief and put the papers back into his briefcase and settled back into his seat.  Tomorrow he was to attend Amy's funeral at St. Bede's in Whitby.  His thoughts were for Amy and her family.

~

Amy's funeral was a quieter, contemplative affair but no less emotional for that. Her mother was grief-stricken, helped by her family. Neil, who had been under suspicion for so long, was equally grief-stricken, introspective in his misery with eyes cast down. He spoke of his love for her in a moving eulogy and how he had plunged the dark depths of despair. He was very eloquent, surprisingly so, despite a face crinkled with emotion, a quivering bottom lip and a tremulous voice.

The release of Amy's body and its cremation had allowed the family to come to terms with her death, to say their final farewells. There was bound to be a formal inquest later where the horrible details of her murder would be made public. But for now they remembered her as she was - a sweet, beautiful, intelligent daughter and loved one.

The ceremony finished, Charles walked to his car, his mind reflective and in a saddened mood. He could hear the sounds of Whitby in the distance. Seagulls, the blaring horns of trawlers and fishing boats, the town traffic and the unloading of catches from the quayside, all the sounds of a busy port. Ironic, he thought, everything that Amy wanted to get away from, to get away to another world of books and literature. It was an act of fate that she was born there, now, through the act of an assassin, she would be cremated there and her ashes strewn over the same waters her father died in. Life has its ironies unfortunately for all of us.

'Chief Inspector,' he heard over his shoulder.

'Mrs Barraclough. Pleased to meet you again, a sad day for all.'

'I just wanted to thank you for finding Amy's killer. It means a lot to the family. Anyone who has lost a child will know there are no words which can express the despair, the disbelief and desolation. Such a death blackens even the purist of hearts. We will miss her every minute of every day in a home that now feels empty. He burnt my heart.'

'I understand and good luck to you.'

Mrs Barraclough's cheeks were wet with tears and she embraced Charles before turning round and running headlong towards her family's outstretched arms. He felt a lump in his throat and choked back a tear himself. A child's death is a monstrous bereavement, a wound that never heals, he was only too aware of that himself.

He continued walking towards his car. He was surprised to see Sergeant Moran waiting for him, standing nonchalantly next to the car. 'Christine, what are you doing here?' he asked with a note of incredulity in his voice.

'Didn't you know, Chief Inspector, I've been transferred to the Cambridge Constabulary. I requested a transfer from the Met and with my good deeds back there it was granted straightaway. I hear that Cambridge is a beautiful part of the country to live in and I'm duly informed that there are some good-looking Chief Inspectors working here, particularly one called Inspector Tae. I wonder who he can be? Can't wait to meet him. I'll see you again some time Chief Inspector,' said Christine as she turned and walked away, glancing back cheekily.

'I believe you will' and a broad smile lit up the Chief Inspector's face. 'She's a right minx if ever there was one,' he whispered to himself, 'here's to the next time!'

A sad rider to this case was that a week after Amy's funeral Neil committed suicide by throwing himself overboard in high seas.

Peter Ebdon, the investment bank's Chief of Staff was arrested for fraud. On bail he committed suicide in local woods at his home. Verdict: self-decapitation due to hanging involving a drop.

skin deep – the second case in the series is not for the squeamish or faint hearted, read on to find out what crime the inspector eventually uncovers...

Cambridgeshire Police
Crime Investigation Unit

# Case 2: skin deep

# One

As night fell, the spirits of the dead, past and present, permeated the building with a reverent silence descending in all of the rooms.

Being alone, Mark Winstanley took no more than the merest of glances into the Chapel of Rest to satisfy himself that everything was as it should be, averting his eyes from the coffin on the opposite side of the room. He grabbed his coat off the peg in the hall, switched out all the lights and hastily headed towards the front door of Dolan & Sons, Funeral Directors. It was closing time and he was in a hurry to leave the haunted building, eagerly looking forward to seeing his new girlfriend at his local McDonald's.

Having activated the front door alarm, he was about to grab the door handle when the door-bell rang. Oh no, not now, he thought, who can that possibly be? Mark hesitated hoping the person would go away. The door-bell rang again and then for a third time. 'Someone's impatient,' he muttered under his breath and cursed his luck, his immediate thoughts lying elsewhere regarding food and girlfriend. He slowly pulled the large wooden door ajar and peered out into the darkness of the cold, wet night.

'Ah, it's you, Mrs Harrington. We're closed. We close at eight o'clock. We did tell you. Sorry, I'm really sorry but we are closed. Can you come back tomorrow?'

The diminutive Mrs Harrington, dressed in all black, looked up at him, closed her black umbrella and whispered in a soft but firm voice, 'Could I see Bert for the last time? His funeral is first thing in the morning and I would like to see my husband, my lovely Bert, just one more time, please!'

'But we're closed, Mrs Harrington, and I can't let you in after eight o'clock. It's against all the rules. It could cost me my job and you don't want me to lose my job, do you?' Mark's impassioned plea fell on stony ground.

'Please, young man. Just this one time, please?'

It was clear that Mrs Harrington wasn't going to be fobbed off so easily. Mark glanced at his watch. Could he spare just a few minutes? It wouldn't take long and Lydia, his girlfriend, he hoped, would understand anyway.

'Five minutes, Mrs Harrington, just five minutes, no more.'

He opened the door wide to let Mrs Harrington through.

'Thank you, young man. I'm ever so grateful,' shaking her umbrella before stepping inside.

'I'll give you five minutes, Mrs Harrington and no more.' This time Mark held up five fingers to re-emphasise the duration as though Mrs Harrington, in her dotage, had lost all sense of time.

'Thank you, young man, thank you. I just want to see Bert's face for the very last time. You know, we were married for sixty-three years. It's a long time you know. A long time.'

'Yes, Mrs Harrington. I know. Now if you take a seat in the arrangement room, I'll switch on all the lights, reset the alarm and check the Chapel of Rest. It will only take me a few minutes. Make yourself comfortable.'

'Thank you, young man, thank you.'

'That's all right, Mrs Harrington. Glad to be of service.'

Mark cursed a little under his breath for missing his date as he watched Mrs Harrington slowly amble to the arrangement room and then just as slowly make herself comfortable on one of the settees. He liked to be on time especially on an important first date. But Mrs Harrington was a sweet, old lady and her doleful eyes were too much to refuse a last look at her husband. After all, they were together for sixty-three years. He wondered how long his marriage would last for, when he did get married that is, but that would not be for a very long time. He was still only seventeen-years-old, too young to be thinking of things like that.

Having put his coat back on the peg, Mark went straight to the Chapel of Rest. He was under strict instructions, because of his age, not to go into the Chapel rooms, the mortuary and the embalming rooms. He was but a student there for six weeks and, because of Health and Safety Rules relating to juniors, was restricted to the office and arrangement rooms only. The terms of his temporary employment were such that he was not to come into contact with the "grief" part of the business, anything directly relating to the dead. The latter point had been drummed into him by both his uncle and Mr Dolan, the proprietor.

Pausing and then taking a deep breath, he switched on the light and entered the Chapel of Rest where Bert was lying. The atmosphere was not to his liking, far from it; it felt stuffy, cold and lifeless, a bit spooky and ghoulish, and more than a little shiver went down his spine. Thinking twice about what he was about to do, he turned round. Perhaps he could persuade Mrs Harrington to come back early the next morning. Yes, that's what he would do. On the other hand, he could be praised by Mr Dolan for his good public relations. In fact, if it was just a quick five minutes no one would need ever to know. What to do?

For a second time, he steeled himself and entered the room. Emboldened, he switched on the two battery-operated incense candles and then, taking out a tissue from his trouser pocket, he waved it over the artificial bouquet of flowers on the sideboard to dislodge any signs of dust and did likewise over the Christian cross in the corner. He dimmed the lights to give the Chapel a warmer ambience. Now for the coffin.

Approaching the coffin very gingerly, he ran his hand over the smooth mahogany lid. This was the very first time he had touched a coffin with someone inside it. It felt cold and somewhat eerie as he recalled the horror movies he'd seen. He backed away to gather his thoughts. He had never seen a dead body before and he did not want to now. Five minutes, he thought to himself, just five minutes. He did not need to look at Bert, just open the coffin lid, keep his eyes closed, and hope the smell wasn't as bad as he imagined.

Trying to move the lid, it suddenly dawned on him that the lid had been screwed down in preparation for the funeral the next day. How could it have slipped his mind? He counted six screws, one at each end and two on each side. They were decorative brass wreath holders which require a spanner to undo. It shouldn't take him more than a few minutes, perhaps five to ten, but where was the spanner kept? In an office drawer he presumed.

'Are you all right in there, young man?' asked Mrs Harrington loudly as Mark went into the office to look for the spanner. He surmised correctly that it was kept in the same drawer with all the different wreath-screw holders. Thank God, he thought to himself, as he opened the drawer, that the simple wooden caps had not been glued over the screws. They would have had to be knocked off and he was not prepared to do that. No way. On the other hand, it would have given him a good excuse to refuse Mrs Harrington's request.

'I'm fine, Mrs Harrington, won't keep you a mo. A few minutes more.'

Mark re-entered the Chapel of Rest and using the spanner removed five of the six screws. They came out readily but the sixth, at the head of the coffin, refused to move. It had caught the lining of the coffin and jammed itself in. There's always one!

Sweating profusely, he removed his jacket and with a few curses and swears wrenched at the screw with all his body's might. To his relief the screw moved first time.

Without looking at Bert he lifted the lid and placed it to one side. It was heavier than he thought and nearly came a cropper, almost dislodging the coffin itself from its stand. Quickly donning his jacket again he pulled several tissues from the box on the sideboard and wiped the perspiration from his forehead.

Feeling pretty pleased with himself, he dimmed the lights further and shouted to Mrs Harrington that she could now view her Bert. As she passed him in the doorway to the Chapel of Rest, again he emphasised, 'Five minutes Mrs Harrington, just five minutes and no more.'

'Thank you, young man.'

'I will leave you to say your goodbyes.'

Mark went straight to the office, sighing with relief and mopping his forehead once more. If he was quick no one need ever know.

Suddenly, there was an almighty, unearthly, ear-splitting scream from Mrs Harrington which pierced the still air such that Mark literally jumped out of his chair. For someone so small, how could she have such a loud scream? He assumed at first that it was Mrs Harrington's reaction to seeing her dead husband. He had been told people react in different ways to seeing their loved ones and to not be surprised at certain utterances they may make. He expected everything to calm down once Mrs Harrington had overcome her first shock at seeing Bert again.

Then he heard a thud. A cracking sort of thud. This time he thought it wise to investigate. He reluctantly levered himself out of the chair to walk reverently into the Chapel of Rest. He found Mrs Harrington lying prostrate on the floor near Bert's coffin. Blood was trickling from her head and pooling around her. She wasn't moving. Without thinking, Mark grabbed a handful of tissues and tried to mop up the blood soaking into the carpet.

At the same time the door-bell rang. Oh hell! What to do? What if it was Mr Dolan? He would be sacked on the spot. Should he check Mrs Harrington's pulse? His mind was feverish and confused.

He decided to answer the door first. It was Lydia, his girlfriend. A big sigh of relief cleared his mind temporarily.

'Lydia, what are you doing here?'

'You were late so I thought I would check if you were still at the undertakers.'

'Something came up and I've been delayed.'

'How long will you be then?'

'Probably another fifteen minutes, is that all right? Why don't you come in and sit in the arrangements room until I've finished.'

'No thanks. You are not going to get me in there. What with all those dead bodies, I mean. No thanks. I'll go back to McDonald's and wait for you there. Be quick. I hate eating by myself.'

'I'll be quick, I promise. See you there in fifteen minutes.'

She blew him a kiss and he smiled back. She was pretty even when she was angry.

Mark wasn't thinking. A voice in his head said there was no way he could be there in fifteen minutes. He had Mrs Harrington to see to. What to do next? He needed assistance. There seemed nothing but problems, problems and yet more problems. Why did it all have to happen today of all days?

He decided on the spur of the moment to ring Mr Dolan on his emergency telephone number. He had never done this before and was not sure how Mr Dolan would react. Mark would normally leave promptly at five o'clock each evening and this was the first time he had been asked to stay until eight o'clock because Mr Dolan had been called away on an emergency and there was no one else to look after the premises, his son also being elsewhere. It was strictly a one-off and he was not to mention it to anyone.

Mark listened apprehensively to the rings and then heard Mr Dolan ask, 'Hello, who is this?'

'It's Mark, Mr Dolan.'

'What is it, Mark?'

'Mr Dolan, there's been an incident here. Mrs Harrington is lying in a pool of blood in the Chapel of Rest and I don't know what to do.'

'Is Mrs Harrington OK?'

'Yes, Mr Dolan. Just a bump and a bit of blood. I'm certain she'll be OK.'

'I thought you said a pool of blood?'

'I meant a bit of blood, Mr Dolan.'

'You silly boy. You haven't opened the coffin have you?'

'It was only for a few minutes so Mrs Harrington could see her dead husband for the last time.'

'Stupid, stupid boy. You were under strict instructions not to touch anything and to lock the front door, and not to allow any visitors, right?'

'Sorry, Mr Dolan. I thought …'

'I don't care what you thought. If I've told you once, I've told you a thousand times that I employ you from the neck down, not for you to use your brain.' Then, after a long pause, 'Have you spoken to anyone?'

'No, Mr Dolan.'

'Have you looked in the coffin?'

'No, Mr Dolan.'

'Then don't,' he rapped. 'Under no circumstances should you look into the coffin. Do you hear me? Don't. I'll be with you in thirty minutes sharp. Wait in the office and don't move. Do you understand? Don't move.'

'Yes, Mr Dolan.'

Mark put the telephone receiver down and breathed a sigh of relief. He had expected instant dismissal but that had not happened. Mr Dolan was an understanding sort of bloke he reassured himself.

Mark sat quietly in the office. His thoughts were of Lydia waiting at McDonald's. He was not allowed to use his mobile at work and was not allowed to use the office phone, except for emergency calls. He hoped Lydia would be understanding. If she liked him, she wouldn't mind waiting a little longer.

He wondered why he had allowed his uncle to persuade him to work in his brother's undertakers. He needed the money but it was strictly against Health and Safety Rules for anyone under twenty-one to work in an undertakers. True, he was restricted to menial tasks like washing the cars and office work but all those dead bodies and things! Lydia did not like it and had said so in no uncertain terms for their future relationship.

Mark wondered how Mrs Harrington was. Perhaps he should go and check to see if he could help in any way. Maybe make her a cup of tea. That was a good idea. He peered into the Chapel of Rest. Mrs Harrington had not moved and the pool of blood around her head was even greater. She might even be dead, he thought. He reassured himself that she was not and would be on her feet in no time. All would be well.

He glanced at the open coffin as curiosity took hold of him. No one would know if he took a quick look at Bert, not even Mr Dolan. He was going to lose his job anyway. What the hell, he might as well see what all the fuss was about and what had upset Mrs Harrington. He advanced slowly towards the coffin, sidestepping Mrs Harrington's body, and then took a good look inside. What he saw would haunt him for the rest of his life.

'Oh my God ...'

For a few moments he was riveted to the spot, mesmerised at the spectacle in front of him. Then he felt his stomach churn and bring its contents into his mouth. He turned away, ashen-faced, holding his mouth as he raced towards the toilet. With his head stuck over the toilet bowl he felt he was going to die. At that moment he wanted to die and the earth to swallow him up.

# Two

'Giz a chip, go on, giz a chip.'

Emma stared blankly at the young girl standing in front of her. She said nothing and continued eating.

'Go on, giz a chip,' said this time with a greater earnestness in her voice.

For a second time Emma casually glanced up, selected a long chip and nonchalantly handed it to her. The young girl grabbed it from her hand and ate it in one go as though she hadn't eaten for a month, savouring every last tasty morsel as she licked her fingers clean.

Emma continued to eat her fish and chips from the carton. For the third time she glanced at the girl who hadn't moved an inch, and who steadfastly refused to move on, hoping obviously for another chip or two.

Emma studied the girl's doll-like face – round, button nose, large eyes with a heart-shaped mouth. A pretty face but drawn, expressionless, neither one thing nor another, as rigid as a doll itself, hiding any inward feeling other than hunger.

'Oh, come on then. Sit down here beside me,' said in a plain-speaking Yorkshire accent. The girl willingly obliged without being asked twice. Emma placed the remains of the carton into her lap. 'Here, you can finish these off.'

Without thanking her, and without saying a word, the girl quickly emptied the carton of its contents, scraping her fingers around the inside edges to mop up the tiny fragments of batter. Having satisfied herself that there were no more, she threw the carton behind her, further into the doorway in disgust. She continued to lick her fingers like saveloys.

'Hungry?' asked Emma.

'Haven't eaten all day,' replied the girl, licking a piece of batter on her finger which had gone unnoticed first time.

'What's your name?'

The girl hesitated and glanced furtively around her as though the walls and windows had ears, her anonymity being her sole protection against the evils of the world and people who would hurt her, before saying, 'Jo'.

'Jo what?'

Jo paused and added thoughtfully, 'Just Jo.'

'Well Jo. My name is Emma, Emma Thompson.'

Both girls smiled tentatively at each other and, realising their mutual circumstances, huddled a little closer for added warmth. The early summer day had been warm but at eleven o'clock at night it was now decidedly chilly. Both girls, sitting in a cold, tiled doorway of a W H Smith shop, just off Leicester Square, watched the passing pedestrians and the one-way traffic, the bright lights of the city reflecting in their eyes. The girls stayed their tongues, their thoughts being elsewhere in far-off places, places they would much prefer to be.

Finally, Emma broke the silence, 'How old are you, Jo?'

'Sixteen, and how old are you?'

'Fifteen. Did you run away from home?'

194

Jo hesitated, not wanting to relate her painful experiences to one so young, but then had second thoughts.

'I was in a Barnado's care home in Reading, separated from my brother and sister. I'd had enough and so decided to run away. I tied my bed sheets together and escaped through the bedroom window. I fell and hurt my ankle and it's still a bit painful when I walk. With the little money I'd saved, I paid for a taxi to the station and then took a train to London. That was twelve months ago. I was the same age as you.'

'Do you regret it?' asked Emma ever more curious about this stranger.

'No. Life was much worse in the care home because I got depressed and cut my arms. I felt so isolated you see from my friends and family and was very unhappy and sad. I felt worthless and unloved. I wanted to kill myself.'

Jo thrust her arms in front of Emma's face to verify the scars. Emma looked closely at the scar tissue and cringed at the extent of the cutting.

'Now I can do what I want, when I want and no one can stop me. There is no one to boss me around.' A brief admission but Jo felt all the better for it as if confessing to a younger sister.

'What about you, Emma?'

Emma sucked in air as if to give her the strength to reply. 'My mum died when I was ten-years-old. I lived with my dad but he was a long-distance lorry driver and was never at home. I had to fend for myself most times, all by myself. We were visited several times by a social worker and I thought I was going to go into care. I decided to leave home and come to London and be my own person just like you rather than someone tell me what to do all the time.'

'Where was home, Emma?'

'In a place called Sheffield.'

'Where's that?'

'It's near Manchester, in the Midlands.'

'Not sure where that is.' Geography was lost on Jo.

Emma continued, 'Where we lived was a dump, a run-down council estate. All the girls got banged-up and only thought of boys and babies, benefits and all that sort of thing. You know what I mean, girls whose only ambition is to be given a council house and to live off handouts for the rest of their lives; girls who can't see beyond their nose. You know what I mean, Jo?'

'I think so. How long have you been here then?'

'I came down yesterday. Slept in a doorway overnight, don't know where, somewhere round Euston station I think.'

'Are the police looking for you?' Now it was Jo's turn to be curious.

'Possibly, but I left a letter for my dad for when he got home. Told him not to worry and would contact him soon. Don't trust the police no way, they're not to be trusted. You know what I mean, Jo?'

Jo nodded approvingly. She had had a few spats with the police authorities herself in her short adolescence.

Both girls listened intently to each other as hurtful memories spilled out of their mouths. Then silence followed. A long silence this time with thoughts of what could have been in their short life-times and what ended up as their lots – a loveless childhood and teenage years filled with meaningless petty arguments, little understanding and even less love.

'What would you like from life, Jo? Asked Emma contemplatively, ending the silence.

'I dunno, a nice man perhaps. He doesn't have to be tall and handsome like in the magazines and on telly, just a nice man. A nice house and a nice family with lots and lots of love. You know what I mean? That's not asking too much, is it Emma?'

'I guess not. Me, too, but where do you find a nice man these days?'

'We're two of a pair,' said Jo, with an element of jubilation in her voice as if finding a long lost friend, a buddy to share her thoughts with. 'Let's stick together for a while. I can show you where you can get a good night's rest, a shower and sometimes a meal. I can help you and you can help me. What do you say? We could become soul mates.'

Emma was about to reply when a young man stopped in front of them, bent down to their height and began to speak. He was a good-looking young man, of Asian extraction.

'Oh! No! Not another do-gooder,' exclaimed Jo, annoyed at his intrusion.

'I can help you girls,' said the man, with an earnest look on his face. 'You look lost and look as though you've been walking the streets. I'm a social worker and if you come with me I can help you find a bed for the night.'

Jo's back stiffened. 'Oh, yeah? Well show me your card.'

The man took out his identity card from his top pocket and showed it to the two girls. Emma looked at it closely to check the photo against the man kneeling in front of her.

'Could be a fake,' said Jo. 'You can't trust any of them. Don't be fooled by any of them. They'll have your knickers off you before you can blink twice. All these men, they are only after one thing.'

'They're not, Jo.'

'I tell you they are. All men are the same. They'd screw a prickly pot plant if it had a fanny.'

'Ugh. Gross. That's a bit crude.'

'That's how men think. They have minds like sewers.'

'Not all of them.'

'It's true, all of them. Men! I hate them.'

'I'm sorry you think like that, Jo. Men are not perfect but then no one is perfect.'

'You'll see. You'll see. My mother was a prostitute and she used to talk to me about men. To her men were wallets and women were holes. All men are the same. You'll see.'

Emma was in two minds to go with the young man. She had spent one night walking the streets and felt tired and dirty. A nice bed for the night wouldn't go amiss.

Jo, noticing Emma's obvious interest, held her back.

'Why don't you come, too?' asked Emma, freeing herself from Jo's clutches.

'I'm not going with a Paki. They're trouble.'

'He's not a Paki.'

'All men are Pakis, you'll see.'

Emma stood up and offered her hand to Jo.

'No thanks,' Jo crossing her hands in front of her in defiance and refusing Emma's hand. 'I'll not go with a Paki.' The determined expression on her face said all.

'See you then, Jo. Take care.'

Emma picked up her holdall with its precious contents and followed the young man, waving goodbye to Jo, hoping the man was what he said he was. If not, she was prepared for the worst. She wasn't as naïve as she might look at times. Her dad had taught her a few of life's lessons as well as to stand on her own two feet when push comes to shove.

She looked back at Jo sitting forlornly in the shop doorway and hoped she would be OK, please God. Lovingly fingering the crucifix around her neck she followed the young man.

A few steps and then she stopped, took out a ten pound note from her purse, turned around and walked back to Jo, handing her the note. With eyes brimful of tears, Jo gratefully accepted the note blubbing a quiet, 'Thank you'. The girls held hands and embraced tenderly.

Catching up with the young man, Emma glanced behind her again. The doorway was now empty of life. The ghost of a smile on her face quickly evaporated, leaving a sense of foreboding as to what the future had in store for her, and for Jo.

~

Emma followed the young man keeping always half a step behind, ready to make a run for it if need be. Not a word was said between them.

She followed him from the bright lights of the city to a darker part of London, to a poorly lit road of large Victorian terraced buildings, their appearance spoilt by refuse bins cluttering small front gardens and pavements. Some of the gardens were neatly kept, most others were not, with overgrown weeds and grass and in some cases rubble from renovations simply strewn in front of the house; many had just been concreted over. The carelessness of the few made the whole road look untidy.

Parked outside each dwelling was car after car on both sides of the road, tail to bumper along the whole length of the road, as far as the eye could see. Now and then a car would rev its motor, switch on its lights and move slowly from the kerb. Each time it made Emma stop with fright, especially when the car was alongside her as the car suddenly jerked into life.

The half step behind gradually became a step alongside the young man, farthest away from the road, seeking comfort from another soul in a soulless road of dark shadows.

London was a big place with many people and vehicles and Emma for the first time felt small and insignificant and lost. Not a single pedestrian passed by which only added to Emma's isolation and fear, further compounded by the echo of their shoes on the pavement and the occasional trip on cracked paving stones.

'Are we nearly there?' asked Emma, breaking the silence for want of a human voice to ease her misgivings about what she was doing in this part of London at this time of night.

'Just a few houses more, on the left here, No 36a. Would you like me to carry your bag? You look uncomfortable switching it from shoulder to shoulder. Let me carry it for you.

'No thanks, I can manage,' said in such a way as to leave no doubt as to her intention to keep it in her possession at all times.

Several houses further along and the young man stopped. 'Here we are.' Emma followed him through the metal gate which swung back viciously with a loud "clang", loud enough to have woken up half the neighbourhood, through an unkempt garden and up a small flight of stone steps to a large front door.

The young man pressed a buzzer from a panel of four on the side of the door and spoke into the speaker, 'It's Paul here, can you let us in.' A crackle of a voice replied but was inaudible to Emma.

A minute later the door was swung open by another man. Without the slightest, even briefest of greetings between the two men, merely a nod of the head, Paul entered followed by Emma. They stepped into a large hallway, dimly lit with a single light bulb still swinging from a gust of wind from the door, casting moving shadows around the hall and stairway. Paul led Emma up a single flight of stairs, pushing open one of the doors and switching on a light. 'Here we are, this is your room for the night. The council pays a fee to the landlord to maintain several rooms for people like you, to give them shelter and safety for the night.'

Emma thought it would never get to this point. She had had serious doubts of the sincerity of this young man, who she now knew was called Paul, and she'd been prepared to run away from him at the slightest sign of misbehaviour on his part. But looking into the room she now thought him genuine enough for her to relax a little and lower her guard.

'It's a single room with a small bathroom, toilet and shower,' said Paul switching on the bathroom light. 'Here is the key to the door and you can also bolt it from the inside for extra security. I suggest you get a good night's rest and I'll see you tomorrow morning at say 10.30am to give you a good lie in. Does that suit you?'

Emma nodded agreeably as she was handed the key, too tired to thank him properly, simply content to be in a warm, dry place for the night. She locked and bolted the door as soon as Paul had left.

Alone in the room Emma was more relaxed, popping her head into the bathroom to take a closer look. It was clean and smelt nice and met with her satisfaction. She switched the light off and closed the bathroom door. She surveyed the main room. It was spartan of furniture with a single bed pushed into the top left hand corner next to the window, a small table and two chairs on the right hand side, a worn rug on the floor and floral curtains on the window. It was crowded but clean and again smelt nice. She had expected a lot worse so she was mildly surprised and quite pleased.

Emma placed her holdall at the foot of the bed, kicked off her shoes and flung herself onto the bed. It was well-sprung, the bed clothes, pillows and duvet smelt fresh as though recently washed and truth be told she could not have wished for anything more at such short notice. She had taken a chance with the young man and it had paid off. She must learn not to be so suspicious of everyone like Jo. There were good people around - you sometimes just had to take them on trust.

Suddenly and strangely, out of the blue, thoughts of home and her Dad slipped in and out of her consciousness together with the dreadful pain he must be feeling from her sudden and unexpected absence. Pangs of home-sickness disturbed her mind as she closed her eyes for a few seconds. Both her mind and body were fatigued from everything that had happened over the last few days and all she wanted to do was to rest and go to sleep and to be at peace with herself and the world.

She felt too tired to shower and wearily lifted herself from the bed, switched out the main light and flopped back again on the bed, curling up into a foetal position as she drifted into a deep sleep, a sleep that was most welcome to shut out reality for a few precious hours.

The noise of road traffic and the beams of moving car headlamps flashing across and briefly lighting up the room caused Emma to stir from her slumbers, but her tiredness was so great that she quickly fell asleep again, pulling the duvet over her for added warmth in the middle of the night.

The loud sounds of increasing road traffic and the start-up of cars nearby eventually woke up Emma from her slumbers. She looked at her watch, it was 9.20am. She had had a good sleep and was now more alert to her surroundings and circumstances, looking around her as though danger lurked in every corner of the room. Satisfied that that was not the case she checked the door was still locked and bolted before stripping naked and going into the bathroom.

The power-shower was most welcome, imbuing a sense of freedom in cleanliness as it sprayed her body, cleansing the dirt away from both her body and her mind. There was also soap and hair shampoo to hand enabling Emma to inhale fresh perfume into her nostrils. Reluctantly stepping out of the shower Emma dried herself with the large, fresh towels conveniently placed on a rack. A hairdryer plugged into the wall allowed her to dry her short auburn hair to her satisfaction, running her fingers through it before tossing it back over her head. Admiring her body in the long mirror from all angles she felt good about herself and that her decision to leave home had been the right one. It was a body untouched by a man's hand and she wanted it to stay that way until the time was right and the man was right, she would have it no other way, defending her honour meant everything to her.

Putting on her old clothes she instantly felt dirty again, all the feelings of insecurity and loneliness returning to choke her throat, feeling wretched as she sat on the bed. She buried her head in her hands as tears welled up. Would it ever get better? She asked herself over and over again whether she had done the right thing in leaving home. At this time in her life she reckoned it was just a case of trying to grin and bear it. Someday, somehow, the sun would shine on her and her loneliness would be banished forever from her life.

Wiping away her tears, Emma carefully packed her holdall and waited patiently for Paul to arrive. She would thank him and then take her leave, chancing her arm elsewhere.

Paul seemed a good sort of guy and her initial apprehension had abated but she wanted no personal involvement with anyone; certainly no relationships at this stage of her life. She wanted to be as free as a bird to do what she liked, when she liked, and how she liked, with no interference from anybody, otherwise what was the point of leaving home.

The knock on the door came at 10.30am, Emma checked her watch.

'Who is it?' shouted Emma.

'It's me, Paul.'

Emma removed the bolt and unlocked the door. Paul entered bright and breezy.

'Morning … You know I don't know your name.'

'It's Emma, just Emma.'

'Well, good morning, Emma, I hope you slept well.'

'I did, thank you, and now I wish to leave.' Emma grabbed her holdall and slung it over her shoulder, brushing past Paul.

'Leaving so soon? Have you eaten? There's a café at the end of the road which makes a really good English breakfast. You must be hungry.'

The mere mention of food made Emma's mouth water. She was famished and the thought of a full fry-up was too good to ignore. But she did not need Paul to accompany her, she was quite capable of going to a café alone and she had enough money of her own to pay for it. She was not looking for handouts from Paul or from anyone else for that matter. Her savings would cover her for the foreseeable future.

'Before you leave, Emma, I just wanted to say that I've arranged for you to stay here for another four nights at no cost to you. You can use it as your base until you are back on your feet and I've arranged a more permanent shelter for you. If you wish you can leave your bag here, the room is secure.'

'No thanks, I'll carry my bag with me, I don't want it stolen.'

'As you wish.' Would you like me to show you where the café is?'

'I'm certain I can find my own way, thank you.'

With second thoughts it dawned on Emma that Paul had gone out of his way to help her and all she could do was to treat him with suspicion and contempt, to treat him as though he had ulterior motives in befriending her, to sexually exploit her at some stage. Her Dad had told her to be aware of such men. Trust your instincts he used to say and if you think something feels wrong, it probably is.

But Paul did work for the local council and could not be that bad a man. She had to stop thinking that all men wanted sex. She blamed Jo for sowing the seeds of doubt in her head.

'OK, just this once. You can walk me to the café.'

Emma locked the door and handed the key to Paul.

'No, you keep it a while. As I said, the room is yours for another four nights if you wish. If you change your mind at any time just drop the key into a neighbour. You are free to come and go as you please. Given a little more time I'll try and sort something more permanent for you.'

Emma placed the key into her coat pocket. Paul was a good-looking lad – smart-casually dressed with good personal hygiene – and she felt she could trust him to do what he said.

In the sunlight the Victorian houses were not as oppressive as at night, thought Emma as they both strolled down the road to the café. It was but a ten minute walk and catching the sun on her face made Emma feel good in herself despite wearing what she considered to be dirty, smelly clothes that she had worn for the last few days.

The café was crowded that time of the morning with patrons being served breakfasts of one kind or another. Paul hesitated before entering but then followed Emma as she waved him in. A table was cleared of used cutlery, plates, cups and saucers then cleaned and laid with fresh serviettes and cutlery. Emma and Paul took their seats.

Emma studied the menu and ordered the English breakfast, the full works minus the beans.

'Aren't you ordering anything, Paul?'

'I've had my breakfast, thank you, Emma. I'm just going to have a coffee.'

Emma looked around the café imagining people were staring at her – they weren't, they were too busy tucking in to their food and, in some cases, reading their morning newspaper. Emma relaxed and stared at Paul.

'You don't look very English, Paul.'

Why? Because my name is Paul you think I should be English? Both my parents are Polish but I was born here and Paul is also a Polish Christian name. That makes me British.

'How old are you then?'

'I'm twenty-six and how old are you, Emma?'

'I'm seventeen.'

'Sweet seventeen, you look a lot younger.'

'Thank you, I'll take that as a compliment.' Emma lowered her eyes somewhat abashed at lying about her age.

There followed a general banter between the two without any more details being asked for or given on either side, a sort of neutral discussion of non-events and life in general.

'Your English breakfast and your cappuccino,' said the waitress taking a good look at Emma and Paul, with feminine suspicions of something not quite right but saying nothing. It was not worth her job to create a fuss with customers on intuition alone. But it was not the first time she had seen an underage girl with this young man whom she knew, through a friend of a friend, to be a Romanian migrant by the name of Darius Dalca. He was also gay.

'Did you not want a drink, Emma?' asked Paul, supping his Cappuccino.

'A tea,' replied Emma, giggling at the ring of milk foam around Paul's mouth.

'I'll ask the waitress to bring over a tea when you're ready,' wiping his mouth with the serviette.

Emma tucked into her food glancing up occasionally at Paul who continued to sip his coffee. She was embarrassed to be eating alone with Paul watching but was equally flattered that she was in the company of a good-looking man who seemed to have eyes only for her. He aroused her with his appearance and his charm.

'Shouldn't you be at work?' asked Emma having finally cleared her plate and in the process of drinking her tea. 'Oh, I was forgetting, it's a Sunday, isn't it.'

'I work shifts, this week its all-night shifts.'

'Oh, I see.'

'Do you enjoy your work?'

'Sometimes yes, sometimes no, sometimes it's good, sometimes it's bad. You know what I mean.'

Emma nodded, which seemed the right thing to do.

All discussion remained at a superficial level with the more pointed questions answered with a curt, dismissive reply. They were strangers and preferred it that way - for the time being that is.

'Is this your first visit to London, Emma?'

'Yes.'

'What would you like to see most in London?'

Emma thought for a few moments, 'Big Ben and the Houses of Parliament, Trafalgar Square and the National Gallery. I've seen them all on television.'

'If you wish I could show you the tourist sights. There's an underground station nearby and we could be in Trafalgar Square in fifteen minutes. What do you say? Would you like that?'

'No, no thanks.' Emma's suspicious demons were at it again.

'On second thoughts, yes, we could go together.'

'And then we could take a tourist bus to see the Tower of London. The treat would be on me.'

'No, I can pay my way.'

'Fine, if you prefer it that way. I was only saying that in case you were short of money.'

'Thank you, I can pay my own way.' To emphasise the point Emma opened her purse, taking out the money for her food and drink. Paul paid for his coffee.

The waitress watched as the man and the young girl stood up and left the café together. All her niggling thoughts were transferred to the back of her mind however as more breakfasts were ready to serve to customers.

The day went as promised by Paul, Emma putting aside her inhibitions and reservations to enjoy the sights of London with schoolgirl relish. When it came to paying however she still insisted on paying her share of the transport costs and the lunch at a McDonald's. She was beholding to no one, making her feel independent and self-assured in other people's company.

Feeling exhausted at the day's revelries Emma decided to return to the comforts of the flat, thanking Paul who saw her into the flat before leaving her, promising the same the next day with a trip to Oxford Street for window shopping.

Taking a shower that evening before bed Emma felt like a girl much older than her years looking forward to seeing Paul at the same time the next day. The traffic noise and lights that night were less of a disturbance as she slept solidly, her mind at ease with itself for the first time for a long time, her home life firmly pushed to the back of her mind.

The next day, Monday, dawned and true to his word Paul took her to Oxford Street where Emma bought some lingerie, the rest of the day being spent at the Tate Modern and St Paul's Cathedral. In the evening they both relaxed over an Indian meal in a restaurant. Emma returned to the flat.

Tuesday morning, Emma showered and waited for Paul due at 10.15am. At 10.45am she became anxious but immediately perked up when she heard a knock on the door, rushing to the door to release the bolt and unlock it. She opened it to find a stranger standing there. Emma stepped out of the room to look for Paul but was forcibly pushed back in.

'Who are you?' asked Emma in a faltering voice, fear now gripping her throat. There was no reply from the stranger. Emma grabbed her holdall and tried to make a dash for it. Her exit was barred and the door was slammed shut in her face. She was then pushed with considerable force back onto the bed. As she fell backwards the handles of her holdall caught her face causing considerable pain.

The man was Asian and gross – big, fat and bald, with a face full of stubble. He smelt of curry, a disgusting smell oozing from every pore of his huge body.

'Who are you?' asked Emma again, smarting from the pain on her face and rubbing it with her hand.

The man advanced menacingly towards her causing Emma to cower in the corner of the bed as far away from him as she could get, sitting with her knees tucked tightly under her chin, her arms wrapped round her legs. 'Please, please mister, don't hurt me,' she pleaded in a high-pitched voice that was cracking with emotion.

The man spoke for the first time, 'How much?'

'How much for what?'

'For sex, you silly bitch.' He took a twenty pound note from his back trouser pocket and slapped it on the table.

Emma shook her head vigorously. Another twenty pound note was added and then another.

Emma shook her head even more vigorously, curling up into an even tighter ball.

The man grabbed back his money and stuffed it into his back pocket. 'In that case I'll take it for free.'

Stepping forward he pulled her legs straight. Emma kicked out and curled up tight again. He slapped her legs hard and pulled her legs straight, this time pulling her body down the length of the bed. Emma started to cry and wet herself, shaking uncontrollably. 'Please don't hit me mister,' she sobbed, deep sobbing that made her chest hurt, causing her to catch her breath.

Unzipping his flies the man leaned over and pulled down her knickers. Emma screamed.

Suddenly the door burst open and Paul entered. Seeing what was happening he grabbed the man by the scruff of his neck forcing him out of the room, kicking his arse on the way out. 'You bastard, get the hell out of here,' he shouted.

Emma jumped off the bed and flung her arms around Paul, sobbing on his shoulder, her body still trembling with fear. 'I want to go home, Paul,' she pleaded, clinging more tightly to him.

'Where's your home, Emma?'

'Sheffield, my home is in Sheffield. I want to go home to see my Dad.'

Paul released her arms from his neck, gently placing his hands on her shoulders to calm her.

'Do you trust me, Emma?' Emma nodded.

'Then I can help you. I have a friend who's going to Sheffield in his van to deliver a load this very day and if I give him a ring I know he'll give you a lift as a favour for me. Give me a second.'

Paul took out his mobile and stepped out of the room. After a few seconds he re-entered and turned to Emma. 'He's agreed but says he has to drop something off in Cambridge. Is that OK with you?' Emma nodded again, too choked to say anything meaningful. All her rational reasoning, something which Emma had always been proud of, thrown to the wind on a spurious whim, all her father's advice ignored in these sort of situations.

'Trust me you'll be tucked up in your own bed tonight, nice and warm.' Emma once again flung her arms around Paul and gave him a kiss on the cheek.

Fifteen minutes later, having changed her knickers, Emma found herself clambering into the passenger seat of a white van driven by a man called Winston. He looked foreign and was not the best-looking of men and in normal circumstances she would never take a lift from someone like that, but she trusted Paul and was just glad to be going home. She waved goodbye to Paul and blew him a kiss as the van moved off.

What Emma did not see as the van turned a corner was Paul talking to the man who had pretended to assault her, the exchange of money and a celebration of high fives with big grins on both their faces.

The van sped away to Sheffield via Cambridge.

# Three

Detective Chief Inspector Charles Waley-Cohen sat behind his desk, head cradled in his hands to shut out the world, eyes closed, hoping for some respite from his pessimistic outlook on life, the grim reality of his police work and a burgeoning in-tray. It was seven-thirty in the morning, his head felt like bursting, he felt like shit and police work was the last thing on his mind.

This temporary stay from reality was not to last very long. Just when his eyelids had adopted a permanent droop, his head jerked up as the office door opened. It was Detective Sergeant Peter Ruskin who entered with a briskness in his gait and demeanour, in total contrast to the way Charles felt at that moment in time. What is it with these "early morning" people, Charles thought to himself. So chipper so early it drives you mad.

'Good Monday morning, sir. God, you look like shit.'

'Thank you, Peter. That's just what I needed. I feel like shit but you didn't have to remind me so soon in the morning. Anyway, why are you in so early?'

'It's my last day.'

'Oh God, yes, I forgot. But why in so early? You could have come in much later.'

'I wanted to pack a few personal items before the staff arrive. A bit embarrassing, you know what I mean.'

'I'll miss you, Peter.   How long have we been together?'

'Four years.'

'Four years.   How quickly time goes by.   You have helped me a great deal and I will definitely miss you.   We made a great team together, you and me.'

'Thank you.'

'I tell you what.   Why don't we have dinner together tonight?'

'I'm in early because I'm leaving after lunch.'

'In that case, why don't we have an early lunch in the pub opposite – on me.'

'Thank you, that's very kind of you'

'Say eleven-thirty?'

'That's fine by me.   By the way, you still look like shit. Would you like to borrow my electric razor?'

'No thanks.   I have one of my own but I take the hint.'

'Would you like a cup of black coffee to wake you up?'

'Not from that bloody machine.   It tastes worse than I feel.'

'I'll make you a proper one from the canteen.'

'You don't have to go out of your way, Peter.'

'It's my last day, sir, and therefore my last contribution to your sanity.'

'That is what I will miss from you, your dry sarcasm and earthy charm.'

'Not forgetting my wit, of course.'

'Of course, what will I do without your wit to sustain me through my darkest hours?'

'You'll think of something, you always do.'

'You know me too well, Peter.   I hope the next man can fill your boots.

'That's doubtful, sir, very doubtful.'

The sergeant left the room. Charles closed his eyes again to clear his head and unclutter his thoughts. He thought of the weekend just gone. A bout of drinking over two days in an all-male bonding party. He should have had more sense than to drink so much and it was a weakness he would need to address more seriously in the future. For now, what the hell, anything goes. It makes the world a more comfortable place to live in when reality is blotted out from the senses.

The pain in his head, like a tightening band, was God's punishment, he thought to himself, as he cradled his head in his hands once again as if that would take away the pain; he would have to mend his ways, sooner rather than later. These morbid thoughts were interrupted by Sergeant Ruskin re-entering his office, coffee in hand in a cup and saucer. Charles harboured his thoughts.

'No mugs?'

'On my final day I thought that a cup and saucer more appropriate. It is very, very strong. If you don't drink it quickly it will set solid. A good shot of whatever to your ailing system.'

'Thank you, Peter. See you at eleven-thirty.'

The sergeant left the room to gather his personal possessions, leaving his inspector sipping gingerly at his coffee.

A cup of strong coffee, a quick dry shave and Charles would be ready to tackle that in-tray; paperwork, paperwork, nothing but bloody paperwork. He hadn't had a decent case to solve since the brutal death of Amy Barraclough. Funny how his mind would still wander back to that case and its ramifications for so many people. He thought again of Carla Bores, the only girl who had stolen his heart and how their love affair had ended the way it did. He was beginning to reminisce. Leave that for another time. There is work to be done. He grabbed the first file from the in-tray, opened the cover slowly and began to read: "Assault of OAP Mrs Grimshaw, aged 86". He closed the file. Nothing like police work to jolt you out of your dreams and back into reality – brutal, gutter reality, embedded in the very DNA of police work.

Just after eleven-thirty saw Charles and Peter in the Red Lion pub opposite the station, known as the "copper den" because of its proximity to the police station. Charles had left a message with George, the desk sergeant, as to his whereabouts in case of an emergency. Not that he expected anything. He had no case requiring his specific attention or even immediate attendance. A brief respite of sorts from what could be intensive police pressure and paperwork.

'They serve a good lamb curry here, Peter. Fancy one?'

'Yes sir.'

'You can drop the "sir" bit. You'll be gone in an hour and I want to talk to you as a friend, as the best man at your wedding would. Now, a pint to celebrate?'

'Just a half. I'll be driving shortly.'

'Very sensible too,' then turning to the barman, 'Two lamb curries and a pint and a half pint of your best ale.'

'Take a seat, Peter, over there near the window, the one that's just been cleared.'

Peter took his seat and sat somewhat impassively looking out of the window, fiddling with his tie as he was prone to do when the subject of his divorce was likely to be on the agenda. Charles took his seat and opened the conversation.

'How are things with you, Peter?'

'Could be better I guess, could be worse I suppose.' A very succinct reply, his inner feelings not inclined to let his tongue move too much.

'Why did you choose the Newcastle Police Force to transfer to?'

'Jane was given custody of Lily and Oliver and is going to go back home to live with her parents in Liverpool. In Newcastle, I can keep in regular touch with the children and at the same time try to strike out on a new life for myself, as far away from Cambridge as I can get.'

'A messy business, a divorce. It can happen to anyone of us. Not me. I'm not married yet and don't intend to for a while, but who's to say what could happen in the future.'

The barman, Ted, brought over the meals and the beer, placing them on the table with the cutlery. 'Enjoy your meals gentlemen,' said Ted with his usual flamboyant grin puncturing the more solemn atmosphere around the table.

'Thanks Ted. You and your good lady well?' asked Charles.

'We survive. Could do with business being a bit better but we survive.' Another rictus grin. 'As long as we keep the punters happy, that's the main thing. Well, enjoy your meal gentlemen.' Ted went back behind the bar, greeting another customer in the same impeccable manner.

The interlude with Ted had helped Peter to relax a little. He stopped stroking his tie and tucked into his lamb curry, sucking in air and waving at his mouth at the intensity of the heat of his first mouthful, his face turning a shade of puce. Peter gulped a mouthful of beer.

'A bit hot eh, Peter? Should have warned you.'

The conversation had been lightened and the two men talked on more trivial subjects, of sport and hobbies, anything but divorce and children. This went on for a good half hour with typical male banter and a hearty guffaw or two, their police ranks subordinate to their friendship, just as it was when Charles was the best man at Peter and Linda's wedding those seven years ago. He had acted as a go-between, an agony aunt, for the couple when their marriage had started to unravel but to no avail when separation became inevitable.

Both men having finished their meals, Peter looked at his watch and rose from the table.

'You will keep in touch, Peter?'

'I will sir, and will follow your career closely. You are destined for high office and I hope you will still remember me then.'

'Thanks for the compliment and the best of luck to you.'

This was the cue for Peter to shake hands and to leave the pub, striding purposely to the door and not looking behind him. He did not want Charles to see his dewy eyes, the pain of love for his family making his eyes smart. One chapter, one very large chapter of his life had come to an end; the next, he hoped, was yet to be written in a nice way.

His heart was in his mouth and it hurt, really hurt as he recalled the question put to him by his young son, Oliver, still ringing in his ears on being told by his parents of their divorce and separation: 'But Daddy, how will Father Christmas know where I am?'

He made a half-hearted, disconsolate wave to Charles as he left the pub for pastures new.

Charles stayed a few minutes longer, supping alone, musing over their police and private repartee and the numbers of criminals they had brought to book. Times go on though, things start and come to an end. Life goes on. One door closes and another door opens. He hoped Peter would find a new life somewhere and with someone. He deserved no less than that.

Having finished his beer, he stood up, smoothed out his jacket and trousers, paid the barman, gave a salutary wave to Ted, 'See you Ted', and headed back to the police station.

Back at Parkside Police Station, George the burly desk sergeant jabbed his pen in the direction of the Chief Constable's office. 'The Chief was asking of your whereabouts and would like to see you in his office straight away.'

'Thank you, George.'

Charles knocked on the Chief Constable's office door.

'Enter.'

Charles entered. 'Father?'

'How many times …?'

'Sorry father … sir.'

'That's better. Take a seat.'

His father muttered under his breath, 'incorrigible, bloody incorrigible,' shaking his head at the same time. It was always the same with his son. Every serious subject reduced to a family verbal jousting contest. The soporific grin on his son's face didn't help matters. He loved his hot-headed son but at work, work was work, and certain principles and procedures had to be maintained. Rank had to be respected otherwise chaos would reign. It was his bounden duty to instil discipline in all his staff.

'Detective Chief Inspector …'

'Yes sir.'

'Detective Chief Inspector,' doubly emphasised, 'I wish to talk to you on a delicate subject …'

'Not when am I going to get married?'

'No, not that. I'll be dead before I have a grandchild from your loins.'

Both men smiled, a perennial subject in the family

'No. No. What I was going to say is that I have appointed a replacement for Sergeant Peter Ruskin.'

'Don't I get a say in the matter? After all, I have to work with the new man and I have someone in mind.'

'No you don't. I am pulling rank, even if you are my own flesh and blood. You will do as I say and make the best of it.'

Charles shrugged his shoulders. He always knew not to argue with his father when he had the upper hand. He had great respect for his father and the responsibility of his office. However on this occasion he had hoped to select his own partner.

Peter had understood his character, his good traits and his bad, and vice versa. They had made a good team and hadn't rubbed each other the wrong way. It was bad enough having to start all over again with another man and so he had hoped he would have had the final say on this appointment.

There was a knock at the door.

'Enter.'

'Detective Sergeant Moran, reporting, sir,' saluting her chief.

Charles practically fell of his chair as his head swivelled round. He … she can't be his new buddy at arms. Surely not. That mischievous grin on Christine's face told him that it was true. A little wink from that minx confirmed it.

'I …,' Charles spluttered.

'I won't hear another word. Detective Sergeant Moran has been appointed to replace Detective Sergeant Ruskin. I believe you know each other from your time in London. You were very successful together then and you can be very successful together now. Now, I have more important things to see to, so if you would both leave my office I can get on with some work.'

As Charles was leaving, following Christine, 'Oh, by the way Chief Inspector, I am holding a party next weekend and I have invited Christine ... I mean Sergeant Moran. Hope you can both come. Dress, informal.'

As the door closed behind them, his father looked up from his desk. He knew there was a chemistry between the two and there was a twinkle in his eye. One day, perhaps, one day.

What he failed to recognise or understand was that he had just lit a crackerjack under his own son's feet.

Charles gently closed the door behind him and then, placing his hand in the small of Christine's back, firmly but gently steered her in the direction of the canteen. Christine objected to being manhandled causing Charles to grab her elbow instead to direct her forward. Christine objected to this as well.

'Christine, I would like to speak to you alone in the staff canteen, if you don't mind?'

'Why didn't you ask me in the first place, sir, instead of pushing me.'

'I'm sorry. Can we please go to the canteen?'

They entered the canteen, Charles still fuming. 'Over there, in the corner. That will do.' Charles directed Christine to a table out of earshot of others.

'Coffee sir? Would you like me to get two coffees?'

'Not now Christine, not now.'

Both being seated, Charles paused to look around him before voicing his thoughts. Looking Christine firmly in the eyes, 'I would like you to resign this position, Christine.'

'Why?'

'Because … because we'll drive each other up the creek and for the sake of both our sanities, your position is untenable.'

'Why?'

'Because … because I'm used to working with a man. Buddy, buddies and all that. You know what I mean.'

'I would never have taken you for a sexist, sir.'

'I'm not. I mean to say that I am not used to working with a female. I need a male deputy to keep me on the right side of bedlam.'

Christine remained cool, calm and unflappable. She was half expecting such a reaction from Charles for her sudden appointment and had already rehearsed her response.

'Women can be just as effective as men, sir. True, they are not men but they can bring other qualities to the position such as female intuition, female sensitivity and female guile. I can be just as effective as Sergeant Peter Ruskin. Times have changed Charles and we must all change with the times.'

'I will have that coffee now, Christine.' Charles knew when to stop blustering and one way or another Christine would have the final say. There was no point in pressing the issue any further at this stage.

'I believe it's white, no sugar, sir?'

'Right. Thanks Christine.'

Charles watched Christine go to the service counter and ask for two coffees. Inside, he was annoyed, very annoyed. It was not so much Christine herself but he disliked being told who his partner would be. He was used to working with a man and had someone in mind. A female, Christine or otherwise, would not have been his first choice.

What to do about it? He could not overturn his father's decision and, in some ways, would not want to. He could resign his own position, but that would be rather rash. He was unlikely to get Christine to change her stance as she was a determined woman whose mind was made up. Best, he thought, to accept the situation no matter what and let sleeping dogs lie, for the moment at least.

Christine placed the two coffees on a tray. She had done her homework. She had had a chance to have a brief discussion with Peter Ruskin and he told her that the Chief Inspector was a mercurial character, to tiptoe gently when he was in a mood, sometimes sullen, depressed and irritable, always prickly. It would take her some time to understand the nuances in his voice and to gain his confidence. Occasionally he drank too much and that had to be taken into account as well.

He was hot-headed, a risk taker, but a friend and confidante, loyal to his partner and would put his life on the line to protect the people around him. He was very professional in his police work even if, at times, police work did not seem to suit him.

Christine had ulterior motives of being with Charles but she, too, was professional in her work and that came before her amorous intentions. She would tread softly and wait for the opportunities to get closer to Charles personally. It was not to be rushed needlessly setting up his defences where they currently did not exist. Softly and gently, that was the way to do it.

Christine placed the coffee in front of her Chief Inspector and resumed her position at the table. She now played her risky but final card.

'I will resign my position, Chief Inspector, if that is what you really want me to do.'

As she expected, her statement took Charles by surprise. He did not immediately reply. He sipped his coffee slowly and said nothing, occasionally looking Christine in the eye, occasionally staring into his cup. Christine waited, fingers crossed under the table.

Finally, 'I do not want you to resign Christine. It was wrong of me to ask you to do so. I have had time to think about it. We worked well together in London and I do not see why we couldn't work together in Cambridge. But, no hanky-panky, mind you. What we did was a one-off and I do not want our personal affairs to interfere with out police work. You do understand that don't you, Christine?'

'Yes sir. No hanky-panky, as you put it. I have already forgotten about our affair. Police work first always.' She lied. She wanted Charles more than ever before. She would need to bide her time though. There was no Miss Bores to get in the way now. His heart would heal following her death and she would be there to pick up the pieces and make him fall in love with her.

Charles nodded approvingly. 'Finish your coffee, Christine, and meet me in my office in thirty minutes. I have something to ask you.' Charles rose from the table and headed towards the canteen door, shaking his head in disbelief at the turn of events.

~

Back in his office there was a present on his desk. He read the label, it was from Peter Ruskin. Opening the box it was a "Newton's Cradle", five small, metal balls swinging together. Charles raised one ball to swing against the others, listening to the "click" as the balls struck each other repeatedly. The monotone somehow soothed his frustration with Christine's appointment as he played with it for the next five minutes. Did Peter know of his replacement before he did? He couldn't help feeling that might just be the case or at least Peter had suspected it to be so. Charles smiled to himself as he put the toy into his desk drawer.

As requested, after half an hour, Christine tapped on the open glass door of her Chief Inspector's office.

'Come in, Sergeant, and close the door behind you. Take a seat. I've spoken to all the staff and they are aware of your new role in the team. At some point you might like to have a word with them yourself. For now, I want you to listen carefully to what I have to say.

'We have heard a rumour that there is going to be a hoist on a jewellers in Cambridge. Our informant is very specific, between 2.00 and 3.00 pm at Bathgate & Sons, near Market Square. Do you know the place?'

'I do. I have been there a number of times. Very classy, very expensive, the shop sells luxury brands including Rolex and Frank Muller, some of which sell for tens of thousands of pounds.'

'Right. You have the option to come with me but this is what I plan. I and a WPC will act as a couple in the shop during this period, looking for an engagement ring. The staff have been informed and they will go along with the ruse. We aim to catch the robbers red-handed. I ...'

'I understand, sir, and if I may, I would like to be that WPC.'

'Are you sure? There are likely to be firearms involved.'

'I am sure.'

'OK. Well, that's settled.'

Christine did not have to be asked twice. This was one of the reasons she loved her Chief Inspector. He was a man of action and it spiked her blood. She could already feel the adrenalin coursing through her body calling her to action. It could be dangerous, very dangerous, but all the better especially with her Chief Inspector by her side. She had total confidence in him and would die for him if need be, but she hoped that would not be necessary or too soon.

From a female perspective, what better place than jewellers to discuss her taste in engagement and wedding rings and all things like that with her prospective husband? Her mind was beginning to wander. She must curb such thoughts if she was to win his loyalty, not to mention his love.

Christine rose from her chair to leave the office.

'By the way, Sergeant, your desk out there is the one that Sergeant Ruskin had. You might like to personalise it with your own possessions.'

'Thank you, Chief Inspector. I already have.'

'Right.'

Charles watched her leave his office and stroked his chin in a questioning way. What had he let himself in for? She was a minx if ever there was one, a cool, self-assured one but still an all-round minx. A devilish smile crossed his face. He would tame her and bring her to heel if need be. He would still rule the roost here, he would see to that. She would soon tire of him and look elsewhere.

~

'Sapphires, rubies, emeralds, but diamonds Charles, diamonds are a girl's best friend and all that. Look, look, look at that diamond cluster ring. Isn't it just beautiful Charles? I would love someone to buy that for me.' Christine sidled even closer to Charles and pressed her hand into his that little more deeply, as lovingly affectionate as she dare without Charles backing off.

'A bit on the expensive side, isn't it?'

'We could afford it, Charles, couldn't we? I mean, with your earnings and my earnings together we could afford such a beautiful ring. Do you think I could try it on?'

'Suppose so. I am not one for ostentatious jewellery, much prefer a simple inexpensive ring.'

'There's one there Charles. That's not so expensive. I could try that one on, too. That would be more to your liking, don't you think?'

The shop assistant opened the locked display case and placed the two rings on the counter. Christine placed each ring, in turn, on her finger and held her hand up high in front of Charles's face.

'Which do you prefer Charles? I think I prefer the inexpensive one. In fact, I think the plainer the better. For my man, if he preferred, I would wear the simplest of rings if that is what he desired.'

Charles thought it wise not to say anything. Christine was lost in a schoolgirl world of her own. The real purpose of their visit to the jeweller seemingly pushed to the rear of her mind. No so. Christine's excitement masked an inner nervousness at what might happen at any time. Her

227

closeness to Charles was part amour and part reassurance. She could sense and feel the tension in his whole body, like a coiled spring ready to be released in an instant.

Christine took Charles's hand and led him to the counter on the other side of the showroom where watches and silverware were displayed.

'Would you like me to buy you a watch, Charles, as an engagement gift? Which one takes your fancy?'

'None really. I'm quite happy with the one I have, thank you.'

'Cuff links? Tie pin? Anything?'

'Not really.'

There were two assistants, one male and one female, serving behind each counter. The proprietor was repairing a watch for an older gentleman, fitting a new battery and cleaning the watch-face. Another young couple were perusing the rings, trying to find one for the future bride and groom which would meet their budget. They smiled at Christine's exuberance and Charles's apparent indifference and pithy riposte.

Charles looked at his watch. It was 2.27 pm. He tapped his watch as the proprietor came from the back room, a given signal for him to usher the two assistants into the back room and the customers from the shop, turning the notice on the door to CLOSED, but not to close the toughened glass door entirely otherwise it would be smashed in the attempted robbery.

The sudden, eerie silence sent shivers down Christine's spine and she experienced those butterflies, the tummy wobbles, whenever she felt impending trouble. Charles released her hand and she felt that much more insecure. She had expected Charles to become more tensed but he did the exact opposite. To her surprise he relaxed entirely and started chatting to her as normal, as though out for a daily stroll. She could only surmise that his previous tension had more to do with talk of engagement rings than it was to do with the expected robbery. He was a man of surprises and the more she knew about him the more she loved him, from the top of his deep-brown, unruly hair to the tip of his polished brogues, even if at times he was loveably taciturn. He was the man for her but in her new position as his deputy her inner feelings had to be well hidden.

Her thoughts came to an abrupt end. They both heard the pop-popping of a moped, which grew louder as it approached the shop and then stopped as if it was being parked. Within seconds, two men wearing hoods and ghoulish masks approached the door intending to smash it open, but seeing it slightly ajar, burst through, one carrying a shotgun, the other a large sledgehammer.

'All of you on the floor,' screamed the man with the shotgun, waving it menacingly at Charles and Christine, the only two in the shop. The proprietor had locked himself and the two assistants in the back room.

The fact that there were only two people and no assistants in the showroom did not register with the robbers. In their haste they were only concerned with a quick hit-and-grab raid. The man with the sledgehammer raised it above his head and brought it down smartly on the glass display cases with an almighty crash.

Their greed was their failing. Both Charles and Christine had dropped to their knees, their hands touching the floor. The shotgun was lowered as the man's eyes surveyed the jewellery. In that instance, Charles leapt up and with his right foot smacked the shotgun out of his hand. A further swivel and the robber bent double as Charles's foot ripped into his stomach. Another swivel and another foot engaged with the robber's chin, knocking him semi-conscious.

In the meantime, the other robber, who had put the sledgehammer down to grab handfuls of jewellery, was taken totally by surprise at seeing what was happening to his mate. He grabbed the sledgehammer again – but all too late. Christine was on to him in a flash, putting his arm in a painful arm-lock from which there was no escape.

'You bastard. You bloody bastard. You wanna make something of it you whore?' Christine tightened her grip and the man went limp with the pain.

'Arghh … Let go of me.' Christine held the position until Charles could put the man's hands behind his back and secure them with handcuffs.

Charles ripped off the masks just as the armed back-up team arrived and looked into their faces. They were middle-aged men, well known to the police and suspected of a spate of such robberies. Until now, no hard evidence was available to convict them.

As the men were led away, Charles shook Christine's hand.

'Well done, Christine. You got him before I did. You did a good job and I seem to have trained you well in the martial arts.'

'Thank you, sir. You were a good tutor.'

Charles glanced at her hand, smeared with blood. 'You've been cut Christine. That will need to be looked at when we get back to the station.'

'I think it was a flying piece of glass when the counter was smashed. It's not too bad.'

'Nevertheless get it checked out.'

'I will check with the doctor when we get back to the station.'

Charles gave her a congratulatory slap on the back, forgetting that she wasn't Peter Ruskin, causing her to lurch forward and almost topple over.

'Oops! Sorry about that, Sergeant.'

'That's all right, sir. You meant well.'

'Well, I think that's our job finished. We can let the proprietor and his two assistants out of the back room now. What do you say?'

'Yes sir. They will be very relieved, as I am.'

'All in a day's work Sergeant,' said Charles as he took out a clean handkerchief, bent down and cleaned his brown brogues.

'Yes sir. We made a good team.'

Christine hoped there would not be too many day's work like that otherwise she would be an old maid before her time.

As they left the shop: 'By the way, Sergeant, I preferred the ring with the cluster of diamonds.'

'So, my initial guess was correct, Chief Inspector.'

'It was indeed, Sergeant, it was indeed.'

These words were said with a wry smile on his face. He knew all along what Christine was up to. It added a frisson to police work, he had to admit to that. What the future had in store for both of them he knew not what, but it was not going to be all plain sailing. His new partner would see to that.

# Four

Hendon Training College, Cambridge
Friday, 29th June 2012, 8.45 am.

Charles drove his yellow Porsche through the imposing wrought-iron gates of the Police Training College at Hendon and headed for the visitors' car park. His reserved space, marked by a blue plaque on the wall of the building in recognition of his sporting achievement, never failed to give a fillip to his ego. Memories of his Olympic gold medal, acquired in Taekwondo at the Beijing games in 2008, would flood his mind. Times now past that seemed increasingly distant with every visit.

Such training days were increasingly infrequent as his police work became more demanding. What used to be a weekly visit was now monthly and even then it was a squeeze to fit it into a work schedule that demanded a lot of his personal attention. Squeeze it in he must if he was to maintain his fitness and to instil in the new police recruits the martial arts of Taekwondo and Karate. Besides, it was always an antidote to his bouts of depression and low spirits when confidence became ever more a distant memory.

True to form and superstition, he alighted from his car, unlocked the boot and took out a pair of Armani shoes, replacing his driving ones; eased on the left shoe and then the right, always in that order; then slipped on his casual, cream sports jacket. Clothes maketh the man was his unconscious mantra. A quick polish of his shoes with two clean handkerchiefs and he was in the right vein of thought for doing justice to his sport and training hour.

Expecting, as usual, to be greeted by his good friend David Blake, the chief training instructor, he was surprised to see Eric Pickles striding purposely towards him.

'Hello Eric, is David about?'

'You haven't heard, Chief Inspector?'

'Heard what, Eric?'

'David is on compassionate leave for two weeks. His wife is undergoing a double mastectomy and he needs to be with her at this time.'

It was like a blow to the solar plexus. He knew Anna well and was godfather to their twin girls, Sarah and Susan, now regrettably deceased. Such thoughts about the twins immediately swamped his mind about their sad passing, thoughts that were always harboured but rarely allowed at sea.

'You OK, Chief Inspector?'

Charles had been taken aback, not just because of Anna, but the fact that he had not known anything about it. The twins, and now Anna. Why hadn't David mentioned anything to him? He had seen him only three weeks ago and no mention of the subject had come up in their discussions. Why does this sort of thing happen to good people? At the first opportunity he would contact the family to offer his condolences.

'You OK, Chief Inspector?' Eric looked quizzically at Charles.

'Thanks, Eric. Lead the way. I will talk to David as soon as I can.' Thoughts other than the training schedule were now uppermost in his mind and pricked his conscience.

Such thoughts persisted as he changed into his Dobok, his white uniform, in the changing room and as he ribboned it with his black belt. They continued to bother him as he was introduced to the new recruits passively seated on the floor.

The applause of fifteen pairs of hands echoed around the gym snapped him out of his reverie. He made an informal bow and smiled a forced smile. He was now in his element, now high on adrenalin, now with an unsullied, one-track mind. The sport was Taekwondo and he was the master. Sport was life and life was sport and he was the king of his sport.

For the first half hour, with the aid of mannequins, he went through his routine of Taekwondo kicks and then the basic movements of Karate. He was not as fit as he would like to be, less to do with his age at twenty-eight and more to do with the never-ending police work which kept him away from the gym and regular physical exercise. When sport fired his blood he always gave it his best, not to his own high standard, but good enough for the new recruits to appreciate both martial art forms.

The following half hour had the recruits practising their own feeble efforts of emulating the master, usually accompanied with howls of laughter as attempted kicks invariably resulted in them sitting on the seat of their pants. Though some were good others couldn't raise their foot above the knee without over-balancing. It all added to a sense of fun even if the underlying purpose of self-defence was a serious matter to all assembled.

Training session complete, Charles took his bow and headed back to the changing-room handing over to Eric to take charge of the remainder of the recruit training, loud applause still ringing in his ears. Applause, like with any actor, lifts the spirit and seals the performance, but being out of kilter with himself it had a hollow ring to it this time.

Driving back home he thought again of the twins. Only death, he thought, would rid him of that particular pain. And now Anna. Poor Anna. What had she done in life to be visited once again by the hideous face of tragedy? How would Anna and David cope? Knowing David as well as he did he hoped the mastectomy would not create a barrier between the two of them. Peter Ruskin's divorce was bad enough, a second de-coupling would be too much. David loved Anna and this would be the antidote in these difficult circumstances, he hoped. He would ring David at the earliest opportunity to see if he could help in any way.

The scudding clouds across a blue sky and warm sunshine did not lift his mood nor did the guttural sound of the Porsche have its usual effect on his senses. He shook his head with disbelief at Anna's wretched luck in life and switched on the radio to try to obliterate his thoughts. The "love" music caused tears to well in his eyes. He switched it off.

~

Charles was in a thoughtful mood as he sat in his office on an early Monday morning, the sobering light of day intruding into his melancholy thoughts. Over the weekend he had spoken to David and visited their home. He was now ruminating on their answers to his questions.

They had deliberately kept it a secret from him not wishing to hurt his feelings, what with the twins and all that. Besides it was personal and private and they were both coming to terms with it. It was a pity he found out the way he did, they knew he would feel it deeply.

Anna explained that it was Angelina Jolie's public announcement of her double mastectomy that gave her the courage to ask her GP for a referral and a DNA test for the BRCA1 gene mutation, making it highly likely she would develop breast cancer. Her family had a history of the disease, her mother dying from it at a young age as well as several aunts.

The DNA test proved positive for the gene. After discussing it at length with David she had decided to have the double mastectomy. It was that simple: lose two breasts and save one's life. Post-operative surgery would do the rest. For Anna, it was all a matter of fact, it was more David's feelings she was concerned about than her loss of sexual identity. They would cope. David had nodded in agreement as she spoke, reassuring Charles that they were and would remain a close-knit couple, as deeply in love as ever. Charles, knowing David well, had his doubts but hoped for the best of outcomes, Anna deserved no less.

'Good morning, sir. I've brought you a nice cup of coffee in your favourite mug.'

'Thank you, Sergeant.'

'You look a bit glum.'

'Just thoughtful.'

'I know a cure for the blues.'

'I am sure you do and I bet it doesn't involve any medicine.'

'Sir?'

'A cheap joke, Sergeant. Sorry for that, I'm not in the best of moods'

237

Christine handed him a file. 'From the Chief, sir. He asked me to hand it to you for your immediate attention.'

'Thank you, Sergeant. I will call you if I need you.'

'Yes sir.'

Christine went out of the office, leaving her Chief Inspector as pensive as when she first entered. Tread carefully was Sergeant Ruskin's advice when he was in that sort of mood and tread carefully she would.

Charles wearily opened the file and read it through. This was no ordinary incident. This was something very different, something to get his teeth into. His police instincts gripped him and all other thoughts flew out of his mind. He read more between the lines than its actual content implied.

He raised himself from his chair and opened the office door. 'Sergeant Moran, could you come into my office please?'

'Yes sir.'

Christine seated herself at the office desk, marvelling at the change in mood of her Chief Inspector. In the dumps one minute, as bright as a button the next. It was a roller-coaster ride for her own emotions but she was strong enough to cope with anything her Chief Inspector could throw at her, or so she hoped.

'Sergeant,' fingering through the file, 'Sergeant, a right arm was lifted out of the river Cam a couple of miles upstream from here. Forensics say it is that of a young white girl, perhaps in her early teens.'

Charles showed her the photograph. Christine studied it closely.

'There is nothing much to go on, sir.'

'True, but what else do you notice?'

Christine studied it even more closely.

'It is heavily tattooed and scarred, suggesting self-harm, possibly?'

'All of those things but apparently it was also severed in one blow using an axe or something similar. No more than perhaps two weeks ago.'

'That adds a new dimension to the investigation.'

'It sure does.

'I want you to arrange for police divers to search the area where the arm was found for any other parts of the body. This arm had been weighted down with stones and had somehow surfaced near some weeds where a jogger, passing by, had noticed it and informed the police. Where is the rest of the body?

'Also make copies of the tattoo patterns on the arm. We will assume, for the moment, she is a local girl who visited a local tattooist. Have your team check out the local studios to see if anyone recognises the patterns and can name the girl. It is a long shot, but worth doing at this stage of the enquiry.'

'Yes sir. I will get the team on to it straight away. We will also check out the Missing Persons Register to see if that can give us a clue.'

'Thank you, Sergeant.' Charles closed the file, tapping his fingers on the cover as if emphasising its importance before finally handing it to Christine.

'Whilst you are doing that, Sergeant, I will talk to forensics to see if I can glean any further information from their DNA tests and will visit the spot where it was found.'

'Yes sir.'

Christine tucked the file under her arm and left the office.

Charles pondered the case. There was little to go on but this is what being a detective was all about. The girl did not sever her own arm and was obviously murdered, and her body cut up. Only by chance had the arm been discovered. Where were all the other body parts and who had done the severing? Like his sport, he had a one-track mind to find her killer.

~

By Friday of the same week, the other arm had been discovered. Like the first it had been crudely severed from the body, but there were no signs of any other body parts. The search by police divers was continuing into the second week. Like the first arm, this was heavily tattooed with the same patterns. Other than that it yielded no more information.

Likewise, the team had not been able to ascertain the identity of the girl. A search of the Missing Persons Register had not revealed any sort of match and local tattooists were unable, or unwilling, to divulge clients' names. In fact, many of them did not complete a register, afraid of a person being underage and getting their business closed down. They were given further warnings by the police that young persons under eighteen need their parents' consent.

Interviews of joggers and pedestrians near the spot where the arms were found also yielded no further information.

'Goodnight, sir. See you tomorrow at the party.'

'Sergeant … Christine, would you like me to give you a lift?'

'That is very kind of you but I can take a taxi to your father's place.'

'That is a lot of money. I insist on giving you a lift. I will be staying overnight but we can get you a taxi home. Where would you like me to pick you up? From your home?'

'No, not from home. I'm visiting friends earlier. Outside the gates of Kings College would do nicely. Say seven-thirty?'

'Seven-thirty it is then. See you then.'

As her back was turned to leave, Charles was unaware of the huge, knowing smile on Christine's face. A private lift by her man to a party – now that was progress! It could even be considered a date!

~

Dress was informal. Charles was wearing white Chinos, suede loafers, a blue check shirt and a pale-blue summer jacket. A close razor shave and after-shave gave his face a slight buff appearance. He was attractive to women and he knew it.

In Christine's case, informal dress meant the opposite. She was dressed to the nines, more appropriate for a ball than a family get-together and barbeque. She didn't get many chances to show off her fulsome figure to Charles and every opportunity had to be taken advantage of.

She had opted for a more demure look with a feminine pastel-pink, prom-style dress, accessorising the look with a grey cape, heels, silver jewellery and a red clutch bag. She looked effortlessly chic with dark nails, smoky eyes and soft curls in her blonde hair. Not always a paragon of fashion, she made an exception in this case.

'You look stunning, Christine,' said Charles as Christine wiggled her way into the passenger seat of his Porsche.

'Thank you kind sir. Just something I threw on.'

'God help the men then when you dress to kill.'

He didn't get it. He just didn't get it. There was only one man in her life and that was Charles. How can men be so thick? What had she to do to get Charles to see that she was head-over-heels in love with him? She would die for him. She would give him babies. She would treasure every moment together for life eternal.

Christine's emotions were running away with her. She ought not to have had those pre-cocktail drinks with her friends.

The Porsche purred along effortlessly. Christine could have sat there forever watching her man, the party being a mere distraction.

'Nearly there,' said Charles as he drove up the long drive to the mansion.

Lulled slightly by the comfort of the car and music, Christine was jolted into reality by the noise of the shingle drive. Her initial reaction was surprise at the splendour of the house in its acres of well-tended gardens and woodland. She hoped her dress was not inappropriate for the occasion but there were nagging doubts she had over-dressed.

Charles parked the car, stepped out and helped Christine, holding the passenger door and giving her a helping hand to clamber out. A quick smoothing of their clothes and they were both ready to enter the house. Christine wanted to hold Charles's hand but she thought better of it. For a moment she had forgotten he was her Chief Inspector, not her beau.

They were greeted by his parents.

'You look beautiful, Christine,' said his father with that same twinkle in his eye as his son.

'Thank you, sir.'

'Drop the sir bit, it's George.'

'Thank you … George.'

'And let me introduce you to my other half, Anthea.'

'Pleased to meet you, Christine,' said Anthea with a courteous shake of the hands.

They entered a large reception room where numerous people were milling around, chattering away, being served drinks and canapés by smartly dressed waiters. It was apparent that an outside catering company was supplying the drinks and canapés and later on a barbecue, with seating in a large marquee in the garden.

Most of the men in the room were in casual trousers or jeans with a mixture of T-shirts and light sweaters. The women, on the other hand, were smartly but casually dressed in top brand names with flashings of jewellery. Christine felt she had over-dressed. Oh well, what the hell she thought to herself as she handed over her cape to one of the servants, you only live once.

'Make yourself at home,' said George to Christine. It is an informal get-together of family and friends. Please make yourself at home.'

'Let me quickly introduce you to everyone,' interrupted Anthea, leading Christine by the hand in determined fashion.

It was a motley group of people. Anthea, being a playwright for the small screen, introduced Christine to her many friends of stage and screen, as well as back-room staff. Then there were George's police colleagues, many of senior rank, from neighbouring police forces, some retired, as well as the Deputy Commissioner of the Met.

The family included George's two brothers and Anthea's sister with a few grand-parents thrown in for good measure. All were on first-name terms. There are some people well connected, thought Christine, and there are some people "Well Connected"!

All the children were in the garden exuberantly playing on a bouncy-castle and gyrating to the piped music. All, that is, except one, Coral. She was the daughter of one of George's brothers and therefore a cousin to Charles. She was not a child but a young woman of seventeen years of age. In contrast to the older women she had adopted a more extreme dressed-down look: black skinny-fit jeans with a hole ripped at the knee, trainers with the laces missing and a lime-green T-shirt under a casual dark jacket. She was lissom, very attractive with a short-bob hairstyle and a complexion to die for - dewy and youthful.

Dressed down maybe but with eye-catching jewellery. In her ears, single diamond studs,  on one finger a gold ring with a cluster of diamonds, and a chunky necklace of beautiful coloured beads from which hung a large black, square stone in which was embedded a  platinum heart. In the heart was an eye-popping diamond, the biggest diamond that Christine had ever seen. Rich relatives or what?

At first it didn't register with Christine that Coral was also wearing the latest must-have trinket for women – Cartier's iconic love bangle to show their devotion to the man in their life, a gold bracelet which is locked with two small grub screws and which requires a screwdriver to unlock it!

In Christine's eyes though, Coral seemed prickly and ingratiating, a femme fatale in elfin disguise, a clothes-horse, a well-perfumed mannequin in Jasmine Noir perfume. And Christine was well versed in knowing what women were thinking before they knew it themselves.

Christine's suspicions were well founded with hackles aroused as she watched Coral sidle over to Charles. Coral's eyes were all over him, batting her eyelashes like a schoolgirl. She overheard their conversation.

'Hello Coral, long time no see. You were just this high when I last saw you,'

'I'm not a little girl now … CHIEF INSPECTOR.'

'No. I can see that.'

'Would you like to come into the music room with me to watch me play my violin?'

'Err …, not at the moment, Coral. Later perhaps.'

'Just for a few minutes. I have practised a lot.'

'Oh, OK. Just for a few minutes then.'

Coral slipped her arm into his to lead him to the music room, glancing back to see if anyone was noticing.

You little whipper-snapper, thought Christine. How can men be so gullible to a pretty face? She was obviously flirting with Charles and it upset Christine who had imbibed a few more drinks, releasing the horns of jealousy.

Christine walked quickly over to Charles and whispered in his ear, 'Your father would like to speak with you.' The glare from Coral said it all as Christine pulled Charles away from her clutches.

'You will have to excuse me, Coral. Father needs to talk to me on police business.'

'Right. See you later then.'

Charles turned to Christine and whispered, 'Thank you Christine, I needed rescuing, I hate the violin.'

Christine whispered back, 'Always the good Samaritan, sir … I mean Charles.'

Christine was surprised at her catty over-reaction to another woman's advances, cousin or not. Charles was still a free agent and she should not get so worked up. Love, though, has a habit of making your mind up for you and she was no exception to that particular rule. Thoughts of Carla however were uppermost in her mind as she watched Coral flounce away into the garden, casting an eye to Christine in a haughty manner, her auburn fringe too short to hide a scowl.

The remainder of the day went well, the ambience of the whole occasion being enjoyed by both Christine and Charles, Christine having been accepted into the bosom of Charles's family and having been a big hit with all the children in the garden, kicking off her heels and joining in the fun. It was with some regret therefore when she stepped into the taxi to take her home. She felt warm and needed inside, and a farewell peck on the cheek by Charles put a final seal on a lovely day.

'Bye Christine. See you on Monday.'

Christine waved back, her heart in her mouth.

Charles stepped back into the house and answered the ringing telephone in the hall. It was Clive, the senior doctor in charge of forensics.

'Chief Inspector, we have made another discovery. I suggest you visit us first thing on Monday.'

'I'll bring Sergeant Ruskin … I mean Sergeant Moran with me.'

'Only if she has a strong stomach, Chief Inspector. And I mean a strong stomach.'

# Five

'Morning, Clive.'

'Morning, Chief Inspector. Good morning, Sergeant.' Clive greeted them both with a warm handshake and then led them to his office, his face as inscrutable as ever, never the one to betray his true feelings in work time.

Charles knew Doctor Clive Dunne well. A two-persona character if ever there was one. At work, this thin, bald, bespectacled, middle-aged man was placid in the extreme, taking his work very seriously and rarely letting a smile cross his face. A man of few words, his apparent cold-hearted demeanour matched and suited his environment. He never referred to people on first name terms whilst in the "office", formalities being always observed in respect for the dead in his care.

Outside of work, on the other hand, he was the exact opposite - amiable, talkative and full of cheer. Charles had joined him sometimes on his marathon runs in London and elsewhere, and played the occasional game of tennis with him. The pallor of his face at work turning instantly into ruddy cheeks at play. A most likeable companion on first name terms with everyone.

At this instant in time, however, he was more than serious with a furrowed brow suggesting what he was about

247

to reveal was most unpleasant, a trait that Charles recognised in other dire situations when dealing with Clive.

'What have you got for us?' asked Charles, in a hurry to get to the nub of the matter.

'The rest of the body, minus the head, and both legs were discovered in local woods by a man and his dog out walking. The area has been cordoned off and the parts brought to the lab by my forensic team. Well, what remains of the body, that is.'

'What do you mean by what remains of the body?' Charles's curiosity was triggered.

'I think you need to see for yourself. Sergeant, do you think you are up to it?'

'I won't know until I've seen it. I've seen corpses before,' replied Christine, tongue in cheek but serious all the same. Like Charles her curiosity was aroused.

'Not like this you haven't,' was the curt reply. 'If it turns your stomach don't be ashamed to leave the room. I have seen students throw up at the mere sight of what you are about to see. I suggest you put on these surgical masks as the putrefaction is overwhelming.'

Clive led them into the mortuary and on his instructions the drawer was pulled out of the freezer by two of his assistants.

'Are you ready, Chief Inspector, Sergeant?' Clive looked at Christine to note the apprehension on her face, not sure how she would react to what was about to be revealed.

Both nodded apprehensively.

Clive slowly removed the sheet and watched their reaction.

The sight before them was of a dismembered body. The arms and legs having been hacked off were placed in their rightful position, giving due respect to the remains. The missing head, which had also been hacked off, gave the spectacle a surreal, even ghoulish appearance.

The sight for the faint-hearted was horrible in the extreme, so much so that after a few minutes Christine felt it appropriate to leave the room, hand over her mouth. Charles steeled himself as Clive explained.

'I know this is not a pretty sight and I can talk to you about it in my office if you wish, Chief Inspector.'

Charles felt a queasiness in his stomach. He had seen many gruesome sights in his short career but this was something else. The sheer revulsion that had been perpetrated on this young girl beggared belief. It was the most extreme kind of murder in the annals of his personal police history of crimes.

'Please continue, Clive, if you would.'

Clive remained unmoved, his face set in place with a firm jaw. Even he had rarely seen a sight such as this.

'This is … was a young girl in her mid-teens. The ribs have been broken and the heart removed. The heart valves have been surgically removed and then the heart crudely pushed back into its cavity. The liver, kidneys and lungs have been removed quite skilfully. Skin grafts have been taken from the upper part of the legs, the central and dorsal trunk - that is the belly and back. Leg bones have been removed together with veins, whole tendons including the Achilles.

'The limbs have been crudely hacked off with something like a butcher's cleaver after all the anatomical material had been surgically removed. Whoever did the surgical work was top class in his field. No ordinary surgeon could have done this. It has taken many years of practice.'

Clive, seeing Charles's unease asked politely, 'Shall I go on?'

'No thanks, Clive. I think I've seen enough.'

Clive carefully replaced the sheet.

'We call them human sock puppets. They are stripped of all their reusable parts, recycled skin, organs and other tissues. So called "anatomical material" to us in the medical profession. The arms were discarded because of the heavy tattoos and scars, otherwise skin grafts would have been taken from them, too. My guess is that when we find the head it will be missing its eyes for the corneas and other parts. It is surprising how many parts of the eye can be reused these days. The same goes for eardrums.

'It is a thriving business, Chief Inspector, the younger the better. Good quality will always command a higher price in the market place, from ten months old and upwards. Of course people donate their organs and that is all legal, but needless to say there is a big black market worldwide which is illegal. This clearly is a case of the latter. A grisly trade, don't you agree?

'You have not just a murder on your hands, Chief Inspector, but possibly many murders. It's your job to catch the criminals, not mine, thank God.'

'Unbelievable,' said Charles regaining his sensibilities, 'bloody unbelievable. How do you surgeons do it? How can you play God in this way?'

'You do get used to it. I tell you what, I have a DVD we use for medical students you can show to your staff. It will give them a better idea of what they are up against in this illegal trade.'

'Thanks, Clive. I think I will do just that.'

Charles took his leave. Removing his surgical mask he thanked Clive who handed him the DVD, meeting up with Christine who was still feeling queasy.

'I'm sorry about that, sir. I don't know what came over me. It wasn't very professional.'

'Please don't apologise, Sergeant. There are fewer things in life you will see worse than that, that's for sure.'

After a pleasurable weekend just gone, it was a shocking jolt to reality for both of them. The uglier, seamier side of life witnessed too often by the police.

The fresh air outside felt good as both inhaled deeply to normalise their senses.

~

Charles addressed his team:

'I have just returned from the mortuary and spoken at length to Doctor Clive Dunne, the senior forensics expert. The body and legs of a young girl, as yet unidentified, minus the head, have been matched to the two arms. The area in the woods where the latest body parts were found has been cordoned off and forensics continues to glean any further evidence from the scene. Police searches continue in the river and in the woods for the missing head.

'This is not a simple murder case. In a nutshell, we are now investigating human organ trafficking. Find the traffickers and we will find the murderers. I say murderers because there is unlikely to be a single person involved but a well-organised team which includes surgeons and others skilled in the art of surgical organ and human tissue removal for transplant purposes.

'I will go into more detail later but for now I would like you to make a preliminary list of all surgeons, dentists and medical research establishments in the Cambridge area.

'In the meantime, I have set up a DVD in the conference room. It is for medical students and shows human organ harvesting and transplants. It is called "Skin Deep". It is not for the squeamish. The operations on cadavers are particularly explicit and gory. I am not forcing you to watch it. It will, however, show you what we are up against. This case takes priority over everything else. Give it your maximum attention. We have never had a case of this magnitude before.

'Fear and revulsion are tangible concepts in cases like this but I ask you to try and put that aside and to keep your investigations professional. I know it will be hard to do but please try.

'Thank you.'

Then turning to Christine asked, 'Sergeant Moran, could I talk to you in my office, please.'

Christine followed Charles into his office, her tummy still feeling queasy.

'Take a seat, Sergeant. It is early days but I don't want the horror of the subject matter to obscure the fact that we are investigating the murder of a young girl. Once the initial shock is over I would like the team to put together a list of all the medical equipment needed to carry out these operations such as surgical implements, refrigerators and coolers, sterile boxes, iodine for cleaning, preservative chemicals and so on. Then a list of the companies in the country producing these supplies for the Cambridge area in particular.

'Ask your team to compile a list of surgeons, concentrate on the top surgeons and, where possible, obtain a photograph from HR departments to match their names. Try not to cause too many waves in the medical profession. We don't want to scare off the perpetrators of this crime. Can you do that?'

'Yes sir.'

'Meanwhile, I will talk to the Department of Health's Human Tissue Authority in London, the governing body in the UK. I will also talk to one of the licensed human bone and tissue banks in Liverpool and Manchester to see what I can glean.

'I then plan to visit a local orthopaedic surgeon to find out what happens on the shop floor, so to speak. Likewise, at some stage, when you have the time, I would like you to visit your dentist. Your teeth need cleaning, Sergeant.'

'Sir?'

'Only joking, Sergeant.'

'Yes sir.'

'Seriously though I would like you to visit a dentist to find out more about the use of illegal bone or any other body parts in modern day dentistry as part of our general investigations.

'Thank you, Sergeant, that will be all for now.'

Christine left his office checking her teeth with her fingers. She was due a check-up anyway but had always found reasons to defer it. She hated the dentist's chair.

With his elbows on the desk, Charles buried his head in his hands and pondered the situation. He would give his team a few days for the subject matter to sink in and to produce the lists. Then the leg-work would need to start. A profile of the organ transplant business would need to be built up, looking for any weaknesses that the unscrupulous could take advantage of, not the most pleasantness of tasks but something that just had to be done.

It was important for everyone, including himself, to set aside their revulsion and imaginings of the murder of this girl and to concentrate on the facts, as they would with any other case. The mind, given rein, can stretch the imagination to breaking point and defeat the purpose of the investigation. How many murders had been committed? Were the boys and girls dead when the organs were removed? How were the remains disposed of? All questions that needed answering but at some later date, the fact-finding had to come first.

'Coffee time,' he said to himself, looking at his watch. 'I have never needed one as much as I do now.'

Christine, too, was contemplating the time being ready for a coffee break to calm her nerves. What she had seen at the mortuary and in the DVD had turned her stomach and she wondered how anyone in the world could do these sorts of things illegally. She had her own donor card and, for the first time, she actually realised what it meant to donate one's organs. Silly thoughts really, but very real, of cadavers being gruesomely cut up. For her own sanity she must concentrate on the facts of the case and lead her team responsibly in their police work. The killers must be found, and soon. She must lead by example. She owed it to herself as well as her Chief Inspector, not forgetting the mutilated teenage girl whose undignified remains lay in a cold mortuary, unknown and friendless. This was a girl who was once the apple of her parents' eye, a girl whose life was cut dreadfully short in the most hideous of ways imaginable.

# Six

'Open wide, Christine.'

'Arrgh.'

'Try not to talk. Just a little longer. Nearly finished.'

'Arrgh.'

'There. That's it. Take some of this mouth wash and spit it into the bowl. You have a good set of teeth but I recommend that you do a bit more flossing. See me again in six months' time. You can pick up the bill from the receptionist on your way out.

'Now in your official capacity, Detective Sergeant, what were the questions you wanted to ask me?'

Christine placed the cool palms of her hands on each cheek, moving her jaws to get them working again. She hated everything to do with dentistry going back to when she was a young girl needing braces. The sound of the drill – oh my! That sent shivers down her spine every time.

In her languid state in the dentist's chair and her innate fear she had quite forgotten she was there on official business. The enquiry from the dentist brought her back to the real world causing her to sit bolt upright and display a modicum of respect for her title. Her mouth felt a bit strange but at least her jaws were now working properly. She cut straight to the chase.

'Mr Pendrew, as an oral surgeon I would like to ask you a few questions on the use of illegal cadavers in dentistry.'

'Wow! That's a big subject if ever there was one. Here was me thinking you were going to ask me about my right to practice, my credentials and all that. Personal questions.'

'No. No. This is a fact-finding mission for reasons I am unable to explain at this point in time.'

'Wouldn't you be better off talking to the National Dentist Association and the Care Quality Commission rather than little old me?'

'Possibly, but I'm interested in your views as a practising dentist.'

'I'm flattered Christine … err Sergeant.'

Mr Pendrew relaxed in his chair, his body less tense now knowing that it was an informal chat rather than a personal grilling. With thirty years of oral practice behind him, he was genuinely flattered that he should be singled out for his view. Not that he knew much about illegal cadavers and all that anyway. He was confident, however, that the Sergeant knew even less.

'Illegal cadavers in dentistry? Now let me think. I suppose you mean the use of illegal human bone in the grafting process. Let me go back one step and talk briefly about human bone.

'Bone grafting is possible because bone tissue, unlike many other tissues, has the ability to regenerate completely but requires a scaffold to do so. This scaffold can be taken from your own body, from cadavers using a bone bank, from synthetic material or from animals, principally cows. Most bone grafts will be reabsorbed by the body and replaced as the natural bone heals.

'The other point to make is that jaw bones atrophy without teeth. Literally within months bone will waste away and shrink. That is why when you see grandparents who have lost all their teeth for over a prolonged period, they will have little jawbone in the mandible – the lower jaw and the maxilla – the upper jaw.

'If I was to remove one of your teeth now Sergeant, the underlying support bone would atrophy before I could possibly replace it with an implant, it is that quick.

So, now you see the need for human bone to be used for the grafting process in dentistry. Most people do not realise that.'

Mr Pendrew hesitated at this point feeling quite pleased with his explanation. He waited for the sergeant to ask another question but Christine stayed silent, listening intently and taking notes. He felt it appropriate to continue. 'Bone grafting in the oral cavity today is a routine, predictable and painless procedure. Bone can be harvested from the chin, the pelvis, the back part of the lower jaw, the pilot holes for the implants, and then inserted into the mouth underneath the new implant. Much of this can be done here in the surgery. Oral work requiring hospitalisation is rare but sometimes necessary under an anaesthetic.'

Christine's obvious displeasure in what she was hearing spurred him on.

'As for illegal cadavers in dentistry: I suppose in the past, in the very far past, bones such as ribs could have been acquired for jaw reconstruction and that sort of thing. That was in the past though. Today, there is much greater regulation. If I was to need bone I would request it from a licensed bone bank, but that would be a rare thing for me to do.  As I have said, most bone can be taken from the recipient, from the hip if larger pieces are needed.

'In the past human teeth also became a prize asset to be bought and sold, the rich paid the poor to give up their pearly whites but with them came a risk of infection and disease.  The transplanting of teeth from the living and the dead became a craze in the late 18th and early 19th centuries.  Grave robbers could make the equivalent of £10,000 a night by stealing teeth from the dead.  The fad reached fever pitch in 1815 when 50,000 men died at the battle of Waterloo.  The sound of gunfire had barely subsided before scavengers arrived on the battlefield to pull out the teeth of the dead and dying.  The market was flooded so even the toothless middle classes could afford new teeth.

'I don't know what your investigation is about, sergeant, but I think you are barking up the wrong tree in the case of dentistry.  I know we still can't seem to forget dentistry's long and bloody past but these are modern times and science has moved on.  For example, the latest research is the use of wood, not bone, for grafting, suitably treated of course.  Sea coral likewise is being experimented with.

'All in all, as an answer to your initial question, I would see no market in dentistry in the use of illegal cadavers.  Does that answer your question?'

Christine stopped taking notes and looked up at Mr Pendrew, giving him a faint smile.

'You have been very helpful Mr Pendrew.  I have always had a fear of the dentist's chair and drill but, in some ways, you have reassured me that many of my fears were figments of my schoolgirl imagination.'

'I am pleased I could be of help. Now make sure you floss your teeth each day.'

A bigger smile lit up Christine's face as she shook hands with Mr Pendrew and took her leave.

On her way out, the receptionist handed her the bill.

'It's how much? You must be joking!'

The receptionist smiled a forced smile and continued with her typing.

~

'Ah, Charles, nice to see you old chap. Like my new office? It is a bit swish don't you think? Take a seat, make yourself at home. Long time, no see. The last time I saw you? Hmm, I can't think when. How is your father these days? Haven't seen him since his knee operation. He was complaining recently about his shoulder. Must make a note in my diary.'

Charles couldn't get a word in edgeways. He sat impassively and let Sydney's gush of utterances wash over him. Mr Sydney Campbell-Knight was his father's orthopaedic surgeon, based in Harley Street. Having attended exclusive Winchester College in Hampshire, he went on to study medicine at Cambridge and, being very athletic, he became a Cambridge rowing Blue.

Sydney was top of his profession and did he know it. He made sure everyone else knew it as well. Smart, dressed in a pin-stripe suit with a shocking mop of black hair for his age, he had a commanding presence.

'Tea, old chap?'

'No thank you.'

'Something stronger?'

'Not while I'm on official business.'

'Sounds intriguing. What's it about?'

There was a reason for Charles's visit. Behind that supercilious veneer, he knew Sydney was well connected with the rich and famous and had both ears to the ground. He was also trying to put two and two together. He now knew that many of the organs harvested from the young girl were not viable for any length of time. Transplants, if any, would have had to be done quickly, within hours. So where were the recipients based – Cambridge, London, where? Perhaps Sydney had heard rumours.

'I'm investigating the illegal harvesting of human bones, tissue and organs. I wondered if you might be able to fill in a few gaps in my knowledge.'

'Sorry old boy. Know little of that sort of thing. Sure you don't want a stiff drink?'

'No thank you. It's too early for me.' Charles knew that Sydney's little usually meant a lot.

'Mind if I do?'

'Not in the slightest.'

Sydney lifted his somewhat corpulent frame out of the chair and poured himself a whisky from the drinks cabinet.

'A nice cabinet, eh, Charles? Lovely Chinese design and very expensive. No point in earning oodles of money if you can't spend it on yourself. What do you say?'

Charles knew Sydney was a life-time bachelor with a countryside mansion down in the West Country. A well-heeled, self-made millionaire, very ebullient at times but a good sort of bloke when you got to know him.

Sydney sat back in his chair, took a sip of whisky and was then gripped by a pensive mood. It was as if the outer shell was being discarded and the real, inner, brilliant self was being put to the test.

'As I said Charles. I am not sure I can help you in your investigation. Human skin is the colour of smoked salmon when it is professionally removed in rectangular shapes from a cadaver. A good yield is about six square feet. It is used principally for burns victims and breast reconstruction after cancer. It has many other uses. The younger the cadaver, the better the quality and the premium paid.

'Bones and other tissue such as tendons and ligaments all have their use. I personally use them of course in my specialist profession for use in knee repairs. Sportsmen are some of my favourite, fee-paying clients, especially the footballers.

'Organs such as kidneys, the pancreas, the liver, heart and lungs, can all be used if transplanted in time. Off the top of my head, I believe kidneys are viable, if stored correctly, for up to thirty hours from harvesting; up to twelve hours for the pancreas and liver; the heart and lungs for up to six hours. It is not common knowledge that a quarter of all transplants are from "high risk donors" – people with brain tumours for example and cancer or hepatitis, or alcohol and drug users, and the elderly. Put into perspective, there are 10,000 patients waiting for a transplant of whom three die every day. They are not too fussy about the source of the organs if they think there is an infinitesimal chance of them surviving their tomorrow. Did you know that up to fifty recipients can benefit from one cadaver harvesting?

'In the US alone, two million products derived from human tissue are sold each year. It is a billion-dollar-a-year industry supplying skin and tissue for one million transplants each year. The skin-crawling fact is that no one knows from whom the bone and tissue was harvested.

'The international nature of the industry makes it easy to move products from place to place without much

261

scrutiny. Once a product is in the European Union it can be shipped to the US with few questions asked.'

Sydney took another sip of whisky. 'Do you want me to go on?'

Charles nodded.

'A dead body can be worth tens of thousands of dollars when dissected for parts. A single, disease-free body can then spin off cash flows of eight-thousand to two-hundred thousand dollars.

For example, cadaver bone harvested from the dead and replaced with PVC piping for burial can be sculpted like pieces of hardwood into screws and anchors for dozens of orthopaedic and dental applications. Or the bone can be ground down and mixed with chemicals to form strong surgical glue.

I have to say, though, that we get too emotive about these things. When we die, our soul leaves our body and what is left is merely a shell. Preserving the body is really only to appease our grief. Far better for it to be used fully for another's benefit. No point in being mawkish about these things.'

Another sip of whisky.

'Where was I Charles? Ah, yes. The illegal side of things. Of course, no one in the medical profession doubts that where there are huge sums of money there will be unscrupulous operators. In the past it would have been grave robbers providing cadavers for medical research, teaching, etc. Nowadays, it may take a different form due to the advancements in science and technology in medicine. However, the demand for transplants easily outstrips the supply in the UK and worldwide. Those rich enough will always find people willing to help in more nefarious ways.

'Then there is the increasing number of products that can be made these days from human tissue and organs. From cosmetics to bladder slings, from wrinkle cures to penis implants, the list is endless.

'In the UK we are very tight on regulations and the audit trails to track the donor and recipient but in many other countries that is not the case. All over the world such products are imported and exported without any confirmation of the original source. The volume of trade is simply too great to regulate.'

Charles, having listened studiously to Sydney, decided to halt the lecture. He asked a more personal question.

'Have you, personally, had any dealings with any of these nefarious activities?'

'Of course not. Don't be stupid, old boy.' The outer shell returned to mask the academic.

'Even if I did, I wouldn't tell you in fear of my life. Rumours and all that. My business would go down the pan and I would be penniless.' Seeing Charles's demeanour stiffen he hastily added, 'Just joking, old boy, just joking.' Another sip of whisky, realising he had pressed a wrong button.

'Seriously though, I have heard of no rumours suggesting anything in London to that effect. If I do, I will let you know. I am always willing to help the police.'

'Well, you have helped me Sydney and I am grateful for your time.'

'No trouble, old boy. Glad to be of help. Remember me to your father would you? I must make a note in my diary.

Sydney saw Charles out of the office and out of the building.

'Remember me to your father.'

'I will Sydney. I will.'

There followed a salutary wave from Sydney, courteous to the end.

~

Charles returned to his office to mull over the salient points from his discussion with Sydney and his discussions with the Department of Health's Human Tissue Authority as well as the licensed human bone and tissue banks in Liverpool and Manchester.

The general consensus was that illegal body harvesting could not happen in the UK, everything being above board, well documented and audited. Procedures were strictly adhered to in order to ensure the legality of the cadavers operated on, consent forms or donor cards required in all cases. There was no room for error in determining who gave what and to whom.

Like Sydney, everyone he had spoken to in senior authority treated the subject in a plain-speaking matter-of-fact way. The human element seemed to be missing with more concern regarding the recipients of the transplants and a lot less on the donors, except for the typical comment of there not being enough of them; numbers rather than human beings being the principal concern of all, the demand always being greater than the supply.

Everyone agreed that illegal body harvesting was possible in other countries but were in denial that it was actually happening here, something they did not really want to think about or talk about, not being a part of their brief, out of sight, out of mind mentality.

The Liverpool tissue bank had invited him to accompany one of their teams to see for himself the harvesting of cadavers but he had declined the offer. He felt that too much of a personal involvement was not conducive to his investigation of the illegal trade. He had to keep his personal, emotional feelings at bay, not to let medical issues cloud his judgement on police fact-finding matters. To do what he had instructed his staff to do, to keep such personal issues at arms-length.

All in all, it appeared the legal and illegal trades were miles apart with most people finding the subject of illegal harvesting abhorrent to think about never mind doing something about it. They all wished him well in his investigations but had nothing to offer of any consequence to point the way forward.

It was a subject swept under the carpet. As a policeman, however, he had to lift that carpet to see what crawled away; then, and only then, could he find the young girl's murderers, a most thankless task.

# Seven

It was sex, nothing more, nothing less. I must stop berating myself, it was just gratuitous sex.

It wasn't Carla. I would have loved her to be Carla but she wasn't Carla. Oh, how I wish she had been Carla. The love inside me for her is still palpable, deep and hurtful. The mere thought of her makes my heart race. Will my thoughts for her never end or will I go to my grave thinking of her and what could have been.

She caught me at my weakest. I was at a low ebb. The times when confidence is a stranger; when you embrace the darkest thoughts of your mind; a paralysis of the mind and body. When getting out of bed of a morning is an effort, dark clouds always obscuring the light of day; when twenty-four hours seems an eternity to survive.

I should have been stronger, much, much stronger but she appeared at my flat brimming with tears. I hugged her for comfort. Her face was close to mine and the smell of her young skin intoxicating, a sort of earthy, raw, musky body odour which set my senses alight. It seemed the most natural thing in the world to give her a peck on the cheek. As her head turned to face mine my lips hungrily searched for hers. It was a quivering sensation to touch her lips gently, to feel her tremors and sweetness, to sense her feminine desires. Such gentle togetherness rapidly gave

267

way to a heightened sexual desire, a basic need to consummate the relationship.

I kissed her forehead, her nose. I kissed her tears away. I kissed those soft cheeks and then a full, forceful kiss on the lips. I didn't mean to do it, but it was Carla again, all over again. She responded willingly and I got lost in my fever.

We spent all Saturday night together making love. I was her first. I shouldn't have done it, I know I shouldn't have done it and I'm cross with myself. But what is a man supposed to do when a girl comes on to you as strongly as that? I'm a man, just a bloody man with all the weaknesses that men have.

Why the hell did I do it? It wasn't right. I should have been stronger, had more resolve.

'A penny for your thoughts, Chief Inspector.'

Christine's voice jerked Charles out of the fog of despair and introspection. Taken somewhat by surprise Charles grudgingly lifted his head from his hands, sitting bolt upright with a weary look in his tired eyes.

'Oh, it's you Christine … sorry, Sergeant.'

'You don't look too good, sir. Everything OK?'

'Thank you, Sergeant, for your concern, the hangover of a cold over the weekend. I'll be fine once I get a mug of filthy police coffee down my throat. I still think we should sue the manufacturer of that infernal machine under the Trades Descriptions Act. What do you think?'

'Would you like a couple of paracetamols with your coffee, sir? You look as though you might need them.'

'Thanks. That might help clear the headache.' Charles looked at Christine with a pleading look that spoke volumes to Christine.

'Why don't you take the day off, sir? I can hold the fort.'

Christine's maternal instincts came rushing to the fore. She would tuck him up in bed if she was given half the chance.

'No, not necessary. Better to keep my mind occupied but thank you anyway.'

'I'll get those tablets and a strong cup of coffee from the canteen.'

'Thank you, Sergeant.' Charles went back to cupping his head in his hands, his eyelids heavy, wanting to close to blank out the world.

Christine thought of what Peter Ebden would have done in these circumstances. Not to overdo the mothering bit that was for sure. Man to man talk, so to speak. That was the way to play it. Keep the mothering instincts at bay.

'Will be back in a mo.'

Charles shook his head as if to clear out his demons and then yawned as the lack of sleep over the weekend caught up with him. Perhaps Christine was right. Perhaps he should take the day off and regain his senses. A day in bed is certainly what the doctor would order.

Then the image of the young girl, dismembered, lying cold in a mortuary, came back to haunt him. He would find her killer or killers if it was the last thing he would do. He would leave no stone unturned until that girl received justice, justice that would leave her soul at peace. Justice that would condemn the perpetrators to infinite hell.

'Here's your coffee and pills, sir.'

'Thank you, Sergeant, and please take a seat.'

Charles downed the pills in one go with a large sip of coffee and stared squarely at Christine, his eyes now ablaze, his chin rigid with self-righteousness.

Christine was taken aback by the sudden change in mood of her mercurial Chief Inspector. The pills didn't work that quickly, did they? They certainly didn't work that quickly with her. Perhaps he knows something that she doesn't. She thought it best to go along with his mood and not to ask too many questions.

'Sergeant. I was thinking of the girl in the mortuary.'

Now she understood his change in mood.

'Sir?'

'Let us spend a few minutes recapping the situation. Oh, by the way, how did your visit to the dentist go?'

'Fine sir. My teeth are in good order. I thought the police might pick up my bill, in the course of duty and all that.'

'No chance. No chance of that. I meant what did you glean from your trip regarding dental practice?'

'I think the conclusion is that very little bone, if at all, is used from third parties. Certainly not enough to warrant a big money business in illegal cadavers. Research reasons, perhaps, but even here it is highly regulated with licensed bone banks. A thing of the past in research and teaching establishments, which used to use parts illegally obtained from dead persons. Modern dentistry has moved on from those times. And you sir. How did your visit go?'

'Not as definitive as yours, Sergeant. There is still a murky business in transplants and in the use of body tissues and organs in the manufacture of medical products. Not so much in this country but certainly worldwide, it is a billion-dollar trade. It is possible that all the parts from the young girl were shipped abroad; it is also possible that parts were used in transplants for clients here in the UK, possibly here in Cambridge.'

'The lists you asked for are now on your screen, sir. There are literally thousands of them in the Cambridge area. I never realised, until now, the degree of medical and research science taking place in this very county, together with the number of companies supplying them with medical equipment. It is worse than looking for a needle in a haystack.'

'We must not let the magnitude of this problem stop us from looking for the obvious and detracting us from the real purpose of this enquiry, and that is to find the killers.'

'Where do we go from here, sir?'

'Leg work, I'm afraid, nothing but leg work at this stage. Start the team making enquiries with names picked at random from these lists. You never know what might turn up when the police screw is tightened. We need to lash ourselves to the mast and plunge headlong into that haystack.'

'That blows the imagination, sir.'

'It sure does, Sergeant, it sure does.'

Both smiled and laughed at the thought. Christine was pleased to see her Chief Inspector was feeling better and back on the ball again. She was never really happy to see him in his more solemn moods and out of kilter with life.

'That will be all for now, Sergeant.'

'Yes sir. Oh, by the way, WPC Jane Wetherspool would like to have a word with you. Is that OK?'

'Show her in Sergeant, she is always worth listening to. That girl has an insight into things we, as mere mortals, can only dream about. Show her in.

'Yes sir.' Christine standing at the open door beckoned Jane to enter.

Jane rose from her desk, smoothed down her uniform, flicking back her loose hair before entering her Chief Inspector's office.

'Come in Jane, take a seat. How can I help?'

Jane always became tongue-tied talking to her Chief Inspector, the difference in rank as well as amorous naughty thoughts causing her heart to jump into her mouth, welding her tongue to her dry mouth. It took a few seconds to compose herself.

'Sir …'

'Yes Jane.'

'Sir, you know I have a photographic memory? This may be nothing, sir …'

'I'll be the judge of that.'

'Well, sir. I spotted a surgeon's face on the television recently.'

'Interesting. Tell me more.'

Jane perked up. This always happened when the Chief Inspector was genuinely interested in what she had to say.

'The surgeon was Mr Brian Claymore, one of the names on our list with their photograph, as you requested. I saw the same face on the local news recently. There was a building on fire and I spotted his face in the crowd.'

'Where was this? Take your time.'

'It was at the Farndale Business Centre.'

'Ah, the Farndale Business Centre. Have you been there, Jane?'

'Yes sir. I went with my mother to look for kitchen tiles.'

'I've been there too. My guess is that several of my team have been there for one reason or another. In fact, I would think half the Cambridge population has been there.'

The change in his tone made her feel embarrassed and her cheeks reddened. She felt stupid and wanted a big hole to jump into.

'Sorry Jane. I didn't mean to embarrass you. You know there is a suggestion-box and I do read them on occasions, some being more plausible than others.'

'Sorry sir. I didn't mean .... Shall I put it in the box?'

'No. No. That's not necessary now.'

Jane stood up to leave the office not wishing to stay a second longer than was necessary.

'On second thoughts, Jane, what is the local news?'

'Look East TV Studios, sir.

Charles thought for a while, running his hands through his hair as if for inspiration. 'Have the Sergeant speak to them and arrange a visit for you and me to look at the footage. I could do with getting out of the office. Some fresh air will do me the world of good.'

Within a heartbeat, from the depth of a deep hole to the surface like an express lift, her spirits rose out of all proportion. She felt valued again like never before, even if, in the end, her observation turned out to be of no consequence.

'Yes sir.'

'And Jane. In plain clothes. Just this once.'

'Yes sir.'

Jane left the office in a more jubilant mood, always pleased to be of help to her boss. Charles settled himself to study the lists on his computer screen.

~

For Jane, the trip to Norfolk in the Porsche was a dream come true. She saw herself as a detective sometime in the future and this was a little taste of what it was going to be like. Sitting beside her Chief Inspector was an added bonus.

The park attendant, having been told of their visit, checked their identities before lifting the barrier to let them through. Jane's sense of importance increased as they entered the spacious foyer and spoke to the receptionist who was also expecting them. Charles introduced himself and Jane.

'Please take a seat. Mr Barrymore is expecting you.' She rang his office to let him know. 'He will be with you in a few minutes.'

Jane's starry-eyed imagination went into overdrive. Would Mr Barrymore, be *the* star of stage and screen? Her feminine reaction was to open her bag and to take out a hand-mirror. Charles stayed her hand.

'Not now Jane.'

Jane hastily closed her bag and sat upright, teasing several hairs away from her face, the wind having ruffled her hair to the point of annoyance. She hoped she didn't look too much of a mess. You never know, there might be cameras and all that wanting to take her photograph and to interview her for the local news. After all, this is where it all happens. Everything we see on our televisions happens right here. She could feel the adrenalin pumping in her body, a delightful frisson to savour.

Her expectations came to earth with a thud as she saw Mr Barrymore, a dwarf, walk purposely towards them.

'I'm Mr Barrymore and I was expecting you. I hope your journey here was pleasant enough.' He shook hands, using both hands to clasp theirs.

'I'm sorry if you were expecting someone senior to meet you or someone from the stage and screen but I did audition once for Snow White and The Seven Dwarfs.'

'Did you succeed?' asked Jane inquisitively.

He deflected such an enquiry with a broad smile and added, 'I was too tall and too good looking. As you can see, I am just a little person of exquisite proportions.'

Such unselfconscious discussion of his stature made both Jane and Charles smile. The ice had been broken this time as it had on many previous times with the same greeting to strangers. It worked every time.

'If you follow me I will take you to my office.'

He led them to a large room in the basement of the building, a sterile room with lots of electrical equipment with racks and racks of spools, some gathering layers of dust, some looking too ancient to use anymore.

'This is where I do my work. We have tapes going back some time but, nowadays, everything is digital and held on discs. I have set up the event you referred to on the monitor. If you sit here you can start, stop and slow the pictures as you please with these buttons.'

Charles indicated to Jane to sit at the operator's desk whilst he sat alongside her.

'I will arrange for coffee and biscuits to be brought. If you don't eat them I will as I'm still a growing lad you see.'

Smiles all round.

'In fact, it only took Jane minutes to stop it at the point where Mr Claymore's face was quite visible in the crowd.

'There sir. I knew I recognised him. That is him for sure,' pointing to a face in the crowd.

'Can we get a still of this frame?' asked Charles.

'No problem.  A few seconds is all it will take.  Wait there a minute.'

It seemed all over in a flash, a bit disappointing really for Jane, as they made their way up the stairs to the foyer.

'I hope you got what you came for,' said Mr Barrymore.

'Yes, thank you,' replied Charles, 'you have been a great help.'

Mr Barrymore shook hands with them both before returning to the basement.  Charles and Jane turned to leave the building.

'Detective Chief Inspector,' shouted the receptionist, raising and waving her arm to attract his attention. 'Mr Patterson, our Chief Executive Office, and Patsy Noble, our senior investigative reporter, would like a word with you if you can spare the time.'

Charles turned to Jane.  'Not a word.  Let me do all the talking.'

'Mr Patterson's PA will be down in a moment.  She will take you to his office.'

Within the minute, the lift doors opened and the PA beckoned them into the lift, pressing the button for the top floor.  She smiled but stayed silent, courteous and officious but not overbearing.

Exiting the lift, they were directed through the PA's office to the CEO's office.  There, sitting behind his desk was Michael Patterson with Patsy Noble sitting opposite him.  They both stood up as the PA introduced them.  Warm handshakes all round.

'Let's all sit over there,' pointing to four lounge chairs around a small glass table.  'My PA will bring in some tea and biscuits.  Please make yourselves comfortable.'

When all were seated, Mr Patterson made his opening speech. 'Welcome to Look East studios where we have been based here in Norwich from …'

Jane wasn't listening. She recognised both their faces from the television, particularly Patsy Noble who had presented a series of investigative reports recently. It was funny to see them in the actual flesh and rather exciting. Charles remained impassive, helping himself to tea and his favourite custard creams.

With the opening address finished, Patsy Noble, forever the journalist, began the more pointed questions just as Charles had expected.

'I hope you found what you were looking for, Chief Inspector?'

'Yes indeed,' replied Charles with a curt reply.

'I believe you were interested in the fire at the Farndale Business Centre?'

'Yes.'

'And a certain person in the crowd?'

No reply.

'Are we allowed to know what the enquiry is about?'

Again, no reply which made Patsy Noble even more inquisitive.

'I know you took a still of one of the people. Are you looking for an arsonist? Perhaps a murderer? Perhaps something more? You have the still in your briefcase. Are we allowed to see it? We can obviously obtain a copy from Mr Barrymore. If the offence is really serious, we, the media, could argue that his identity should be made public. What are you not telling us, Chief Inspector?'

Enough was enough. Charles took a final sip of tea and swallowed the remaining crumbs of the biscuit.

'With great respect, you know I cannot answer your questions. This is an ongoing investigation and I am not at liberty to disclose such information at this stage. At the appropriate time, and only then, will we make a public announcement. Any meddling in police affairs and inappropriate speculation would result in a caution and possible arrest for wasting police time. You understand?'

'I do, Chief Inspector.'

In view of his brusque reply, Patsy Noble knew she would make no inroads with the Chief Inspector, but she smelled a story, a big story. She made one final attempt but this time directing her questions to Jane.

'Shouldn't you be in uniform, WPC Wetherspool?' The question was asked in an intimidating way to unsettle Jane, which annoyed Charles.

Jane was about to reply but Charles intervened. 'WPC Wetherspool is in plain clothes at my request. We did not wish to bring undue attention to ourselves when visiting your studios for reasons I cannot disclose.

I would be grateful if we could close this meeting as we have pressing engagements to attend. We are grateful though for your co-operation and your time in this investigation. Let us leave it at that.'

Patsy Noble coughed a false cough having been firmly put in her place.

'Thank you Chief Inspector,' said Mr Patterson, standing up and shaking both their hands, Patsy Noble did likewise. 'My PA will see you out.'

Once again in the foyer, Jane recognised several more familiar faces from the small screen which made her day. Her only regret was that they were not shown around the studios. She was certain they would want to take her photograph, perhaps another time.

~

Back in the office, Charles discussed the visit with Christine, showing her the still and then slipping into the file.

'Should we arrest Mr Claymore? Bring him in for questioning?'

'No. There is no evidence to justify that. He is just one of many who have visited the Business Park. He has probably got an innocent reason anyway. No. We need to keep up the leg-work. However, just in case there is anything to it, I want you to ring the PI firm we use and to put a two-week tail on Mr Claymore. I wouldn't want it on my conscience if he was the needle in that proverbial haystack and we had overlooked it. Can you do that, Sergeant?'

'Yes sir. I'll get onto it straight away.'

Christine left the office leaving Charles to ponder whether Patsy Noble would prove to be a thorn in his flesh in the near future. The last thing he wanted were the details of the young girl's brutal death to be made public knowledge at this stage of the investigation. The sheer brutality of her death would cause a public outcry to find her killers and which could only hinder progress.

# Eight

'Georgio.'

'Georgio.' This time a little louder and more demanding.

It was an open-plan office, second floor of an office block, sparsely decorated with five desks and chairs, three metal filing cabinets and a couple of nondescript pictures of aerial photographs of the area hanging on plain walls.

Georgio put down his half-finished Mars bar and strode over to Wendy's desk, the receptionist-cum-organiser-cum part owner of the firm.

'Here is a job for you, Georgio. It is a 24/7 assignment for two weeks. If you take the midday to midnight shift I will get Robin to take the midnight to midday shift. The afternoon shift will be easier on your advance years as you keep moaning about your aching body parts in our British climate. Is that OK with you?'

'No problem, Wendy.'

Good. Well here is the dossier. You will find his name, address, photograph, etc. with other relevant details we have gleaned from public records. The assignment is to shadow him and to report on his whereabouts. He is a Category "D", not considered dangerous or a person who has committed a felony. It should be an easy stroll for you on your last assignment with us, Georgio.'

'Thank you, Wendy. I will always hold a special place in my heart for you when I am back in Greece thinking about your lovely charming ways, while supping my ouzo and staring up at the cloudless, starry sky. You will be forever in my thoughts and always in my heart'

'Get off with you.' Wendy playfully waved him away from her desk. She had heard it all before, a thousand times or more, but his flattering comments and smiles were always welcome to brighten many a drab day.

Georgio took the dossier back to his desk and read its contents whilst finishing his Mars bar. No specific reason was given for tailing this individual so he assumed it was yet another pending divorce case. He could not recall the number of such people he had reported on in his fifteen years stint with this company and, thank God, this was to be his last. What a lot of unhappy people he had met in his life; what a lot of heartache for so many parents; what a lot of misery for so many children caught up in things they did not fully understand. It was a sad, sad world at times.

The next day, day one of the assignment, followed the usual pattern: a short briefing with Robin and then to settle into the routine of waiting for the person to appear, then to follow him in his car, shadowing the subject, being as inconspicuous as feasibly possible. Day after day, reporting into the office at the beginning of the shift to tell them he was still alive and on the job, and then at the end of the shift to report events. Wendy would record the telephone conversation and then type a report for the client. It was not the most glamorous of jobs. On the contrary, it must be one of the most boring jobs ever devised, although he had learnt to enjoy it and the money was good if not brilliant. As for the danger – he knew you can't insure yourself against everything but you can frighten yourself to death with what could be. Many a time he had found himself in a sticky situation but never anything life threatening.

The first changeover was on a Wednesday outside St George's Hospital. Robin, not his real name for reasons of confidentiality and possible future victimisation, filled him in on the subject's location, his car licence number and other relevant trivia to be minded of.

Georgio, real name Petros Kritikos, an Athenian by birth, parked his car in the hospital car park and took a position to watch the hospital exit. There were two exits but Georgio assumed that the subject would take the nearest to his car.

He was right. After several boring hours of watching and waiting, he recognised the person from his photograph, dashing back to the visitors' car park to be out in time to follow at a safe distance. At the exit the pre-paid ticket refused to lift the automatic barrier resulting in it being queried by the park attendant as to the amount paid. Georgio paid the difference and watched with annoyance as the subject's car drove out of the staff car park and then quickly out of sight. By the time the barrier rose it was too late for him to follow.

A small curse under his breath but his experience had taught him not to get stressed over these situations. The law of Sod was many times a companion to a private investigator. You just had to get used to it. Things never went to plan always, in truth they rarely ever did.

Instead, he drove to the subject's house to wait for him there, parking close by to observe the entrance to the car drive. Switching off the engine he slithered down the seat to make his profile as inconspicuous as possible to passers-by. He then made himself comfortable, opening one of his many books to while away the time. Fortunately he was an avid reader with plenty of time on his hands to indulge his passion for books, both fiction and non-fiction. He saw it as another means of education having never had the opportunity to go to University. It was one of the few perks of being a PI – plenty of time to read!

It was getting on for five hours before seeing the subject's car turn into his driveway – five hours he could not account for, which would not go down well with Wendy. These things happen, unfortunately, just as well he had his ready excuses to hand to placate Wendy.

With a flask of coffee and a lunch box of sandwiches he was ready to settle down for the evening, pulling a blanket over his legs for added warmth.

It started to rain. 'Bloody English weather,' he muttered to himself. He blamed the cold and damp for the early deaths of both his parents, his greying hair and for the bald spot on his head, getting ever larger. He fingered it to see if it had got any bigger that day. Satisfied that it had not, his thoughts drifted towards Greece and its warmer climate, his other passion.

For economic reasons, his parents had emigrated from Greece to the UK, settling first in London and then in Cambridge. He was ten-years-old at the time but could vividly recall swimming in the sea with his parents under a hot sun as well as the warm, balmy evenings whilst taking their main meals of an evening. As a child he never realised or was made aware of the negative side to his family's fortunes, not that he would have understood anyway at that age. It was with great sadness that he had left Greece.

He intended to return. After this assignment it was "pack your bags and head for Greece time". He knew exactly where he wanted to go. It was the beautiful, mellow island of Samos in the Aegean Sea, to a small village called Kokkari on the northern coast. An idyllic cove to semi-retire. After several visits he had spotted a run-down building on the sea front which he knew he could convert into a taverna – a Traditional Greek Taverna. That was his aim. It would take a little money but, being single and unattached, he had saved sufficient funds, the money going a lot further in Greece in these straitened times. In the tourist season he would work hard and then relax for the rest of the year. It sounded like bliss and some of his bags were already packed. The time couldn't come soon enough.

At thirty-nine he was not too old to meet a nice Greek girl and have a family of maybe three or four children. That would be nice, that would really be nice. He must cut down on the sweets though if he was to keep his figure in trim. He blamed the English weather for his sweet tooth and portly frame.

A tap on the driver's window made him jump. It was Robin, somewhat po-faced.

'Why the hell haven't you reported in. You know you have to ring in within half an hour of the end of your shift. Where were you? You are losing your marbles, Georgio. Now report in and I will take over from here.'

Georgio reported in giving some feeble excuse for the missed five hours to Wendy's admonishment. Then, with a heavy heart, he drove back to his flat for a good night's sleep.

The next day was the same. And the next. For both days, the subject drove straight from the hospital to his house directly. He remained in the house all evening.

There was little to report.  Robin's sparse reports were similar.

The following day, Saturday, Georgio followed him to the Farndale Business Centre and to a tile shop.  He seemed to stay there for an inordinate amount of time but he thought it of no consequence, house renovations and all that.  That evening the subject had dinner at the local Indian restaurant with his wife, and then drove back home.

Sunday was obviously a family day.  Georgio could hear the children playing in the back garden and then the ritual of them washing the two family cars.  A few pangs of regret in thinking of his own circumstances.  With a little luck, and God's help, he too would have his family in Greece, his car, his own house, his garden and above all – love by the bucketful.

Monday and Tuesday had nothing special to report either from him or from Robin.

Wednesday, a week into the assignment, on the other hand, was different from the norm.  After his work at the hospital, Georgio followed the subject to the tile shop.  Nothing new there but that evening at 9 o'clock, the subject made another trip to the tile shop.  This time Georgio suspected there was more to it than tile hunting and all his investigative powers and experience came to the fore.  Something deep inside him told him to beware, however.

The Business Park was effectively closed.  It was dusk with only a few lights dotted here and there to light the way on the principal roads through the park and some security lighting outside a number of the buildings.

The car park remained open but Georgio decided to park his car outside the main gates and to shadow the suspect on foot to the tile shop, stopping occasionally if he thought he was being spotted.  There was a handful of people milling around, presumably business people working late, so he didn't stand out to any great degree at that time of night. He followed the suspect and saw him enter the tile shop from a side entrance. The shop was now in semi-darkness with blinds drawn, a faint light possibly coming from a back office penetrating the gloom.

Georgio slipped into position within the darker shadow of a building opposite where he could observe without being seen, settling himself for a long wait. A glance at his watch told him it was 9.45 pm.

One hour slipped by, and then another. The Park, now in pitch darkness, was still and absent of any activity, either people or vehicles. An eerie silence with only the park lights making a slight buzzing sound, casting a soft, yellowish glow over the surrounding area. A fox made its appearance but scurried away on seeing Georgio. Other foxes barking in the distance produced a piercing sound at that time of night which Georgio always found unnerving.

Should he call in now, it was nearly the end of his shift. No, he thought. He would leave it for a few more minutes when, hopefully, both he and the subject had left the park. He pulled out a Mars bar from his pocket and chomped on that to boost his flagging energy levels; he stamped his feet to improve the circulation, again cursing the English weather for all of life's ailments.

It started to rain and he found a spot giving better shelter. A quick glance at the tile shop told him there was still activity taking place there. He resigned himself to one of those nights, those never-ending nights, the bane of every private investigator. Another Mars bar would help him through it.

His mind began to wander for lack of stimulation. Those glorious sunrises in Greece of an orange ball rising in a cloudless sky, over mountains clothed in cypress trees; of olive groves; of warm, still evenings with the sound of cicadas; of terraced vineyards and pine forests. He couldn't wait to pack all his bags. Soon he would be on his way to a sun-kissed country.

He stepped forward again to take another glance at the tile shop and then looked at his watch. It was 11.58 pm. With no sign of the suspect emerging he decided it was time to ring in and fished in his raincoat pocket for his mobile. He touched the illuminated screen and listened to the dialling tone.

It was all too late. As he was about to speak, a large suffocating hand closed around his mouth and nose and he felt a deep, piercing pain in his side. Then another in his back. His legs gave way like a rag doll and he tasted blood as it gurgled in his mouth.

His last conscious moments were of four hands dragging him towards the tile shop.

# Nine

Charles knocked on his father's door.

'Come in.'

'You wanted to see me, sir?'

'Yes, Chief Inspector. Take a seat. Close the door behind you if you would.'

The Chief Constable put down his pen, sat back in his chair, adjusting his posture to give his son his full attention. He spoke with a hint of anxiety in his voice.

'You might like to know that I've heard on the grapevine that the murder of the young girl will be on the front pages tomorrow. They will report that she was butchered and there could be others. Who and how it was leaked I do not know but the media is on our trail for an explanation. In an ideal world the press would wait until we were ready to disclose our findings, but this is not the world we live in where everyone expects instant communications and answers. As policemen we have to find that fine balance between the privacy of our findings and public disclosure.'

Without knowing for sure Charles could hazard a guess that Patsy Noble was involved somehow. He was in two minds to meet up with her again to warn her off for a second time or to charge her accordingly. But all that would do would be to waste further police time and to incite her further, an unnecessary distraction at this point in the investigation.

'Do you want me to hold a press conference?' asked Charles. 'I can make the necessary arrangements.'

'No. That is, not unless you have made serious inroads in your investigations to justify one.'

'Not really. We are still wading through piles of data. We are up to our necks in the stuff. We know a lot more about what we are up against but nothing at this stage that directs us to arrest anyone. We are a long way from solving this murder.'

'In that case, I suggest we issue a bland statement that states that the police investigation is on-going and we will inform them as and when we have something positive to say. Agreed?'

'Agreed.'

'I will arrange that. As you know, this changes the complexion of the case. I am going to be under pressure from my seniors and I will need something from you soon. I hate to make life more difficult for you but you know how police pressures can build up from on high, especially when the press are involved.'

'Understood.'

'Do you need to increase the numbers on your team? Would that help?'

'Not at this stage. We need more of a breakthrough than extra hands and feet. I will let you know though if that is the case.'

'Let's leave it at that then. I will deal with the press, you continue your work and let us hope that breakthrough is soon forthcoming.'

Charles left his father's office. The lack of the usual family banter between the two of them told his father that his son was under pressure and somewhat depressed. He knew his son liked to get early results and a slog through reams of data was not his forte. He also knew that his son was a realist and that there were times when there was no alternative to police work other than to keep one's nose to the grindstone.

Charles returned to his own office and slumped into the desk chair. His head was bursting with all the reports from his team piling up in a burgeoning in-tray. Nothing, but nothing pointed to an arrest, never mind a charge. Annoyingly there seemed to be an almost accepted veil of secrecy surrounding medical practitioners and their use of human tissue and organs. They appeared not to care where the spare parts came from because they knew their patients, on the whole, did not care as long as they were made better. The authorities likewise were all in denial of the extent of the illegal trade and proffered no insights that were worth pursuing. A pall of secrecy hung all over the subject of illegal body harvesting.

His team had done a splendid job so far but wherever they looked and whatever they did drew a blank. How long could he maintain their morale?

His thoughts were interrupted as Christine burst into the room. 'I think you should take this call, sir. I've put it through to your desk phone.'

'Hello. This is Chief Inspector Waley-Cohen.'

'Chief Inspector, this is Wendy Baker from the PI firm you hired.' Her voice was breathless and emotional.

'Yes Wendy. What can I do for you?'

'Chief Inspector, one of our operatives working on your case has gone missing.'

'How long missing?'

'Over thirty hours.'

'That's not long, Wendy.'

'But he is one of our most experienced operatives and it is unlike him not to report in. I think something might have happened to him. His name is Petros Kritikos, known to us as Georgio. I ... ' Charles interrupted to reassure her.

'Let us not think the worst, Wendy. Why don't you fax over his photograph, his details together with your interim report and we will see what we can do.'

'Thank you, Chief Inspector. I'll send them over in the next few minutes,' her voice now sounding a little calmer but still very anxious.

'Bye for now, Wendy.'

Charles replaced the receiver, fully expecting another call from Wendy within the day to say the operative had reappeared. He went back to his previous ruminations.

Fifteen minutes later, Christine handed Charles the faxed material. He studied the photograph and then read the interim report. There was nothing of note. Wednesday, 22nd July, there was a five hour gap of zero report because the operative had missed his target. On Saturday, 25th July, Mr Claymore had visited Smiths Tile Shop at the Farndale Business Centre. Nothing unusual in that except for the length of time he was there, a total of three hours. Then on Wednesday, 29th July, there was no report except that Wendy had noted a recorded dialling tone late at night on her machine, one minute to midnight to be precise.

This was not much to go on but this, together with the fire recognition by Jane, suggested our Mr Claymore was making a lot of visits to the Business Centre. Equally, there could be an innocent explanation and he should not jump to hasty conclusions.

'Sergeant,' shouted Charles from behind his desk.

Christine entered the office. 'Yes sir.'

'Could you ask the telephone operating company to put a trace on this dialled tone, when and where?'

'Yes sir.'

If this didn't help with his own enquiries it would go to placating Wendy's anxieties about her missing operative.

Thirty minutes later Christine re-entered the office.

'The call was attempted at 11.59 pm at the Farndale Business Centre.'

Charles did not need to be told twice. This time, two plus two did make four.

'Grab your coat, Sergeant. We are going to pay a visit to this Smiths Tile Shop and it is not for tiles. Have a back-up team on standby.'

'Yes sir.'

~

The journey to the Business Park, on the outskirts of Cambridge, took fifteen minutes. With the speeding squad car flashing its blue light and shrill alarm, the road traffic quickly gave way. They entered the park at speed.

'There sir, on the left. That's the tile shop.'

Charles stopped the car directly in front of it, coming to a screeching halt. They both exited the car together and tried to enter the shop. The door was locked and the blinds closed on the windows.

'There's a side entrance, sir.'

The side entrance was an aperture within two large, warehouse doors but again this was locked. Charles tried to kick in the door. It would not budge. He pushed against the warehouse doors but they held firm.

'Sergeant, I will stay here. You go and get the Park manager with the keys. We passed his office at the entrance to the park. Be quick about it.'

'Yes sir.'

Christine ran the short distance to the office. The manager was already on his feet somewhat startled by the sudden commotion. He had the master keys ready to hand.

'Police,' shouted Christine, showing her identity card to the manager. 'If you would come with me, sir, and bring the keys.'

The manager did not need to be asked again. Like a scared rabbit in the headlamps, he followed Christine, puffing like a train engine as his corpulent frame could only go so fast.

'Open the door,' demanded Charles, waiting impatiently at the front of the shop.

The manager did not say a word. Sweating profusely, he juggled the keys on the ring to find the right one.

The door opened and Charles and Christine entered.

'You stay there, sir,' said Christine to the manager. 'Please stay outside.'

'But it's just tiles, nothing but tiles,' blustered the manager.

'I won't ask you again, please stay outside,' bellowed Christine, forcibly yanking him back by the arm.

The firmness of her voice made the manager gulp and mop his brow with a dirty handkerchief, now rooted to the spot, trembling with the suddenness of it all.

Charles and Christine looked around the shop. The manager was right. Nothing but tiles – floor tiles, ceiling tiles, kitchen tiles, fireplace tiles, every imaginable tile to suit the most discerning of tastes.

They peered into the adjoining office. A desk, two chairs and a filing cabinet. That was all.

Charles tried to open the door leading from the office to the warehouse. It too was locked.

'Ask the manager, Sergeant, if he has a key to this door.'

The manager heard Charles's request and simply shook his head. 'Only the front door.'

Charles kicked the lock and latch vigorously and they eventually gave way. Both Charles and Christine entered the warehouse. There was sufficient light coming from the two skylights for them to see clearly about the place.

A few tiles were stacked here and there but not many, not as many as was expected. To the left were the large warehouse doors leading to a small parking bay in which was parked a white Ford van. A short walkway from the bay and they were confronted with yet another door. This time, a heavy security door.

'Check with the manager, Sergeant. See if one of his master keys can fit this lock.'

Christine beckoned to the manager to enter. He stood firm not wishing to enter, gripped by fear. Christine beckoned more forcibly and this time the manager reluctantly stepped forward. He handed over the set of keys to Charles.

One key after another was tried to no avail. Charles was on the point of asking for the back-up team when the door unexpectedly unlocked. The heavy security door swung open with a screeching of the hinges. A smell of flesh assailed their nostrils and a blast of cold air made their faces smart.

'Tell the manager to go outside,' shouted Charles. There was no need to ask. He was already hot-footing it away from the foul air.

In front of them was a heavy plastic curtain. They both squeezed past it, Christine following closely behind her Chief Inspector.

The sight before them was half-expected by Charles but was no less of a shock for all that. It was a makeshift operating theatre, small but fully equipped with an operating table, lighting and other paraphernalia needed for surgical work within a sterile environment.

To the right was another large plastic curtain and behind that another security door. The same key opened this door.

Charles levered the door open and indicated to Christine to stay, pushing her behind him. It was in total darkness. Searching for a light switch he managed to turn on two fluorescent ceiling lights. It took a few seconds to illuminate the room fully. There were no windows in the room.

What the light revealed was truly astonishing. It could only be described as a butcher's parlour. To the left were stacked sterile boxes for transporting body parts, together with drums of chemicals. In the middle was a bloodied, stout wooden table with an assortment of knives and cleavers positioned close to hand on a wall rack.

To the right he counted three refrigerated units, each with a capacity for two bodies, similar to the ones used by mortuary morticians. To the side of that were boxes of polythene bags stacked against a commercial ice maker.

The nauseating smell of rotting flesh, gore, and chemicals was overwhelming. Charles took two clean handkerchiefs from his pocket, one to cover his nose and mouth, the other for Christine to do likewise.

Christine backed off initially, the odour being too great, but then curiosity got the better of her. She entered, pushing the heavy security door to give more space. What she encountered would haunt her dreams forever.

Behind the door, hung on a metal hook by his collar, was the dead body of a man, fully clothed, a man she instantly recognised as the reported missing private investigator. Her shriek caused Charles to spin round to see the spectacle for himself. He quickly ushered Christine out of the room.

'You OK, Christine?'

Christine nodded, holding the back of her hand to her mouth as if wanting to bite it.

'Christine, go outside for some fresh air and ring for the back-up team and forensics.'

Where he felt it necessary and personal, Charles would always call someone by their first name, a spontaneous reaction to seeing one of his colleagues in trouble, his or her rank being of secondary importance.

Christine nodded affirmatively and left the room in a hurry.

With Christine gone, Charles looked at the body again. The clothes were soaked in blood. He could see the signs of a side wound and the throat had been slashed. The face was peaceful though, despite the obvious horrendous ordeal the victim had suffered.

He turned his attention to the refrigerated units and opened one of the drawers. He reeled back in horror at the sight of the naked body of a young girl, whose skin had been harvested and whose eyes had been removed. He quickly closed the drawer.

On opening a second drawer his skin pricked. It was the remains of a young boy who had also been skinned, and with legs and arm bones removed leaving empty tissue. The chest had been opened. He closed the drawer in sheer disgust.

The third drawer he opened contained the grisly sight of butchered body parts. A sight of unconsciable horror.

It was all too much. Charles closed the drawer and exited the room. Never in all his days as a policeman had he seen a sight of such carnage. Was it for real? Police sirens wailing outside assured him it was.

On leaving the building a gulp or two of fresh air was sufficient to revive his policeman's senses. He turned to Christine who was equally trying to find her feet.

'Sergeant, put out a police warrant for Mr Claymore. Bring him in for questioning.'

'Yes sir.'

Turning to the office manager, 'I would like you to accompany us to the police station. You also have a few questions to answer.'

The office manager was riven with fear. He had not seen inside the warehouse but, in view of the increasing police activity, he could only assume it was bad, very bad. How could this happen on his patch? Would he lose his job?

Charles watched as the back-up team cordoned off the area and held back the ever increasing crowd. Within minutes the shop was swarming with police and forensic teams in their white apparel. After briefing the relevant persons on the crime Charles took his leave with Christine, the office manager following, handcuffed, in another police car.

~

Back at the Police Station Charles updated his father and his team on the discovery in the warehouse, also the arrest warrant for Mr Claymore. He knew once the news broke the national and international press and media would have a whale of a time clamouring for more and more information to satisfy their readers and viewers, heaping more pressure on the police to come up with answers.

Whilst his father was dealing with the press he must now direct all his attention to finding the perpetrators of this horrendous crime as quickly as possible, leaving no stone unturned in the quest to close this case.

Locating the seat of the operations was one thing, a very important discovery which would put a halt to further murders, but there was a lot of work still to be done to bring all the perpetrators to book. This case had moved on to a new phase.

With a saddened heart Charles picked up the telephone to tell Wendy about the news of her operative – Petros Kritikos aka Georgio.

# Ten

In the interview room, sitting opposite Charles and Christine, the office manager twitched nervously, shuffling his bottom on the chair, unable to stay still for more than a few seconds. He scraped his fingernails on the palms of his hands and clicked his knuckles, making Christine cringe with the sound. Beads of sweat ran down his fat cheeks and he used the same dirty handkerchief again to wipe his brow and to smooth the few hair strands on his head. His cheeks were flushed, his shirt didn't look as if it had been changed for a week and his body odour was not to Christine's liking. Christine almost took pity on him but the enormity of the crime under investigation reined back any such sentimental thoughts.

'You are Thomas Watching and you are the manager at the Farndale Business Centre,' stated the sergeant, fixing the manager with an icy stare causing even more nervous twitching and knuckle clicking.

'I am.'

'And you have been in your job how long?'

'Three and a half years.'

'I presume you know who was renting the premises in question?'

'Of course.'

'Describe them to me then.'

301

'Hmm.'

'Describe them to me.' Her tone of voice emphasising it was more than a request.

'It's difficult to describe them but they were east Europeans.'

'What were their names?'

'David Smith, Paul Jones and Winston Churchill.'

'But you just said that they were east Europeans.'

'I know but they thought it best for their business if they used English names, if you know what I mean.'

'No, I don't know what you mean. What were their real names?' Christine's voice became ever louder.

'I don't know.'

'But you must know. They must have signed a rental agreement.'

'They did, but under the name of Churchill.'

'I don't believe this. You are trying to tell me you did not query their real names.'

Silence on the part of the office manager was very tangible. Then, after some thought and considered reflection, he spluttered, spraying spit everywhere, 'They were good payers. They were large premises, a large square footage and they paid twelve months in advance.'

'Could you do an e-fit of the three men?'

'Well, I only saw one and he had a moustache.'

'Is that all?' Signs of exasperation were all over Christine's face.

'All these East Europeans look the same to me. I know he had a moustache. Yes, he definitely had a moustache and a stubbly chin.' He smiled at Christine's obvious irritation, clicking his knuckles once again to deliberately annoy her.

Christine looked ready to wallop him for not understanding the gravity of the situation, to wipe that offensive, surly smile from his obnoxious face.

'Can you please stop making that sound!' asked Christine politely but sharply enough to make the manager stop and to bury his hands in his pockets.

Charles thought it timely to intervene in the discussion, the initial sternness of his voice causing the office manager to stiffen his body and recommence his twitching, glancing away not to catch the Chief Inspector's eyes. His surly smile disappeared in a thrice.

'Look at me when I'm talking to you,' bellowed Charles. 'Did you take a back-hander from these men, a bribe in other words, not to ask too many questions?'

The office manager sat bolt upright. He was in it to his neck and knew he had to come clean or all hell would break loose. He did not know what was going on in the warehouse and had not been told but he knew it was serious, very serious, and he was implicated whether he liked it or not.

'They paid me £10,000 in cash each year not to ask too many questions and to forge the rental agreement. I was not to enter the warehouse even though it was my right to do so. I was to stay clear.'

'And you had no idea what they were up to?'

'There are two hundred and forty businesses in the Farndale Business Centre. How can I be expected to know what they are all up to? My job is to find clients for the premises and to collect the monthly rent. OK so I took a bribe, you can do me for that, but I still say I was not aware of what they were doing and still don't. You haven't told me what the crime is. It seemed a legitimate business to me. I know they only opened their shop for one to two hours a day and, when passing, only saw a few people in it. I assumed their business was going down the tube with that sort of footfall, but they reassured me it was not and were concentrating on trade business, housing estates, blocks of flats and that kind of thing.'

'Sergeant, can I have a word with you outside,' asked Charles.

Christine switched off the recording machine, only too eager to leave the room, to distance herself from this cretin of an office manager with his annoying habits.

Charles and Christine left the office manager to contemplate his future in prison.

'Shall I book him, sir?' There was an eagerness in her voice to lock him up for a long time if she had her way.

'No Sergeant. His is a petty crime which I am not really interested in. His employers, on the other hand, may take a totally different view when they are informed of his misdemeanours. Let them deal out the justice by sacking him. A word of advice, Sergeant, try not to let his mannerisms get to you in the interview room, I've known a lot worse characters than him.'

'Do you think he is telling the truth about not knowing these east Europeans?'

'Funnily enough, I do.'

'What about getting him to do an e-fit?'

'Wouldn't be worth the paper it's printed on. 'No, let him go. We have bigger fish to fry.'

'Yes sir.'

'Oh, one other thing. I noticed a CCTV camera at the entrance to the business centre. I want you to get your hands on it and any other CCTV in the area of the tile shop. Then get WPC Wetherspool to analyse the footage and take stills if need be. We might get images of these three east

Europeans on camera. We know the registration number of one of their vans. See if you can find others registered in the same name. These three men are crafty buggers and will have gone to great lengths to hide their real identity.'

'Yes sir. Shall I bring in Mr Claymore for interview?'

'No. Not for a couple of hours. Let him stew in his cell. It might loosen his tongue.'

'He has asked for his lawyer to be present.'

'By all means. He is certainly going to need one where he is going.'

'Yes sir.'

~

Two hours later, Mr Claymore faced Charles and Christine in the interview room. His initial demeanour was the total opposite to that of the office manager – confident, relaxed, self-assured and full of himself. Charles spoke first.

'It is 6.00 pm on Friday, the $3^{rd}$ of August, 2012. In attendance are Detective Chief Inspector Waley-Cohen, Detective Sergeant Christine Moran, Mr Brian Claymore and his lawyer, Mr James Entwhistle.'

'Mr Claymore, let me first start by asking you to state your name, your address and where you practice.'

As cool as a cucumber, as if speaking to one of his patients, the surgeon replied, 'Mr Brian Claymore, 30 The Avenues, Hillstock, Cambridge and St George's Hospital.' This statement was followed by a steely, withering glare at Charles.

'And how long have you practiced there, Mr Claymore?'

'For about six years, on and off.'

'And what do you specialise in?'

'Mainly organ transplants and a little orthopaedic work.'

'Let me be blunt.  We know that you are a regular visitor at the Farndale Business Centre.  What was the purpose in your visits?'

'I was looking for tiles for the kitchen.  My wife is keen to change the kitchen décor.'

'Did you find any that were suitable?'

'No,' and looking at the sergeant eyeball to eyeball, 'you know what women are like.'

'We'll ignore that remark,' said Charles, annoyed with the flippancy of the comment.

Christine wasn't going to ignore that remark, especially when made with a smarmy smirk.  She fixed Mr Claymore with a venomous look that spoke volumes.

'Mr Claymore, how many times did you visit this tile shop to select tiles?' asked Christine with an unmistakable firmness of voice.

A shrug of the shoulders by Mr Claymore, 'Three or four times, I guess.  I wasn't counting.'

'And why did you visit the tile shop late at night when the shop was closed?'

The surgeon turned to his lawyer and whispered something, hiding his mouth behind his hand.  The lawyer whispered back doing likewise.

'No comment.'

'We have evidence that you entered the premises through the side door.'

Another consultation with the lawyer.

'No comment.'

Charles realised they were interviewing a very cool customer indeed. The same coolness, no doubt, he showed when carrying out many of his operations. A new approach was needed if they were to get the surgeon to confess to his horrific crimes; a more vexatious opening gambit was needed to unsettle his cavalier indifference. Charles spoke again.

'Mr Claymore, you are being charged with the murders of young girls and boys which are so gross you will be incarcerated for the rest of your life. We have evidence of your numerous visits to the warehouse for which the tile shop was but a front. We have evidence that you attended sometimes late at night. We have evidence that you worked in the operating theatre there from DNA samples taken at the scene.'

This latter statement was not, as yet, true but Charles reckoned it was just a matter of time.

'You carried out the most horrific of operations including the harvesting of skin, bones and other tissues whilst the victims were still alive.' Again, this last statement was conjecture on Charles's part, but it did have its impact. The lawyer winced at such an accusation.

'No comment.'

Frustrated with the obfuscation and denial, Charles turned to Christine, 'I suggest Sergeant that you and I leave the room and let Mr Claymore and his lawyer, consider their position.'

Charles and Christine left the room and watched behind a one-way mirror at the heated discussion between lawyer and client, the lawyer being the more agitated and expressive at the enormity of the charge, the client remaining impasssive and unperturbed.

The lawyer seemed to win the argument. Charles and Christine re-entered the room. James Entwhistle spoke as soon as they were seated and Charles had switched on the recorder again.

'My client pleads "not guilty" to murder but pleads "guilty" to a lesser charge of manslaughter. He denies any knowledge ...'

'Could Mr Claymore speak for himself,' interrupted Charles.

Mr Claymore shuffled uneasily, the veneer of coolness and self-assurance being slowly stripped away. He paused, looking down at his hands clasped tightly. The surgeon knew in his heart that his career was ruined. There was no hiding place any more. Sooner or later the truth would come out.

'I admit that I harvested the organs, skin and tissue from cadavers. Where the material went I was not privy to. They were not used for any of my own patients. I did not ask questions as to the source of the cadavers and how the remains were disposed of. I was paid to harvest the bodies and to ask no questions. I wrestled with my conscience but I needed the money. My divorce and all that. I swear by Almighty God that the bodies were cadavers. I did not, and would not operate on a body that was alive. I was asked to do so once but refused. It is beyond belief that anyone would do such a thing.

'I would receive a coded telephone call on my mobile when needed day or night. I was shown into the operating theatre and was not allowed to visit any other part of the warehouse. I did my job and then left. I kept my mouth firmly shut, in fear of reprisals if I did not.'

'You knew what you were doing was illegal?' stated Charles.

'Yes, and wanted out, but my life was then threatened and so it went on.'

'And were other medical people involved in this illegal activity?'

'Not to my knowledge. I believe not but it's possible.'

'Can you name the men who hired you?'

'No. Real names were not exchanged.'

'In that case how did you first meet?'

'It was by coincidence. I was in the tile shop looking for tiles for the kitchen and I happened to mention I was a surgeon. After several visits one thing led to another and I was offered £100,000 for doing a small job for them - £50,000 up front and the rest after the operation. One small job led to another and so on. I know it sounds corny but it was easy to get sucked in. I needed the money.'

'How many men were involved?'

'There were three, all east Europeans.'

'Would you recognise them?'

'Yes.'

The surgeon was half the man now than when the interview first began. It was as if the admission of his guilt had assuaged his conscience and the process of telling the truth after all this time was cathartic. Divorce pending, career ruined, he had no more to look forward to than a very long spell in prison.

'I would like you to complete an e-fit of these three men. Can you do that?'

With head bowed, 'I will co-operate as best I can.'

'Then this interview is concluded but expect to be interviewed again.'

Outside the interview room, Christine spoke to Charles.

'Do you think he knows more and is not letting on?'

'No. The men he was dealing with are ruthless. They would have no hesitation in carrying out their threats if he had said anything to anyone. Look at what they did to the private investigator.

'It's a shame though, what an incredible waste of a God-given talent. Now he is a broken man, confused and foolish.'

They both watched as Mr Brian Claymore, surgeon, was taken back to the cells, head bowed even further, being patted on his back by his lawyer.

~

The following week, Charles was called in to his father's office.

'Enter.'

'You wanted to talk to me, sir?'

'I do, I do, please take a seat. I have something to tell you which gives a new twist to this gruesome saga. First bring me up to date with your findings so far.'

'As you know, we charged Brian Claymore, the surgeon, with first-degree murder. We have interviewed him several times now and under that cool exterior he is a deeply troubled man and delusional. He believed strongly that the more money he could make, the more he could patch up his failing marriage. Money, by whatever means was all that concerned him. It all made sense in his befuddled brain. The horrific nature of his crime didn't seem to enter his head. He is to undergo psychiatric tests to determine if he is fit to stand trial.

'We have a watertight case against him. We have his confession of course, but CCTV evidence of numerous visits to the Business Centre and also DNA evidence of him being in the operating theatre.

We know from records that the operations were set up over three years ago by three east Europeans. Mr Claymore confesses that he has been doing their clinical work for two and a half years, an average of one cadaver a month. This would equate to the unbelievable total of about thirty bodies – young adolescent boys and girls, picked up from the streets no doubt.

'Forensics has some eighteen DNA patterns so far of the teenagers. Boys and girls we are unlikely to put names to, but we will try.'

'Do you think there were other medical personnel involved?'

'We have no evidence to suggest so. We have looked at CCTV footage of car registration numbers entering the park over the last three years and cannot link any with known doctors or surgeons. I believe that Mr Claymore was the only one.'

'What about these three east Europeans? How did they equip their warehouse?'

'We have found no evidence of direct shipments from medical suppliers to their address in the business park. We can only assume that they did it indirectly from a storage depot, perhaps in another county. They obviously went to great lengths to conceal their clandestine operations.'

'Well, I think you and your team should be congratulated on the work you have done so far, and the busting of this operation is a feather in your cap, you should be proud.'

'Thank you father … sir. As far as the other three perpetrators, the three east Europeans, are concerned, we have drawn a blank. We also do not know how they disposed of the bodies after harvesting. The e-fits from Mr Claymore are unreliable in view of his mental state, DNA evidence does not put a face to the person and CCTV footage is somewhat sketchy. They were very clever in that they hired couriers for the vans so that their facial exposure was minimal.

'I'm not sure where we go from here. Eastern Europe is a big place to track these individuals down, even if I knew their names.'

'On that very subject, I have had a call from the Deputy Commissioner of the Met. He would like you to pay him a visit as soon as possible. He has something to say to you that might help you to further your enquiries.'

'I hope so. It would be fitting if we could bring these perpetrators to book.'

As Charles was leaving his father's office, 'Keep me informed, Chief Inspector. I will need to arrange another press conference very soon.'

'Yes sir.'

Charles returned to his own office ever more determined to identify these three east Europeans, to extradite them from their own country and to bring them before the British courts for justice to be seen to be done. In his current frame of mind he would have liked to see these three men hang for their crimes, though on second thoughts hanging was too good for them, a more medieval form of torture being more appropriate.

An eye for an eye and a tooth for a tooth punishment, doing the same thing in return seemed the only way to deal with a crime of this nature, to let the perpetrators suffer in the same way as their victims. Drag them through hell as they did their young victims.

A pity, he thought, that capital punishment no longer applied in this country.

# Eleven

This was a deja-vu experience for Charles as he stood outside New Scotland Yard. It was only seven months ago he had first met the Deputy Commissioner in an official capacity. How time flies he thought to himself, it seemed only like yesterday.

Not surprisingly memories of Carla Bores came flooding back, her name resonating with him to haunt his mind yet again. If only things had worked out differently, life could have been so different being with the one he loved and cherished.

He pulled himself together, smoothing his jacket, straightening his tie, running his hand through his hair to make it respectable. Entering the building he approached the receptionist who instantly recognised him from his previous visit.

'It's Detective Chief Inspector Charles Waley-Cohen, I believe,' remarked the girl sitting at the desk, perking up at the sight of Charles.

'It is, and I have an appointment with …'

'I have already put a call through to his secretary, sir, and he will be down in a few minutes. Please take a seat.'

Charles was impressed. They were awaiting his visit and it did his ego the world of good. He was making his mark in the bigger world and that was satisfying to his self-belief and confidence.  Being a more parochial policeman, quite happy at times to be in Cambridge, he felt more like a stranger and an outcast when it came to the political and Machiavellian world of the Met.  His visits to London and New Scotland Yard always brought the comparison more sharply into focus.

'Are you in London long, sir?' enquired the receptionist, throwing him a glance or two of the "girlish" kind.

'No.  Just the one day and then back to Cambridge.'

'Could I get you a coffee while you are waiting?'

'No, thank you.'

'It is a lovely part of the country, Cambridge, isn't it?'

'It is indeed.'

The receptionist was keen to engage in more personal conversation but Charles stayed silent.  He wasn't entirely immune from female advances and the thought went through his mind that he wouldn't kick her out of bed if he had half the chance.  He was relieved of such carnal thoughts however as the Deputy Commissioner, Robert Wyatt, stepped out of the lift.

'Nice to see you again, Charles.'

'You too, Robert.'

The Deputy Commissioner gave Charles his usual vigorous and warm handshake and directed him to the lift. There he patted Charles's stomach in a playful way.

'Is the job keeping you away from exercise, Charles?'

'Cheeky bugger.  You are not so lean yourself.  Still a stranger to exercise I see, Robert.  You get bigger and better every time I see you but definitely bigger.'

'The older I get the more weight I put on.  I blame it all on the office work but it seems a fact of life these days.

Unlike in my youth when I was slim and handsome and attracted all the girls, now I'm podgy and past it.'

'It's all in the mind, Robert. It's all in the mind.'

Both men laughed as they exited the lift on the top floor, exchanging friendly banter as usual.

Charles was directed to the Conference Room. They entered.

Two men in the room stood up, holding out their hands to greet him.

'Can I introduce you to Andrew Lonsdale from MI5, and to Douglas Home from MI6. Oh, I forgot, Charles, you have already met Douglas.'

'I have, on a previous occasion. I had the pleasure of working together.'

Charles shook hands and all four men sat round the table, Robert at the head, Charles to his right and the two agents on his left.

Charles glanced at the MI6 agent whose body language had not changed from their first encounter – deadpan facial expression, staring straight ahead, poker-faced, hardly blinking. Not the most sociable of characters but he had learnt to look beyond initial impressions, to appreciate that they were really good at their jobs.

The MI5 agent was very officious, sitting erect with a straight back, staring at Charles as if suspicious of anyone new in his life. A brusque demeanour, he took off his glasses, cleaned them with a cloth from his pocket, put them on again adjusting them to his liking on his nose. Having satisfied himself that he could see properly he took a fountain pen from his inside pocket, scribbled something on a piece of paper in front of him, finally staring at Charles once again.

They do have some strange characters, thought Charles to himself. They really do. It must be a characteristic they look for when recruiting, the greater the oddball the better being the prime recruitment mantra. On the other hand it could be the agency itself that changed these people into nervous wrecks, a life of subterfuge eventually taking its toll.

The meeting started with Charles briefing them on the case and reporting on the progress so far. With the interjection of questions from the agents and the Deputy Commissioner in particular, the briefing took longer than expected, a good hour in total. Charles was surprised at the interest of the Intelligence Agencies but at the same time was pleased at the depth of their knowledge in the subject of organ harvesting. Either that or they were just curious.

Having finished his briefing the Deputy Commissioner sat back in his chair and gestured to the MI5 agent to speak. There was a pause as the agent filled his glass with water from a jug on the table, taking several sips to clear his mouth. He then seemed to come alive, speaking with a somewhat drawling accent, his hands doing most of the talking!

'I must first congratulate you, Chief Inspector, on finding the seat of operations of this despicable crime and closing it down so promptly. If the mutilated body of that young girl had not been fortuitously discovered then God knows how many children would have been murdered. When the sorry details of this crime are fully released to the press there will be an outcry by the public, a baying for revenge and a scapegoat to pin the blame on. The Home Office is not going to look good and we will need to prepare a statement for public consumption by the Home Secretary.'

Was that it? Was that his total contribution to this meeting? Charles assumed he would have something more important to say than Home Office politics. Not even a mention of illegal organ harvesting had passed his lips. Surely they were not also in denial of what was going on right in front of their noses.

The Deputy Commissioner, sensing Charles's reaction to the MI5's comments, quickly asked the MI6 agent to speak.

The MI6 agent coughed to clear his throat to speak with his usual monotone delivery.

'Your contribution, Chief Inspector, in finding these operations is more significant than you think. Our feedback from MI5, MI6 and GCHQ is that a similar operation was to be set up in south London, in the Lewisham area we believe.

'We suspect, but as yet have not sufficient proof, that such operations were contemplated in several European countries, the British one being but the start of a European-wide setup. Why do we think this? A rhetorical question, because, as you know, Chief Inspector, the skin trade is big business especially between European countries and between Europe and America. It has been going on for a number of years, increasing each year with advances in medical practices. Controls are fairly lax between countries and this has spawned a huge black market which is very lucrative for the Mafia and the like, but also for political funding purposes. Have you heard of the DPR?'

Charles shook his head.

'It stands for Donetsk Peoples Republic, a self-proclaimed state in eastern Ukraine. Its activities are headed by the Donetsk Republic Organisation, a group which has been banned in the Ukraine since 2007. This year, it was classified as a terrorist organisation. It is seeking separation from the Kiev government and, by all accounts, aided and abetted by Russia with money, arms and military personnel.

'I assume you read the papers and know what is happening in that region of the world, the civil war there between Ukrainian government forces and pro-Russian rebels.'

Charles nodded. He was not that politically minded but he knew the general gist of what the agent was saying.

'We know that the Kiev Government have intercepted large shipments of human skin into their country for converting into various medical products, these finished products then being shipped to Germany, from where they are shipped to other European countries and to America with a European stamp. With this stamp few questions are asked at border controls.

'Sympathisers in the Ukraine pass the funds to the separatist rebels for arms and other military supplies, buying them from the black market and from Russia.'

The MI6 agent paused at this point to let the enormity of what he was saying register with the Chief Inspector.

'The finding of their operations in Britain will have curtailed their expansionist policies in Europe because of tighter controls now being imposed at border crossings. So you see, Chief Inspector, your contribution is more significant than you realise.'

Charles thought for a moment. He was getting used to his cases going from the parochial to global importance in a matter of a few words; likewise with his previous case concerning the Bores family. He gave a measured response.

'I appreciate your concern gentlemen on Cold War issues and all that, but my case concerns a young girl who was brutally murdered. It now includes many other young boys and girls who were also brutally murdered in the most horrendous of ways. We have found the surgeon who carried out the clinical work but have not apprehended or even identified the men who ran the operations. My case will only be closed when I have brought these murderers to justice. I owe it to their victims.'

'Well said,' said the Deputy Commissioner, 'but let Douglas speak further.'

'MI6 has spoken to the police in Kiev. If you go there they will assist you in your enquiries. They have mug-shots of most of the criminals and will be only too pleased to help you sift through them. If you can identify them they will apprehend them and extradite them to this country. Can you identify them?'

'Not yet. We do not have their names and are still working on their profiles with people who may have met them. They have been very clever, have kept themselves to themselves and covered their tracks well.'

'Well, I will leave that to you but the offer in Kiev to assist will be open for a while, details of which you will find on this sheet of paper.

The MI6 agent passed a sheet of written notes marked "confidential" to Charles.

'What I would like to add,' said the MI5 agent in that same drawl, 'is that we will never stop the very rich from illegally acquiring tissue and organs, and there are many unscrupulous medical practitioners willing to oblige without asking the source of the donors. We can tighten up procedures, audits and checks to try and stop such a thing ever happening again in this country but we will never eliminate it entirely. Thanks to you, Chief Inspector, we all need to be on our guard if good things are to come from the bad.'

'On that note,' said the Deputy Commissioner, 'I think we should end this meeting. Thank you for coming everyone.'

The two agents left the room. Robert indicated to Charles to stay. They both sat down again.

'Charles. You realise the Ukraine is a very explosive place at the moment and it's a very dangerous place to be at this time. There are many factions keen on toppling the Ukraine government, many sympathise with the east of their country. Think twice before you go. I do not want to see you hurt or be killed.'

'Thank you for your concern, Robert, but I will follow my conscience and see the case through. I couldn't sleep at night otherwise. If we stop, the bad guys win.'

'Well, good luck to you, Charles, and remember me to your father.'

Robert accompanied Charles to the lift entrance.

'Back to Cambridge?'

'Back to Cambridge.'

As Charles passed the receptionist's desk, the girl slipped him a piece of paper.

'My telephone number if you are interested.'

'Perhaps on my next visit.'

Charles noticed her wedding ring.

'Married?'

'We have an understanding.'

Not bloody likely thought Charles. An unfaithful wife with a wandering eye, inclined to indulge in a spot of extramarital hanky-panky is one thing, one with a semi-attached husband in tow is something else. He screwed up the piece of paper to dispose of it later.

~

Back at the police station, Charles updated his father and Christine on the meeting. On his travels back to Cambridge on the train he had mulled over the need to identify these three east Europeans. He needed to strike while the iron was hot and accurate e-fits were taking far too long. He decided to take a gamble. It was a long shot but it could work. It was risky but danger had never been an excuse to sit on one's hands and do nothing.

He asked WPC Wetherspool to come into his office.'

'PC Wetherspool, I believe you trawled through the CCTV footage at the front gate of the Farndale Business Centre?'

'Yes sir.

'Do you think you could recognise these three men we are after if you saw their police mug-shots. Could you place them on the CCTV footage?'

'I think so.'

'In that case, I want you to pack a small bag for two to three days and come with me to Kiev.'

'Kiev in the Ukraine, sir?'

'That's the place.'

'When sir?'

'We leave on Monday.'

'Yes sir.' Jane's emotions went through the roof.

Christine had the job of booking the flight and hotel for the two of them. She was not happy. She was annoyed that she wasn't going with Charles but kept it to herself, knowing it was Jane's photographic memory which was the key factor in the relationship. It still didn't stop her hoping upon hope that there was nothing else to concern herself with. Oh, how love can conjure up such infidelities from nowhere and trysts where none exist. The jealousy demon was at it again! She must keep her real feelings under lock and key whilst keeping the fort in his absence. She was a professional after all and professionals do not let their imagination and emotions go wild. Or do they? Christine pondered her dilemma. Reluctantly she made the bookings.

# Twelve

Heathrow Airport, Flight to Kiev
Monday, 13th August 2012, 6.00 am
Flight time 3 hrs 10 mins;  Kiev 2 hours ahead of
London

It was a British Airways flight to Boryspil International Airport.

The weather was not so kind on this early Monday morning being overcast, cold with a strong, blustery wind, a feeling of early autumn rather than late summer.  Drizzle was in the air threatening heavy showers.

Jane clambered up the aeroplane steps holding down her coat and dress with one hand, holding her tote bag in the other, attempting all the time to shield her face and hair from the elements. For the first time in her life she was directed to First Class.

Helping her to take off her coat the air stewardess folded it neatly, placing it in the overhead locker with her tote bag.  Having tidied up her somewhat bedraggled look in the aisle, Jane took her seat next to the window.  Already flushed with the VIP treatment at the airport prior to the flight she was ready for more.

Sitting next to Charles she revelled in the hospitality and wished she was rich enough to travel like this every time.  She looked around the cabin to see if she could see any famous faces but there were none so, somewhat disappointed, sipped the early champagne on offer.

Breakfast dining finished, she looked at Charles adoringly as he adjusted his watch for the new time zone, then reclining his seat to snatch a few minutes shut-eye. She had always admired him from a distance but never this close-up, she considered him a handsome brute of a man, the stuff of her dreams with his windswept look.

She was about to ask him a question.

'Sir.'

'Call me Charles, Jane. Sir is too formal in the present circumstances.'

Jane felt embarrassed and self-conscious to call her boss Charles. She was from a council estate and he was part of the huntin', shootin' and fishin' set. There was an insurmountable gulf in their social pecking order as well as their official police rank. She admired him and had a "bit-of-a-thing" for him, but felt he was out of her reach. The prejudice was all on her part however as he seemed to have no such inhibitions.

Still, she certainly felt important being so close to him in the air at 30,000 feet. Having drunk a little too much so early in the morning, something she was not used to, naughty thoughts swamped her giddy mind. She had been told often enough that love knows no boundaries so why should she create them? If given half the chance she would grasp it with both hands, especially with someone like Charles.

'What did you want to ask me, Jane?'

'It's OK sir.'

'Call me Charles,' said with a firmer tone of voice this time, eyes still partially closed, hoping to drift into sleep.

'I would prefer not to, sir, if you don't mind.'

'It's up to you. Now relax and enjoy the flight.'

As Charles let his head loll back, Jane sipped at her champagne, nodding to the air hostess who was offering to refill her glass. If it was on offer it seemed sensible to take advantage this one and only time, it might never happen again. Jane settled herself for the flight, too excited to think of sleeping, her mind going to all places in its heightened state.

Jane's self-importance sprang to new heights when a black limousine was awaiting them as they exited the aircraft, avoiding Passport and Customs Control, to be driven the 29 km to their luxury Hilton Hotel in Kiev. Importance indeed for a mere council girl to be given such VIP treatment.

'What about my suitcase?' asked Jane of Charles, as they both took their seats in the back of the limousine.

'It will be sent separately, direct to the hotel. Don't worry.' Charles placed his overnight case on his lap, keeping it close to him at all times; Jane did likewise with her tote bag.

There was something very reassuring about her Chief Inspector which she revelled in, especially being in a foreign land, in a civil war country where tensions were high. She sat as close to him as she dare without suggesting she was a little concerned for her person. They were driven directly to their hotel, the driver not saying a word, not even looking round, his dark sunglasses and jet black hair giving him a somewhat sinister appearance. Jane was about to try to converse with him but the atmosphere in the limousine was of preferred silence so she thought it wise to say nothing and take her cues from Charles who simply smiled at her, a reassuring smile which settled her nerves temporarily. Jane whiled away the time staring out of the window at the passing countryside looking its best on a bright, sunny day.

Arriving at their hotel the chauffer opened Jane's door, again not a word being said. In fact, to Jane's surprise he seemed to deliberately turn his head away avoiding any eye contact. What a surly character Jane thought to herself, I hope the natives are a bit friendlier than this miserable soul! Charles just seemed to take everything in his stride - maybe she should try and do the same.

Once the formalities were completed at the reception desk of the hotel, around midday local time, they went directly to their rooms in the lift, to the third floor, where Jane's suitcase was waiting for her outside the door of her room. Charles's room was a little further down the corridor.

Charles called to Jane, 'Half an hour Jane, and then the limo will take us to our meeting at police headquarters. Dress informal but business-like.'

'Yes sir.'

~

In the limousine, Charles briefed Jane on their visit.

'The Kiev police force is one of the oldest police departments in the Ukraine. It is part of the Ministry of Internal Affairs, located at Volodyingr Street in Kiev.

'The top man, the Kiev City Police Commissioner, is Yuri Leonidovich Moroz, head of Kiev's Internal Affairs Department and the Kiev City Police Department. MI6 has cleared our visit with his Department. We will be meeting Vladimir Andreichenko, police rank 10. You can address him as Captain or sir. Everything has been arranged so don't be overawed.'

'Yes sir.'

Deep inside, Jane was nervous but did not show it, smiling at Charles, hiding her fidgety hands from view.

For the rest of the short journey Charles stayed quiet which only added to Jane's nervousness. She was reassured, however, with Charles's presence alone, casting him furtive glances now and then to calm her jangling nerves.

The limousine came to a stop outside a large, officious-looking municipal building, the chauffeur then darting out of the car to hold the passenger door open again for Jane. Nothing was said, only an exchange of black looks which did nothing to reassure Jane.

They walked up a flight of stone steps, through marble-faced pillars to a large marbled foyer with low-hanging crystal chandeliers; opulence reminiscent of a former time. The chauffeur followed closely behind, the limousine having been driven away by someone else.

Charles had known beforehand that the chauffeur was both their driver and a security agent for their protection from the airport to this building. But to allay any fears he had not mentioned this to Jane.

The chauffer stepped smartly in front of them to direct them to a reception counter to the left of the foyer behind who stood a small but well-built, officious-looking female police officer in uniform.

'We have an appointment with Vladimir Andreichenko,' said Charles, pronouncing the name as best he could.

The police officer gave them both a good hard look, looked up her list, waved the chauffeur to leave in peremptory style and came out from behind the counter. Neither a greeting nor a smile crossed her lips.

'Could you come this way,' leading them to an adjoining office. 'If you could wait here for a few minutes,' said in slow but good English whilst holding the door open.

Both had barely sat down when a taller, more slightly built female police officer entered, asked them, in good English, to stand up with their hands in the air and began to frisk them all over. Charles didn't mind, thinking it amusing, but Jane found it highly embarrassing to be touched in such a way in front of Charles. Charles, on seeing Jane squirm slightly turned his head away which helped Jane a little.

Just as promptly, and without saying another word, the officer left the room to be followed immediately by another more senior male officer in uniform who also spoke very good English.

'Sorry about that. This war makes animals of all of us. Let me introduce myself. My name is Vladimir Andreichenko and I am here to look after you.'

Charles introduced Jane and himself and they all shook hands.

'If you would follow me to my office?'

He led them up two flights of marbled stairs and into one of the many offices on either side of a long corridor.

'Please be seated. Sorry again for the frisking but you can't be too careful these days. Spies and terrorists are everywhere and in a building of this importance procedures have had to be tightened. All visitors are vetted. It is not nice but these are dangerous times and we all have to adapt. I have already been given an outline of the reasons for your visit but if you could fill in the details I will see if I can help.'

Charles ran through his case notes, explaining again the reason for their trip to the Ukraine. Vladimir listened intently. Although his English was good he liked to hear it from a well-spoken English man.

'Thank you, Chief Inspector. We will get on to it right away as you English would say.'

He rose to his feet, went to the door and beckoned Jane to follow. Jane looked at Charles for approval before following. Charles then heard muffled voices in the corridor as Jane was introduced to others in the Ukrainian language and English.

Vladimir returned and sat at his desk again. 'I have arranged for your constable to visit our central information unit where we hold many, many photographs of known criminals. We do not have the means for DNA comparisons. That is for the future. With your photo-fits I am certain we can find these three men. English is spoken well here so they will put your constable at her ease.'

'Thank you, Captain.'

'Now tell me, have you been to Kiev before?'

Charles shook his head.

'Well, while your constable is doing her job, I can help you get more acquainted with our glorious city. Please come with me.'

Vladimir led Charles to another office further down the corridor and opened the door.

'Let me introduce you to Miss Hanna Goraya, police rank 5, a senior sergeant in your Britain.'

'Pleased to meet you, Sergeant,' said Charles shaking her hand.

'The sergeant will show you the tourist sights. I will leave you with her and we will meet up later. She will give you a good time.'

'Thank you, Captain.'

Vladimir left the room and disappeared down one of the many corridors, leaving the two of them searching for their initial words.

Hanna was in police uniform and had a pretty face, if somewhat stern-looking at this moment in time, blonde-haired, tied back in a severe bun. She stared at Charles from behind her desk as if weighing him up and assessing this stranger before her. Rather than putting him at his ease, she waited for him to speak. Charles hesitated for a few moments but then realised her silence was probably because of his superior rank so he spoke first.

'Sergeant, I hope I'm not a burden for you to show me around your city. If you have more pressing police work I am quite prepared to go by myself or even to stay here.'

'No. No. It is all arranged. If you give me five minutes I will change. I will make myself more presentable for you. We will draw too much attention if I stay in uniform.' It was bluntly said but with a good accent.

Hanna went into a side room. After a few minutes another woman emerged. It was the same woman but with the face and the body of another female. Dressed in casual clothes, with her hair loose and with a little make-up, she was stunningly beautiful. Charles's eyebrows lifted in surprise, pleased with what he saw from this female metamorphosis!

Posing in the doorway with her hand on her hip: 'You like?'

Charles was lost for words although his eyes and smile told her all she needed to know.

'Come. We will paint the town red as you would say in your country.'

Flinging a coat over her arm, she led Charles out of the building.

'We will take an official company taxi, the gypsy cabs are too dangerous. You never know who is in them these days.'

And so started an afternoon tour of Kiev. First to the main square on Khreshchatyk street where the posh cars and people could be found; then to St Sophia's Cathedral, followed by St Michael's Golden-Domed Monastery; then to the Mariyinsky Palace with a stroll in the park; and finally, to the Golden Gate of Kiev – a nice spot to learn about the town walls and some nice buildings there.

It was a whirlwind tour with Charles flagging from the day's travelling and the sweltering weather but determined all the same to keep up with Hanna.

'I will take you to a nice restaurant for a late lunch now. You like?'

'I like.'

'You must try the Chicken Kiev, like you have never tasted before, and the borscht, a Russian soup, very tasty.'

Lunch and visits to two more tourist spots went well, the tension of officialdom between the two of them receding into the background as they both relaxed in each other's company. Charles took a liking to this sassy beauty and she to him. Those feelings he had for Carla were rising to the surface again and he was beginning to feel pleased he could be affected in that same way by another woman. Perhaps a little too much drink at lunchtime had fuelled his emotions.

While being driven back to the Ministry of Internal Affairs, Charles turned to Hanna, 'If you ever come to London, please look me up. I would be only too pleased to return the compliment.'

'Thank you, Chief Inspector. I might just do that one day.'

Back in the building Hanna directed Charles back to Vladimir's office, returning to her own office with a cheeky grin on her face and a little wave goodbye. She'd taken quite a fancy to this Englishman.

Charles met up again with Jane who was with Vladimir in his office. Her crest-fallen face and shake of the head told him immediately that there was no luck to be had that day.

'Never mind, Jane. Perhaps tomorrow will bring better luck.'

'Yes sir.'

'I hope you had a good time, said Vladimir with a knowing smile on his craggy face. 'A limousine is waiting to take you back to your hotel. Early morning, same place tomorrow, *tak?*'

Vladimir escorted them out of the building to the waiting limousine with the same chauffer in attendance.

'We'll be back,' said Charles, 'see you in the morning.'

'See you in the morning,' repeated Vladimir in parrot fashion, a huge grin on his face.

~

Dinner that evening in the hotel was a subdued affair with Jane picking at her food feeling she had let her Chief Inspector down; Charles foolishly thinking of Hanna and his city visit. An awkward silence at times.

Little was said that evening and they both retired early to their rooms.

Jane took another cooling shower still miffed at her lack of success, retiring early to catch up on her sleep. With hundreds of mug-shots still reeling through her mind sleep came very quickly.

Charles lay on his bed, reminiscing about his day and fantasising about Hanna. He knew he was a sucker for a certain kind of lady, especially of the foreign kind, with enigmatic and intriguing airs and graces, one with higher cheekbones and fuller lips.

However, the policeman in him had never gone away for a second and he was conscious that they were being trailed through the city, someone observing their every move. It could well have been another security agent hired by Vladimir to protect their backs but equally it could just as well have been a pro-Russian agent or sympathiser spying on their whereabouts. He suspected the latter since he felt Vladimir would have at least mentioned it to him. He needed to stay on his mettle at all times if he and Jane were to get out of this country alive, or at least in one piece. This is a country riven with politics, prying eyes and fear of what your neighbour might say or do; all symptoms of a nasty civil war brewing with innocent people caught in the middle.

He slept heavily that night from physical exhaustion and jet lag.

~

The next morning went like clock-work after an early morning call – breakfast, limousine, Vladimir's office and Jane to the information unit.

Charles looked at Vladimir across his office desk. Silver-haired, clean-shaven with a craggy, slightly pock-marked, leathery face. A face animated with silvery, bushy eyebrows. He was a handsome man who looked as though he kept himself in good physical shape. Charles reckoned he was in his mid-forties or thereabouts.

'I ask a favour of you today,' said Vladimir, leaning forward in his chair.

'Yes Captain.'

'You know of Stanislav Tkachenko?'

The name rang a bell but Charles shook his head.

'I did not think so.'

'You remember when you won your Olympic gold medal? Can you now remember who you beat in the quarter-final?'

'That Stanislav Tkachenko? The Ukrainian contestant?'

'That is the man. He now heads our cadet training. On hearing of your visit he asked me to ask you if you would be so kind as to demonstrate your skills in the martial arts to the cadets. They would be honoured to observe someone with your reputation. What do you say?'

'I, too, would be honoured, but must admit I'm not as fit as when I won the gold.'

'Excellent. I thought you would agree so I have arranged everything. A limousine will take you to our cadet training school and there you will meet Stanislav. We will meet up again after lunch, yes?'

'The pleasure will be all mine, Captain. I'm only too pleased to help out.'

'Excellent. I will show you to your car.'

~

The cadet training school was just twenty minutes away, the same chauffeur doing the driving. On entering the grounds through a sentry post, manned by two armed soldiers, it was obvious that the police training was shared with the military.

A long driveway led to the cadet training school entrance where the limousine stopped. Stepping out, Charles watched the soldiers marching in the large quadrangle, performing arms drills, sergeants barking out orders, remonstrating with soldiers out of line. Then he heard a half-familiar growl behind him and, turning, saw Stanislav Tkachenko approaching, waving his arms as if greeting a long lost friend, then giving him a bear hug which almost squeezed the living daylights out of him.

'Charles Waley-Cohen! Nice to meet you again my good friend. My school is very honoured to have you visit.'

Charles had a little difficulty in understanding his words as his broken English was peppered with the vernacular. It was good enough to just interpret though and Stanislav was clearly overjoyed to see him again, that much was obvious.

Stanislav was a brute of a man, a barrel-chested man, tall with strong shoulders and body. He had lost most of the hair on his head since Charles last saw him six years ago but had compensated with a full, grizzly beard and flamboyant moustache. He looked slimmer and fitter than ever. He was fearsome enough in the tournament and a very difficult opponent to overcome but now, he thought, it would take a super-human effort to beat him.

Charles shook his hand, 'Pleased to meet you old friend.'

'Come, come, come inside. Let us have a coffee and talk about the good old days.'

Stanislav led him to a canteen bursting at the seams with military and police personnel. The chatter, more like a din, was deafening with voices, crockery and cutlery mixing in a cacophony of sound. Grabbing two coffees he was then led to the back of the canteen to a cobbled courtyard with benches dotted around a small fountain where water, by the look of it, had been turned off for some time, leaving smelly algae to proliferate. The main thing was that it was quieter here, out of earshot of others.

'Tell me Chief Inspector … I am told I should call you Chief Inspector now … tell me about yourself and did winning the Olympic gold make any difference to your life?'

Charles spent the next half-hour giving Stanislav a potted history of his life since their first meeting in Beijing, recalling more of the good times than the bad, not going into too much detail.

Stanislav listened intently and then reciprocated in his broken English, recalling mainly how the events in his country had taken a turn for the worse, some of the bloodiest battles with the pro-Russian faction. He was careful to keep his voice low when talking about his own opinions on the recent elections and made sure no one but Charles was listening.

He was getting more sombre by the minute when suddenly his emotions went into reverse, slapping Charles on the back and making a welcome speech again.

'Nice to see you again old friend,' glancing at his watch. 'I have twenty cadets waiting to greet you in the training gym and to watch you. Only, of course, if you feel up to it.'

'I will give it a try but I'm not as fit as I was when I beat you in the quarter-finals. Age has thickened my muscles in places not conducive to making high kicks.'

'I understand. Me likewise.'

In actual fact, Charles was looking forward to a good workout, his current regime was too infrequent for his own liking as more and more office work was piled onto his shoulders.

'Lead the way, Stanislav.'

The rest of the morning was to Charles's satisfaction. Having changed into a Dobok and black belt, he stunned the young cadets with his repertoire of high kicks and movements to continual applause, Stanislav discussing every move he made in his own language with great enthusiasm and joining in the applause.

Then ensued a great time by all as the young cadets tried to emulate his moves with the guidance of both Charles and Stanislav, especially when Stanislav himself ended up on his bottom trying a very high kick to the chin.

The session finished with a reverential bow from Charles, a standing ovation and the hollering of young voices.

When showered and dressed, he was entertained royally but frugally, being put at the head of a long trestle table in the canteen with Stanislav and all the cadets in attendance. More talk, more memories, this time about their encounter at the Beijing Olympic Games. A simple meal with wine culminating in Stanislav holding Charles's arm upright to signify him as the winner with all the cadets standing to toast the master of Taekwondo.

This encounter with Stanislav Tkachenko would not be forgotten for many a year!

~

Escorted by a uniformed policeman to the Captain's office, Charles knocked apprehensively on the door. He knew in his heart of hearts that it was a big ask of Jane to identify three eastern Europeans from her memory banks of the CCTV footage. He was expecting the same response as the previous day and for his gamble to have failed miserably.

He was invited to enter and again saw Jane sitting opposite Vladimir. He need not have worried - Jane's broad smile told him she had been successful this time which was a huge relief to him. He returned Jane's smile, thanking her for the successful outcome, shaking her hand enthusiastically, praising her for her diligence in identifying the men.

Vladimir beckoned Charles to be seated. In front of him were three photographs which he passed one by one to Charles.

'This is Alexei Kamkin ... Bogdan Yevzov ... and Vladimir Andropov. All are Ukrainian born in Donetsk and identified by your constable. They have all been in prison for petty theft and common assault at some time in their lives. Kamkin is the eldest and, we suspect, the leader of the three.'

Charles studied their faces and thought of how he could bring them before the English courts.

Vladimir seemed to read his thoughts.

'Do you want the good news first or the bad?' He continued without waiting for a reply. 'We have identified them so you can rest your mind easy on that, but here comes the bad news, as far as you are concerned. All three were fighting with the pro-Russian separatists. We know this for a fact because all three were killed by government snipers. Their bodies were taken back to Donetsk for burial.' He handed three more photographs to Charles showing their bullet-ridden faces. 'Their burial took place three days ago.'

Watching Charles's face, he added, 'I know this is not the outcome you desired and would have preferred to have had them extradited to your country for their horrible crimes there. These things happen unfortunately in this war-torn country and God has decided their fate here.'

Charles was flummoxed by this turn in events and looked blankly at Jane and Vladimir. He quickly regained his composure but still registered annoyance on his face.

'Thank you, Captain. I can't thank you enough for your cooperation in this matter.'

'I suppose you and your constable will be flying back to the UK tomorrow? As you are leaving for the airport ask the hotel receptionist to give me a ring and I will have the limousine pick you up from your hotel.'

He handed Charles a piece of paper with his telephone number.

'Ask her to ring this number and to use the code 30. She will know what you mean. I will know then that it is you calling. Better to play it safe knowing that you are well-protected. I would not want a black mark on my own records, you know what I mean.'

'Thank you again, Captain, your cooperation has been invaluable.'

'The photographs are for you, for your files.'

Charles and Jane stood up, shook hands with the Captain and were escorted by Vladimir out of the building to the waiting limousine ready to take them back to their hotel. Vladimir saluted Charles as he entered the limousine. Charles returned the salute.

Jane was in an exuberant mood while Charles, on the other hand, was getting maudlin, brought about by the sudden and unexpected emptiness he felt about not being able to bring the perpetrators to justice. It would need time for it to sink in that they were stone-cold dead and there was nothing else that he or anyone else could do.

~

Back at the hotel Charles was feeling a little better, more relaxed and accepting of the situation as he knocked on Jane's door, signalling for them both to go down together to the restaurant for their evening meal. He had arranged for an early flight home the following morning.

He was even more perkier when Jane opened the door. She looked stunning. Dressed in a bright, floral-patterned chiffon shirt and mini-skirt, with heels, a chunky necklace and bracelets, she looked the bees' knees. Her brunette hair was lustrous and loose, touching her shoulders. Her blue eyes were sparkling, her smile captivating.

'You look beautiful, Jane.'

'Thank you, sir.'

'Please call me Charles, just for this evening, just this once.'

'Yes sir … yes, Charles.'

It still seemed strange for Jane to call him Charles. It made her self-conscious but she reckoned that she would get over it with a few drinks inside her. One thing was for sure: she planned to enjoy her last swish meal with her Chief Inspector as it may never happen again with such a man as her Inspector Tae.

The conversation throughout the meal was about Charles telling her how his day had gone at the cadet training school; Jane telling him about the thousands of police photographs, how she had been looked after with tea, coffee and biscuits to keep her alert at all times, pumped with so much liquid she had had to make frequent visits to the ladies ruining her concentration. They both laughed, clinking glasses, toasting the successful outcome.

Several drinks later, the talk drifted to more personal matters as Jane described her time as a beauty therapist and masseuse and her clients, both male and female, who misinterpreted her intentions when first advertising as a "tantric massage therapist".

Charles was all ears as Jane went on to explain tantric massage as a Western form of the ancient art of Tantric involving erotic massage or sensuous massage by one person on another person's erogenous zones to achieve or enhance their sexual excitation or arousal.

Unabashed, Jane continued, 'By using touch and intuition, practitioners can tailor the massage according to individual needs and desires, ensuring the most erotic experience possible.'

Charles went silent for a while and Jane wondered if she had been too forthright in her explanations. She hoped not as the last thing on her mind was to embarrass Charles.

Then Charles took her by surprise by coming up with an unexpected comment of his own.

'That explains Jane, being a beauty therapist, why you have such a natural look with no make-up. Such a beautiful complexion.'

What Jane did not want to say, was that women take years to perfect the "no make-up" look. It takes a lot of skill requiring subtle blusher rather than rouge. Charles was happy with what he saw and that was all that mattered, there was no need to explain further the ways of women.

However, Charles's comment was a red rag to a bull. Emboldened, she asked Charles if he would like a massage. After a few moments hesitation, Charles declined the offer, feigning an evening's workload.

Jane did not press the matter, still astonished at herself to have the temerity to make such a suggestion in the first place. The mere act of doing so had sent a frisson throughout her body and naughty thoughts again clouded her mind, as they tended to do with several alcoholic drinks inside of her.

After the meal, they went to the cocktail bar where they drank, talked and listened to the piano player. Several couples gyrated on the small dance floor tempting Jane to ask Charles but thought it too pretentious, thinking it best to listen to the music instead.

They both retired to their rooms together later, Charles seeing Jane safely to her room.

'Do not open this door to anyone but me. Goodnight Jane.'

'Sure you don't want a massage, the best there is?'

'Thank you Jane. Not tonight ... too many things on my mind.'

Jane closed her door and Charles walked further up the corridor to his room. He was about to put the card-key into the lock when he stopped himself. He put the card-key back into his pocket and re-traced his steps back to Jane's door. He tapped on the door.

'Who's that?'

'It's me, Charles. Are you still up for that massage?'

Jane opened the door and a broad smile lit up her face, her pulse racing wildly.

~

The next morning Charles settled the hotel bill, then went to Jane's room and knocked on her door.

'We leave in five, Jane.'

They both emerged from their rooms five minutes later, Jane holding her tote bag in one hand, wheeling her suitcase with the other; Charles holding his overnight case.

'Good morning, Jane.'

'Good morning, sir.'

They walked along the corridor exchanging pleasantries when two men advanced towards them from the opposite direction. Charles recognised one as the chauffeur and was on immediate alert. He had not asked the receptionist to ring Vladimir and no code had been given.

Jane also recognised the chauffeur and stepped ahead of Charles, bending down slightly to fold the handle of the suitcase, attempting to hand the case to the chauffeur.

The chauffeur grabbed her by the nape of her neck and swung her around as a shield forcing her to drop her tote bag. At the same time he drew a hand gun from his coat pocket. He pointed it at Charles to shoot, Jane wriggling to release his grip on her neck.

Seeing Jane in danger, Charles hesitated, not knowing which of the two men to tackle first. A red mist blinded his normal reasoning.

Jane had the presence of mind to drop her case onto the foot of the chauffeur and, as he partially released her, brought her elbow sharply up and into his groin area, the way she'd been taught.

The gun was lowered for a second. But that was all the time Charles needed to go manic with the two men. With fist-clenched defiance he kicked the gun out of the chauffeur's hand and with a spinning turn, smashed his foot into his solar plexus. As the chauffeur bent double another high kick thudded against his jaw felling him unconscious.

The other man was startled and drew a serrated blade. He too was quickly disarmed with a kick and another swivel kick. A Karate punch felled him also unconscious.

It was all over in a matter of seconds.

'Are you all right, Jane?'

'Yes sir. Should we call the police?'

'We are the police. Let's get the hell out of here. There could be more.' Charles kicked the gun and knife further down the corridor.

Charles grabbed Jane's suitcase and his overnight case, Jane grabbed her tote bag. They both ran towards the lift. Changing his mind at the last second, Charles led Jane down the six flights of stairs to the ground floor, entering the foyer in a hurry. They threw their room keys towards the receptionist and dashed to the hotel doors.

'Should we ring for the limousine, sir?'

'No time for that.'

They exited the hotel and hailed a passing taxi.

It was a gypsy cab that arrived first. It could be anything, thought Charles, but the risk had to be taken. He bundled Jane into the cab with the cases, jumped into the front seat and shouted to the driver, 'Airport, and hurry man.'

The driver heard the word "airport" and blithely continued at his leisurely pace, not realising the urgency of the situation.

Jane shrieked at the top of her voice, '*Po bih strey ye, pit dee syat* Euros,' whilst still catching her breath.

'What on earth did you say, Jane?'

'I think I said, in Russian, hurry up, fifty euros.'

'But I don't have fifty euros.'

'I do. Just in case of emergencies. Their own currency is in free-fall at the moment. Better to be safe than sorry.'

'Is there no end to your talents, Jane?'

A slight blush revealed her conscience of the night before.

'I speak six languages, sir, but know only a smattering of Russian. I am hoping he understands.'

She repeated the words to the driver, frantically waving a 50-Euro note in front of his face. This time the driver got the message.

The taxi sped to the airport, breaking the speed limits occasionally, with Charles hoping they wouldn't be stopped by the traffic police patrols. That was the last thing he wanted. He looked back to see if they were being followed. After several minutes, he knew they were.

At last, in what seemed an interminable journey, they arrived at the airport - the car following coming to a halt as they entered the Departures hall.

At that same moment a man in a white raincoat advanced towards them with his hand in his pocket as if to retrieve a gun. Jane stopped and froze, bewildered with the whirlwind of events beyond her comprehension.

'Don't worry Jane. You're safe now. He's a security agent here to protect us. It was all arranged with Vladimir except that he did not realise the chauffeur is a mole for the pro-Russians.'

Jane let out a deep sigh of relief and puffed out her cheeks.

'Being with you sir is quite an experience.'

'Thank you. It's all in a day's work, Jane.'

They both smiled at each other and headed to the Check-in desk, the security agent in close attendance guarding their backs.

The flight back to the UK was even more pleasurable for Jane. She could finally relax knowing what she now knew about her Inspector Tae, a secret she would guard closely and not disclose it to anyone. They clinked glasses and smiled again at each other.

'Here's to your good health, Jane.'

'To yours also, sir.'

The champagne flowed freely throughout the flight with Jane sporting a permanent soporific grin. This was one dream of hers which had actually come true. She was in seventh heaven.

# Thirteen

Back early in his office, Charles was preparing his speech for his team, bringing them up to date with events, when Christine entered in her calm, reassuring way.

'Yes Sergeant?'

'How did it go, sir?'

Without looking up from his writing, 'All's well that ends well, Sergeant. I'm just finishing these notes and will address the team. Could you arrange a staff meeting for fifteen minutes time, please?'

'Where's WPC Wetherspool?'

'I've given her the day off. She will be in first thing tomorrow morning.'

Christine was in two minds to ask why but decided not to delve further into something she might regret later. Instead she dealt with the matter in hand.

'The Desk Sergeant has just rung through, sir. He has a young lad by the name of Mark Winstanley, seventeen years of age. Wants to see the policeman in charge of the murders he's read about in the national newspapers. Should I show him into the interview room?'

Charles stopped writing, glancing up at Christine.

'I wonder what that could be all about. No, Sergeant, bring him to my office. You stay with him. We'll defer the staff meeting to another time.'

'Yes sir.'

Charles put down his pen and waited for the youth to arrive.

'This is Detective Chief Inspector Waley-Cohen,' said Christine as she brought the youth into the office. 'Please take a seat here. I will sit next to you if that is all right by you.'

Mark Winstanley gave her an affirmative nod and then sat himself down.

Charles stood up, shook the boy's hand which was trembling, and sat down again, pushing aside his notes to give the youth his full attention.

'What can I do for you, Mark?' asked Charles politely.

There was no response for several seconds as Mark settled himself, feeling a little self-conscious in front of two detectives, directing his eyes everywhere other than at Charles or Christine. Finally he found sufficient confidence to speak.

'My name is Mark Winstanley. I am seventeen-and-a-half and want to speak to the policeman in charge about what I saw.' The words were uttered in a shaky voice and were almost inaudible.

'What did you say, Mark?'

'I said I want to speak to the policeman about what I saw.'

'What did you see, Mark?'

'Will I go to prison?'

'Let's not worry about things like that. Tell me, what did you see?'

'I read about it in the papers. My boss, Mr Dolan, was found dead. He had been murdered.'

Charles looked at Christine for some sort of explanation.'

'I believe he is referring to a body found in another county, sir.'

Tell me more Mark, about this Mr Dolan.'

'I worked for him, sir. He is the owner of Dolan & Sons, Funeral Directors. He and his son run the business. I just helped out there as a student for six weeks, cleaning the cars and things like that. I know I shouldn't have been working there because I'm under-age. You have to be twenty-one. Will I go to prison?'

'I don't think so, Mark. Now tell me, what did you see at the undertakers?'

Preparing to recount his experience, Mark's nerves were frayed and he fidgeted uncomfortably as if to vomit. He struggled to compose himself, shoulders heaving uncontrollably.

'Can you get him a glass of water, Sergeant.'

Christine left the room, returning in a couple of minutes with a glass of water. Mark sipped it and regained some of his composure.

'I can't help you, Mark, until you tell me what you saw at the undertakers.'

Mark plucked up the courage to recall his experience.

'There was a coffin in the Chapel of Rest and I opened the lid to let Mrs Harrington see her husband, Bert, for the last time. I know I shouldn't have done it but I felt sorry for her and there was no one else around at the time.

'Mrs Harrington looked in the coffin and fainted, hitting her head on the corner of the sideboard. I thought she was dead but she later recovered and was taken to hospital. She didn't attend the funeral the next day.

'I looked into the coffin and saw the dead parts of another person wrapped in plastic bags. It was a boy. His head had no eyes and his other parts were packed around Bert. His ...'

'Let me stop you there, Mark. The sergeant will take you to a room where you can write down what you saw. She will contact your mother and father who will be brought to the station to look after you, and to witness your statement. Don't worry. Nothing will happen to you. We are immensely grateful to you for coming here to tell us all about it.'

Charles stood up and shook Mark's hand. Christine led the boy out of the office.

Once out of the room, Charles flung his arms upwards, punching the air. 'At last, at last,' he enthused, 'the final piece of the jigsaw has fallen into place.'

He now knew how the bodies had been disposed of. They were cremated with cadavers, leaving no trace, no trail. By a fortunate coincidence, Mark, in all his innocence, had opened a coffin lid and exposed the racket.

Christine returned to see a jubilant Chief Inspector, eyes ablaze, still punching the air.

'Why oh why, Sergeant, did we not think of that before; so simple, so beautifully simple, yet so macabre in its execution.'

'Normal people don't usually think like that, sir. You have to have a warped mind to do that sort of thing.

'On the way to the interview room, Mark was saying that he was under strict instructions from Mr Dolan not to say a word about what he saw. He was in fear of his life. Mr Dolan gave him a huge bonus to keep his mouth shut and told him that he would go to prison because he was under-age to work there. He was told to man-up and put a brave face on it. After reading of his murder, he decided to go to the police. He did not go immediately because he feared he would be charged with being an accomplice to murder but his girlfriend urged him to tell all or she would leave him.'

'I now know who is an accomplice though,' said Charles - 'Mr Dolan's son. Have him arrested and brought to the station asap.'

'Yes sir, with the greatest of pleasure.'

~

Charles was reading a copy of the forensics report on Mr Simon Dolan, faxed over from Essex County Police. His throat had been slashed and he had several knife wounds, similar to that of the private investigator. It was his conclusion that before fleeing the country the three east Europeans had murdered the undertaker to stop him from revealing their identities. Mr Nolan and his son were the final link in the chain that disposed of the young boys and girls. Charles presumed there must have been some dispute with the undertaker which would explain why the body parts of the first young girl were hurriedly disposed of in the river and in the woods. He was certain that Mr Dolan's son would tell him all he needed to know.

That same day, Charles joined Christine in the interview room where Mr Dolan's son sat on the opposite side of the table. Charles switched on the recorder and went through the preliminaries of date, time and those present.

'Can you speak your name,' asked Charles politely.

'My name is Simon Arthur Dolan.'

'How old are you, Simon?'

'I am thirty-five.'

'And what do you do for a living?'

'I run ... I ran the family business of Dolan & Sons, Funeral Directors of Cambridge with my father. The business was closed down on the recent death of my father.'

Charles realised immediately that this was a confident young man, used to death and all its horrors and would not confess readily to normal questioning. Instead he went straight for the jugular, showing him the horrific forensic photographs of the dismembered bodies. Simon reeled back in disgust, pushing away the photographs, turning his head away.

Charles pushed them back into his line of sight. 'Look damn you, take a good look. These are the body parts of young boys and girls. Their bodies were harvested for skin, bones and organs, and then what was left was cut up, wrapped in plastic bags, put in coffins with other cadavers and incinerated. Your father was responsible for the last link in this chain. Were you aware of this?'

'Absolutely not. I had no idea. My father wouldn't do a thing like that.'

The initial ploy of using shock tactics had failed to work on Simon Dolan so Charles waded in with the evidence to extract a quick confession.

'We have a witness of such body parts in one of your coffins.'

'That would be Mark Winstanley. He is just a young student. He fantasises about these things, makes a pig's ear of everything he does. He is an unreliable witness. I tell you, my father would never do a thing like that. Never.'

'I would think very carefully about what you say next, if I was you.' The inflection in Charles's voice took on a more serious tone.

'We have evidence of you collecting body parts from the Smiths Tile shop in the Farndale Business Centre. You acted as one of the couriers and we have you on camera entering and leaving in one of their vans. DNA and fingerprint evidence will place you in the van. We have enough evidence to send you to prison for life. It would help your case if you confess all.'

'All right, all right,' he blustered turning redder in the face. 'I will tell you all you need to know.'

Charles sat back, folding his arms, waiting for the explanation.

'I was coerced into it by my father. I didn't want to do it but my father was a very domineering character and could be very persuasive at times, you ask anyone who knew him.'

Simon realised the game was up and there was no point in trying to give false statements. There was too much evidence against him. He reckoned a quick and full confession might help his case in the courts.

'My father told me he was approached by someone from the Ukraine. I never knew his name. He was to dispose of body parts from the Smiths Tile shop at the Farndale Business Centre. My father took a lot of persuading, so he said, with threats on his life. Our business was in no great shape and the regular amounts of money we were promised came in useful and kept the business afloat.

'He was told that teenagers were being picked up from the London streets and brought to the Business Centre. I was not told and did not want to know what happened there. All I was instructed to do was to pick up body parts, sealed in plastic bags, and to place them in our coffins before being taken to the crematorium.

'Once a month we took it in turn, my father and me, to pick up the load and then place them in our refrigerators. We packed them into coffins as and when we had a cremation. No one would know and no one would suspect anything different from a normal cremation. The coffins were never opened once the lid had been screwed down not even at the crematorium. When Mark Winstanley discovered the parts, my father told him a bull-shit story which he believed. We gave him a bonus not to say anything and to keep his mouth shut. He was quite willing to take the money, more money than he had ever seen in his life, but he blabbed about it to his girlfriend and developed a conscience.'

'What happened to Mrs Harrington,' asked Christine.

'Mrs Harrington was taken to hospital with mild concussion and a cut to the head and couldn't remember anything anyway. She was a soppy old cow.

'The death of my father changed everything. I know he wanted to pull out. He'd had enough, he couldn't sleep at night and his health was failing. He feared for his life and he was obviously proved correct. I was asked to identify his body.'

At this point, Simon Dolan broke down. He was in floods of tears. Tears it seemed for his father rather than the fate of all the boys and girls murdered. With those, he still seemed to be in denial. To him dead bodies were dead cadavers to be disposed of whole or in part, it didn't matter one way or the other, but that of his father was something else, to be mourned over and to shed tears for.

Charles stopped the recorder.

They watched as Simon Arthur Dolan was taken to the cells still crying over his father's death.

'Charge him, Sergeant, as an accessory to murder. He is going to go down for a very long time, a very long time indeed.'

'And good riddance,' whispered Christine, moved almost to tears herself by the confession, thinking of all the boys and girls who had passed through his hands, money being his only concern. What kind of man is that?

# Fourteen

The following day Charles addressed his staff in a firm but emotional voice. His father was in attendance.

Charles spoke of events in time-line order, starting with the discovery of an arm and then other body parts of a young girl. A girl whose head was still missing and whose name had still not been identified; of the foot-slogging of his team to understand the nature of the crime; of the private investigator and the raid on the warehouse; of the diabolical crime committed there and the sheer magnitude of the forensic report; of the trip to Kiev and the role WPC Wetherspool had played, a vital role which deserved further praise and commendation; and finally, of the statements made by Mark Winstanley and Simon Dolan which exposed the crude disposal of body parts by cremation.

He finished by saying, 'We now know who did it, why they did it and how they did it. The perpetrators are now dead but many boys and girls died at their hands in terrible circumstances, many of whom have yet to be identified and the total number confirmed. Possibly the number may never be known. No doubt they were some of the 12,000 teenagers who have run away from home for whatever reason and doss down on our streets and in our parks every night. It is a sad state of affairs, an awful indictment on our present society but regrettably a fact of modern life.

Other than trying to find the names of those girls and boys murdered, this investigation is effectively closed. Thank you for all your work.'

The team listened intently and then broke out in spontaneous applause at the end of the speech, clapping their own endeavours as much as their Chief Inspector's.

The magnitude of what his son had achieved and in such a short time was not lost on Charles's father. He asked him back to his office.

'Please be seated, Chief Inspector. I have first to congratulate you on the solving of this horrendous and gruesome crime. But I can see from your demeanour and detect in the sound of your voice that you are still downhearted and in low spirits. Why is that?'

'I don't know why, sir. I feel the same sense of emptiness as when I was told the perpetrators were dead. There is a sense of injustice which weighs heavily on my mind. As with the first girl found, we still do not know her name or what she went through before her death. The same with the other boys and girls. A horrendous crime solved maybe, but it leaves me cold with a sinking feeling and relief at the same time.

'The other nagging factor is that this is still going on in one form or another. There are gangs of men out there who are grooming and sexually exploiting young children and teenagers. But, worst of all, is the thought that in this particular case the boys and girls were deliberately brought to the warehouse alive to be killed there, as and when, to maximise returns from the harvesting of fresh body parts. It's inconceivable that such a thing can happen on our own doorstep here in Cambridge without us knowing about it.'

'Let me talk to you as a father to a son. I have a lot more years in this "business" and I can offer up some advice which might help you cope in these situations. Life delivers knock-backs and traumas to every one of us, particularly in this profession. It is our choice whether we let our down-times define us or help us to grow wiser and stronger. Bad times do not have to become a blueprint for life. We owe it to ourselves to learn and heal from the rough times and move on to pastures new.

'Policemen are human beings like everyone else facing situations they could never imagine when they first sign up. Some cases involving criminal masterminds, career gangsters, drug kings, mega swindlers, terrorists, paedophiles and those like the one you have just dealt with can make you introspective, bordering on depression and even self-pity.

'Pity is corrosive and toxic when not used properly and self-pity is a poisoned palliative for a life less lived. Everything in life is a risk. As a policeman you have to learn to live with these pernicious emotions on a constant basis. Learn to draw a line under it and live your life as you wish it to be lived, not by the cases you are involved with. Police work with society's dross can blacken the purist of hearts.

'There, I have said my piece and I hope it helps.'

'Thank you father. Sound words indeed. I will try to live up to your expectations.

'Good. Now off you go. Remember that your team goes through these same ups and downs as you and look to you as their role model. Always have the welfare of your staff uppermost in your mind at all times.'

'Yes father ... yes sir.'

'Let me just repeat again, congratulations on an excellent piece of detective work by you and your team.

My seniors would also like me to pass on their congratulations for a job well done.'

'Thank you sir, but all the congratulations in the world does not bring back the murdered children, nothing can do that.'

'That is one way of looking at it, Charles. Another way is to think about all the other children you have saved by your timely intervention. This is not a perfect world and never will be. As a policeman you have to put these things into perspective and to look on the positive side of your work. Remember, your work will always come after the crime, it will always be thus being a detective.'

Charles went back to his office to mull over his father's words. He glanced at his in-tray and had that sinking feeling once again. Was he really cut out to be a policeman? At this particular moment he had his doubts.

Christine entered his office. Charles looked up at her enquiringly.

'You look a bit despondent, Sergeant, anything the matter? Anything I can help with?'

Charles assumed it was the case that was making her look glum and chose his words to cheer her up.

'We make a good team, you and I.'

'Yes sir. I always said we would.'

But it wasn't the case that was making Christine sour. It was the fact the she had seen Jane's face on her return to work and knew, as a woman, what had taken place in Kiev.

At that moment, she hated her Chief Inspector, but knew in her heart that it would never stop her loving him any the less. She would bide her time knowing the main enemy of women is other women and Charles could not be blamed for what is natural for a fickle man.

Christine reasoned that love is as destructive a force as it is harmonious and that it can take you on a circuitous route to one's destination. All would be well that ends well, but she needed to up her game. Try just that little bit harder and not let the hare run too far ahead, so to speak.

'I just wanted to congratulate you personally, sir.'

'No need for that, Christine, you did your bit and it was a good team effort.'

'Yes sir.'

Christine left the office. Charles was not the only person with that sinking feeling!

---

A rider to this case was that, several weeks later, the head of the young girl was found in woods just south of Cambridge near the M11 motorway, spotted by a young courting couple. From teeth and DNA evidence she was identified as Emma Thompson from Sheffield.

Charles and Christine attended her funeral at the crematorium in their official police capacity. They felt that saying "sorry" to her father was not a big enough word in such a crime as this, but what else could they say to alleviate the pain of losing his only daughter in such a manner.

Mr Claymore, the surgeon who carried out the body harvesting, was deemed fit to stand trial and was sentenced to life imprisonment, not to be released for a minimum of thirty-five years.

Simon Arthur Dolan, the undertaker's son, was sentenced to twenty years imprisonment.

Thomas Watching, the manager of the Farndale Business Centre was sacked from his job.

The waitress in the café, having seen the headline in the national press regarding the murders, spoke to the police who arrested Paul and his accomplices. Emma's DNA was matched with that found in the flat. Paul, real name Darius Dalca, was sentenced to fifteen years in prison for procuring boys and girls for organ harvesting.

To date, the number and names of some of the young persons murdered remains unknown.

Rob Roy is the third and final case in the series - follow the chief inspector and his team as they try to solve the mystery surrounding a vagrant tramping the streets of Cambridge...

Cambridgeshire Police
Crime Investigation Unit


# Case 3: Rob Roy

# One

'Aha! The Good Lord has sent us an angel in tramp's clothing. Is there austerity in heaven as well as on earth? Has the Good Lord finally given up on you, my friend?'

'Very droll, very funny, I think not.'

'By the way, if you don't mind me asking, don't you have the courtesy to knock any more, just come barging in as and when you like, as if you owned the place.'

'Don't be so bloody stupid, this isn't a proper office, just a derelict room in a derelict church ready for demolition soon. It may have been God's house once but its current occupants are not here on the Sabbath seeking redemption for their sins or concerned with salvation, the soul and the hereafter.'

'I don't care what it is. I have to enforce discipline of one kind or another or it's not going to happen. Now, go outside, knock on the door and wait until I call.'

'Bugger off!'

'Whoa there tiger! The book worm has morphed into a forest cat! What would your students have said if you'd spoken to them like that? The spell in the gutter has clearly broadened your colourful vocabulary.'

'I've had enough of this silly nonsense. I can't go through with it. It's nothing more than mass anarchy which could lead to the numerous deaths of innocent people. I don't want it on my conscience. I no longer want to be a part of it.'

'What do you mean you can't go through with it? You silly sod, you prat, you're up to your neck in it and you can't chicken out at this point of the operation, not when we're so close to attaining our goals.'

'Your goals and yours alone, they're not my goals. I don't want anything to do with it, not any more. It's fucking ridiculous.'

'Listen, calm yourself, take a seat, I'll pour you a drink of the hard stuff.'

'I don't want a drink. I gave that up months ago.'

'Go on, another small drink isn't going to harm you.'

'I said no and I mean it. I'm not going there again.'

'As you wish my friend. Let it not be said that I was the one to lead you down the path to hell again. Now take a seat or I'll forcibly have you pinned to it. You get my meaning?' The atmosphere in the room blackened immeasurably.

'You've changed, Robbie, you're not the same man you were.'

'We've all changed, including you. Life changes, we change with it or perish. I never had you down as a coward.'

'I'm not but my life has changed for the better. I've met a girl.'

'You've met a girl. Well, there you go. You've met a girl so all our two years of meticulous planning is all for nothing. We abandon everything, all the hard work that everyone has put in; all the money that has been raised; all the clandestine meetings of which you were a part. All abandoned, and for what? - because you have a new girl in your life.

'Take a look at yourself, a bloody good look. You are the same pathetic vagrant tramping the streets as you were then. You were penniless, a lush, a discredited member of society, a person who couldn't stop putting his hand up girls' skirts as a so-called professor of linguistics. You were pathetic then when you lost your job at the University and your wife threw you out, and you're pathetic now. Yes, take a good look at yourself; you're a right dork, a right berk, a right Judas.'

'I know and I'm ashamed of myself. How could I ever have let you talk me into something like this? I must have been mad at the time, mad with drink.'

'You were certainly that. But you were a willing partner at the time. I didn't hear too many complaints then when I took you off the streets and gave you a purpose in life, some self-respect after you had lost your job, your house, your kids, your wife – everything, every bloody thing. No one but us was interested in you, in your undoubted talents. We gave you a future.'

'I was grateful at the time.'

'Yes, yes, you were grateful at the time, but not now, not now that you have met a girl. Life has totally changed. Well, let me tell you that life hasn't changed for any of us; it's getting bloody worse – more fucking immigrants taking our jobs, our schools over-flowing with their offspring, our health service paralysed with their numbers, our police service stretched to their limits; more fucking austerity, more fucking rich bankers and more sleazy politicians. Nothing has changed. Nothing has bloody well changed. Get that into your thick head. We're an island sinking with the ever-increasing burden of too many people.'

'It is still mass murder. If we kill these people how are we any better than them. I want out. I'll talk to the police.'

'I'm afraid we can't let you do that. You know we can't let you do that. You're a bosom pal, you've done the lion's share, your linguistics skills have been invaluable, but you know we can't let you do that, the whole of Europe is waiting for our signal. I'm sorry but that's the way it has got to be. Nothing can stop us now. Our target is well defined and we won't stop until it is achieved, come hell or high water, police or military. Europe will be set alight and democracy returned to the peoples.

'Those who govern only look after themselves. It's payback time, no more than they deserve.'

'You're mad, I'm leaving whether you like it or not.'

'Afraid not, old chap.'

'Who's going to stop me?'

'We are.'

'Not you, a cripple. The Taliban should have blown your head off instead of just your legs; perhaps your big, black, bug-eyed bodyguard, the drunk and sacked ex-bouncer. You make a right pair. Or maybe you'll set your dog on me. What's it to be?'

'Take one step towards the door and you're a dead man.'

'I'll take that risk. Let's see what the police have to say.'

'That's your individual right but the group's prerogative under rules agreed at the outset, and we shall carry them out.'

'I'm leaving right now.'

'Goodbye my friend. See you in hell sometime since I know I'm not going to heaven.'

'You're not just mad, you're delusional and a curse to humanity.'

'No, you're the delusional one believing you can set the world to rights with academic thought. I'm the realist, the pragmatist, the army taught me that. You don't defuse an Improvised Electronic Device by thought alone; you have to get your hands dirty, to feel God's earth under trembling fingers and to pray to the Almighty that this isn't your last bomb. For many it was and I saw the result - a jigsaw scattering of human bone, flesh and gore that someone had to clean up.

'I was spared for greater things.

'I wanted you to be a part of that but it seems you want to go back to your wasteful ways. You will always be a disgrace to your profession. I, on the other hand, will die a hero, what's more, a people's hero.'

'I've heard enough. I'm off and don't try to stop me.'

'As I said before: goodbye my friend, I can't say it was nice knowing you. Enjoy the dark; it will embrace you for evermore; a suitable shroud for one such as you.'

A signal to the bodyguard was all that was required.

# Two

'Morning Sergeant, have a good weekend?'

'Not too bad sir. I had a few games of tennis with friends. Good for toning up the muscles and that sort of thing. What about you, sir?'

'Nothing special: just a family get-together to celebrate my mother's birthday. You know, we must get together and have a game of tennis sometime, just you and me. What do you think?'

'That would be nice, sir. I can think of nothing better.'

'Don't take your coat off, Sergeant, there's work to be done. We have a house to visit.'

'You're in a good mood this morning, sir, if I may say so.'

'You may say so. It's a sunny spring day, a warm sun in the sky, what's there not to like about life. Feel on top of the world.'

Christine wondered how long this particular mood would endure. But, nevertheless, such high spirits were welcome at any time, particularly first thing on a Monday morning. His mood always affected her mood even if sometimes she pretended it didn't.

'Where's the house, sir?'

'It's a large Victorian house twenty minutes away. We've had a tip-off that the smell from the street is more than that of squatters.'

'Couldn't we just send a constable instead to investigate?'

'We could but I feel like a run-out in the sunshine. Let's go, Sergeant.'

A few minutes later, Charles found himself at the wheel of a patrol car as it sped to an out-lying Cambridge district, some ten miles away from the City centre. For the whole of the journey Charles whistled and hummed his favourite tunes, occasionally bursting into song to Christine's amusement. Christine plugged her ears with her fingers only for Charles to sing that little bit louder in friendly annoyance, a big smile creasing his face.

'Should I contact the back-up team, sir, just in case?'

'Not necessary, Sergeant, let's see what the problem is first.'

Christine was always wary in situations like this. She admired her Chief Inspector for his get-up-and-go attitude but his ebullient, hot-headed approach to some aspects of police work made her nervous. She had every confidence in him and knew he could handle himself in difficult situations but there were times when more caution and self-preservation would not go amiss.

The car stopped outside No.18 Worley Street, a street of detached Victorian houses, up-market, prime real estate in their time but now showing their age, some in need of some tender loving care. Charles drove into the gravel driveway and parked in front of the house. Through the windscreen they both surveyed the property, craning their necks to look up at the upper reaches of the building.

'What do you think, Sergeant, three storeys and an attic?'

'Looks like it. Amazingly large these Victorian buildings close up. I see most of the windows are shuttered to keep out vagrants. Pity, it must have looked good in its prime. I bet a bit of restoration would soon return it to its former glory; no doubt, in these days, being subject to the process of de-gentrification and then demolished for a block of retirement flats.'

'Looks vacant, there's no sign of any activity. You stay in the car. I'll check the front door.'

Charles exited the car, strolling to a large oak door. Turning the door handle he expected it to be locked but, to his surprise, the door swung ajar. A slight push of his shoulder and the door opened wide. He beckoned Christine to come to the door.

Christine joined her Inspector who was busily sniffing the porch entrance like a bloodhound smelling for its quarry. 'You stay here, Sergeant, whilst I investigate.'

'Sure you don't want me to come with you?'

'No, you stay put whilst I'm inside.'

'Yes sir.'

Charles entered the building, still doing his imitation of a bloodhound, extending his right arm backwards with open palm signalling for Christine to stay put until directed otherwise. There was enough light to see into the ground-floor rooms. They all appeared empty with furnishings previously removed. There was a dank, musty smell in these rooms, somewhat unpleasant but typical of rooms not lived in for a while.

There was no carpeting on the stairs, each step creaking as he proceeded up the first flight. Unlike the ground-floor rooms there were signs of life, or at least people having lived there recently. The light switches worked in each room revealing in more detail four un-made single beds, an assortment of tables, dirty rugs covering bare floor-boards, and two electric heaters. A scattering of cutlery, cups and mugs, a pile of empty cartons of food and other waste heaped in one corner of each room – all suggested recent squatters. The foul smell suggested likewise.

'You OK there, Chief inspector?' shouted Christine from the hallway, venturing in a little further from the porch, wanting to be by his side rather than obeying his instructions. Her sixth sense told her that danger lurked behind every closed door.

'I'm fine, Sergeant,' shouted Charles back down to her, leaning over the bannister rail for maximum volume effect.

Charles proceeded up the next flight of creaky stairs. He immediately recognised the strong aroma assailing his nostrils – mature marijuana plants, class-B drugs, very strong, very pungent.

Though this was his first case of "cannabis farming", he had read of many such cases so he knew what to expect as he opened one of the doors. But even he was taken by surprise at the sheer number of plants in three large bedrooms knocked into one, too many to count but must be in the hundreds. The sight of the plants flourishing under specialist growing lamps was unbelievable.

Leaning over the bannister rail again he shouted down to Christine, 'Cannabis, call for back-up, Sergeant.'

'Will do,' was the curt reply.

Having seen enough Charles descended the flights of stairs. Christine framed the porch doorway talking into her mobile.

'There are lots of plants, Sergeant, a veritable "forest", some five feet tall. No sign of human life though. Well, not at the moment that is, but there's evidence of habitation on the second floor. Forensics should have a field day.

His foot had barely touched the bottom step when three men mysteriously appeared from the ground-floor room to his left. Unfazed, Charles studied their faces and physique – East European at a guess and all slightly built. He braced himself for what was to come.

One of the men turned and fled the house, brushing aside Christine as he did so, totally taking her by surprise, almost toppling her over in the process.

'Chase and arrest that man, Sergeant, I'll deal with these two.' Christine, regaining her balance went in hot pursuit.

One of the men was armed with a baseball bat, the other with a crowbar. They advanced menacingly towards Charles who calmly stood his ground. Quite simply they were no match for a Taekwondo and Karate expert on top form. With kicks and punches they were soon disarmed and lay moaning with hurt on the floor within a couple of minutes of starting the fight.

What Charles failed to see, and only caught sight of him in his peripheral vision, was a fourth man armed with a knife standing on the stairs behind him. Charles turned sharply to confront him but it was too late by a split second. He felt a searing pain as the knife entered his left shoulder and stayed there.

Now in an ugly mood and pain, Charles set about this fourth assailant, summoning all his strength to leave him prone on the stairway. Charles could feel his body's energy being sapped as blood poured out of the wound, his knees began to buckle.

As he fell he was conscious of being cradled in Christine's arms breaking his fall, and then the voices of the back-up team as they set about arresting the men.

His last conscious moments were of Christine saying, 'I've got you, Charles, love you.'

# Three

Saint Mary's Hospital, Cambridge
Tuesday, 22<sup>nd</sup> April, 2014, 3.00am

'Where am I? Charles stuttered the words through dried lips and a parched mouth, trying to focus his eyes in the semi-darkness of the ward.

'You're in a private ward in Saint Mary's hospital,' replies the nurse checking his pulse, 'you are just waking up from the anaesthetic, from an operation on your shoulder.'

'What time is it?'

'It's about three in the morning.'

'Can I have a drink?'

The nurse poured a small drop of water into a glass and gently pressed it against Charles's lips. 'Just sips mind you, not too much.'

Charles attempted to move for greater comfort in the bed but the pain in his shoulder was acute, making him wince and lay still.

'Try not to move too much. The surgeon has left a drain in your shoulder which we'll remove tomorrow for you. In the meantime try to get as much rest as you can, you had lost a lot of blood before you came into hospital and the body needs to rest to repair itself.'

The nurse held the glass of water to his lips again, 'Sip it only.'

Charles's mouth was still parched and the water tasted good.

'I need a pee!'

'I have just what you need here,' passing a urinal bottle to Charles, 'I'll leave you to do your thing and be back in a few minutes.'

'Thank you.'

Charles carefully positioned the bottle under the bedclothes and relieved himself to his great satisfaction, wincing once again as his left arm inadvertently moved. The nurse returned and he sheepishly handed the warm bowl to her, filled to the brim.

'Sorry about that, a bit full.'

'No problem. Now try and get some sleep before the morning. I'll be waiting outside should you ring. The button is there on your right.'

'Thank you, nurse.'

'Let me make you a little more comfortable.' The nurse plumped his pillows before leaving the room.

Charles stared into the semi-darkened room, the only light coming through shuttered blinds from the brightly-lit corridor. It was deathly quiet other than for a slight humming noise coming from somewhere, and very quiet muffled whispers between nurses. He closed his eyes but his mind was racing, reprising the previous day's events. Why did ne not see the man behind him sooner? In the scuffle with the other two assailants he had not noticed the third man coming down the stairs or even the creak of the stairs forewarning him.

The man was on the bottom tread when he had lunged downwards with the knife to his back. He had turned to confront him but had felt the knife penetrate his shoulder instead. He knew he was lucky to be alive. Why hadn't he listened to Christine and called for back-up sooner? She was right about expecting the unexpected in all police situations. It was a lesson he would have to learn all over again.

As he berated himself his eyelids grew heavier. He fought the tiredness and bleary-eyes for a few moments until sleep over-powered his thoughts and rested his tired body.

~

'How are you this morning?

'My name is Arthur Rathbone, the hospital surgeon. You came into A&E yesterday morning with a knife firmly embedded in your left shoulder. You had lost a considerable amount of blood. We operated on you immediately to remove the knife and to stitch-up the wound.

'You're a lucky man, Chief Inspector. If the blade had been a little further to the right it was deep enough to have penetrated the heart and that would have been a different story. As it is, the wound is serious but not life-threatening and you'll be on your feet in a day or two.

'Mind you, the shoulder will be painful for a while and rather stiff, but with the right physiotherapy and rest you ought to recover all your arm movements over the next six months.

'The main problem was that the rotator cuff, the group of four muscles and tendons that surround and stabilise the shoulder joint was partially severed. We've stitched it up as best we can but it will take time for it to heal. Expect a healing period of some six weeks. In the meantime take it easy. I'm told you are right-handed so it shouldn't be too much of an inconvenience to your police work.

'Have you any questions?'

Charles shook his head. Having just woken up he felt groggy and couldn't think of anything to ask at that point in time.

'Good, then I'll be off to visit my other patients. I'm certain your police doctor will advise you further. I'll ask the nurse to remove the drain from your arm later today or tomorrow; that will make you a little more comfortable.'

As the surgeon was leaving the room, Charles overheard his conversation with the nurse, 'Take good care of him, I've never operated on a Taekwondo Olympic champion before, the lucky beggar came close to losing his life but should make a complete recovery. His sporting days however may be over with a shoulder injury as bad as that.'

Such a comment both raised Charles's spirit, not to mention his ego, and left him deflated at the prospect of not participating in his beloved sport. He was determined that that would never happen.

His thoughts then turned to the admonishment of his father, which would surely come as day follows night, once he was back in the office. He'd been warned often enough by his father of going it alone and now his father would have been proved right. Ah well, he thought, in this case he must take it on the chin and accept he was in the wrong.

He looked forward to breakfast being served though – he was famished.

~

Come the visiting hours there was no reproach from his father. Both parents were naturally sympathetic, simply overjoyed that the injury was not any more serious than it was. They had spoken to the operating surgeon who had assured them that the drain would be removed the following day, the wound re-dressed and the patient allowed to get back on his feet for a wash and a shave. He suggested Charles stay another night in the hospital and, if all was well, he could go home the next day, that day being Thursday.

'We will pick you up on Thursday at 10 o'clock,' remarked his father, 'and then we insist you stay at the family home for the next two weeks. I will hear no complaint. You will do as you're told this time. Your mother will take care of all your needs as you build up your strength.'

There was no point in Charles saying otherwise. He was not in much of a position to argue anyway.

'We have arranged for the physiotherapist to visit you each day to get your arm moving again. It will take time but we are told you should regain your arm movements in full.'

Charles nodded affirmatively to his father's diktat, his arm stiff and painful to the slightest movement.

'Patience, that's what's needed.'

Charles nodded again.

The rest of the visiting time was spent in family banter until Christine appeared carrying a bunch of flowers. His parents acknowledged Christine's presence and then made their leave, his father warmly shaking his son's hand, his mother kissing him on the cheek.

Christine sat next to Charles on his right hand side, placing the flowers on the bedside cabinet – for them to be immediately scooped up by the nurse.

'Flowers are not allowed in the wards,' said the nurse quite sternly, giving Christine one of those "you-should-know-better" stares. 'But they're very pretty and smell delightful,' burying her nose in the bouquet of flowers. 'I'll leave them in reception and you can pick them up on the way out.'

Christine looked apologetically at Charles, a slight flush of embarrassment on her cheeks. Charles looked at Christine. They both laughed nervously after the nurse had left. 'Naughty woman, assume you have been suitably ticked off,' said Charles to Christine, wagging his finger at her and turning his head away to hide his smile-cum-grin.

Regaining some decorum, 'How are you, Charles?' asked Christine, handing him a "Get Well" card from the team and another one from herself. Charles was touched as he read all the kind messages and his eyes glazed over with emotion. Even more so as he read Christine's poignant message from the heart.

'Thank you, Christine,' leaning over to give her a peck on the cheek but then jerking back with pain from his shoulder. Christine winced in unison, his pain was her pain.

There was no reproach from Christine either and little discussion of police work except to tell him that the four men were Albanian, illegal immigrants, and all had been arrested and charged. The three men in the downstairs room had been hiding behind a moveable room partition which had served as a secret hideaway from visitors who would assume the room was empty. The fourth man, who had jumped Charles from the stairway, had hidden in the attic, the one place Charles had not looked. He had taken off his shoes and crept down the stairs in his socks making little noise; he was being charged with attempted murder.

There were a total of 1200 cannabis plants being farmed with mature plants, some five feet tall, ready to harvest, bound for the streets. The dope factory was using enough electricity to power three streets of houses. But the "cannabis farmers" had bypassed the meter to hide the operation. It was a sophisticated operation, all four men insisting they were being held against their will, all refused to name the person or persons in charge.

Charles listened attentively to Christine who was now dewy-eyed, her professional veneer hiding her innermost feelings. Charles patted Christine's hand. 'Thank you, Christine, for all your help. I owe you one.'

'You don't owe me anything, Charles. I'm just glad the outcome wasn't worse for you. That would have been awful.' Christine gulped as her emotions rose in her throat.

'Now don't think like that, Christine.' Charles affectionately patted her hand again seeing that Christine was deeply upset and about to burst into tears, holding back for his benefit.

It was another twenty minutes before Christine took her leave, waving goodbye as she left the room. She'd been in two minds to give him a kiss on the lips but had thought it an inappropriate time to show her true feelings for her Chief Inspector. Out of his sight though, she let her tears flow freely. It could have been so much worse for him; for her life, too, coming to an untimely end. She loved him so much she couldn't think of life without him, a life without colour, without meaning was no life at all without Charles by her side. She had fallen in love with him at first sight. It was as simple as that.

~

Two weeks at his parents' home was more than enough for Charles. Daily the physiotherapist had re-dressed the wound and exercised the arm, bringing back movement to an otherwise stiff arm and neck; painful, boring, but all for the best.

No, it was not the physiotherapy that had bored him silly; it was the constant reasoning by his mother, Anthea, who clearly perceived that this was her opportunity to persuade her son to leave the police force and to take up a less dangerous profession. All said in a nice way, of course, but grindingly obvious as to her intentions. The City, the theatre, she could name a dozen occupations which did not involve criminals, well, at least not the thuggish kind of criminal he was used to. He had only to say the word and she would open many doors for him.

Her enthusiasm for a change in her son's career, at this point of time, was understandable. One of her plays for the small screen was to be adopted for a West End theatre. She was bubbling over with excitement at the prospect of talking to the producer and director regarding the casting and stage sets. She could see an entry point for Charles in her own world, if only he would grasp it with both hands.

Charles had given careful consideration to what his mother had said, to reflect on other careers as well as the theatre. But, however tempting, his heart was to follow in his father's footsteps. The more cogent his mother's reasoning and persuasive her arguments, the more convinced he was doing the right thing.

So, two weeks into his recuperation, Charles found himself sitting at his desk, staring at his empty in-tray, his arm in a temporary sling. It was good to be back, or was it? Perhaps his mother was right all along. No more self-doubts as a tap on the office door signalled the entry of Christine.

'Good morning, sir, I wasn't expecting you back so soon.'

'I couldn't stay away one minute more from your bright, beaming face first thing on a morning, Sergeant.'

'One minute, sir,' Christine held up a finger to indicate a temporary halt to the conversation as she left the office.

Charles was amused wondering what was going to happen next. He did not have to wait long as Christine ushered in all of his team to his office. They assembled around his desk spontaneously clapping their Chief, caterwauling, 'Inspector Tae, three cheers for Inspector Tae.'

'It's their way of showing their appreciation of what you did in the migrants' case, sir,' shouted Christine above the noise, joining in the clapping herself.

'That's enough, that's enough,' cried Charles, holding up his right hand, slightly embarrassed but, at the same time, moved by the depth of feeling and generosity within his team.

'That's enough, thank you all, now back to your desks, there's work to be done.' They all trooped out of his office wishing him well. Christine stayed behind.

'Thank you, Sergeant. If I ever had doubts about my police work you have put me straight.'

'I'm not sure how to interpret that, sir.'

'In a nice way, Sergeant, meant in a nice way.'

Christine was delighted to see her Chief back in the office, fully expecting him to be away for a much longer period of time than two weeks.

'Are you still staying with your parents, sir?'

'No, I'm back in my flat.   I took a taxi here. Everything OK with you, Sergeant?'

'Yes sir, everything's fine but we missed you.'

'Good, then perhaps when you get a few minutes you can bring me up to date with what's been happening.'

'I can do that but first the Chief Constable would like to see you in his office.'

'Right, I'm ready.   Let me just thank you once again for what you did, Sergeant, much appreciated.'

'As you would say, sir, it was all in a day's work.'

'It was more than that, Sergeant, and you know it.'

'The Chief Constable is waiting, sir.'

'Right, I'm on my way.'

Christine left the office as Charles prepared himself for his father's admonishment.  Being at home was one thing, in the office was another, rules were rules and the penalty for flouting them had no respect for rank in the police force, as emphasised time and time again by his father.

As he knocked on his father's door Charles braced himself for his dressing-down.

'Enter.

'Take a seat, Chief Inspector.'

His father was signing invoices, not even bothering to raise his head to acknowledge the presence of his son; for several more minutes he continued signing, leaving his son to fidget uncomfortably in the air of silence.  He studied the last invoice, perusing through its details for an inordinate amount of time.  Finally he put his pen down.  He stared at his son with a fierce look, tempered only by seeing the sling, a look that even as a child Charles knew when to stay silent.

'What the hell were you doing going into that building alone? The raised, rasping tone made Charles jump slightly, an involuntary reaction harking back to his childhood days when the letter of the law was read out to him for his misdemeanours; and loud enough for everyone in the police station to hear!

Charles was about to answer when his father's raised finger signalled to him to remain silent for longer, fixing his son with a judicial stare.

'What on earth were you thinking? You not only jeopardised your own life but that of your Sergeant. What do we teach our young constables? I'll tell you what we teach them. Discretion over valour – that's what we teach them. Do you think your rank makes you somehow different? Or that simple rule no longer applies to you because of your undoubted wisdom and experience?

'You came within an inch of your life, literally. Another inch or two the wrong way and you were a dead-man, and what is more, a dead son of mine. If the men had succeeded they could well have set about your Sergeant and left her for dead, too. Where was your professionalism? You're a fool, a bloody hot-headed fool. What are you?' The tone of delivery was now emotional accompanied by a withering look.

His father paused to gather himself, sitting back in his chair, garnering his thoughts, undecided whether to temper his tirade. His finger told Charles not to say a word.

'When am I ever going to get through to you?' said in a quieter tone this time, taking the heat out of the initial outburst, his heckles lowered for the moment to normal levels..

'If I've said this once to you, I've said it a thousand times. You have an appetite for risk-taking and your hot-headedness not only endangers your own life but that of your colleagues. It has got to stop, I tell you. Your shenanigans have got to stop.

'Your colleagues admire you because you take a lead in everything you do and are prepared to put your own life on the line before others. I find that commendable and must praise you for that.

'But you are giving me and your mother nightmares and this latest incident confirms our worst fears. As your police senior it is my formal duty to give you a warning. As my son I beg you to heed my advice, to take a more cautious line in the future otherwise you'll put me in an early grave.

'There, I've said my piece, now what do you have to say?'

In his heart of hearts his father knew his son only too well to know that anything he said was like water off a duck's back, the words went in one ear and out of the other. But this was a big scare for him and his words said were more for his own benefit than that of his son's. His son was a born leader of men and it was always in his nature to lead a charge; it had always been a question as to whether his son would survive to old age in his police career and enjoy its benefits just as he had.

'Well, speak up! What have you to say for yourself?' A question posed as if to an errant son rather to a Chief Inspector. But the question was asked in an almost apologetic manner as his fatherly feelings now outweighed his police officer's duties.

Charles felt suitably chastened as he listened to his father but all the time he had been berating himself for not having seen the fourth man sooner. He really must improve his reaction time to unforeseen events, just as in his sporting days; that was now his new mantra in life.

'I was wrong. Sergeant Moran suggested we get back-up earlier but I thought otherwise, preferring to see the lay of the land, the nub of the matter, so to speak, before calling them out. It was a sunny morning and I was feeling good in myself, I felt I could conquer the world. In retrospect ...'

'... In retrospect you could have lost your life and that of your Sergeant's. Not the wisest of moves on your part, don't you agree?' His father just couldn't stop himself from interrupting his son, not liking what he was hearing.

'Yes sir, in retrospect.'

'The back-up team are there to assist you in situations like this. That is their job. Whether it had come to nought was no skin off their teeth. You get my drift? It is always best to err on the side of caution. Remember it for the next time or one day there won't be a next time.'

His father, as father's do, felt he had said enough, and seeing his son wince as he moved his arm in the sling only brought about a total softening of the heart, from the initial anger at the possibility of losing his son to a father's love for an only son. Without wishing to hear any crass, puerile explanations from his son, he decided to bring their conversation to an end.

'I've said all I have to say. I'm due back at Headquarters soon and I've left you an empty in-tray. Clearly you need time to regain your strength and for the arm to heal, so I've distributed the crime files to others. Instead you will be given some administrative work to be getting on with. It will tie you to your desk for a while and for now I see that as a good thing, it will keep you out of harm's way.

'I suggest you continue your training at the College as and when you see fit, a respite from your desk now and then, so to speak. Yes, I know I am all heart.' His father allowed a smile to cross his lips at his son's reaction to his desk-bound duties.

'Oh, and by the way, I have asked your Sergeant to give you a lift to and from your flat, since you insist on staying there rather than with us, as well as on all police business.'

'I can take a taxi.'

'Too much expense. We have to cut down on all police expenses.'

'I can pay from my own pocket.'

'Won't hear of it.'

'Surely not in the Sergeant's old, rickety Ford Fiesta.'

'No, no. Since I wouldn't expect you to allow her to drive your Porsche I have authorised the use of an unmarked police car.'

'But …'

'There's no more to be said. I will hear no argument. The sooner your arm is better the sooner you can drive yourself. Understood?'

'Yes sir.' Charles knew he was on a losing wicket and the less said the better. He knew not to try and humour his father when in his business mood and uniform.

'Right, then, I'll leave you with the station's budget file, forecasts, invoices, payments and ledgers. Check the spreadsheets are all up to date and audit the invoices well; we need to reduce the station's overall expenses. Your right hand is working perfectly OK I believe so I expect to see everything shipshape when I return in a week or two.'

Charles's face dropped. His father noticed his son's reaction knowing full well he hated admin work of any kind but this was the only way he knew of tying him to his desk whilst his arm healed. It was for the better, the end justified the means.

As Charles was leaving with a bundle of files under his arm a wry smile crossed his father's face, 'By the way, Chief Inspector, that was a hell of a bust with the Albanians, it made a big splash in all the local and national newspapers, brings credit to the police force and to this station in particular. Well done.' With that compliment he gave his son a pat on the back, forgetting for a second that the arm was in a sling.

Almost a glimmer of a smile appeared on Charles's face mixed with a grimace from the pat on the back. He returned to his office cursing his wretched luck with the Albanian who had jumped him, he swore to himself that it would never happen again. He needed to be that much fitter and that much more alert, improvements, he hoped, which would result from extra stints in the gym. But, above all, he must keep his wits about him in the future and to expect the unexpected, just as he did in his Taekwondo bouts.

Christine tapped on his door, entered, and seeing Charles in a gloomy mood, sat on the chair opposite his desk. Her heart went out to him, as it did at the hospital, but this time with greater composure.

'Are you good at accountancy, Sergeant?'

'No sir, but I know who is.'

'Who's that?'

'WPC Wetherspool, sir.' With Kiev still uppermost in her mind that was Christine being more than just catty.

'Good, I've got a number of jobs for her.'

'What time would you like me to pick you up from your flat, sir?'

'Say 8.30 in the morning and leave here about 6.00. Is that OK with you?'

'Yes sir, no problem.'

Christine left the office, a big smile creasing her face. The thought of escorting her man to and from work was a dream come true; the thought of WPC Wetherspool slaving away over figures was an added bonus.

# Four

Hendon Training College, Cambridge
Thursday, 15<sup>th</sup> May, 2014, 9.30am

At the first opportunity Charles requested Christine to drive him to the Hendon Training College.

Desk work drove him barmy; it robbed him of all reason to get out of bed first thing of a morning; it was soulless work and drained life of its free spirit. He was such a free spirit and intended to stay that way; being tied to a desk was not his thing, certainly not at this point of his career, perhaps sometime in the distant future, but not now. His father meant well but Charles needed to get up and about.

Christine drove the car through the wrought-iron gates of the College and up to the main building, Charles pointing out his reserved parking space with its blue plaque and Olympic logo. If ever he needed a boost to his ego and confidence the mere sight of the plaque did it for him, time and time again without fail. He could feel his quickening heartbeat, his face wreathed in a permanent smile, his blood warming to the challenges ahead.

For Christine, too, it brought back memories, nice memories of her training at the College before transferring to the Met in London, and of seeing her training instructor, Charles, for the very first time. She had admired him then but had never dreamed she would, one day, be this close to him.

'I suggest, Sergeant, you have a coffee in the refectory if you wish, then drive back and pick me up later,' glancing at his watch, 'say, in two hours, make it midday.'

'Yes sir. I'll go for a coffee first. It takes me back a few years being here.'

'Yes, of course, I was forgetting, you did your police training here.'

They both stepped out of the car and were greeted by Police Sergeant David Blake, the chief training instructor. From his office he could view the cars entering the grounds and on seeing Charles rushed to greet him, as always, with a cordial invite.

'Nice to see you again, Charles.'

'You too, David. Have you met my new Sergeant, Detective Sergeant Christine Moran?'

'Pleased to meet you, Sergeant Moran.'

'Me likewise, sir. We met once when I was a young cadet here, a few years ago now.'

'I can't say I recognise your face, we get so many recruits here every year. But nice to see you all the same.'

'Thank you, sir.'

Christine headed to the refectory as David pulled Charles to one side.

'Could we go to my office for a few minutes, I have something to tell you.'

The speed with which the smile left David's face, to be replaced by a sad, mournful look, told Charles all was not well with his friend. With his hand on Charles's back, propelling him forward with uncanny haste, it was clear to Charles that this was a man in a rush to get something off his chest.

Once in the office, David slumped languidly into his chair. 'Take a seat Charles, please.' He then blurted out -

as though offensive words were burning his mouth and the sooner they were spit out the better - 'Anna and I have split up, we've separated.'

David looked at Charles's face, scrutinising it for feedback, not sure quite what to expect but clearly hoping for some kind of sympathetic acknowledgement, not a harsh judgement from a close friend.

Charles's face was impassive, his brain trying to take in the awfulness, the finality, of that curt statement; a few words which rendered Charles speechless. What eventually came out of his mouth was an equally bland statement, 'I'm sorry to hear about that, David, really very sorry.'

Charles was upset by the suddenness of it all, his immediate thoughts being for Anna, David's wife. But not entirely surprised. Knowing David as he did, he had suspected all along that Anna's double mastectomy would take its toll on David's affection for her.

Although never openly discussed between friends, Charles had believed it more than likely that David had always been repulsed by imperfection in people, the body's imperfection in particular. He was a stickler for pointing out the failings and shortcomings in the recruits and to some degree that was to their advantage if, in Charles's opinion, he took it too far at times. As for the opposite sex: Anna was beautiful when she and David had first met, representing his idealised image of womanhood. Anna's disfigurement and reconstruction would have been difficult for David to accept, even if he gave the impression initially to the contrary. Charles knew David had a fetish for purity in all its forms.

'Do you think you'll get together again, sometime in the future perhaps?' questioned Charles, not wishing to probe too deeply and to delve too much into the reasons for the separation.

'I don't think so, it's over between us,' answered David without thinking twice. Then, after a few moment's pensive thought: 'I think it's for the better.'

'Where's Anna now?'

'She's living in the family house; I'm sharing a flat with a friend – a girlfriend if you would like to know. The house is up for sale.'

It was all said as a matter of fact, years of marriage reduced to a cold, emotionless summary of a few words.

Charles did not wish to hear any more from his friend. What with his younger sister, Faye, Peter Ruskin, and now David Blake, it was all too much in his current state of mind. He abruptly changed the subject from separation and divorce.

'I'm here today to improve my fitness - if you could leave me to my own devices.'

'Yes, of course. How's your arm? I heard about what happened.'

'Getting better, the sling is a temporary measure whilst the wound is healing.'

'Well, take it easy.'

'Will do.'

Charles wanted to quickly absent himself from his present company and the ever increasing stifling atmosphere, to fill his lungs and mind with fresh air from a long run.

'Look me up when you're ready to leave the College.'

'I'll do just that.'

Charles spent the next two hours exhausting his body with a long run followed by leg exercises in the gym. It helped to cleanse his mind from his negative, nagging thoughts of romance, marriage and divorce. Not a path he was keen to follow himself, not now, not ever.

Having showered he looked into David's office. Seeing David still in a depressed state of mind, he made his excuses not to linger.

'See you again, David.'

'See you, Charles, still friends I hope?'

'Still friends, David.'

Christine was waiting as agreed, standing patiently by the patrol car with a smile on her face.

'Good workout, sir?'

'Very good, must do it again soon,' answered in a resigned sort of way which made the smile on Christine's face promptly disappear.

As Christine drove back to the police station she was puzzled at her Chief's pensive mood. She refrained from asking him any further questions fearing he would snap back at her no matter what she said.

He was still in the same mood as she drove him that same evening to his flat. Not so much a pensive mood now but a grouchy one, tense and prickly, ranting on about marriage and relationships and anything else which had stuck in his gullet over the last few years, anything and anyone.

'We're here, sir.'

'Thank you, Sergeant, would you like to come in for a coffee?'

This was the first time Charles had invited Christine back to his flat. Christine thought it wise not to in his current mood but, seeing him swing into a more depressive phase again, reluctantly agreed, 'Thank you, sir, just a quick one.'

'Call me Charles. We're not in office hours now.'

They both stepped out of the parked car, Charles leading Christine to the entrance lobby, pressing the button for the lift. Christine remained silent. The lift was of the old-fashioned type with heavy metal gates which Charles clanged open and then shut. They exited on the third floor, Charles taking out his key to unlock the door to his flat. Christine entered his abode for the very first time. She usually just dropped him off to drive a further fifteen minutes to her place so this was a seminal moment for her, a moment of nervous expectation.

Charles turned on the lights and, without saying a word, headed straight for the kitchen leaving Christine wandering in the lounge.

Christine looked around. It was a spacious flat, very "brownie", very masculine with darkish, chunky furniture, cushions casually thrown here and there. It was not to her taste. But there were some nice paintings on the walls, even an early Salvador Dali sketch which she thought must be worth a few bob; various figurines and objet d'art littered the place with no sense of placement or presentation. She could do a lot to this flat with a deft woman's touch she mused as Charles busied himself in the kitchen to make the coffee. Knowing how fastidious he was with his clothes she had expected the same in his flat but that did not seem to be the case with newspapers and magazines strewn haphazardly.

Christine wandered into the kitchen to find Charles still fiddling with the coffee machine. She could not help noticing a heap of cartons from takeaways around the waste bin, some still containing left-over food, not a pleasant sight or smell.

'Charles. Why don't you go into the lounge and pour yourself a stiff drink to drown your sorrows whatever they may be. I'll make the coffee.'

'Would you like a Chinese takeaway, Christine?'

'No thanks, Charles. Look, you go into the lounge and I'll make you something to eat instead.'

As Charles left the kitchen Christine checked the cupboards. They were full of food, she presumed bought by his mother to ensure her son did not starve himself to death in returning to his flat. She made two coffees and then set about making the meal – a spaghetti Bolognese would be quick and nourishing. She had a girls' night out with friends that evening so wanted to leave early.

Having set the table for one; cleared away the cartons to make the kitchen a little tidier; washed-up a few items of crockery; she placed the dish on the table shouting, 'Dinner, Charles, your dinner is ready.'

Charles entered the kitchen, lurching towards her, more for comfort than with alcohol in his veins. He pulled her towards him in a roughish manner, bending his head down to kiss her.

Christine, at the last second before their lips could meet, placed her finger between their lips. 'No hanky-panky, Chief Inspector, remember?'

'Quite right, Christine, but you shouldn't be so beautiful.'

Now she knew it was definitely the drink that was talking.

'Charles, I want to be kissed by you but in love not lust.'

'What does it matter these days, Christine. Love, lust, romance, marriage, divorce, nothing really matters these days it seems.'

Christine had a hint now of what was upsetting him.

'Love and marriage is for fools. Don't get married, Christine, it's not worth it.'

'It is, Charles, some couples stay together all their married lives. Take, for example, my parents and your parents. Not everyone breaks up and sometimes there are good reasons, not necessarily infidelity.

'I have seen several very difficult marriages endure through decades of problems, for the couple involved to find solace in their old age. Surviving their very difficult years they have forged a bond which has sustained them through their later years. Romantic love cannot last for ever but companionship can.

'We would not want to go back in time when women were trapped in marriage but nowadays couples seem to divorce on nothing more than a whim.

'In the first flush of love there is a feeling that anything and everything is possible. We have to learn to lower our expectations.'

Christine surprised herself with her unexpected outburst on love and marriage, thoughts and emotions that had been brooding inside of her for a very long time, waiting for the moment, the person, to say it to in a heartfelt way.

Charles responded, deliberately enunciating his words: 'for better, for worse; in sickness and in health; for richer, for poorer; to love and to cherish till death us do part. What happened to these vows, Christine?'

'At times I don't know, Charles, many of my friends are divorced, with one partner walking out for no other reason than the going got tough.'

'Some marriages are made in Heaven; some are the Devil's play. But how do we know, Christine, who's pulling the strings when we get married – God or the Devil?'

'We don't know, Charles. But we have to believe that God walks down the aisle with us.'

'That is very philosophical, Christine. I like that,' words now increasingly slurred.

'Now I suggest you eat your meal before it gets cold, have an early night and I'll see you first thing in the morning. I'll see myself out.'

'You're the best type of woman a man could wish for, Christine, and very beautiful with it.'

'I know, Charles, now see you in the morning.'

Christine closed the door behind her and headed for the lift. She smiled to herself. She was not averse to a bit of lust herself but preferably when both parties wanted it, not when one party wanted to drown their sorrows in it.

But she loved Charles even if he was too blind at times to see it. His physical desire for her gave her an idea though. She smiled again to herself as she thought of what could be in store for him, but she must time it right. If planned correctly he would know the true meaning of the word "lust".

# Five

Parkside Police Station, Cambridge
Friday, 16<sup>th</sup> May, 2014, 8.30am

Christine picked up Charles the next morning at the usual time.

'Sergeant, I'm sorry about what happened last night. I...'

'No problems, Chief Inspector. Nothing happened and I've already forgotten about it. Just remember in the future that "no hanky-panky" applies to the both of us.'

'I will, Sergeant, I promise.'

'Good.' Christine smiled inwardly seeing her Chief Inspector so sheepish-looking but wanted to hug him all the same as with a little boy lost in his emotions.

In the office Charles looked at his burgeoning in-tray of the admin completed by Jane. She's one hell of a proficient assistant, thought Charles to himself, a woman of many talents and he was lucky to have her in his team. He grabbed the invoice file just as Christine entered the room.

'We have just had a call through of a suicide in a Methodist Church – a vagrant by all accounts.'

'Good. I mean let's get to it, Sergeant.'

Christine drove the patrol car to the gate of the Church. Clive from Forensics was waiting for them inside the police cordon.

'Pleased to meet you again, Chief inspector, Sergeant,' shaking them both vigorously by the hand. 'Come this way, we haven't cut him down yet, thought you might like to see him first.'

Clive led them through the Church gate to the main Church door, then down a long aisle to another door on the right leading to a small underground chapel.

'Take care, Chief Inspector, Sergeant, there's just one flight of stone steps but they are steep and damp. The electricity to the Church was switched on for the viewing but the bulb in the chapel has been broken. It's very dark down there with no outside windows.

'We'll be setting up lights soon but I thought you might like to see the place first. Take these torches, you will need them.

'Now, watch your step. There's a hand-rail to your right.'

Charles turned to Christine, 'I'll go first - you follow, and take the steps slowly. I'll break your fall,' said amusingly but with sincerity.

'I'm OK, sir. Thank you, sir.'

All three descended the steps into a black hole with the beams of their torches illuminating the sides of the narrow, steep passage. The air was thick with damp and mould, almost choking to the throat. Christine coughed unexpectedly, the noise vibrating off the walls.

'You OK, Sergeant?' asked Charles.

'I'm OK, sir, thank you.'

'If it's too much, you can go back.'

'Really, I'm OK, sir, please don't worry about me.'

Having descended the steps, all three torch beams focused on the corpse hanging by its neck from a horizontal, wooden beam. Being in a chapel the body was given a surreal, religious significance; the dancing beams of light playing on the corpse only adding to the macabre spectacle; even more so as Christine's torch picked out a small cross on the wall behind the still corpse.

Clive spoke first:

'At a guess I would say the man had climbed onto the chair and then hung himself by means of his scarf tied to the beam, kicking over the chair. The beam probably had, at one time, a larger cross or figure of the Crucifixion.'

'I suppose if you're going to kill yourself it's as good a place to do it,' said Charles, moving closer to the body, shining his torch on a wretched face, its eyes bulging, mouth open but twisted and distorted. Not a pretty sight. Both Charles and Christine took a deep intake of breath. Clive in his typically unperturbed manner showed no outward signs of disgust, though even he was affected a little by the surroundings to this suicide being a religious man himself.

Further inspection by Charles showed the figure to be dressed in old, tatty clothes with holes in the shoes.

'How long?' asked Charles.

'At a guess: twenty-four hours at the most. Will give you a more exact time when we have the body back in the lab. OK if we now set up the lights and take him down?'

'Be my guest.'

Having seen enough, all three clambered back up the steps with Christine leading the way followed by Charles and then Clive. Clive set about giving instructions to the forensics team whilst Charles and Christine looked around the dilapidated Church.

The Church was one big space, empty of pews or of any other furniture or ornaments save for an altar. There were signs, here and there, of vagrants having used the building to doss down for the night – cigarette butts, beer bottles, food cartons and other miscellaneous litter including the odd syringe and needle and foil indicating drug use; in one corner what looked and smelled like human urine and faeces.

'I'm told,' said Clive, joining them again, 'that the Church was up for sale although there is no sale or sold sign outside. I am told it was bought recently by a young couple to convert into a domestic building, the chapel into a wine cellar. It was they, when inspecting the property, who contacted the estate agent, who in turn contacted the police. I wonder whether they will still be interested after what has happened in their wine cellar.'

'It wouldn't be my cup of tea,' replied Charles, still surveying the sorry sight of what used to be a fine Church, his eyes glancing up at the shattered stained-glass windows; a sight both nauseating and religious at the same time.

Charles opened the door to an office, Christine followed.

'Probably a verger's office,' said Christine, holding her nose because of the smell. The office too showed signs of vagrant activity. The light coming through the one window was poor but sufficient to see a table and three chairs, no other furniture being in the room.

Charles closed the door, thanked Clive, and then strolled with Christine down what used to be the aisle towards the front door, glancing back occasionally to see the body being carried out in a black body-bag. 'It's funny,' said Christine, also looking down the aisle to the altar, 'that this still remains consecrated land and will always be so no matter what human beings do to it. I can understand why people buy this sort of property if you are religiously inclined.'

'I understand where you're coming from, but as I said before, it wouldn't be my cup of tea,' replied Charles, trying to lighten Christine's serious and thoughtful expression.

'We are all different, sir.'

'We certainly are, Sergeant.'

On the way back to the station Charles spoke to Christine.

'Do the basics, Sergeant. Get the team to identify the man, his background, his usual haunts including any night houses. Tragic it maybe, but he's just one of many tramping the streets who are friendless, homeless and penniless; too many of them these days. Not the best way to end your life but, there again, what did he have to live for?'

'What priority should I give it, sir?'

'Low, Sergeant, fit it in with the rest of the work. In the meantime, whilst I'm waiting for the forensics report, I'll finish off the admin on my desk.'

'Yes sir.'

'Let's close the last chapter on this unfortunate soul's life.'

'Yes sir.'

~

Within a week the information was to hand, presented to Charles by Christine in a dossier.

Charles flicked through the documents with raised eyebrows.

'Take a seat, Sergeant. It says here he was a professor of linguistics at Cambridge University. Aged forty-two he was expelled for misdemeanours regarding girl students. Following several harassment claims he was asked to leave forthwith. Neither the University nor any of the girls took legal action against him. God, I wonder how many teachers and professors in the land come into this category?

'His wife of twenty years - gosh he married young - threw him out of the house, the house being in her name. She has since remarried. Did anyone interview her?'

'Only briefly, just to establish his name as Andrew Falconer-Smith and to obtain a photograph of him.'

'A double-barrelled named professor, who fell on hard times! I'm surprised he couldn't get employment elsewhere. But, I suppose teaching was his thing, and with a black mark against his name and no letter of recommendation from the University, no other teaching establishment would take the risk. Still, I am surprised he ended up on the streets with his impressive academic credentials.'

'How the mighty fall, sir.'

'In the twinkling of an eye, Sergeant. It's a warning and a lesson for all of us.'

Charles continued to peruse the dossier.

'It seems it wasn't too difficult to find his usual haunts. He was well known on the streets and by various publicans who could recall his shabby appearance as well as his thirst, many a time being ejected from the premises for being drunk and disorderly. Where did he get the money from for all his drinking?

'His life seems to go from bad to worse.

'He was a regular in several night houses, staying over for a meal, a shower and a shave. At least he tried to keep himself clean and free from disease.

'He was known as "The Falcon" by the other dossers and vagrants but that was some time back. He hadn't been seen of late, not for some considerable time, presumed dead by many.'

Charles closed the dossier. 'We'll wait for the forensics report and then close the file on Professor Falconer-Smith.'

'Yes sir. I was thinking, sir.'

'Yes Sergeant?'

'Well, it's such a nice day with the sun shining I thought you might be interested in a game of tennis as a break from your admin work. We could go now if you're up for it.'

'I'm always up for it, Sergeant. It would be good exercise for my arm; it's feeling a bit stiff. If we could stop off at my place I can pick up some tennis shorts. What about you though?'

'My tennis outfit is in my kit bag in the car, just in case you said yes.'

'I'm saying yes alright. Let me first have a word with the desk Sergeant to tell him where we're going and then lead the way, I'm raring to go.'

'Yes sir. Thank you, sir.'

Christine smiled to herself. Her Chief had no idea what he had let himself in for.

~

'Where are we going, Christine, to your tennis club?'

'Not this time, Charles, we're heading to a friend's house. She has loaned us her house and gardens whilst on holiday. Set in about two acres of land it has two tennis courts – one hard, one grass – with a swimming pool, a Jacuzzi and a hot tub. The tennis courts are beautiful to play on. She used to play tennis professionally until struck by a knee injury. Pity about that, she could have made a real name for herself in the tennis world, as it is she teaches others these days.

'It's not far, about a fifteen minutes-drive into the country, a very secluded place away from prying eyes. She preferred it that way.'

Arriving at the house, Christine unlocked the front door and beckoned Charles to enter.

'There's a changing room there to the left, Charles, if you would like to change I'll go upstairs to the bathroom and change. The tennis courts are a couple of minutes-walk to the back of the house, next to the swimming pool. See you down here in five minutes.'

Charles quickly changed into his tennis shorts and was looking out of the back window from the lounge area to the lawns and flower borders as Christine descended the stairs. Looking under the stairs cupboard and switching on a light, she fished out two tennis rackets with several tubes of tennis balls. She handed the rackets to Charles as she unlocked the back door.

'You come here quite often, Christine?'

'Quite often, we enjoy a game together, good for keeping the weight off as well as for picking up a few tips.'

'I'll follow you. By the way, you look very fetching in your tennis kit – all white suits you.'

'Thank you, Charles, and you cut a dashing figure in your white shorts and red shirt, too.'

They both laughed out loud at each other's praises as they walked through the grounds to the tennis courts, Christine in a somewhat abashed manner knowing full well the game she was about to play on Charles.

Entering the hard tennis court, Charles removed the sling from his arm and began to exercise the serving arm, wincing slightly as he did so.

'Do you think you're fit enough to go three sets, Charles?'

'I think so. The arm should get easier as the game goes on.'

'Game on then. I'll serve first to give your arm a little time to adjust.'

'Don't worry about me, Christine, you serve your hardest, my right arm isn't affected.'

'Here we go then.'

Christine was a good tennis player, a very good tennis player, and she had Charles flailing around trying to return the ball. The first game was forty to love in Christine's favour.

On Charles's serve, Christine watched with concerned eyes as Charles constantly misjudged the flight of the ball, the arm clearly painful in its upward throwing motion.

But Charles persevered, his throwing action improving all the time as the game progressed. Christine made some deliberate mistakes but still won the first set.

Charles edged the second set as his throwing arm improved, his returns of serve now being more physically powerful.

The final set was about to get underway when Charles, for the first time, noticed Christine was wearing no panties. He had been so wrapped up in his own discomfort and keeping the score he had not seen the blindingly obvious.

Seeing Charles observe her nakedness for the first time, Christine exaggerated her body movements, which caused her skirt to show tantalising glimpses of what was underneath.  Charles stopped playing, pointing his racket at her accusingly.

'You sassy minx, Christine!  You temptress, showing me your hidden weapon, eh!  I'll have you for that.' Charles advanced towards Christine with just one thing on his mind.

'No, no, Charles, not now, this is a three-setter, remember.  Fun only after the tennis match, and only if you win.'

Charles frustratingly walked back to his line determined to make this set a short one.

Christine giggled and flirted with Charles as he desperately tried to concentrate on his serves.  To no avail, with one eye on the ball and the other on Christine's skirt, with sweat dripping down his face from both lust and exertion, his shots went astray more times than she could count.

It was a foregone conclusion: Christine won the third set, claiming victory with a whoop and a holler, throwing both arms high into the air and leaping up and down, motions that caused her pleated skirt to ride even higher.

Charles, disappointed at losing, sulked for a moment, but was now beyond the point of no return.  With an added spring in his step, he vaulted over the net charging towards Christine.  Christine waited momentarily and then ran to the other side of the net giggling and goading Charles to get her.  Charles ran after her only for Christine to dash again to the other side and goad him further still.

They both did this several times more before Christine, seeing her man totally exhausted, backed herself into one corner of the court, leant suggestively against the chain-link fence, parted her legs slightly and began raising and lowering her skirt to titillate further.

'You lost, remember! Fun only if you win; that was the rule of the game.'

Charles could bear it no longer. He caught up with Christine, pulled down his shorts, casually throwing them away to one side, embraced Christine, and in a moment of feverish excitement entered her, moaning and panting with pleasure, catching his breath, all at the same time. His thrusts became more and more vigorous as Christine responded to his every movement.

Feeling her man inside of her brought out both the lust and the love she felt for Charles; love that was like a warm towel after a shower, all enveloping and embracing and cosy – transcendentally sublime.

As her man climaxed inside of her she climaxed too, holding him close to her by his buttocks, not wishing to ever let go. In that moment, as a woman, she felt complete; a feeling she had never experienced before with another man; a feeling of unheralded joy.

Charles withdrew. Both were exhausted as they sat down, smiling and laughing, giving each other pecks on the cheek as love tokens. Moments of infinite happiness – al fresco style!

'What am I going to do with you, Christine,' said Charles, shaking his head, 'you're doing my head in with your shenanigans. You had this in mind all along, didn't you?'

'A little bit, just a little bit, you didn't mind, did you?'

Charles's smile turned into a big grin. And then to a more serious look.

'Oh hell, Christine, I didn't take any precautions, in the heat of the moment I forgot myself.'

'Not to worry, Charles, I'm on the pill, no problems there.'

'Thank God for that, I wouldn't want you to get pregnant.'

Those last words somehow hurt Christine. Would it be that bad if she was pregnant? A baby made in love was surely the most desirable thing for a woman, in or out of marriage. But she could see Charles's point of view, so her rational mind told her. That was something to discuss for the future, not now, not following irrational lust on both their parts.

They both showered later together, making love again in the shower and on the bathroom floor. In a closed world of their own they kissed and explored each other's body, whispering sweet nothings to each other, rolling around laughing uncontrollably, tickling each other until both were screaming for mercy.

~

By the time the car had returned to the police station both had sobered up their emotions with their most officious-looking faces they could muster despite both flushed pink. Play was play and work was work, not to be mixed or confused in police time. Christine couldn't help the occasional outward smile though, grinning inwardly like a Cheshire cat as she recalled the game of tennis.

And yet, as she sat at her desk, negative thoughts intruded on her happiness. Had she cheapened herself in the eyes of her Chief Inspector? Would he see her differently? Was she someone to have a good time with and nothing more? Had she been too adventurous in her love-making for Charles to think twice of her now? Would what she had achieved be her moment of cheap triumph?

She told herself not to be so silly and to concentrate on her work, to think instead of that warm towel feeling – of love in its purest form.

Charles sat at his desk, composed himself, and then opened the forensics report in front of him.  He rose immediately and asked Christine to come into his office.

'Sergeant, the forensics report says his neck was broken before the hanging.  Our suicide case it seems has just turned into a murder enquiry!'

'Yes sir.'

# Six

'Clive, I thought I would give you a quick ring to go over the bullet points of your report sitting on my desk concerning the vagrant, and whether you had anything more to add.'

'Fire away, Chief Inspector.'

'The first concerns the bruising around the neck. Forensically you can show that his neck was broken before the hanging?'

'The bruises are consistent with a headlock and the pressure applied would have been sufficient to break an arthritic neck. There is no doubt this happened before the hanging.'

'The second point is about his clothes.'

'Yes, I've done many autopsies on vagrants. This is the first one though with shabby outer-clothes and pristine clean underwear, including a recently ironed shirt. Even his socks appeared new, unaffected by the holes in the shoe soles.'

'Next: the body itself.'

'There were no signs of any malnourishment or emaciation as one might expect, his stomach contents even suggesting he had had a good three-course meal. He was recently clean-shaven and there was no dirt under his fingernails; his toenails had been recently cut; his hair was clean and his teeth white. There were no signs of disease either inside or outside the body – he was a very healthy man, probably healthier than you or me.'

'…Except for his arthritic neck.'

'Except for that.'

'And what is your conclusion, Clive?'

'I don't speculate, Chief Inspector, I leave that to you. All I've said is that the body and appearance is not that of a vagrant walking the streets for years and the neck injuries are not consistent with suicide.'

'You think he was murdered then?'

'As I said, I don't speculate, just present the facts of the autopsy. That's your job, Chief Inspector, I'm glad it's not mine.'

'And how long was he dead, Clive?'

'Well, there's the rub, Chief Inspector. It's a mystery we are still trying to solve. His broken watch says the 20th of April, broken we presume in the scuffle, and his body shows little sign of decomposition. But, after three to four weeks, from then to now, it should be nothing more than a skeleton with little flesh on it. Can't understand it, it's either the cold of the chapel that has preserved the body or God has had a hand in it somewhere. Never come across this in my whole career, must talk to my colleagues again.'

'Thank you, Clive, and thank you for your swift report.'

'Good luck, Chief Inspector.'

'Thanks, Clive.'

Charles put down the receiver and pondered Clive's words, flicking through the report once again. There were so many anomalies to this suicide it had to be treated as murder. But why the disguise in vagrant's clothes and what could possibly be the motive for his murder? He could speculate all day long about the time of murder but that wouldn't solve this mystery. He needed facts, hard facts, and names, people who might have come into contact with him or had a grudge against him.

There was an oddity about this case which stirred his curiosity and set his police instincts on high alert. But, until a motive could be established it would be nothing but informed guesswork and a trawl down many redundant pathways. The prospect of the challenge, however, was what being a detective is about – and he was up for it.

His first task was to talk to his team.

Assembled in the conference room he outlined the forensics report and his conversation with Clive, the case now being that of murder.

He followed this up with a review of the dossier on Professor Falconer-Smith they had compiled for him.

He threw open the question of motive to his audience.

'One of the girls he molested at University sought revenge,' was one suggestion.

'Possibly,' replied Charles, 'but remember this was a healthy individual over six feet tall, not easily overpowered by a woman. Though I do accept she could have hired someone. Check this out as best you can with the University authorities and the girls names, if forthcoming.'

'Insurance policies,' was another suggestion.

'Good one, check with his former wife on policies outstanding.'

Christine's hand was raised.

'Yes Sergeant?'

'He was in a fight with another vagrant, perhaps?'

'Could be, I suggest we talk to other street users who may have come into contact with him and anyone with a reason to kill him.'

Jane Wetherspool raised her hand.

'Yes Jane?'

'The Professor was mixing with the wrong sort on the streets, drug dealing and all that?'

'Hmmm, that's an interesting one.  We know he was clean of drugs, alcohol being his thing.  But drug dealing or the falling out, for some reason, with a street gang, mafia or underworld, now that's a distinct possibility.  Again I suggest we question our contacts in these areas.  Nice one, Jane.'

Jane was pleased to be praised by her Chief in public – to Christine's chagrin of course, a residual discomfort still with Jane's apparent bonhomie with her Chief.

'Are there any more suggestions for the motive?'

A heavy silence ensued.

'In that case let me re-emphasise.  We need more facts, more names, photographs if possible.  We need to paint a picture of this individual – his likes, his dislikes, who he came into contact with in the last two years since he lost his job and tramped the streets.  Then, perhaps, we might be a little closer to his killer.

'I notice from the dossier that the name of Lord Hutton came up when the publican of the "Black Lion" was interviewed.

'As you might or might not know, Lord Hutton is on the Board of the Police Federation and is a very influential person in these parts.  I plan to talk to him if only to clear his name from our investigations.

'We will leave it at that for the moment.  We will reconvene when we have more information to hand.  It's going to be hard work but we will find the killer of the Professor one way or other.  Thank you.'

The meeting broke up to a hubbub of noise, speculation rife.

~

Charles thought it appropriate to give his father a ring before seeing Lord Hutton.

'Hello father … sir.'

'Hello Charles … Detective Chief Inspector. What can I do for you?'

'I'm planning to interview Lord Hutton and thought it wise to give you a ring first.'

'Lord Hutton, you mean Lord Hutton on the Board of the Police Federation?'

'Yes sir.'

'Why's that?'

'His name came up in our general enquiries of the murder of Professor Falconer-Smith. It's a routine interview to eliminate him from our enquiries.'

'I don't see any problems but take care, he's an important person in these parts as well you know. As useful background information: he was our Member of Parliament for about twenty years before losing his seat, rising briefly to be a member of the Cabinet. When his party lost power he was demoted, as you might say, to the House of Lords.

'He made his fortune through upmarket property development but there are rumours, and I must emphasise they are only rumours, that he has serious financial problems.

'What I'll do is to give him a ring first and then ring you back. Is that OK?'

'I'll await your call.'

Charles did not have to wait long.

'Chief inspector, I've spoken to Lord Hutton, told him what it's all about and he's agreed to be interviewed. He's currently at home in his town house, number five Mews Crescent.'

'I know where that is, just a ten-minute walk from here.'

'That's right. He will see you at ten o'clock tomorrow, if that's all right with you.'

'That's fine. Thank you father ... sir.'

'By the way, Charles, how's your arm?'

'The wound has healed and I don't need to use the sling any more. The arm movement is still a bit restricted but coming along fine.'

'That's good news but no driving meanwhile, do you hear?'

'Yes sir, no driving.'

'See you soon.'

The next day Charles instructed Christine and the Desk Sergeant as to his whereabouts and left for Mews Crescent.

Mews Crescent was an expensive property development of stables originally in an exclusive part of town. As he knocked on number five he admired their quaint frontage with thoughts that he wouldn't have minded a property there himself if he'd been rich enough that is. Lucky beggar thought Charles to himself as he patiently waited at the door.

Lord Hutton answered the door.

'Pleased to meet you, Detective Chief Inspector,' holding out his hand to greet Charles. 'Come in, come in and tell me what this is all about.'

Charles entered, to be then guided to a surprisingly spacious lounge, not obvious from the small frontage and cottage-style windows.

'Take a seat. Would you like a drink?'

'No sir, not whilst I'm on duty.'

'You don't mind if I do?'

Charles shook his head, watching as Lord Hutton poured himself a large glass of whisky.

'Good stuff this whisky. It's not Scottish, it's Japanese called Yamazaki. Heard of it?' He thrust the bottle, label-side up, into Charles's face.

'I can't say I have,' pushing the bottle away after reading the label.

'I'll give you a bottle to take back with you.'

'That's very kind, sir.'

'Now, Chief Inspector, tell me how I can help in your enquiries.'

Lord Hutton remained on his feet, strutting around the room, gulping back his drink, staring at Charles occasionally as if weighing him up in order to attach some degree of importance to his visitor.

'We're investigating a suicide – now a murder case – and in our interview with the publican of the "Black Lion" pub he listed a number of patrons who frequent his premises and your name came up.'

'Oh yes, I know the "Black Lion", one of my favourite drinking holes the "Black Lion". They have a good selection of my favourite wines as well as beers, you know; a fine establishment, yes indeed, a fine establishment.'

'We're trying to add more names to our list and wondered if you could remember who you might have had a drink with.'

'How far back do you want me to go?'

'Say, two years.'

'Two years, that's a long time. My memory isn't that good now. I talk to a lot of people without asking their names, a habit from when I was canvassing for votes, bonding with my constituents and all that. But that was all in a previous life when I was a young whippersnapper, making a political career for myself. I made it to the Cabinet, you know.

'Names ... Names? Let me think about it.'

Whilst Lord Hutton was thinking about it and pouring another drink for himself, Charles studied the man, unperturbed by his Lordship's apparent need to dominate the room and to emphasise his social superiority.

He was of average height with a portly frame; fleshy jaws with a turkey neck; a ruddy complexion with a purplish nose; all features suggesting his imbibing was one of his favourite pastimes. He had a mop of thinning fair hair, more distinctly yellow with bushy eyebrows to match. He gave the impression on the outside of being a jocular sort of person, courteous and affable, one of the lads so to speak. On the inside, who knows? Clearly an astute politician with a keen business brain who had mellowed with age, or is that with the drink?

'Look here, Chief Inspector,' glancing at his watch, 'I'm due at my country estate in an hour to do some shooting and all that. Why don't you come along whilst I'm doing all this thinking? I see my chauffeur is preparing the Rolls. It takes about an hour's drive. He'll drive you back. What do you say?'

'Err ...'

'I won't take no for an answer.'

'I was just thinking of what I had on today.'

'I'm certain whatever it is it can wait. Give your station a ring, tell them where you'll be and who you are with.'

Lord Hutton was very persuasive and Charles knew that if he was to get any information from him he would need to cajole him, to catch him before drink scrambled his brain entirely.

Charles rang Christine to tell her where he would be. Lord Hutton's smile widened at the sound of his own name.

'My diary for the day has been cleared, Lord Hutton, for your benefit.'

'There, I told you so. Now let's get in the Rolls.'

~

On the journey to the estate Charles was on the receiving end of a potted history of Lord Hutton's political life mingled with his business interests; how he had overcome adversity in his childhood days to make it to the top and become mega-rich in the process.

The drinks cabinet in the Rolls was well-stocked and well used! The more he imbibed, the more lucid he became, but not about the information Charles was seeking.

The most Charles got from him was of a soldier in a wheelchair with his dog who he'd spoken to from time to time; he could not remember the soldier's name but the dog's name was "Tally". There were also a few Smith's and Jones's – not very helpful! Charles knew this whole episode was a total waste of police time. He would just have to hope that Lord Hutton was a bit more forthcoming over time, perseverance being needed on Charles's part rather than a heavy-handed approach which could upset his seniors and other persons in high-office.

Arriving at the mansion house they were greeted by the gamekeeper dressed in his tweeds with a double-barrelled shotgun slung over his shoulder, ready for instant action. A retriever had sprung to its heels, its tail wagging ten to the dozen as it greeted Lord Hutton who bent down to give it a big, soppy cuddle; man and his dog reunited once again.

On entering the house Charles was struck by how cold and uninviting it was and except for a few servants, uninhabited – Lord Hutton never having married and with no offspring. Clearly the residence was used solely for his second passion to drink – shooting!

'Can you handle a gun, Chief Inspector? Look, can I call you Charles, Detective Chief Inspector is too formal and it makes me feel like a felon let out on bail.'

'No problem, Lord Hutton.'

'Can you handle a gun, Charles?

Whether he could or not Charles was handed a gun by the gamekeeper.

'Need to change into my shooting jacket and hat. If you go with the gamekeeper he will fit you out. By the way, the chauffer's name is "King" and the gamekeeper's name is "Cole". Get it? - loved that crooner!' A bellicose laugh erupted which followed him as he strode purposely towards where he was to change.

On his reappearance the same laugh hung around him and seemed to continue for the next hour or so as the three of them – Lord Hutton, Charles and Cole - were driven by King in a Land Rover to the more wooded part of the estate; the dog sitting on Lord Hutton's lap, frequently looking up and licking his master's face, slavering with excitement which seemed to bring out the Lord in fits of giggling, patting the dog's head to try and calm it.

'A couple of thousand acres, prime acreage, Charles,' bellowed the Lord to Charles as he struggled to placate the beast, 'mainly meadow and woodland. Use it just for shooting, not interested in any agriculture. We breed our own game, mainly pheasant and partridge with a few quail thrown in for good measure. We'll bag a few for tonight's dinner.'

The shoot continued for three hours, Lord Hutton being an excellent shot as he stalked the gamekeeper beating the bushes and tall grass. Charles tried his hand but winced with the gun's recoil affecting his left shoulder. He managed to shoot one pheasant but that wasn't too difficult from a flock of a dozen birds flying out of the grass together.

'I was forgetting, Charles, about your injury,' said the Lord, interrupting his shooting for a minute to reload, 'nasty business. Your father keeps me informed. Hope the men who did this to you are locked away for a good length of time.

'Let's head back, my back's beginning to moan with all this standing around. Not getting any younger, you see. We've got enough for dinner with three braces of pheasants for us and the servants, a good day's haul, don't you think?'

At that instance a hare popped its head and long ears above the grass and scurried across the field. With unerring accuracy, Lord Hutton, in one motion, darting on a sixpence, swivelled, took aim, fired off a single shot, dropping the hare in its tracks.

'Nat, fetch!' The retriever lived up to its name.

'We'll have hare and pheasant for dinner tonight, Charles. That should fill your belly.'

Lord Hutton had clearly felt great pleasure from hitting a swift moving target, more than that of shooting the birds. Holding the hare up by its ears and taking another drink from his hip-flask to celebrate the kill, his florid face lit up with a huge smile; this was followed by yet another bellicose laugh that seemed to last until dinner time.

Dinner being over, they both retired to a lounge warmed by an open fire. Supping whiskies and brandies, Charles took the opportunity in Lord Hutton's relaxed state to ply him with more questions regarding the names of people he had come into contact with in the "Black Lion".

But it was like getting blood out of a stone. His prevarication was annoying as if deliberately avoiding answering, using drink and his languid posture, his staring into the fire and the rubbing of his eyes, as an excuse to deflect questions and to go off at tangents. He let his head loll back and closed his eyes, the drink and warmth of the fire finally taking their effect.

Charles knew at this juncture there was no point in continuing. He asked the chauffeur to prepare the Rolls for his journey home. Yet he felt there was something Lord Hutton wasn't telling him, something important and relevant to his inquiries - but what? He was back to the guessing game again and it left him devoid of even the merest hint of progress. He could interview Lord Hutton back at the station but felt this was a step too far without a good enough reason; his Chief Constable wouldn't sanction it. Charles would have to wait for another day.

# Seven

'Where is everyone, Sergeant?'

'They're all in the conference room, sir, watching the events in Europe on the BBC. They've projected it onto the big screen.'

'What's happening in Europe, then?'

'It seems there are riots on the streets of Athens, Rome, Lisbon and Milan – all the southern countries. Mainly anti-austerity, populist groups but other extremist factions of both the left and the right appear to have joined in, mass protests of the people marching on government buildings and their parliaments. The police are having problems containing them and the armies have been called in to quell the riots and looting. Lots of ugly scenes and clashes with the police using tear gas and batons. They're like scenes from a war!'

'Let me take a look.'

Charles entered the conference room to find all his staff there staring at the big screen. Christine had remained in the office to answer any telephone calls.

Charles watched with his staff. According to the BBC the protests had all started peacefully with marches to centre city squares but had rapidly deteriorated to mass rallies to parliament buildings, resulting in live ammunition being fired by the police and army. Baton charging was being resisted by factions wielding clubs and other weapons.

The fact that all the protests in all the countries were occurring at the same time in four major cities was unnerving to say the least. Clearly there was a degree of coordination between the anti-austerity groups for maximum impact on their governments and on the ruling bodies in Brussels, if the banners were anything to go by.

The peaceful mass rallies were now degenerating into riotous behaviour as cars were set on fire, shops broken into and pillaged, and barricades erected against charging police lines. It was rioting on an organised scale; a cauldron of insurrection.

After a few minutes viewing Charles had seen enough.

'Come on, back to work you lot, you can catch up with the news on the evening programmes. Remember there's work to be done here to find a killer. This has nothing to do with us so concentrate on what you're paid to do. I need names, names and more names in the life of our Professor Falconer-Smith.'

Charles switched off the television as he watched his team troop out of the conference room discussing between them, in an animated fashion, the incidents they'd seen on the broadcast.

Returning to his office Charles asked Christine to join him.

'Sergeant, I would like the team to do three things for me, but first tell me of any news your end.'

'We've drawn a total blank, sir. There was no insurance motive to speak of, his main life policy being annulled when he left the University as stipulated in his contract.

'The University, understandably, was reluctant to discuss his dismissal and would not divulge any of the girls' names since no one had brought any charges against the Professor, citing the disclosure of the Private Information Act.

'We've received similar blank stares from everyone we've interviewed on the streets as well as the known criminal community. No one wants to say they knew him or can relate anything about him, his habits, his whereabouts, anything. They all give the impression he was a loner when not in the pubs.

'And what about you, sir, did you get anything out of Lord Hutton to advance the case?'

'No Sergeant, like you I drew a blank. For a man who mixed well with the community he knew surprisingly little, using his alcoholic state as a cover, a smokescreen for what he does know. I would need more information on him to bring him into the station for questioning further.'

'So you think he's hiding something?'

'I do, Sergeant, but haven't a clue as to what that might be.'

'These three things, sir, you wanted us to do?'

'Ah, yes. Lord Hutton mentioned a soldier he'd spoken to quite often in the "Black Lion" pub. He couldn't recall his name but he was now in a wheelchair having lost both legs in Afghanistan. He had a dog – an Alsatian – which he called "Tally". I'd like you to check with the MOD so we can put a name and a face to this character. May mean nothing but we're clutching at straws anyway.

'Secondly, and this really is clutching at straws, I want you to investigate some dog poo for me.'

'Dog poo, sir?' Christine started chuckling to herself.

'Stop laughing, Sergeant, I'm serious, well I think I'm serious.' Christine's chuckle was catching.

'No – listen - seriously, I noticed some dog faeces in the verger's office at the church. I believe, but I'm not certain, I read it somewhere I think, that you can determine the breed of dog from its DNA and that includes from its poo, its saliva, its hairs and other things. Have it checked out with the local vet could you and if so arrange access for them to the verger's office. Best to check first with forensics in case we're treading on their poo, if you get my drift.'

Christine looked at Charles. Charles looked at Christine. They both burst out laughing and got a fit of the giggles.

Regaining some of his composure, Charles blurted out, 'And could you find out how old the poo was.'

This time, side-splitting laughter from both of them, loud raucous laughter that spread from the office to the team outside, bringing smiles all round wondering what was so amusing.

'There was a third point, sir,' said Christine, wiping tears from her eyes.'

'Ah yes. On a more serious note, could you ask forensics to check for any tyre marks in the verger's office made by a wheelchair, I suspect any such marks may have been scuffed out but there may be small traces left. It's worth checking since we have nothing else to go on.'

'Except for poo, sir.'

'Except for poo, Sergeant.

A more restrained bout of laughter this time from the two of them.

'Yes sir, anything else, sir?'

'No, that's all for now, Sergeant. But after you have instructed your team I would like the two of us to visit the publican once again at the "Black Lion" to see if we can jog his memory a bit further for the names of his clientele.'

'Yes sir.' Christine left the office still wiping her eyes. In the serious business of police work, perhaps too serious at times, it was good occasionally to see the funny side of things.

~

Arriving at the "Black lion" both Christine and Charles entered the premises together. It was an old establishment with large oak beams dating back God knows how many years. It was one of the oldest pubs in Cambridge, small, intimate, frequented by students as well as the usual regulars. The smell of beer was everywhere, from the soaked tables over the years to the constant flowing pumps at the bar. It was tempting to order two drinks but common sense prevailed.

They approached the man serving behind the bar, levering their way between thirsty clients.

'Mr Harrington?' asked Charles raising his voice above the din, holding out his identity card, Christine doing likewise.

'Yes, that's me,' shouted another man pulling a pint at the other end of the bar, 'what can I do for you?'

'I'm Detective Chief Inspector Waley-Cohen and this is Detective Sergeant Moran. Could we have a few words with you in private?'

'You could have chosen a better time. You can see how busy we are.'

'Sorry about that, in private if possible?'

'Come through to the office,' responded the publican, drying his hands with a clean cloth and beckoning them to follow. 'It's a bit of a cubbyhole I'm afraid, not much room.'

Charles and Christine managed their way past others and followed the gentleman to a small room designated as an office with not much room for a table, a chair and a single filing cabinet. They all squeezed in together.

'It's a bit quieter here, cramped but quieter. Now what can I do for you? I've already spoken to the police several times and I've exhausted the list of names I can remember. We don't ask for names, we just serve beer and wine. Lots of students, of course, who are blank faces to us; we also have our regulars, some we know by name such as lord Hutton; others we do not, nor are we interested in finding out.

'I've already pointed out to your police officers that the premises are under new management and I've only been here for six months. I suggest if you want to interview someone with a good memory for names you speak to the publican here before me. He was here for twenty years before retiring from the trade. He's got a rollickingly good memory.'

Charles turned to Christine, 'Did we interview the previous publican, Sergeant?'

'Not to my knowledge, sir.'

Turning again to the publican, 'What's his name and where can we find him?'

'His name is …err … Mr Bainbridge. You can find him most times on his allotment at Westley Gardens. You know where I mean? I would try there first.'

I know where that is, sir,' said Christine, 'about fifteen minutes away. It's worth trying.'

'Thank you, Mr Harrington. We'll take your advice. Thank you for your time. Nice pub you have here.'

'I think so, Chief Inspector. If I can be of any further help please let me know.'

'Thank you, we'll be in further touch if need be.'

Charles and Christine managed their way to the pub door, leaving Mr Harrington hurriedly dashing to the bar to help his flustered assistant, shouting in a loud voice: 'Gentlemen, gentleman, I'll be with you in a minute.'

A short drive later Charles and Christine were at Westley allotments.

There they questioned a number of gardeners as to the whereabouts of Mr Bainbridge's patch. Eventually they received a positive response.

'You mean Freddie, he's over there,' responded one of the gardeners as he forked a barrow-load of manure into his soil, pointing to a potting shed on the other side of the allotments.

This meant a five-minute walk over muddy, squelchy, wet grass paths after overnight rain, to eventually find Mr Bainbridge with sleeves rolled up, wearing an old pair of muddied jeans – ripped in parts – and clodhoppers, bent double nursing an aching back after sowing some sweet peas.

'Mr Bainbridge? Charles asked politely.

'That's me, who's asking? Freddie partially straightened his back with some considerable effort.

'I'm Detective Chief Inspector Waley-Cohen and this is Detective Sergeant Moran of the Cambridgeshire Police; both flashed their identity cards in front of his face to avoid him straightening his back even further.

For some reason Charles had expected a large, broad-chested, big-bellied, bald ex-publican. He got the bald bit correct but not the other features. He was the exact opposite: thin, wiry and slim; the redness of his face having more to do with exposure to the elements rather than with drink.

'Call me Freddie, everyone else around here does.'

'Freddie, they say you have a good memory. We'd like you to recall for us some of your clientele's names when you were the publican of the "Black Lion".'

'What's it in aid of?'

'We're investigating the death of Professor Falconer-Smith who frequented your pub. He was known on the streets as the "Falcon", I don't know if that helps to jog your memory.'

'Ah, Falcon the tramp, yes I know that name, several others as well. Look, do you mind if I sit in my shed, my back is killing me. Not getting any younger, you know.'

Freddie dug the spade into the earth with some relish as if a break was on the cards anyway; a pot of brew waiting to be made to succour the spent body from gardening. He made himself comfortable in an old lounge chair and then braced himself to get up once again to make himself a cup of tea with an instant tea bag and a primus stove.

'Would either of you like a cup?' Both shook their heads.

'Perhaps a chocolate digestive then?'

'No thanks.' Both shook their heads again.

Charles sat on a wooden stool and looked around the potting shed as Freddie busied himself. The shed was a typical "man-shed" with all its paraphernalia together with some creature comforts and personal objet d'art. The smell of compost, earth, earthenware pots, grease and insecticide, together with the oil fumes from the primus stove, gave the whole place a distinctive though not unpleasant smell; an acquired smell all the same!

After having made a cuppa, Freddie relaxed back in his chair and lit a cigarette. After a few deep draws he was ready to put his memory to the test.

'Professor Falconer you say, yes, I knew him well, not personally that is, but he was a regular in the pub, someone down on his heels. Pity about that, he was a very intelligent man who had lost his way. He took to drink to erase the past, whatever that might have been. Sometimes drink got the better of him and he had to be escorted, if that is the word, out of the pub on more than one occasion. Found dead you say?'

'We're investigating his death,' replied Charles, not wishing to say any more than he had to.

'Died in unusual circumstances, eh; pity, he didn't deserve that.'

'Cast your mind back, perhaps two years or more. Can you recall other names who he might have associated with – friends, other vagrants, anybody he spoke with?' asked Charles, hoping for a positive response with a gentle probing.

'Oh, sure, no problem, got a good memory you see, always had a good memory for names and faces. Now let me think.

'There were a number of groups who met regularly, putting the world to rights and all that. Good for business, you know, more talk, more drink, good for business.'

'Can you recall a soldier in a wheelchair with a dog,' asked Charles, trying to prompt Freddie in putting names to faces.

'Oh, that group! I never knew the soldier's actual name but everyone referred to him as "Robbie". From his broad accent I would say he was undoubtedly Scottish. His dog, an Alsatian, was called "Tally"; used to give it a drink of beer occasionally, nice, good-looking animal.

'Then there was Cecil, don't know his second name either, remember him because his name didn't match the stature of the man. He was a tall, black, beefy-looking man who used to be a bouncer at the Astoria night-club; looked powerful, a man not to be messed with, probably was a real softie at heart belying his outward appearance.

'Ah, yes, there was another soldier, name of John something … yes, John McPherson. I believe the two soldiers were mates, served together in Afghanistan, real buddies if you know what I mean. The way they looked at each other sometimes I would say they were more than good friends.

'There were two others in the group. Let me think. I know one was an engineer, something to do with the internet, the dark web I overheard him say once, or something like that, don't know what that means. Never knew his name but he had a distinctive cleft palate. The other was from the banking world, didn't understand what he did, Neil something or other … Neil Soames, an investment banker or something like that.

'They all used to huddle together in a corner out of earshot. Don't know what they talked about, used to be joined by the professor; funny, I thought that odd, and oh, yes, the peer of the realm, Lord Hutton, I nearly forgot him. The good Lord was a right regular, especially when he was canvassing for votes, he also liked his drink, would see him often in conversation with the group.

'But all this is going back some time, two years or so. I saw less and less of them as time went by; preferred another pub obviously, except for the professor, he's always been around.

'I see your Sergeant is taking notes so if you have the time I can give her fifty more names, the pub was always a hive of politics.'

Freddie rattled off twenty more names before feeling exhausted, slumping back in his chair as if to catch a bit of shut-eye. He stubbed out his cigarette in a plant pot and lit another, his eyes glazing over.

Charles decided that was enough for the day.

'Well, thank you for your time, Freddie, you've been most helpful. We'll let you know if you can help us further.'

Freddie acknowledged Charles's gratitude, slumping further back into his chair, gardening could wait a little while longer.

'Nice plot you have here, Freddie,' said Christine, closing her notebook, 'there are lots of healthy plants. You certainly have green fingers.'

Such a compliment had Freddie rising to his feet reinvigorated, instantly ready to show and discuss with Christine every plant in his garden.

'Another time, Freddie, perhaps,' said Charles, holding out his arm to signal Freddie to sit back in his chair, 'time is pressing and we have other engagements. But thanks anyway.'

Charles and Christine took their leave.

'He's quite a character, Sergeant.'

'He certainly is, sir.'

Charles handed one of his handkerchiefs to Christine to clean her shoes before getting back into the car, another he used to clean his own of the grass and mud. When it came to shoes Charles was very fastidious, one of his many superstitions.

# Eight

'More riots in Europe, Sergeant? Couldn't help but notice the empty desks again as I came in.'

'Yes, this time in the northern countries. Riots in Paris, Berlin, Brussels, Amsterdam, Stockholm and Dublin; really ugly scenes on the streets with rampaging mobs looting and burning, confronting the police lines at every turn. Peaceful rallies of solidarity seem to have turned into violence against all forms of authority.'

'What about the UK?'

'Nothing reported so far. But then we're not part of the Eurozone and the austerity isn't biting enough compared to some places where the unemployment is so high, particularly amongst the younger element.'

'What is the world coming to?'

'Time for retribution of the peoples of Europe, perhaps?'

'Could be, Sergeant, could be.

'Look, I know it's not easy but let's try and concentrate on the matters in hand. What did the MOD finally have to say about the soldiers?'

'John McPherson was a private in the 19<sup>th</sup> Regiment, now known as the Scottish Gunners.

'The other soldier was Captain Robert Roy MacBeath of the same Regiment, a born leader by all accounts. He led a specialist unit searching out IEDs until his luck ran out. The blast severed both legs below the knees. On leaving the army he put in a request for his dog, "Tally". Such a request is normally refused but an exception was made in this case.

'Both soldiers are now living in Cambridge at the same address according to their pension records.

'Cecil Homes was a bouncer at the Astoria night club. He was sacked after being found drunk at work and abusive to the public. A big, strapping ex-boxer who some say had a heart of gold, but not a man to pick a fight with.'

'Was there any feedback regarding the verger's office?'

'Both negative. There were no wheelchair marks and the faeces, which were several months old, were not that of an Alsatian but that of a mongrel.'

Charles swivelled his chair to stare pensively out of the window. Christine knew he was disappointed at the lack of leads over this length of time and stayed silent.

He then stood up. Putting both hands in his trouser pockets he tapped his head repeatedly on the window glass in utter frustration.

Without thinking Christine asked, 'Should we arrest the two soldiers, sir?'

The response was more than tetchy. 'What for, Sergeant? ...For being gay? ...For talking in a pub? ...For being soldiers? We cannot place them at the crime scene and they're no more suspects than any of the hundred names we've interviewed over the last few weeks.'

After a moment's hesitation Christine asked tentatively, 'Where do we go from here, sir?'

''I don't know, Sergeant, I really do not know.'

Charles regained his seat, putting his elbows on the desk, burying his head in his hands. He stayed silent for a couple of minutes before raising his head and addressing Christine again.

'Sergeant, this case is a total enigma. We haven't the slightest evidence to place anyone at the scene and no motive whatsoever as to why someone should kill a vagrant.

'On the one hand we could dismiss this case as being the unfortunate death of yet another vagrant tramping the streets. But I ... we don't work like that. Forensics says he was murdered and there is a killer out there, a killer we have to find and find fast.

'Why? Why am I not seeing the wood for the trees? We've done the basics of police work and sifted through reams of information but it's gotten us nowhere, we're going around in bloody circles. But ... But there is something, something that is ruffling my police feathers, I just can't put my finger on it. What is it, Sergeant?' Charles stared at Christine as if hoping she had all the answers.

'Perhaps, sir, we're looking too deeply into this case and being swamped with the information we've collected. At the same time we're being too parochial, not seeing the wider picture.

'We're treating this vagrant as a tramp, therefore dismissing his intelligence, his knowledge, his experience, concentrating instead on his shortcomings and misbehaviour.

'Why don't we treat his murder as being that of a murder of a gang member, someone who has fallen out with its leader and has subsequently been "silenced"; we have experienced such cases many times.' Christine paused to take breath and to see what affect her words had had on her Chief.

'Keep talking, Sergeant, you're giving me ideas.'

Christine continued with greater confidence. 'If he was part of a gang or group of felons what did he bring to the group? Why would they tolerate a smelly, down-on-his-heels tramp?'

'His linguistic ability maybe?'

'Yes, that's what I believe. You need someone like that if you have operations on the continent. English is widely spoken but it's always best to have someone who can speak the local lingo.

'I suggest, sir, we study his recent travel movements abroad. He did not have a passport on him or at his ex-wife's home but these days it is easy to travel on a false passport.'

'Christ, Sergeant, I think you're on to something. Let's check with customs and passport control; also his bank statements, if any, he needed to be funded somehow and by someone; and let's refer to him as "Professor" in future.'

'Yes sir, good reasoning. We'll get on to it straightaway.'

At that moment the office door opened and a member of the team handed Christine several papers. She studied them and a huge smile crossed her face.

'What is it, Sergeant?'

'Have you listened to the BBC news recently?'

'Not recently.'

'Well, yesterday the news channels reported on the deaths - the assassinations - of two British men in Italy, found in a ditch, shot through the head.

'What's that got to do with our case?'

448

She handed the papers to Charles. 'We asked Interpol to fax over their names and faces and they've just arrived.'

He studied the photographs and then thumped his desk. 'Oh, my God, I don't believe it ... I simply do not believe it.' He took a deep intake of breath, staring once again at Christine but this time with fire in his eyes.

'Their names are John McPherson and Robert Swaine, two of the names in our group. And would you know it, Robert Swaine has a cleft palate mentioned by Freddie.

'Brilliant, Sergeant, brilliant work. Let's get on to it straightaway. I want you to find out the travel arrangements and bank statements of these two men, too; also of MacBeath and Homes and to bring them in for questioning. Also let's find out more about Lord Hutton's financial affairs.'

'Do we need the Chief Constable's permission to proceed with Lord Hutton?'

'Not this time, Sergeant, I'll take the risk. Whilst you're collecting this information I'll arrange to talk to Lord Hutton again. My gut feeling is he's more involved in this group, more than he's letting on. I won't let drink get in the way of our discussion this time. I'll also find out what I can on Lord Hutton's financial affairs from my contacts in the City.'

'Yes sir.'

And as Christine turned to leave the room: 'Excellent work, Sergeant, I feel we might be getting somewhere at last.'

She smiled at her chief. 'We make a good team, sir.'

'Yes, Sergeant, I believe we do.'

~

Armed with more knowledge of Lord Hutton's business affairs, Charles decided to pay him a surprise visit at his country estate, driving himself there in his Porsche, his arm by now feeling a lot better. He knew his Lordship was in residence all that day.

He entered the open gates to the gravel drive of the mansion house and couldn't help but notice a figure – a woman in a cape and hood – in the wooded area of the drive. Slowing he hoped to get a better view but the furtive figure appeared to disappear amongst the trees as if hiding. A modern red riding hood he chuckled to himself, either that or he was due for an eye test soon.

Having arrived at the house he exited the car, peering back towards the woods to see if he could see the figure again. But there was no one to be seen. He dismissed it from his mind as he rang the door-bell. Lord Hutton opened the door.

'You again, Chief inspector, what's it this time?' It was a less than cordial greeting.

'I thought a second visit was necessary to tie up some loose ends, to ask some further questions. I did not get the opportunity the last time since you were inconvenienced by fatigue, nodding off in front of the fire.

'Oh, yes, sorry about that. Not getting any younger, you see. Come on in.'

'Thank you, sir.'

'I can't remember you making an appointment.'

'I was passing so I thought I would drop in on the chance you were at home.

'Right … well, come in.'

They both went into the lounge.

'Drink, Chief Inspector?'

'No thanks, I'm driving.'

'You don't mind if I help myself.'

'No, go ahead.' Charles did mind but hoped to get some answers before drink deliberately clouded Lord Hutton's memory.

'Fire away, Chief Inspector.'

Charles noticed that Lord Hutton was not his usual ebullient self. He was solemn, his actions slow and deliberate with a face that seemed to bear a permanent frown. Gone were the smiles and the hilarious quips that gave rise to bellicose laughter. He was a different man, very introspective and deflated for some reason, a person likely to erupt at the slightest provocation. Instead of drink masking the questions Charles felt it would be coarse anger this time.

'Do you know a Mr Neil Soames of the Alveco Investment Trust?' Charles had tried to choose his opening words carefully but knew instantly that Lord Hutton's fuse had been lit. His Lordship slammed down his whisky glass onto the table spilling its contents with the force.

'Of course I bloody well know him. We are co-directors of the company. What relevance has that got to do with your case? I'm a director on half a dozen boards. Have you been investigating my financial affairs? How dare you? Am I a suspect in this case? If not then I suggest you leave my house immediately. I will speak to your Chief Constable to have you reprimanded for police harassment.'

Charles was unperturbed by him ranting on, he had half suspected it would happen. One of the rumours from the City was that the Investment Trust had degenerated into a Ponzi scheme, a fraudulent operation offering new investors abnormally high interest rates, achieved by paying its investors from new capital rather than from profits. Another rumour was that a lot of Russian money was involved.

Charles happened to glance out of the window as Lord Hutton hurriedly filled his glass - taking a large swig in doing so - to see the same woman, in cape and hood, approach the house. The hood hid most of her face but what he did see, together with the gait of the woman and her pert derriere, made her seem familiar to him but he couldn't think of whom.

'Who is that woman?' asked Charles.

Lord Hutton turned sharply to look out of the window and then, just as swiftly, turned back to pour himself another drink.

'Probably one of the servants,' he mumbled.

The effect of seeing the woman had a startling effect on his mood though. He became calmer and introspective again, staring into his whisky glass, swilling the liquid around as if to gain precious moments to garner his thoughts. Charles took advantage of his quietened mood.

'Did you hear the news regarding the two British men killed in Italy?'

'I did. What about it?'

'Their names were John McPherson and Robert Swaine. Did you know the men at all?'

'Never heard of them. The "Black Lion" is well known for spawning political activists and is a nest of sedition. Men with drink in their bellies always want to put

452

the world to rights, many are redundant and rebel against all authority.'

Charles had not mentioned the "Black Lion" pub. He sensed that Lord Hutton knew these men and would continue to deny such knowledge, however hard pressed.

'Did you know Captain Robert Roy MacBeath?'

'Likewise - never heard of him. Oh, was he the ex-soldier in a wheelchair with an Alsatian dog? Didn't know his name but had seen him several times in the same pub.'

Charles now knew that he was lying. He had known the name of this soldier all along but would deny any degree of familiarity despite Freddie, the ex-publican, saying he conversed often with the Captain.

Lord Hutton's guilt was etched on his face as his cheeks reddened, his body stiffening as if about to explode, preparing himself for another bout of rage.

Charles sat back waiting for the diatribe. He was not to be disappointed.

'Today's bankers and politicians, I hate them with a passion. They are all parasites. Together they have ruined this country, brought it to its knees. From the 50s to the 70s we were happy then, people had a job and prospects of a house and family; we had a Christian upbringing and its values; we had a hope for the future. Now look at us, what an un-Godly country we have become, subservient to the diktats of the little "Hitlers" in Europe; undemocratic and unelected civil servants telling us how we should live our lives. The overwhelming urge of EU administrators is to increase their control over more and more territory, aided and abetted by politicians who regard democracy with contempt.

'Germany: a defeated nation in two world wars, once again putting other countries to the sword, but this time by economic means. The euro is a disaster - any blind fool can see that. But no, the politicians of other countries don't see it, don't see that the austerity measures imposed on them by Germany are ruining their peoples, subjecting them to such punishment for decades to come. And, whilst this is happening, Germany uses the Euro to its advantage by increasing its exports at prices lower than the Mark. It's all a bloody political mess. It's time for a political uprising of all of Europe, blood spilled if necessary to eliminate this false democracy that's spreading like a cancer.

'And bankers: I hate them more than the politicians. Whatever happened to the traditional banking profession? I tell you what: replaced by salesmen who, by their greed, have reduced their banks to the point where they look for handouts from their governments, from you and from me.

'They have always been fair-weather friends, knocking on your door when things are going great to lend you more than you need, and disappearing from sight when you need their assistance. But now their activities are bordering on the criminal. Currency rate rigging, interest rate rigging, takeovers that bankrupt their bank, dealers rigging the markets to their personal advantage, enriching themselves. And what is the result: big fat bankers taking home big, fat bonuses - that's what. Nothing changes, nothing bloody changes, let the little man in the street, the likes of you and me take all the knocks. Who cares? But the bankers, they're completely immune from prosecution. They get bailed out and then go back to the same fraudulent practices.'

Charles listened intently until the storm had passed and Lord Hutton had cooled down. A delivery of such vehemence had surprised him somewhat, but, as he had listened, he couldn't help but link it with the recent events in Europe. A tenuous link maybe but there was more to Lord Hutton than met the eye. His gut feeling was that the Professor's death and the assassination of the two men in Italy were somehow linked directly or indirectly to the very same man standing in front of him. What that link might be he hadn't a clue.

Charles stood up, about to take his leave, when the door to the lounge opened. He blinked hard to see if he was imagining things.

'Hanna, is that you?'

'Yes, Chief Inspector.'

'I didn't recognise you at first with your dark hair and all that. What on earth are you doing here?'

Hanna sauntered into the room, her presence filling the space. She sat down next to Charles, crossing her legs in a deliberate way and smoothing out her dress. She turned her head demurely to face him, flicking her hair from her eyes and staring him long in the face.

'I knew Lord Hutton from a delegation he led to the Ukraine on a fact-finding mission, showing him around Kiev as I did with you. I thought I would kill two birds with one stone - as you would say in your country - by visiting Lord Hutton and then you. I was about to give you a telephone call to say I am in your country. Surprised?'

'You bet! I thought I recognised you earlier in the woods.'

'Yes, that was me. I was going for a stroll.'

Hanna smiled a warm smile at Lord Hutton who was helping himself to another whisky. Her smile was not returned; his face now more ashen than ever, his ruddy cheeks disappearing in a thrice, jaws clenched, eyes firmly on the floor, his only response being a grunt; Charles noticed his hand was shaking uncontrollably. What was the true relationship between Lord Hutton and Hanna, he asked himself; yet another mystery with this idiosyncratic man, which would only come to light over time.

Charles rose smartly to his feet. 'I have to leave now, Hanna, but give me a ring, Lord Hutton knows my number, and we'll arrange a get-together at the weekend. I'll show you around Cambridge.'

Hanna also rose to her feet, holding out her hand for Charles to shake. 'That would be nice, Chief Inspector … Charles. You see, I still remember your name. Until we meet again then, Charles.' Her smile grew even wider, holding on to his hand for as long as possible.

'Bye Hanna, goodbye Lord Hutton.'

There was nothing but another deep grunt from the po-faced Lord Hutton as he turned his back on the Chief Inspector, mumbling something inaudible.

~

Back in his office Charles listened to Christine as she relayed the initial feedback from the team's enquiries.

'Over the last two years the Professor's travels to Europe were extensive taking in most of the Capitals. He used false passports in false names but his photograph was recognised by passport control using facial recognition technology. He used cash each time to pay for his travel and hotel expenses, his current account having been dormant for some considerable time.'

'So someone was funding him?'

'It seems that way.

'The two men killed in Italy were also travelling regularly together it seems, many of the dates of travel and destinations coinciding with the Professor's. Their bank statements showed no exceptional credit items or disbursements.'

'All three were regular companions, then?'

'That's the way it seems.

'MacBeath and Homes, on the other hand, appear not to have made any foreign trips in the last two years. Their bank statements also showed no unusual debits or credits.'

'It seems someone was funding the whole group in cash to hide any traceability. Have we brought them in yet for questioning?'

'We can find no trace of them. We've checked at their home addresses but no one can tell us where they are or where they could be. We're at a loss to know where they're hiding out.'

'It's very strange … very strange. The plot thickens. The more we study this group the more disturbing questions it throws up.'

'What about Lord Hutton, sir? Did he throw any further light on the problem?'

'Only indirectly. He was his usual belligerent self, venting his anger to the world. He lied through his teeth concerning his knowledge of the men in the group but was highly sensitive when I mentioned the name of Neil Soames, his co-director of Alveco Investment Trust. That might be because the Trust is being investigated by the Serious Fraud Office for fraudulent transactions.

'So, summarising, Sergeant: we appear to have a group of seven men, being funded, we know not how; involved in activities on the continent, we know not what.'

'Could it have something to do with what's happening in Europe at the moment with all these protests and riots?'

'That seems difficult to believe. Politically they wouldn't have the clout and very large sums of money would need to be involved in any coercion of populist parties.

'Let's think ... who else, besides the political parties, benefits from these riots?'

'The answer is obvious, sir – criminals, organised criminal activity, the Mafia and the like. Since Europe opened up its borders there's been a huge increase in the movement of stolen goods between the West and the East. I was reading about it recently how the Russian Mafia and the Italian Mafia have cooperated in the black markets of diamonds, antiques, paintings, drugs, counterfeit currency, luxury cars and aggravated money laundering. These riots are a blessing in disguise for them.'

'Assuming you're right, Sergeant, how do we link this small group, so to speak, with organised criminal activity?'

Christine paused for a while. 'We need more answers, sir.'

'We certainly do, Sergeant. Let's keep probing, we'll only get more answers when we find these two men who are holding out somewhere. But your idea of organised criminal activity is an interesting one; this group could certainly fit into that scenario.

Charles looked quizzically at Christine.

'I don't wish to be personal, Christine, but are you feeling OK? You look a bit peaky.'

'I feel a bit under the weather, sir. I might have a touch of the flu coming on.'

'If that's the case why don't you take a few days off and take to your bed with a couple of hot drinks?'

'Thank you, sir. I might just do that.'

Now showing more concern for her welfare, Charles asked concernedly, 'Are you well enough to drive yourself home, Christine?'

'I think so, sir.'

'You're sure you wouldn't like me to drive you home?'

'No sir, I'll be all right, but thank you, sir.'

Christine left Charles's office feeling unwell, holding her left side as if to ease the pain. Charles watched as Christine tidied her desk, put on her coat, and left the room, giving her a salutary wave goodbye and shouting after her, 'Take care, Christine, hope you're feeling better in the morning.'

# Nine

Charles had a light breakfast and then showered. He was expecting Hanna within the hour, an incentive therefore to tidy the flat a little, to plump the cushions, to get the vacuum cleaner out and to do a little dusting. His weekly house-keeper was not due for several more days and this was a chore he hated above most things.

Satisfied with its appearance he settled down on the settee and waited impatiently for the door-bell to ring.

His feelings for Hanna were strangely mixed. It was if there were boundaries he shouldn't cross in his flustered desire. There was an instant physical attraction, mutual he believed, but, at the same time, there was an element of caution inside of him which seemed to hold sway.

With Carla there had always been a freedom of expression of both the heart and the mind, an expression that had no boundaries, a freedom of the soul of loving someone, a soul-mate in every sense of the word. The freedom of shouting out to the world: "I love you, I love you," with no self-consciousness. Carla had felt likewise, manifesting itself occasionally in tears of joy. Together they had been on top of the world looking forward to a long future in each other's company. But it was not to be, the Devil pulling the strings and parting them for ever.

It was nice to have similar feelings of love for Hanna, something he thought would never happen again, but they came with a warning sign. He had only known Hanna but briefly and it was probably the policeman in him that exaggerated the negativity in such a brief acquaintance. He ought to learn to give every relationship time to develop otherwise he would end up a bachelor for life like many of his friends. Such a life without marriage and children – lots of children – was an anathema to his way of thinking.

The door-bell rang causing his heart-beat to race. Expectation was often the downfall of many a suitor, were the strange thoughts that passed through his mind at that instance.

He opened the door to be greeted by Hanna in the same pose as he had first met her in Kiev.

'You like, good sir?' A shy flutter of the eyelashes together with the impression of wide-eyed innocence was her calling card.

'Good morning, Hanna, please come in, take a seat.'

Hanna sauntered in, taking off her coat and handing it to him. Then, making herself comfortable on the settee, she smoothed out her dress before brushing her hair from her wind-swept face.

'Have you had breakfast?' asked Charles being ever so courteous.

'Yes, thank you.'

'A cup of coffee then?'

'Yes, that would be nice.'

Hanna surveyed the flat whilst Charles busied himself with the coffee machine. The flat was not to her taste – too masculine, too little light penetrating the heavy atmosphere of the place. It desperately needed a woman's touch; those curtains would definitely need changing and more pastel shades introduced on the walls to replace the heavy browns; as for the furniture: a total change from leather was needed giving a much lighter appearance to the room.

'How long have you lived here, Charles?' raising her voice for him to hear in the kitchen.

'Oh, several years now, about five I think. You like black coffee, don't you, no sugar?'

'You remember well, Charles.'

He brought in two coffees. Placing the cups carefully on the coffee table to avoid spilling he sat in the chair opposite Hanna.

'Tell me, Hanna, how did you know Lord Hutton?' It was not the opening line he had had in his mind prior to her visit but somehow it just came out of his mouth without thinking. Having realised what he had asked he tried to change the question to a nicer one but it was too late. He could visibly see Hanna's body stiffen and her whole demeanour change from her relaxed pose, now sitting upright on the edge of the settee, pushing her coffee away from her slightly, fixing him with a glare.

After a few seconds thought she spoke in a calm manner. 'As I said before, he was part of a delegation of Lords on a fact-finding mission about the war in the Ukraine and the business opportunities when the war ceased. They were all very kind, very gentlemanly, wanting to help in any way they could. I speak English well and my role was to show them around our capital city.

'I was invited by several of your Lords to visit them when I was in your country. I wanted to visit you and knew that Lord Hutton also lived in Cambridge. So, when my holiday was due, I contacted Lord Hutton who said I could stay for as long as I liked. That was very kind of him, don't you think?'

'Yes indeed,' said almost apologetically for his initial faux-pas.

They spent the next hour in general banter, cutting out the serious stuff, nothing of great importance, a period of time to lighten the atmosphere, to establish their acquaintance and to see if the flame of passion still burnt brightly on both their parts – it did! Hanna took on her more relaxed pose again smiling coyly at Charles.

He was smitten for the second time in his life and those boundaries he thought of earlier had evaporated completely from his mind; they were now a long, long way away, out of sight, out of mind at this moment of time.

The rest of the daylight hours were spent visiting the tourist sites of Cambridge when laughter was the order of the day, taking lunch at a McDonald's and punting on the Backs. An evening meal at Charles's favourite restaurant completed the day.

Back in the flat they both flopped on the settee totally exhausted after a day of play. They looked at each other lovingly, longingly, and their lips met, first oh so gently and then with fevered passion, all rules of conduct swept aside in unbridled lust for each other.

Their frenzy of undressing was interrupted in one moment of absolute hilarity however. To Hanna's horror and to Charles's utter astonishment, Hanna's wig was dislodged, revealing her natural blonde hair which flopped over her face veiling its delicate features.

Saucily brushing it aside and holding several strands under her nose for effect, Hanna whispered in her best pillow-talk voice, 'Which you like, Charles - me blonde or brunette or ménage-à-trois?'

For just a few seconds there was an air of embarrassment, all lustful thoughts suspended as they stared blankly at each other, before both of them fell about laughing, Hanna plonking the wig onto his head as they fell to the floor in one long, loving embrace. All thoughts of her dangerous loveliness banished from his mind, replaced by the act of vigorous love-making.

Sunday was spent mainly in bed like newly-weds wishing their wedding night would never end; the afternoon and evening rustling up an evening meal – Ukraine style – between periods of robing and disrobing and moments of tenderness.

Early Monday morning Hanna was picked up by King to be taken back to Lord Hutton's estate with Charles returning to his office. They both planned to meet again the following Saturday for a trip to London to see the sights there and to take in a West End show, staying overnight in a London hotel. They blew kisses as they parted.

~

'Is Sergeant Moran in today?' asked Charles of the Desk Sergeant, 'she was feeling a bit poorly last week.'

'No, Chief Inspector, she rang in earlier to say she'd be off work for a few more days, a bad bout of flu I believe.'

'Sorry to hear about that, thank you George.'

As Charles sat at his desk that Monday morning, his thoughts initially were more about Hanna than his police work. But police investigations put fire in his belly and were the reason for getting out of bed first thing of a morning, so his thoughts soon swung to this intractable case of the Professor, to Christine's theory of organised European criminal behaviour in particular.

If her theory was correct there had to be huge funding involved, millions of currencies changing hands, much more than the simple cash funding of a group of individuals; but where and how to obtain such information? Lord Hutton and the Alveco Investment Trust were implicated somehow, he was sure of that, but without evidence and without a good reason to investigate their financial affairs his hands were tied.

MacBeath and Homes were still on the run hiding somewhere. They can't run forever and one day soon they'll be caught, their statements throwing light on the group's purpose and activities as well as the murder of the Professor. Setting aside what was happening on the continent, his role in this murder investigation was to find the killer of Professor Falconer-Smith, and only that. Any other information gleaned that could be useful to Interpol was of secondary importance in this case. It was important to stay focused on finding the Professor's killer or killers.

First thing Wednesday morning Charles checked with the Desk Sergeant again.

'Is Sergeant Moran in today, George?'

'No sir. She rang in to say she'd be off for the rest of the week.'

'It sounds serious. I'll give her a ring to see if she's OK.'

Back in his office he rang Christine who answered the telephone.

'Christine, this is Charles. Thought I would check with you to see if you're OK and getting over your bout of flu, it sounds nasty.'

'I'm OK sir, on the mend.'

'Anything I can do? Mop your fevered brow with a cold towel perhaps or make you a hot meal?'

'No, thank you, sir, I should be in on Monday.'

'Well, don't rush things; take as much time off as you need. Your desk will still be here on Monday.'

'Thank you, sir.'

'Take care, Christine, see you on Monday.'

'Yes sir.'

He put down the receiver. It was obvious to him that Christine was not in a talkative mood, her voice sounding a bit crackly and emotional. He hoped she would be on the mend soon; he did miss her presence in the office.

Sitting at his desk mid-morning on the Thursday, Charles received a call from George.

'Yes, George, is it about Sergeant Moran?'

'No sir, we've just had a call from Headquarters regarding Lord Hutton, he's been found dead.'

'Dead, you say!'

'Yes sir, paramedics, the local police and forensics are at the scene now, at his country mansion.'

'Right, I'm on my way. Thank you, George.'

As Charles drove his Porsche, he tried to absorb the magnitude of the news of Lord Hutton's death and its implications for his investigations. He had hoped to interrogate him further believing he was the brains and fund-raiser, but now that avenue of evidence was cut off for good.

There was also Hanna to consider. How had she taken the news? Was she the one to have found Lord Hutton, and how did he die. His death gave rise to another set of questions that plagued this particular case.

Arriving at the mansion house he was confronted with two police patrol cars, an ambulance and several forensic investigation vehicles. Clive was there to greet him and to lead him through the melee outside, to inside the mansion, up the stairs to one of the bedrooms, and to the en suite bathroom where Lord Hutton lay naked on the bathroom floor; he lay face-down, his head surrounded by a pool of blood.

'It looks as though,' said Clive, 'he probably slipped on the wet floor having had a shower, hitting his head on the sharp corner of the basin.'

'How long ago?' asked Charles surveying the prone corpse.

'My best guess at the moment is about thirty-six hours, around 9 o'clock Tuesday evening.'

'Who found the body?'

'It was the cleaner, apparently. It was the gamekeeper who rang 999. I'll let you know more after the autopsy but at this stage it looks like a straightforward accident.'

'Thank you, Clive.'

'I will give you a ring, Chief Inspector, with the autopsy result; it should be early next week.'

Charles retraced his steps down to the hall to look for Hanna. She was nowhere to be seen. Noticing King he shouted over to him, 'Where's Hanna, King?'

King shouted back, 'She left early yesterday morning. I gave her a lift to Heathrow airport.'

'Did she say where she was going?'

'To Moscow.'

'Moscow!'

'She asked me to give you a message.'

'What was that?'

'Sorry. That's all she said – sorry.'

Charles was left speechless. They were so close and now this. What the hell was happening? Why had she left so suddenly? Did she know Lord Sutton was dead before leaving? His head was spinning with questions whilst his heart was in his mouth at not seeing Hanna again. He was so looking forward to their trip to London having already booked the hotel, to a romantic weekend and an even closer relationship. Why…Why had she left without seeing him? Why had she not given him a ring?

He was still coming to terms with his feelings as he drove back to the police station, wracking his brains for some kind of explanation in the sudden turn of events, both in the case he was investigating and in his personal life. The word "sorry" from Hanna was not a big enough word to lessen his deep-felt sorrow.

Such machinations continued the next day, and now Hanna was part of this disparate mix. A simple case of the death of a vagrant had somehow morphed into a complex investigation involving his own personal life. What next?

The telephone rang. It was George again.

'We've received a call from a Ralph Burnell from the Serious Fraud Office in London. He would like to speak to you.'

'Put him through, George.'

'Detective Chief Inspector Waley-Cohen?'

'Speaking…'

'My name is Ralph Burnell from the Serious Fraud Office here in London. I was asked to speak to you concerning the Alveco Investment Trust.

'The trust has been closed down for operating fraudulent financial transactions but that's not the main reason I'm ringing you. It concerns a Mr Neil Soames, a director at the Trust, who has disappeared without trace. He cannot be contacted anywhere.

'Should he come your way could you give us a buzz. We would like to speak to the man.'

'I'll do that.'

'Thank you, Chief Inspector. Likewise if we find him first we will let you know.'

'I would appreciate that.'

'Goodbye, Chief Inspector.'

Charles replaced the receiver. The whirlwind of events seemed to be continuing as if the whole case was imploding in front of his very eyes. With these three men apprehended - MacBeath, Homes and Soames – he might finally get answers to some searching questions.

He thought about ringing Christine to bring her up to date with this week's events, picking up the receiver. But on second thoughts he placed it down again, he had no desire to upset her delicate state of mind whilst recovering from the flu; it could wait until Monday.

# Ten

Christine checked her watch - the time was 9.15am. Her appointment with her GP was at 9.30am.

The waiting room was crowded, not a smile to be seen on any face, not even the slightest glimmer of a smile; even the small children in the play area seemed to sense that this was not the place to talk to their mothers or to show too much exuberance. When they did speak the response would be a typical "shush", as if not to disturb the accepted reverent silence of the place. The puzzled face of the child would give way to a muted acceptance while playing silently with the toys, glancing up at his or her mother now and then for reassurance.

The oppressive silence was broken occasionally by the entry of another patient who would recognise and then hail a friend. The animated greeting would then be followed by a relatively loud discussion which would abate very rapidly as all eyes were focused on them, everyone wanting to say "shush" but using their eyes instead, hushed silence being the order of the day for patients who were there because of being so-called "poorly".

All eyes would then turn to the large screen on the far wall where a piercing "ding" would precede the name of the doctor's next appointment. One person would recognise their name, rise and exit the waiting room, no doubt sighing with relief that their wait was over. For everyone else their eyes would return to a blank stare or whatever else they were doing to pass the time until the next announcement, hoping it would be their turn soon.

Christine surveyed the room out of boredom rather than read one of the many out-of-date magazines stacked on the small tables. The children's play area was set against a mural of wild African animals, quite cleverly done in her opinion. She amused herself by trying to remember all the animal names and in the case of the hippopotamus trying to spell it backwards with her troubled mind.

Two of the walls of the waiting room were adorned with paintings from an amateur painting group with stickers showing their price and a telephone number to ring if interested in buying. Several of them, she observed, were very good, especially that of a dog, someone's pet obviously, which was certainly worthy of the price tag.

Christine also recalled the last week gone. This was her second visit to see her GP to discover the result of her blood test, her first visit being to discuss her unusual symptoms.

It wasn't just the pain in her side; she had noticed changes in her body, too. Her breasts were more taught and her nipples slightly enlarged; she had also felt nauseas at times. They were all the signs of pregnancy, she was at least aware of that having discussed such issues with many of her friends.

But she couldn't be pregnant because she was still on the pill and she had had her last period, albeit not as heavy as usual.

Furthermore when she had tested herself with a pregnancy kit using both testing sticks, the first was negative and the second positive though with very faint symbols. She had followed the instructions and was in two minds to buy another pregnancy kit to double check. But the pain in her side was unusual so she had thought it time to visit her GP.

Having explained her symptoms and her confused state of mind to her GP on the first visit the doctor, having first examined her, had requested a blood test to put her mind at ease, one way or the other.

So she waited anxiously for her name to go up on the screen, every minute's delay seeming like an eternity, creating yet more confusion in her mind. Was she or was she not pregnant, if not what was happening to her body?

When the time eventually came for her appointment she felt this was the moment of truth, striding purposefully to the doctor's door and tapping on it gently.

'Come in.'

She entered, her blood pressure rising now and flushing her cheeks.

'Take a seat, Miss Moran.

'Your blood test has come back and it says categorically that you're pregnant.'

The female doctor smiled and was about to say congratulations until Christine blurted out, 'But it can't be, I'm still on the pill and I'm still having my periods!'

The doctor looked again impassively at the blood test results on her screen.

'The blood test doesn't lie, you are pregnant.'

'Could it be something else?' asked Christine nervously.

'Look, let's not speculate. I will refer you for an ultrasound scan. Are you going private?'

Christine nodded, lost for words; it was exciting, nerve-racking and unexpected, all at the same time. Her mind was a whirlwind of thoughts and apprehension.

'I'll arrange for you to have one tomorrow, is that early enough?'

Christine nodded again. You could have said anything to her at that point of time since her ears seemed deaf to the outside world, her own thoughts blocking everything else; a mixture of happiness, anxiety and dread, all rolled into one thought – she was pregnant!

'You will get a call from the hospital for the timing of your scan tomorrow.'

'Thank you, doctor.'

Seeing the way Christine had reacted to the news, the doctor gently stroked her hand, 'Don't worry, Christine, I'm certain everything will work out just fine.'

Christine managed a feeble smile and took her leave, her mind still fazed by the prospect of being pregnant. Despite all her precautions with Charles her blood test was telling her she was pregnant. She couldn't believe it. She wouldn't believe it. There had to be another explanation for her symptoms other than pregnancy.

That evening and night such thoughts were churned over and over again until sleep over-powered her anxiety, putting her mind to a fitful rest at best.

The following day she found herself in another waiting room, this time awaiting her ultrasound scan. There were only two people waiting this time but with trepidation written large on their faces – a male partner reassuring his woman with his arm around her shoulders. For the first time she was conscious of not having a man by her side, her loving feelings for Charles welling up inside of her. She dabbed her eyes to prevent any tears revealing her true feelings to the outside world; she was good at that, she had had to be in her profession. But it didn't come easy, especially at times like these. Stupidly she was feeling that the other woman's eyes were saying: 'Where's her man at this important time in her life?'

'Christine Moran?'

Her name was being called and she followed the nurse into the room, removing her coat.

'Just hang it there on the peg and lay on the trolley if you would. I'll be with you in a minute.'

The young nurse smiled a comforting smile but had an air of clinical efficiency about her; that together with the starkness and sterile nature of the room made Christine nervous as she took off her shoes and lay awkwardly on the trolley.

The nurse returned to wheel the ultrasound equipment alongside the trolley, then adjusted Christine's clothing to access her tummy.

'Do you want to see the screen?'

Christine nodded but really wanted to say no.

'This will be a little cold at first as I apply the lubricating gel. Now just relax.'

Christine stared at the ceiling and not at the screen as the nurse searched for the foetus. The nurse was about to say something when she abruptly turned the screen away from Christine's view.

'I'll be back in a minute, just need to have a word with the consultant.'

The nurse hurriedly left the room to return several minutes later with a male consultant. Christine continued to stare blankly at the ceiling not wishing to be distracted by their obvious concern.

'Hi, Christine, my name is Adrian Blakewell and I'm your consultant gynaecologist. I'm just discussing with the nurse what we're seeing on the screen. This will just take a few more minutes.'

Christine's stolid demeanour remained the same, still staring at the ceiling but out of the corner of her eye she could see the consultant and nurse nodding in agreement at whatever was the issue.

'Christine, the nurse will clean you up and then I will see you in my consulting room.'

The consultant left the room, the nurse busying herself removing the gel from Christine's tummy without saying a further word, her rictus smile betraying little. Christine was then led to the consulting room where the consultant was meticulously studying the scan images. She simply did not know what to think but all indications told her that things were not right, not as they should be. She had probably been right all along and that she wasn't pregnant, one of those scares that would be quickly forgotten. Her mind was now calmer as she sat down and awaited the verdict from the consultant, the nurse remaining in attendance.

'You are about six weeks pregnant, Christine,' said in a very calm, dispassionate manner.

'But I can't be - I'm very regular with my pill taking!'

'The pill isn't fallible, Christine, you should know that, there is still a one in a thousand chance of becoming pregnant even with correct usage; one in twenty with incorrect usage. You are pregnant, I can assure you.'

All the suppressed emotions welled up inside of her once again.

'But you have a very rare condition. You have what we call a "bicornuate uterus", commonly known as a "two-in-one womb" or "heart-shaped womb".

The consultant paused to allow the news to sink in.

'The main risks to a woman with this condition are miscarriage and premature labour. It can also cause fertility problems and breech births as well as malformations in the baby.'

The consultant paused again. The nurse remained silent.

'Are your periods painful, frequent and heavy?'

Christine nodded. Her mind now numb to what he was saying.

'This is because effectively you have two wombs. It means you have double the amount of bleeding, pain and frequency. I'm surprised it wasn't picked up at an earlier stage in your life. But the contraceptive pill can mitigate many of these effects, controlling and regulating the cycle, so these things can be missed.

'The chance of you going full term with this pregnancy is very slim, very slim indeed. There is nothing we can do; there is no cure or treatment for this condition.

'Let me explain further,' drawing a rough sketch on a piece of paper: 'When development takes place in the womb the uterus comes from two tubes which fuse in the middle. When the tubes fail to fuse they become like two horns and the baby can only develop in one of these horns. There is insufficient space for the baby to grow leading to early onset of labour and miscarriage and the baby not developing properly.

'At six weeks we cannot tell if the baby is malformed. But usually with this condition the foetus does not attach to the womb properly and to determine that you would need to come back for an eight-week scan.

'I, personally, have only encountered this condition twice before. In both cases there was an early miscarriage and the foetus had not developed correctly. My colleagues have had similar experiences.'

Christine was stunned, her mind reeling with the consultant's matter-of-fact, medical terms. She looked at the nurse but there was no comfort to be gleaned there. She gulped before asking him the most important question in her mind, the answer to which she really didn't want to know.

'Does that mean I can't have a baby in the future, ever?'

'I'm sorry to say it's highly unlikely. It's been known in very rare cases but not to my experience. I'm sorry, Christine.'

'What do I do now?' Christine held back the tears.

'You have two options, Christine. You can continue with this pregnancy with all the risks I have outlined or ... '

'Or have an abortion?' Words that Christine never thought she would ever utter.

'... Or have an abortion. Think about it, give yourself time. But the final decision is yours. I can only advise you one way or the other.

'I'm sorry to be the conveyor of such bad news, Christine. You can seek a second opinion if you wish.'

Christine shook her head, paralysed by the thought of never having her own child, the world suddenly turning the colour of grey, all other colours banned for ever from her life; a childless woman, an end to her life as she knew it, all her dreams of motherhood dashed on a few medical terms.

'I would like you now, Christine, to see the nurse and arrange for an appointment tomorrow. Her name is Irina,' the consultant swivelling his chair to engage the nurse in the conversation. 'Irina is here to give you any support you wish and to be available to answer your questions 24/7.' Christine looked at the nurse for a woman's comfort but was only met with a semi-reassuring, medical smile.

'Irina will discuss with you your situation and should you decide to have an abortion, she will discuss the different methods available – chemical and surgical – most suitable for your stage of pregnancy and their related risks and complications.

'She will take a blood test to see if you are anaemic and, if appropriate, a cervical screening test; a check for STIs, again if appropriate.

'You will be asked to sign a consent form.

'On this first visit, if you opt for an abortion, you will be given an abortion pill. This blocks the hormone that makes the lining of the womb suitable for the fertilised egg. You can continue your normal activities though you may feel a bit sick at times and diarrhoea is not unknown. A few women have cramps and a little bleeding but most do not.

'Irina will then book you a second visit thirty-six to forty-eight hours later. You will be given a second medicine which you can take at home if you so desire. Within four to six hours your womb lining will break down along with the embryo and be lost through your bleeding. This part can be painful but you can take a painkiller.'

The consultant looked at Christine's face and his heart went out to her.

'I know this is all medical speak, Christine, but I do realise this is a major shock to you, a massive upheaval in your life and your dreams, but you must believe there is life after this and life does go on. Life may change dramatically but doesn't stop. You're only twenty-five-years-old, not all that many summers behind you, and you have your whole life ahead of you, try to be positive.

'I've said all I want to say. I suggest you go home and think on it. Irina will clarify tomorrow any of the issues I've mentioned and answer any of your questions.

'Once again I would just like to say how sorry I am. Thank you, Christine.'

The consultant stood up, shook Christine's hand, and held open the door. Christine left the room feeling sick in the pit of her stomach, her face drawn and her steps faltering. The nurse held her hand as they discussed the next day's appointment time and how she could be contacted.

~

The rest of the day and night Christine felt she was floating on air but not in a nice way. Her situation wasn't for real; she was dreaming it all and would wake up thinking it all a silly nightmare. It was not her but an impostor who had stolen her identity and the truth would come out in the end; she would then be able to resume her normal life.

One of her first instincts was to go to the drinks cabinet to drown her sorrows but, at the last moment, rationalised it unwise with a baby inside her.

The foetus growing inside of her was a baby, a real baby, not distinguishable as such at this early stage but nevertheless a real baby growing inside her body. She was a pro-life person and always had been; she would see it to term or however long it took for her to miscarry. Wasn't that better than to abort at this stage without giving the baby a chance for life, however infinitesimal that may be? Let God determine the outcome and wipe away her tears, be they of joy or of grief. That is the way it should be.

But, and it was a big but, what about the father? Would it be fair to Charles to subject him to an inevitable period of hurt; he was bound to find out at some stage and he might feel obliged to be with her, even marry her. He was that sort of man.

On the other hand he might feel in his heart that he'd been tricked into marriage, a childless marriage with no prospect of fatherhood and come to despise her in time. Would it not be better in this case therefore to have an early abortion so that no one gets hurt; she was a strong enough personality to take it in her stride and, you never know, there might be a cure for her condition one day with all the medical advances. She shouldn't be so negative and to start looking at the more positive side of life. As the consultant said it wasn't the end of her world, life does go on.

Such thoughts, one way or the other, tormented her all through the evening giving her a restless night with very little sleep.

The next morning, Wednesday, she had made no decision, torn between having the child whatever the outcome, and thoughts of Charles.

That is, until Charles rang early to ask of her health. The sound of his concerned voice melted her heart and after the briefest of responses to his questions, she broke down into floods of tears, scalding tears that hurt her eyes and her cheeks. The decision had been made for her.

Later that same day she swallowed the abortion pill.

She felt no ill effects but emotionally did not feel it appropriate to go into work.

On the Friday morning she took the second medicine at home. Her bleeding that evening was heavy and painful and she took a painkiller to ease the pain. She dared not look at what she flushed down the toilet later that evening.

That night, in bed, her mind was at ease as if a huge burden had been lifted from her shoulders; light-headed and relaxed it was as if she was at peace with herself and the decision she had made. Sleep was most welcome, soothing her whole body, cleansing it of all impurities from the medicines and the effects of sleep deprivation these last few nights. She would wake up a new woman were her last thoughts as she closed her eyes.

That is what she thought. But that was not to be. She woke up the next morning with an immense sense of soul-bearing, searing emotion – intense grief for an unborn child. Her heart swelled with misery. What had she done? How could she have been so cruel? If she had made the right decision why did she feel so wretched? Why was the pain of losing a child so strong in her; would it ever ease? She felt she had joined the legion of lost souls.

Her suffocating grief was unbearable, so deep and hurtful, something she had never experienced before. Her tears scalded her cheeks once again and she felt like crying herself to death for her wickedness to her unborn child who was now floating in the sewers underneath the earth, gasping for its last breath. Her imaginings were grotesque and knew no limits.

The stress was painful and had come to her like a bolt from the blue. The relationship between mother and child was never as strong as she felt at this very moment for her lost child.

Should she ring someone for counselling? The nurse had given her a number to ring if she needed an ear to listen to any post-abortion problems. The nurse had also discussed post-traumatic stress but she had never thought it relevant to her. After thinking about it for a while she decided not to ring Irina, perhaps some other time.

As Sunday dawned the tsunami wave of grief had abated to a few ripples and was much more manageable. Her pragmatic and logical persona was now the dominant force in her reasoning, quietening her grief and mental stress. Her emotions however still swung uncontrollably from belligerence to lucidity to head-in-hands weeping.

She could see things clearer and the logical decision she had made now held sway. It was for the best all round – for her, for Charles and for the baby. Gradually she would come to terms with losing the baby and with her condition, and be able to move on in her life. Things could be a thousand times worse, health-wise, and did not preclude her from trying again to have a baby, or for that matter, to adopt a child if need be. She hadn't been cut off from motherhood altogether; she needed to be more rational and patient with herself.

Work the next day would also take her mind off things and have a sobering effect on her tribulations. In police work there wasn't much time to think about oneself but to think of others less fortunate who came before the courts; to develop a thicker skin against personal attacks of both the mind and body. A good policewoman kept her private life separate from her work. She was mentally ready for Monday's workload, looking forward to seeing Charles and the team again.  Yes, work was the antidote to her troubles and a salve to her febrile mind and guilty conscience.

# Eleven

'Good morning, Christine, are you feeling better?' asked Charles as Christine was about to sit at her desk.

'Yes, thank you sir.'

'Sounds like it was a nasty bout of flu you had.'

'Yes sir.'

'Glad to see you're better, I missed you. I think we all missed you.'

'Thank you, sir.'

'Now, grab your coat we have an urgent job on. Just an hour ago, Neil Soames, the co-director of Alveco Investment Trust, asked for police protection. We have him in police custody.

'He's disclosed where MacBeath and Homes are hiding out – in a farmhouse on Lord Hutton's estate. Whilst the team are taking down his statement I'm in a hurry to apprehend these two. Are you up to it?'

'Yes sir, I wouldn't miss it for the world.'

'Good, let's go then. I've informed the local police and they're already on their way. En route I'll bring you up to date as to what happened last week; it was one hell of a week resulting in Lord Hutton's fatal accident. I hope your week was better. Sorry, you know what I mean.'

Christine responded limply, 'It could have been better, sir.'

'Let's go then. I know the farmhouse's exact location. We'll use a patrol car to clear the traffic instead of the Porsche.'

With blue lights flashing and siren blazing they reached the farmhouse in double-quick time, screeching to a halt next to all the other vehicles surrounding the farmhouse.

'What the hell,' blurted out Charles, 'what the hell have we here?' There were several police cars and vans, several ambulances, armed response units, a forensics unit and a police liaison unit.

Exiting the car, Charles looked around asking, 'Who's in charge here?'

There was no initial response until a plain-clothes officer strode up to Charles.

'I'm in charge, I'm Detective Sergeant Bell.'

Charles shook his hand.

'I'm Detective Inspector Waley-Cohen and this is Detective Sergeant Moran. What's going on here? My instructions were to apprehend two men – MacBeath and Soames. I need them alive for questioning; why the firearms officers and negotiators?'

'They've surrounded the building with instructions to shoot to kill if necessary.

'Following your instructions a WPC with a police constable went to the house to apprehend the occupants. Approaching the house the WPC was gunned down, we believe with a double-barrelled shotgun. Her wounds, thank God, aren't fatal and she's been rushed to hospital. We laid siege to the place and I called in the armed response unit. They've been asked to come out and surrender but their response was another volley of shots at a police car smashing the lights and windscreen. There have been no further casualties.'

'You did well, Sergeant Bell. I would like to try everything possible to get them out alive before the armed response units rush in.'

'We've tried negotiating with them but they respond each time with another volley of shots.'

'Well, we'll just have to sit it out for a while; maybe they'll come to their senses and give themselves up quietly.'

'Yes sir. Do you mind if I call in my superiors?'

'No, please go ahead.'

Christine turned to Charles, 'What now, sir?'

'It's just a question of sitting tight for a while. I'm not optimistic though, having shot one policewoman the armed police will be trigger-happy to end this siege one way or the other. I don't see it ending amicably if they don't surrender within the next hour.'

~

In the farmhouse MacBeath sat in his wheelchair as calm as you like, feeding the dog with biscuits. Homes stood by the side of the broken window from where he had fired off several shots from his double-barrelled shotgun; empty cartridges lay at his feet, smoking from the residue and giving off an acrid smell. He kicked them to one side.

'That was a bloody silly thing to do, Cecil, shooting at that policewoman. Haven't you any sense in that thick head of yours? We could have got off scot-free, talked our way out of things but, no, you knew best, you are the one with the brains. You thought, without asking me, that you'd shoot at the police. Now, if we get out of this alive we'll spend the rest of our lives in jail. You're a right wally.

'I panicked!'

'You're not paid to panic. You're paid to look after me and obey my every command. Do you understand?'

Homes rolled his eyes as he reloaded his gun, his manner deferential yet faintly superior. His attitude annoyed MacBeath.

'I said - do you understand?'

'Shut it, can you! I've had enough of all this and with you in particular with all your blabbering,' replied Homes through gritted teeth as he glanced out of the window for signs of police movement.

'Oh, another worm has turned. That's what I like to see, a bit of spunk in my men.'

'So much for your men - the Professor is dead, Lord Hutton is dead, McPherson is dead and Swaine is dead. Soon we'll be dead.'

'They are the inevitable casualties of war, Cecil. Men die for what they believe in. Sacrifices have to be made sometimes.'

'Why did the Professor have to die then?'

'Because he was a turncoat, a police informant, and in war you have to execute traitors, and, don't forget, you were the executioner.'

'But only on your command, against my better judgement.'

'There you go again, questioning my authority. In the army you have to obey commands from your superiors however distasteful.'

'A group of seven men, you call that an army?'

'Seven men or seven thousand men, it makes no difference, you have to have a leader for others to follow.'

'What a joke! Captain MacBeath - our masterful leader, eh? Our "Rob Roy" of the glens! The only thing you have in common with the Scottish hero is your red hair.'

'Don't you dare sneer at your Captain; in a few weeks when the third phase happens, I will go down in history as the "Rob Roy" of the modern era, the people's champion, a legend in my lifetime like Robert Roy MacGregor of the early 18th century. He was a folk hero and I, like him, will be known as the Scottish Robin Hood.

'Whereas you, Cecil Homes, are nothing but dirt to be trodden on like dog shit under one's shoes, to be cleaned off immediately to avoid the foul smell; a scumbag of the worst kind.

'I, Captain Robert Roy MacBeath, will be spoken of in years to come as the man who lit the fuse to set Europe alight. The first man in history to ignite the people's wrath against the bankers and politicians of Europe and to change the whole course of democracy – government of the people by the people and not by unelected, behind-closed-doors, faceless Eurocrats, who are lavishly overpaid, massively powerful and wholly unchallengeable. I will cripple Europe and claim the countries back from Brussels. Nothing worth having can survive undefended.'

'You're mad, consumed with hatred.'

'Listen, who are you to call me mad? With respect, you're nothing more than a brainless, big black nigger, with more brains in his arse than in his head.'

'What did you call me?'

Homes was now teeth-grindingly furious, his anger at fever-pitch.

'I called you a fat, bastard nigger.'

Homes in his fury, with fist-clenched defiance, pointed the gun at MacBeath's stumps and pulled the trigger, blasting the lower half of MacBeath's body with shotgun pellets.

'With respect, this fat, bastard nigger has just blown your Scottish git balls off to kingdom come. That's for the bastard bit. Now this is for the nigger bit.'

Hearing the blast of the first gunshot, MacBeath's dog, "Tally", first cowered before springing to the aid of its master. With fangs bared it ran headlong to Homes who turned the gun on the dog and pulled the second trigger. The dog barked and then yelped as it fell to the floor in obvious pain and distress.

Homes then reloaded the gun and blasted MacBeath's head and body with both barrels, the force of which sent the wheelchair to the other side of the room, crashing and up-turning against the wall.

'That, my friend, is for the nigger bit. I never did like that word and you will never say it to me again, ever.'

In the heat of the moment Homes forgot about his exposure at the window. The crack of a sniper's bullet deafened his ears before the bullet passed through his brain. His legs crumpled as he fell heavily to the floor – dead, as dead as "Rob Roy"!

~

Charles feared the worst as he heard the shots ring out and saw the armed police unit with guns and shields storm the farmhouse. There were no more shots and it was all over in minutes, the melee of armed police on entry quickly subsiding to an orderly exit.

The Captain of the armed police unit was the last to leave beckoning to Charles to enter the farmhouse. Christine followed Charles warily.

The Captain, without saying a word, just pointed to the two bodies and the dying dog.

The upside-down face of MacBeath had been partially blown away giving it a ghoulish appearance, the rest of the body riddled with pellets, many weeping blood. A dog was slumped by the side of the wheelchair, its legs still twitching in its final death throes, its tongue protruding from a bleeding mouth.

Homes's body had fallen to its knees and there it had stayed, like a kneeling statue of Pompeii frozen in time. An exit wound in the forehead made the reason for death apparent.

Christine could not stop herself. She dashed over to the dog, bent down and stroked its head and ears until the twitching stopped. She finally rose with a brimful of tears in her eyes.

'Sorry, sir, it was just the sight of the dog dying.' That was a half-lie; her problems went much deeper than that and the tears were not all for the dog.

Charles handed her a handkerchief to dab her eyes and another one to clean the traces of the dog's blood from her hand.

Charles surveyed the room. On the wall behind the wheelchair and MacBeath's body a large blackboard had been erected, now covered with splashes of blood. The chalk writing listed European cities, including London, with dates and crowd numbers in thousands. Cities ticked indicated where riots had already taken place; against all cities was the same future date. The last column read: "Bankers and Politicians killed", but there were no entries.

In the other corner of the room were placed two computer screens still live and flashing with rolling lines of meaningless symbols and characters; also two television screens, one tuned in to the BBC news, the other to a foreign station.

The whole scene could be likened to a movie set where the actors would suddenly come back to life, congratulating each other on a scene well done, wiping away the make-up from their faces; a scene of an operations room on a "B" movie set.

'Weird, it beggars belief,' were the words that came out of Charles's mouth. Christine just stared dumbfounded, her mind not able to take it all in.

Neither in their wildest dreams had either of them imagined the goings-on of this disparate group of individuals they were investigating. This was more than just organised crime, there appeared to be a political element to their intentions which gave this case a sinister twist. Charles was now even more interested and motivated in unravelling the plans of these people.

All three of them – the Captain, Charles and Christine – moved aside as the forensics team entered the room to do their duty of photographing and marking the crime scene.

The captain turned to Charles: 'We had listening devices on the outside walls. We will send you a transcript and a recording of what was said by the occupants during the siege.'

'Thank you Captain, it will be of great interest to our investigations.'

Charles and Christine took their leave, heading back to the police station. Little was said between them as they mulled over in their own minds this sudden turn of events.

'You OK, Christine? You look as though you could throw up at any moment.'

'I was thinking about the dog, sir; that poor animal to be treated that way. Having survived Afghanistan it was cruel for it to die in such macabre circumstances at the hands of a crazed gunman.'

'It wasn't a pretty sight, especially on your first day back after being poorly yourself. Sorry you had to see that.'

'Not your fault, sir. Life can be awfully cruel at times.'

'It certainly can, and you and I have seen more than our fair share recently, but as policemen we are supposed to absorb it into our psyche and lock it away out of sight and out of our mind of our personal lives. Not an easy thing to do but we're professionals and have to accept that goes with the job. We should seek another profession if we can't handle it. Don't you agree, Sergeant?'

'I do, sir, unfortunately.'

# Twelve

Back at the police station more revelations were yet to follow as Charles and Christine sipped their coffee in Charles's office.

Charles was about to ask Christine about her absence and to check she was feeling well enough on her first day back when his telephone rang. It was Clive from Forensics.

'Hello Clive.'

'Hello, Chief Inspector, I've got the results of the autopsy on Lord Hutton. You are not going to believe this.'

'What am I not going to believe, Clive? Before you answer I have Detective Sergeant Moran in my office and if I may I would like to switch this call to the speaker. Is that OK with you?'

'The more, the merrier. What I've got to say concerns her also.'

'Fire away, Clive'

'As I was saying, I now have the autopsy report on Lord Hutton.

'He did not die from natural causes from hitting his head on the basin. He died from acute renal failure from the ingestion of poisonous mushrooms. The blow to his head was the result of his fall after his heart had stopped.

495

'Looking through his medical history he had had a diseased kidney removed in his forties and the other was therefore more susceptible to catastrophic failure when flooded with poison.'

'You think he was murdered then?' Charles's eyes widened at the unexpected news.

'I've told you before, I don't speculate on matters like that. That's your job.

'The poisonous mushrooms could have been there by accident or been deliberately served to him. All I can say is that he died from mushroom poisoning, also medically known as mycetism. Over to you, Chief Inspector.'

'Thanks, Clive. Can you tell us what sort, what type of mushroom?'

'I can't say definitely. Many of the poisonous mushrooms have the same chemical elements. But a reasoned guess, at this stage, would be something like the mushroom "amarita phalloides" – the "death-cap" mushroom. Will let you know when we have done more analysis.'

'Thanks, Clive. Hope to speak to you again soon.'

The call was ended. Charles and Christine stared at each other with blank expressions. Now, it seemed, six of the seven persons they were investigating had been murdered. No wonder Neil Soames, the seventh member of the group, had asked for police protection to save his skin.

A niggling question though in Charles's mind, which would not go away, was whether Hanna was involved in some way with Lord Hutton's death. Her sudden departure raised the stakes that this might be the case. He needed more answers and quickly.

'Let's talk to Neil Soames,' said Charles, 'he's got an awful lot of explaining to do.'

'Yes sir.'

As Christine followed Charles to the interview room she was pleased the day was working out as it was with little time for introspection. On first seeing Charles a love swell had surged through her breast making a lump come to her throat and her eyes smart. Her instinct was to reach out to him, to blurt out what had happened to her, hoping he would have comforted her by holding her in his arms and saying how much he loved her and in the end everything would be all right. However, the events of the day so far had allowed no such lingering thoughts.

In the interview room Charles and Christine went through Neil Soames's statement. It was brief and concise, a précis of his time at Alveco Investment Trust and little much else.

'Not good enough,' said Charles out loud, 'no mention of any of the group. I realise he doesn't want to implicate himself with any of their deaths, preferring to be prosecuted for financial fraud rather than for murder, but the fact he is seeking police protection means he knows a lot more than he is telling us.

'Let's have him in, Sergeant.'

Christine left the room to return a few minutes later with Neil Soames. He was the archetypal respectable business man, dressed in a smart, expensive, pin-striped suit with a white shirt, a blue tie, a gold tie-pin and gold cuff-links. He was clean shaven with sleek, dark hair combed neatly back.

Charles beckoned him to be seated opposite Christine and himself. He sat bolt upright as if at a General Company Meeting, staring straight ahead. Christine switched on the recorder.

'For the record,' said Charles, 'this is Monday, the 6th of July, 2015, at 11.45am and those present are: Detective Chief Inspector Waley-Cohen, Detective Sergeant Christine Moran, and Mr Neil Soames of Alveco Investment Trust. Also for the record Mr Soames does not wish to have legal aid or legal representation.'

Charles pushed the statement towards Soames.

'For the record can you state your name, age, and occupation.'

Soames acidly responded, 'My name is Neil Richard Soames, I'm forty-five years of age and I'm the co-director of Alveco Investment Trust headquartered in London.'

'Thank you.' There was a deliberate, long pause before Charles spoke again.

'Mr Soames, I'll give it to you straight. What you say to us in this interview will determine whether I hand you over to the Serious Fraud Office or keep you here and charge you with murder, or both. Think and think well before you answer our questions.'

This opening statement had no perceptible effect on Soames's business demeanour, his face expressionless as if at a business conference or discussing terms with a client.

'I want you to start at the beginning,' said Charles politely.

'Lord Hutton and I set up Alveco ... '

'I want you to start at the very beginning,' said Charles in a more commanding tone of voice this time.

'Where do you want me to start?'

'Let's start at the "Black Lion" pub could we and what happened there before you set up the Trust.'

'I met lord Hutton at the "Black Lion" pub and we talked about setting up Alveco ...'

'I've tried to be nice to you, Mr Soames, but now you're beginning to annoy me. I gave you the opportunity to come clean but I see I'm going to have to lead you by the nose.

'What do you know about Captain Robert Roy MacBeath, John McPherson, Cecil Homes, Robert Swaine and Professor Andrew Falconer-Smith?'

'I've never heard any of those names.'

'This is a waste of time, Sergeant, take him away and book him for first-degree murder of Professor Falconer-Smith and Lord Hutton.' Christine stood up. It had the desired effect.

'I'm not a murderer. Yes, I did know these men but I'm not a murderer.' This is exactly what Charles wanted to hear.

'Sit down, Sergeant. Now this time start at the very beginning. I will not ask you again.'

'It...It all started so innocently, a group of men in the "Black Lion" pub discussing politics, football and every other subject under the sun over a pint or two. We had all been made redundant so bankers and politicians were high on the list of people to hate and to vent our spleen on.

'Lord Hutton was a regular in the pub and he took more than a passing interest in our group, particularly with Roy MacBeath. We put this down to his interest in military history, MacBeath having served in Afghanistan.

'Over time the discussions became more heated and we were all surprised when he invited the five of us  - not the Professor who wasn't a member of the group at this time - back to his farmhouse on his country estate. As I said, we had all been made redundant and were penniless, living off benefits. So, what the hell, we had time on our hands.

'The visits to the farmhouse became more regular and it transpired that Lord Hutton's investments were haemorrhaging money and he feared he would go bankrupt. He told us he had made contact with the Russian mafia on his visits abroad and they were prepared to pass money to him if he was able to launder the money through his investments, particularly his property portfolio. This Lord Hutton had agreed to do; receiving many millions via a Maltese bank.

'But the Russian mafia had insisted on one more thing: to set up a master cell, a group of political agitators in the UK to coordinate the many such similar cells throughout Europe; the intention being to rock the establishments in the various countries by bringing about a concerted, simultaneous campaign of rioting in the streets, allowing roaming gangs of the mafia criminals to take advantage.

'Europe's porous borders meant it was easy to move stolen goods from west to east where there were huge black markets with no questions asked. Luxury cars – Aston Martin, Bentley, Rolls-Royce, Jaguar, Land Rover – were in demand in China, premium cars with a strong brand heritage. Antiques, paintings, jewellery, agricultural plant, you name it; it was all up for grabs.'

'How did the Professor become involved?' asked Charles.

Soames poured himself a glass of water to moisten his lips, his calm, business demeanour now fraying at the edges.

'MacBeath took it on himself to be the leader of the group, treating it as a military operation. But he needed someone with the linguistic ability to talk to groups on the continent. The Professor was a down-and-out tramp at the time but gradually with the promise of free drinks and spending money he was roped in.'

'And why was the Professor killed?'

'I was told by MacBeath, I wasn't there at the time, that prior to the start of operations he was going to go to the police and to inform on the group. Some girl or other had pricked his conscience. MacBeath had ordered Homes to kill him in the church. We used several disused buildings to hold our meetings, the church being one of them. Homes was the lackey and the muscle of the group.'

'And what were the roles of the other members of the group?'

'John McPherson was an ex-military man whose role was to organise the flow of military equipment to the groups abroad. Swaine was a telecoms engineer whose role was to set up a "dark-web" illegal internet for communicating with others, everything being deeply encrypted to avoid detection by the authorities; the use of mobiles were banned between group members, between cells, and with the Russian mafia.'

'And why were they assassinated?'

'I don't really know. I mean that. Something went wrong there with the Italian mafia perhaps or some misunderstanding with a criminal gang, I just don't know.'

'We know a lot of travel was involved. How was it funded?'

'Oh, easy, they were given wads of cash from MacBeath who, in turn, received it from Lord Hutton. They were all to be given a lump sum of cash on successful completion of the operation, again from Lord Hutton.'

'So far, so good. Now tell me about your role.'

'Being a redundant investment banker, I was asked by Lord Hutton to set up an Investment Trust. It was not part of the deal with the Russian mafia but Lord Hutton saw it as a way to safeguard his estate by siphoning money off and trousering it. Russian oligarchs were also contributors, as were others.'

'What went wrong?'

'The finances were sound initially and the investments good despite Lord Hutton's pilfering. But then the Trust was made to pay, under his instructions, monies to leaders of populist parties and criminals, against false invoices. Some of the investments also turned sour. We ended up with a Ponzi scheme to keep going which we knew would eventually break down but would last long enough to make our escape from the financial mess and the country.'

'Did you kill Lord Hutton?'

'No! Absolutely not! Whilst he was alive there was always the chance he could rescue the Trust from his laundered money from the mafia. I certainly did not want him dead. Anyway, why are you asking me that question? I thought Lord Hutton died from natural causes, or so I hear.'

'Did you know Miss Hanna Goraya?'

'Who? I've never heard of her.'

'You're sure about that?'

'I have no idea who she is. Should I know her?'

'I have one final question. On a blackboard in the farmhouse there were dates against cities. What did they signify?'

'These were the dates for synchronising the riots. The first phase was successful with the southern countries and the second phase was also successful with the northern countries. The last date was the third phase when all the countries would rise up together against their governments, their bankers and politicians, including London this time.'

'I see, and the column listing the number of dead bankers and politicians?'

'For Lord Hutton it was all about money. He would rant and rave against bankers and politicians but it was mainly money he was concerned about – money and his precious estate.

'MacBeath, on the other hand, had a hidden agenda partly funded by Lord Hutton. He wanted to kill as many bankers and politicians, with the riots being a diversionary tactic from his main objective. For the third phase he was in the process of hiring ex-military and mercenaries to do the killing and was in contact with Islamic State cells to create further panic throughout Europe. He was a mad man with sinister intentions, not to everyone's liking. He had a target of one hundred deaths – fifty bankers and fifty politicians. Hackers, for a price, had hacked into the computers of the European Parliament in Brussels and the European Bank in Frankfurt and supplied him with names and addresses. The most senior were the main target wherever they were vulnerable. The man was paranoid and a psychopath suffering more than post-traumatic stress from his time in Afghanistan.'

'Well, thank you Mr Soames, we may need to interview you again so you will stay here in police custody until we decide what to do with you. I'll inform the Serious Fraud Office of your whereabouts.'

'I didn't kill anyone, I swear.'

'Probably not but you could be charged as an accessory to the murder of Professor Falconer-Smith.'

Christine closed the proceedings and Soames was led away, back to his cell still pleading his innocence.

'Wow. That was some interview, sir.'

'It certainly was, Sergeant. It's been a busy morning. Let's go down to the canteen and have a late lunch together, you can tell me all about your bout of flu last week. I feel in the mood to give you a sympathetic ear to all your ills.'

'Yes sir. Thank you, sir.'

Christine knew in her heart what she would like to say but she also knew that her head would rule her heart for the foreseeable future, possibly for ever. It was kinder to Charles that way.

And who was this Hanna Goraya? Charles had never mentioned her name before and she was afraid to ask for being hurt once again. Were they having an affair? Was she part of his life? There were many such questions in her frazzled brain as she headed to the canteen.

Charles turned to Christine and jokingly quipped: 'You should take a holiday break, Sergeant, somewhere nice and warm, do you the world of good after your flu.'

Christine made no reply but thinking: I wish I could take a break from myself sometimes, both body and mind; to remove myself from myself and to look at myself to clear away the fog of despair which is clouding my every judgement; now that would really be a nice break!

# Thirteen

Charles sat in his office waiting for a visit from MI5 and MI6.

Having brought his father up to date with Soames's statement he had contacted MI5 with regard to the third phase of riots due in five days' time. Real or imaginary the date had to be taken seriously by higher authorities.

The two agents had arrived earlier that morning and had made a courtesy call with his father before wanting to see Charles to discuss the case in more detail. There was another reason to talk to him but that was secondary to their main purpose of validating the date of the expected insurrection throughout Europe.

His father showed them in to Charles's office and introduced Peter Turnbull from MI5 and Graham Petty from MI6. His father then left the room.

'Gentlemen, please take a seat.'

'Thank you, Chief Inspector,' said in unison.

'Can we get you a coffee?'

'No thanks,' said Petty, 'We've been well-watered in your Chief Constable's office.'

'Let me start then by playing the recording by the armed police unit during the siege of MacBeath and Homes in Lord Hutton's farmhouse. It will give you a sense of the gravity of this case as well as the thinking of the men involved.

'I will then play the interview with Soames taken by myself and my colleague, Detective Sergeant Moran. In this interview he clarifies the purpose and intentions of the group. It is the third phase of insurrection which is of concern to us and obviously to you.'

'This is why we're here, Chief Inspector,' said Turnbull, pulling his chair a little closer to the desk.

Charles switched on the recorder and then watched as the two agents listened intently and took notes.

Turnbull was the older of the two with a deadpan expression, showing little emotion. Petty, he got the impression, was relatively new to his role in MI6 and squirmed a little at the heated exchange of MacBeath and Homes prior to the shooting; even more so when he showed them the photographs of the scene after the shooting, particularly the close-ups of the bloodied corpses of both men and the dog.

'And now the interview with Soames,' showing them first a close-up photograph of the blackboard, 'it's for you to gauge the importance of the same future date against all of the countries together with Soames's explanation.'

As they listened Charles smiled inwardly. He'd had contact with a number of MI5 and MI6 agents in previous cases and was always surprised at how ordinary and insignificant they looked - you would have difficulty in identifying them in a crowd. Both wore business suits and ties but were indistinguishable from thousands of other business men; perhaps there was a deliberate policy to merge in with the crowd, sober dress being a prima facie requirement of any agent.

But one thing he had also learnt: such men were not to be underestimated. They were recruited for their intelligence as well as their looks and had powerful support operations throughout the world; they were always a force to be reckoned with.

The interview finished, Charles switched off the recorder.

'What do you think, gentlemen?'

'Can we get a copy of the two recordings?' asked Turnbull, putting his notes into his briefcase.

'Already done, I have them in my drawer, I will give them to you when you leave.'

The recordings had made quite an impression on the two agents and although they did not discuss anything between themselves it was clear to Charles from their now animated expressions that they were taking the third phase very seriously. It was Turnbull who spoke first.

'First, Detective Chief Inspector, I must congratulate you on your investigation into this case. In view of recent events in the Far East there's been a crackdown on Russian spy cells in Britain. A policy change has seen MI5 stepping up counter-espionage efforts.

'This cell you have uncovered has somehow slipped under our radar and will need further investigation by ourselves. I will be reporting back to my superiors but I believe this third phase of insurrection has to be taken very seriously. I would expect the COBRA committee to be assembled once again to be chaired by the Prime Minister.

'As I'm certain you are well aware, COBRA is a crisis response committee set up to coordinate the actions of government bodies of the UK in response to a national crisis or events with major implications for the UK. There have been several meetings due to the recent riots on the continent. The puzzle was: why was it not happening in the UK? Now, from your investigations we know the answer. Thank you, Chief Inspector. Your work has been invaluable.'

It was now the turn of Petty from MI6 to have his say.

'Again, like my colleague, I must congratulate you on your work, Chief Inspector.

'MI6 was aware of radical splinter cells throughout Europe, set up for both political and criminal activities, and the recent riots have led to many arrests. We have seen a huge increase in organised criminal activity from west to east, from drugs to diamonds, and from east to west in money laundering to counterfeit goods. The porous borders have encouraged the mafia gangs to expand their activities with a vengeance.

'And not just criminal gangs: Populist political parties have seized their opportunity to expand their aims. Formed from socialist academics, former Trotskyists, Maoist revolutionaries and many other extreme groups, the austerity regime throughout Europe has given them a cause to group and work together, many believing that only by overthrowing their governments can they truly find themselves. It's an extremely corrosive mix of views.

'For example, Greece has the Leftist Syriza party, which has just taken power and are an untried, unstable grouping of various types of Communists, fun-revolutionaries and Greens. Spain has the Podemas party, Italy the Northern League, Germany the EU-sceptic Alternative for Germany party.

'The danger facing all of us is that the Islamic State militants, radical Islamists and local extremists who have aligned themselves with the so-called Islamic State will take advantage of the uprisings to further their cause in the bloodiest of ways and to foment anarchy throughout Europe.

'So, you see, Chief Inspector, your work has been invaluable to uncover this cell right under our noses. I, too, will refer this case back to my seniors and they will alert Interpol and the Governments concerned. They will all take the appropriate measures. To be forewarned is to be forearmed - don't you agree, Chief inspector?'

'Quite so!'

Petty might be new to his job but no one should doubt his credentials, thought Charles as he was about to take the recordings from his desk drawer.

'Oh, there is one other thing,' said Petty with a serious-looking face, not knowing how the Chief Inspector would take what he was going to say next.

Charles sat back in his chair.

'Hanna Goraya is a Russian KGB spy.' Petty paused to allow the words to sink in. Getting no response from Charles he continued.

'We know she was working in Kiev. We had her shadowed by undercover agents when she came to these shores. We know she stayed with Lord Hutton and she visited you in your flat.

'We believe, but cannot prove conclusively, that she murdered Lord Hutton in a Russian mafia revenge for his, let's say, nefarious financial dealings. A lot of Russians lost a lot of money.

'Even if we could prove she poisoned him we know Russia would not extradite her to face trial here.

'I don't know what your relationship with Hanna Goraya was but she was not what she appeared to be. There are two other unsolved murders on our books involving the same person – in France and in Italy. Men were easily duped by her good looks but the devil exists in many places including beauty. You will let us know, of course, if you should ever see her again.'

Charles did not reply; his vacuous stare told Petty all he needed to know regarding his relationship with Hanna Goraya.

Both men stood up thanking Charles for his time, Charles shaking their hands and then opening his desk drawer to give them both a copy of the recordings. The agents took their leave.

Charles slumped back into his chair, trying to absorb what Petty had said about Hanna. How could he have been so foolish to have been taken in by a pretty face? There had always been a nagging doubt in his mind but the amorous mix of love and lust for the woman had overridden his common sense. He was stunned by the revelation she was a spy, tapping his forehead as a sign of disgust with himself. What happened to those well-honed instincts which should have alerted him?

He did not have time to think of it further as Christine popped her head in, 'The Chief Constable would like to see you, sir.'

'Thanks Sergeant.'

Charles, in his father's office, relayed the gist of the meeting with the two agents together with the suspected involvement of Hanna Goraya with Lord Hutton's death.

'Amazing, isn't it,' said his father, 'that such an apparently simple case of suicide should escalate in such a way. It shows how shear bloody-minded determination can unravel the most difficult of protracted cases. You have to be congratulated.'

'I didn't do much,' replied Charles, 'the case unravelled itself as the gang imploded on itself. Six of its members are dead and fortunately one was left to explain all. I was just the conduit through which it happened.'

'You were more than that, Chief Inspector, don't underestimate your achievement. You found the killer of Professor Falconer-Smith and that alone should be reward in itself. You completed your part of the brief, let others now complete theirs.'

His father looked quizzically at Charles, knowing well his son's moods.

'You sound despondent Charles, anything the matter?'

'It's nothing to do with work, sir.'

'Something personal then, OK I won't probe any further. But I have something here that might cheer you up. You may not be, but my seniors are impressed with your work and there's a promotion in the offing to Chief Superintendent should you wish to accept it. Think about it could you. It's likely to involve more desk work, something I know you're not happy with, but give it some thought. It's up to you, it's your decision.

'Something else may be more to your liking. I have been informed from on high, and the source is very reliable, you are to be awarded an MBE for your services to Taekwondo in the next Queen's Honours List. Watch out for the letter from the Palace. Not a word, mind you, to anyone before then.

'I'm very proud of you, son.' His father stood up to shake his son's hand.

'I'll look forward to the letter and let you know as soon as it arrives; it's a great shot-in-the-arm for the sport of Taekwondo.'

'Oh, I nearly forgot!' He took out a letter from his desk drawer. 'I have a letter of resignation from Detective Sergeant Moran.'

'She did what!!'

'I thought you two were getting on well so I am surprised she has asked for a transfer back to the Met. Do you know what's happening?'

'I have no idea. Let me have the letter and I'll discuss it with her. What on earth has caused her to ask for a transfer?'

Charles stormed out of his father's office carrying the letter and when passing, angrily asked Christine, who was sitting at her desk, to see him in his office.

'Close the door, Christine, and take a seat.

'What the hell is all this about,' waving the letter erratically in front of her face.

'I thought it for the best, sir.'

'Drop the sir bit, Christine, call me Charles. I'm really angry with you for putting me through this. I thought we were working well together, you said so yourself.

'And best - best for whom? Not for me, you're my right-hand man and I need you. If I haven't made that clear in the past then I can only apologise. So who is it best for? Best for you, why?'

'It's personal, sir … Charles.'

'And you can't tell me?'

'No Charles.'

'I'm sorry to hear that, Christine. Has it anything to do with me or any of the team?'

'No sir.'

Realising it was a personal matter Charles did not want to push the matter further. He could see from Christine's crest-fallen face that she was upset and almost ready to shed tears. His heart went out to her and his initial anger gave way to sympathy.

He looked at her for a few minutes not saying anything. She was mute with eyes lowered, choking with emotion.

He placed his hand on her shoulder. 'Christine, promise me one thing could you. Before I accept this letter, promise me you will think it over for the next two weeks and if, after that, you still want to resign, I will, most reluctantly, accept your decision. Will you do that for me?'

'Yes Charles, I owe you that after springing it on you this way.'

'Thank you, Christine, and whatever is ailing you I hope it goes away.'

'May I go now, Charles?'

'Yes Christine. You will think about it?'

'Yes sir ... Yes Charles, I will think about it.'

Christine left Charles's office and headed straight for the Ladies toilet. There, sitting on the toilet seat, out of sight from everyone, she bawled her eyes out; tears not of grief but tears that dragged up the past, present and future as far as she could see.

# Fourteen

Parkside Police Station, Cambridge
Friday, 11<sup>th</sup> July, 2014, 10.00am

The animated noise of staff in the conference room abated as Charles entered. As he looked at his team total silence fell other than the occasional cough or the clearance of a throat. Christine took her seat and shuffled nervously. Her resignation was a private affair between the Chief Constable, Charles and herself. There was no reason for Charles to mention it to the staff but nevertheless it made her uncomfortable.

Charles surveyed his team once again, looking at their individual faces before lingering a little on Christine's. His smile told her there would be no announcement on that particular matter. He glanced at his notes.

'I have assembled you all together to go over the case of the death of Professor Falconer-Smith, a case that has thrown up a number of police issues and has dumbfounded even the most intelligent amongst us.

'First, I should tell you that I have been personally congratulated by my seniors in Head Office, by MI5 and MI6, by the National Crime Agency, by New Scotland Yard, by the Serious Fraud Office and by the Counter Terrorism Unit. Quite a barrage of praise, wouldn't you agree?

'But it is not I who should be praised – it is you, the persons assembled around this table. You are the heroes to be congratulated. I was a blind man leading the blind until Detective Sergeant Christine Moran opened my eyes to the possibilities of where this seemingly parochial case might be heading. Christine is singled out for particular praise. But all of you deserve praise for your contributions in the collection of data from numerous sources, which allowed a picture to emerge from a miscellany of facts.

'A picture that identified a group of individuals - a cell for a better word - which had evil intentions beyond normal comprehension; a cell that had moved from idle talk over a few pints to action on a large scale in Europe. That is a huge transformation and I am certain psychiatrists and psychologists will have a field day when they get their teeth stuck into this case. Good luck to them, I say, but for us, as policemen and policewomen, that is not our concern. Our concern is to bring villains to book and to face justice in our courts, not to wonder what turned their minds to such evil thoughts.

'And this is the point I wish to make: your foot-slogging for names associated with the Professor, the innumerable interviews and seemingly endless collection of facts, which at the time seemed to have no relevance, has, in the end, allowed the pieces of the jigsaw to fit together and expose the picture we were all seeking. It is a reminder of the relevance of your work which, at times, is boring and meaningless but without it so much police work is helpless. Detective work, sometimes, is nothing but a hard slog. I say, once again – thank you.

'Now, let me go back to the beginning of this case - the suicide of a vagrant in Cambridge. Not exactly headline news. We are all aware of the increase in food kitchens, in food banks, in hostelries, in overnight houses, yes, even in Cambridge when austerity times hit hard. We see beggars and tramps every day on our streets and we have arrested many drunks for overnight stays in our cells. So the suicide of a vagrant who has given up on life is not a surprise to any of us.

'What was a surprise, however, was to see a vagrant committing suicide by hanging himself in a church. We have had lost souls drinking themselves to death, slashing their wrists, throwing themselves in front of trains and many other ways of ending their lives, but hanging oneself in a church – never!

'It was a very strange case right from the start. But even stranger when it came to the forensics report: that the Professor was murdered before hanging and even stranger as to what happened to the decay of the body. His broken watch during his murder told us he died on the 20th of April, which was a Sunday, but the body wasn't discovered until three or four weeks later, the 16th of May to be precise. The corpse by then should have been well-decayed from autolysis, the self-digestion of enzymes and from putrefaction, the melting of the body by bacteria. But it wasn't! The decay had somehow been suspended whilst in the church. Forensics remains baffled, putting it down to the cold temperature in the chapel.

'The more religious amongst you will have your own thoughts on the matter and have come to your own conclusions. In the paths of life and death and of love, God can work in mysterious ways. It is not a policeman's lot to unravel the mysteries of the universe; we'll leave that to forensics!'

There were smiles and mirth all round but not for Christine. Charles's comment about life, death and love made her gulp.

'Please bear with me. I know this is a long speech but I think it important.

'The Methodist Church in question had been derelict for almost a whole year and had been vandalised. The front door was very stout and had been permanently locked over this period. The door had not been damaged in any way. Access by vagrants was by the verger's office to the side which, after the murder, had been boarded up to prevent further entry.

'The body had been discovered in a room underground, used as a chapel, by a couple wishing to renovate the church into a home. The sale has now fallen through, not surprisingly.

'There was no forensic evidence to point us in the direction of a particular individual or individuals either in the church, the chapel, or the verger's office. We were so short of evidence we even had analysed a dog's excrement! And even that didn't tell us anything!!'

The laughter in the conference room was audible at the other end of the corridor; it broke the tension in the room which was Charles's intention.

'So, with no evidence to hand we had to rely on the scattered information from interviews. What emerged from this hazy picture was the "Black Lion" pub, a pub renowned for its subversive characters and political agitators. Of the groups studied we fortunately focused on the MacBeath group. Why? There was no evidence to suggest this group was involved in the Professor's death. It was simply one of those strokes of luck. Many of you will put it down to a policeman's hunch, an intuitive guess.

'We knew Lord Hutton was friendly with the group but he was a politician by nature who involved himself with all and sundry and the "Black Lion" was his favourite drinking hole.

'Still, there was no evidence to arrest anyone for the Professor's murder. It wasn't until two of the group were assassinated in Italy did we suspect it right to focus further on this grouping of individuals. I, personally, couldn't see the wood for the trees. It was Sergeant Moran who opened my eyes to the possibility it was organised crime related.

'When I interviewed Lord Hutton for a second time I realised his involvement with the group was both criminal and political, linked to the failure of Alveco Investment Trust. The extent of this involvement I could only guess at.

'It was at Lord Hutton's mansion that I met Miss Hanna Goraya. I had met her once before in Kiev where she was given the responsibility, because of her good English, to show me the tourist sites in the city. I reciprocated showing her around Cambridge.

'It turns out she was a KGB officer known to MI6. The Intelligence Agency has linked her to Lord Hutton's death but there is no direct evidence to extradite her from Russia, if that was at all possible.'

Christine listened intently to this passage of the speech and inwardly sighed with relief. It was not what she had expected; assuming Charles had been more than just a tourist guide. The fact that there was no other woman in his life somehow gave her comfort.

'Again, at even this stage, there was no evidence to arrest anyone for the Professor's murder. We had suspicions but no evidence to bring to court.

'What gave us the evidence eventually was the siege at the farmhouse and Soame's confession to the group's activities and intentions; also to the person who killed the Professor; job done, so to speak! This is where we can all congratulate ourselves on a job well done. We found the killer, end of story.

'But the ramifications of this case are far-reaching. There have been two phases of riots in Europe with a third phase, involving all those countries, including the UK this time, being planned. This third phase is due on Wednesday, the 23$^{rd}$ of July, from evidence gained by us.

'I am duly informed that European Governments have been put on their mettle against riots which could develop into bloody conflict, with extreme party activists involved and IS factions taking advantage of the confusion throughout Europe. In the UK contingency plans are being ramped up to cope with feared terrorist attacks.

'Be aware therefore of serious media coverage and a thirst for information from police sources. You are not to say anything and anything you might say has to have clearance from the highest police authority, in your case that would be our Chief Constable.

'Finally, I would like to draw this meeting to a close and to congratulate you all once again for your efforts in solving this case.'

There was a spontaneous round of applause for their Chief Inspector as well as for themselves.

Charles shuffled his papers together, smiled at Christine, and went back to his office. Sitting in his chair looking out of the window, he felt emptiness in the pit of his stomach at the prospect of Christine resigning her position. He had come to rely on her in his private as well as his business life, more than he had ever realised.

He could only keep his fingers crossed, and everything else for that matter, that she would stay. He would be bereft without her.

That same evening when Charles was working late his father popped his head in.

'Do you mind if I have a word with you, Charles?'

'No, take a seat, father.'

Charles put down his pen.

'Son, it is not my intention to interfere in your private life but if you would listen to me for a minute I have something to say about the opposite sex.'

'I'm a bit old, father, for you to talk to me about the birds and bees.'

'No son. Not about the birds and bees - but about shoes.'

'Well that's a new one on me, when did you ever take interest in my shoes?'

'I know you like shoes for a start.'

'At least I agree with you on that and I've got a wardrobe full of them to prove it.'

Charles wondered where this conversation was going.

'In my simple way, son, shoes are a good analogy to love.'

'I am fascinated, father.'

'There is a certain frisson in looking at new shoes, smelling the new leather, trying them on, and buying them. But this shouldn't blind you to the fact that the one's you already have and worn in like a pair of well-worn slippers can be even better for your feet. You get what I'm saying, you get my drift?'

'I haven't a clue, but keep on talking.'

'Let me spell it out: at times I have seen how you and Christine Moran get on privately and in business. I don't know what is wrong with the girl for her to resign her position because I thought the two of you were getting on so well.'

Charles now knew where this conversation was going.

'Let me put it very simply, not from a father to a son but man to man: if you love the girl, for God's sake, go after her and tell her you love her; a faint heart never won a fair maid. Go now and knock on her door, have a heart to heart talk about what is upsetting her.

'There, I've said my piece.'

His father expected a pithy, comical riposte from his son as usual. But this time it did not happen to his obvious relief. Instead his son had a rueful expression on his face.

'Father, believe it or not, but I think you're right, even if you went about it in a cack-handed way.'

Charles leapt up out of his chair.

'Where are you going?'

'I'm going to see Christine right now and have it out with her, by hook or by crook.'

'And to tell her you love her?'

'…And to tell her I love her.'

Charles was surprised how easily those words tripped off his tongue.

# Fifteen

With his father's words still ringing in his ears, Charles left his office, said goodnight to the new Desk Sergeant on passing, and left the building. Sitting in his Porsche he started the engine, paused, collected his thoughts, and then switched the engine off. Should he or shouldn't he drive to Christine's flat? After a few more minutes of contemplation he switched the engine on again determined to find out what was troubling Christine, what was causing her so much pain. She said it was personal so perhaps he shouldn't interfere in her private grief. But damn it, he needed to know why she had resigned and he would take the risk of her wrath for his uncalled intrusion into her private life. Holding her in his arms he felt he could bring her some comfort from her angst, whatever that might be.

Charles knew Christine lived in Bewley Court, a discreet building of residential flats off Bewley Gardens Road, no more than a fifteen-minutes-drive away from his own flat. But what was the number of her flat? He couldn't remember. Was it 36 or 37, maybe 38? But some number in the thirties he knew that much. He racked his brains for confirmation. 'For Christ's sake, think man and calm yourself,' rebuking himself out loud for not recalling her flat number. With more reasoned thought he was certain it was 36. But to be sure he pulled over to a side lane and rang the Desk Sergeant on his mobile.

'Tony, this is Charles speaking, can you give me Sergeant Christine Moran's home address from your screen.'

'Evening Chief Inspector.' And then, after a brief pause, 'I'm not allowed to give you those details over the phone, Chief Inspector. You know the rules.'

'For Christ's sake man, this is Chief Inspector Waley-Cohen making the request. What is her address?'

'I'm sorry, sir, I cannot give out personal addresses over the telephone. You will need to come back to the office.'

Charles in a petulant rage ended the call. He knew the Desk Sergeant was correct not to divulge such information over the telephone, cursing himself for stupidly asking for it in the first place. But something in his head was telling him to get to Christine as soon as possible; there was no time to lose. He started up the engine once again and headed for Bewley Court, he would seek out her flat number somehow when there. His foot hit the accelerator pedal more than it should do.

~

Christine poured herself another coffee, all the while looking at the aeroplane ticket in her hand. The ticket was for a one-way flight to Melbourne in Australia. There she would stay with her friend, Alice, who had invited her to stay for as long as needed in order to help her clear her head and to sort herself out.

At work she was able to bury her darker feelings under the load of police work. That is until she had tendered her resignation. Suddenly, like a pressure-release valve, her feelings flowed from the depths of her heart bringing uncontrollable tears and yet more introspection and guilt.

She needed to get away from it all, to a different environment, to a different social atmosphere; even a female shoulder to cry on might make all the difference; the further away from Charles, the better. She loved him to bits but after losing his baby he would never forgive her once he knew the truth. It was better this way to put distance between them, as much distance as possible; it was for the best, for both of them.

Christine glanced at the packed suitcase with a twinge of regret. It was not what she wanted and she was not one to run away when things did not go her way. Throughout her life she had faced up to her problems, presenting to the world a confident, self-assured persona which had always stood her in good stead. But somehow this was different. It seemed impossible to control her inner feelings and especially when close to Charles it just made things that much worse.

Her mobile rang. The taxi had arrived to take her to Heathrow. Putting on her coat, she washed out the coffee cup in the kitchen, and then proceeded to take her suitcase out of the front door. Taking a last look around the flat she switched off all the lights and with a heavy heart locked the front door.

~

Charles had forgotten the new one-way system around Bewley Gardens. He had not been this way for a long time and cursed as the road signs directed him away from where Christine lived. The detour had cost him another five minutes before he finally drove down Bewley Gardens Road. He knew Bewley Court was but a few minutes away, somewhere on the right-hand side. Was it number 36 where she lived? He was still unsure of the number.

All such thoughts went out of his head however as he spotted in the semi-gloom the figure of Christine. She was getting into the back seat of a taxi as the taxi driver was loading her suitcase into the boot. Without a moment's hesitation he drove his Porsche in front of the taxi, coming to a screeching halt with the car skewed to prevent the taxi from moving. The taxi driver's instinct was to remonstrate with the unruly driver but as Charles exited the car he shouted, 'Police,' and flashed his Identity Card. The taxi driver backed away and then stood his ground, terrified, bemused and somewhat apprehensive, all at the same time, not knowing what to do next. A reassuring smile from Charles settled his nerves a little.

Charles went round to the side of the taxi, tapping on the window to gain Christine's attention. He mimed the words, 'I love you,' against the glass. Christine, interpreting his mouth movements, her face lit up like a beacon and then just as suddenly became despondent again as she settled back into her seat. Charles mimed the words again, tapping that much harder on the window. He signalled to her to open the door.

Christine reluctantly opened the door allowing Charles to push in beside her. She was flummoxed, not knowing what to do, what to say, whether to hug him or to back away. Charles was more forthright: 'I love you, Christine.

Look at my lips,' gently turning her face to his, 'I love you, Christine,' said even more deliberately with loving feeling. She flung her arms around his neck and the two embraced briefly, Christine suddenly retracting from Charles's tight embrace and folding her arms. The tension between the two reappeared.

'What is it, Christine? Have I said something or done something to annoy you? Is it my fault?'

Christine shook her head.

'Then what?'

Christine found her tongue, if somewhat falteringly.

'No, Charles, it is not your fault.'

'Then tell me what it is that's upsetting you.'

'I can't Charles, I really can't.'

'No such thing as can't, Christine. Look, there's a park nearby, let's go for a walk and sit in the park for a few minutes.'

'...But the taxi, Charles?'

'Where are you going?'

'To Heathrow, to catch a flight to Australia.'

'Australia!'

'Yes, Australia, Charles.'

'Come on, let's have this walk.' Charles's tone was now more assertive.

They both exited the taxi, Charles asking the taxi driver to stay put for a few more minutes, his fare being covered for the delay. The taxi driver shrugged his shoulders and sat in his cab. He had resigned himself to the fact that he could not move anyway until he was given the all-clear by the police, and that he was not the person the police were after, more likely a domestic affair possibly to do with his passenger.

Charles and Christine entered the park, sitting on the nearest bench. At that time of the evening the shadows were lengthening as the sun dipped to the horizon, but the air was cool and fresh after the earlier rain, the atmosphere peaceful. Charles turned to Christine who was sitting stiff and erect wearing a solemn face without a smidgen of a smile, her eyes fixated on her hands in her lap.

'You said it was personal, Christine. I understand that but I want to be part of your life so perhaps we could try and share your problems. A problem shared is a problem halved and all that. What do you say?' He placed his hand on her hand.

The dam holding up Christine's emotions finally burst. She blurted out, still staring at her hands: 'I can't have children, Charles. I know you want lots of children, you told me so. I can't have children and I'm no good for you.'

'Why can't you have children, Christine?'

'Because I have two wombs and the chance of bringing a baby to term is very slight if not impossible.' The words were spit out as though the Devil was in those very words.

Christine glanced at Charles, half-expecting him to be moved by her impassioned outburst. Charles was unmoved. She went on to describe her condition in more impassive medical terms.

After listening patiently, Charles asked in a quieter tone of voice, squeezing her hand just that little bit more: 'But there is a chance?'

'A very, very slight chance.'

'But a chance, Christine. It's not like you to give up so easily, it's not in your nature. What with modern medicine that chance is getting greater each day. In any case, I want to be with you for who you are, for you alone, not for the children you can bear me. I love you and that's more important to me than anything else. Let's take the risk together and if the worse comes to the worse we can always adopt. There are always ways around these problems. Charles squeezed her hand again, a flicker of a smile appeared on Christine's face, but that was all.

Charles playfully nudged her in her side causing a tickle-smile to fill Christine's face. It also caused tears to flow.

'You're better off without me, Charles,' she sobbed.

'I'll be the judge of that, Christine.' He took a handkerchief from his pocket and handed it to her. 'Wipe away your tears. I think you have probably shed enough to drown your sorrows ten-fold.'

Christine wiped away her tears giving Charles a lukewarm smile. He cupped her face in his hands and kissed away the remaining tears; then a kiss on her moist lips. She responded more fully as if the kiss was an antidote to all her ills. He pretended to gasp for air making her smile a fuller smile. She kissed him on the lips again that much more tenderly.

'You know, Christine, said Charles hugging Christine, 'it's in bad times when life is at its lowest ebb that we need to turn to others for comfort and support, and I can be here for you to ease your pain and suffering. Love is at its highest and most welcome when life is at its lowest.'

'Thank you, Charles, for those kind words. I love you too but I never knew how to approach you to express my deep love for you.'

They hugged once more and then hand in hand left the park. Charles paid the taxi driver who by this time had a broad grin, bemused but not surprised at the travails of love in his cab. He reversed the taxi and drove away leaving the couple still holding hands, giving each other reassuring kisses.

Charles proceeded to park his car correctly by the side of the road.

'Would you like to come in for a coffee, Charles,' asked Christine tapping on his car window.

'I would love that, Christine,' replied Charles scrambling out of his Porsche, stubbing his toe in the process and falling into Christine's arms. They both saw the funny side of it and burst into laughter.

With his comforting arm around her shoulder they entered Bewley Court, to flat 36.

That evening gave both of them the time to open up to each other and to discuss the issues in much greater detail, to Christine's obvious relief as she unburdened her deepest sorrows.

But the abortion was not discussed that evening. Christine left that for another time, for another tomorrow when both of them were less emotional. But she would tell him soon, very soon.

Christine cancelled her trip to Australia and at work withdrew her resignation.

---

---

As a rider to this case, the 23<sup>rd</sup> of July saw riots throughout Europe including the UK. A total of 150 people lost their lives including the murder of 36 senior bankers and politicians; not the 100 MacBeath, the second coming of "Rob Roy", had targeted, but a sufficient number to make people in these professions more afraid of public disgust with their policies and banking scandals; they were all made aware of the power of the people. At the time of penning this rider a European-wide hunt continues for their assailants.

Neil Soames was charged with the assisted murder of Professor Falconer-Smith and fraudulently running a Ponzi scheme. He was jailed for 16 years.

The WPC shot at the siege of the farmhouse made a full recovery.

Charles's father could only guess at what was said between his son and Christine when he had dared to intervene between the two, but was delighted to see Christine at his son's side outside Buckingham Palace with his MBE, arm in arm, a glow of love between the two, an ocean of mutual love and respect.

**Also by Peter Wadsworth**

**Adult fiction**

The Fairy Slipper Orchid

ISBN 978-178035-0950-0

The life story of a soldier in the American Civil War of 1861

Inspector Tae - the intern

ISBN 978-150078-194-1

Crime series: No 1

Inspector Tae - skin deep

ISBN 978-151739-709-8

Crime series: No 2

Inspector Tae - Rob Roy

ISBN 978-153282-297-1

Crime series: No 3

**Children's Stories (Illustrated by Mark Lee Jones )**

The Wicked Witch of the Woods

ISBN 978-178035-481-1

Grandad's Stories

ISBN 978-178035-685-3

Six Short Stories for Schoolchildren

ISBN 978-1-5237-4655-2

Made in the USA
Charleston, SC
11 August 2016